Dunster's Calling

A Novel

ॐ॰॰ॐ

Tracey Gemmell

First Printing, 2016

ISBN 978-0-9976137-0-4
ISBN 978-0-9976137-1-1 (eBook)

Tracey Gemmell Publishing
W5317 Highland Drive
New Glarus, Wisconsin 53574

Cover design: Anita B. Carroll, Race-Point
Cover illustration air balloon and flags © Eisfrei/Shutterstock Images
Cover illustration rose branch © Marya Kutuzova/Shutterstock Images
Cover illustration heather branches © Alexander Potapov/Dreamstime
Cover photo USA/UK flags © Mark Gabrenva/iStock. Getty Images

Author photo: Steve Howes

Website: www.traceygemmell.com
Facebook: www.facebook.com/author.traceygemmell/
email: tracey@traceygemmell.com

To Betty, my real-life Mrs. Althorp, with love

There are no foreign lands. It is the traveller only who is foreign.

—Robert Louis Stevenson

Preface

This novel was written using British English spelling and American punctuation. When you non-Brits see a double L in *cancelled* or *marvelled,* an S in *realise,* or the word *centre*, you may be taken aback. When you Brits see an unhyphenated *midlife* or quotation marks outside punctuation at the end of sentences, you may feel a little … off. Well, welcome to Samantha McClintock's world. This work sits somewhere in the Atlantic between the United States and the United Kingdom, like a literary Bermuda.

Prologue

Exmoor, England. 1960

The mare's nostrils flared with each rapid breath as she lay, fore and hind legs stretched out straight and rocking back and forth in time with her contractions. The light frost was slowly being vanquished by lemony rays as they stole into the valley below the farm. But the early spring dawn went unnoticed in the paddock except for the glint reflecting in the sweat coating the Exmoor pony's neck and flanks. The single observer noted the calmness of her demeanour. He remembered childbirth looking and sounding different during the birth of his own children.

She'll kill me, he thought.

"Merv! Wha' 'av you done?" He could already hear her voice as she interrogated him later, hands on hips, head on one side. But how was he supposed to know the foal would come early? No time to get the mare in the barn. No time to fetch his wife back to the farm. And besides, he didn't think she'd approve of being disturbed at her father's sickbed.

Should I call the vet? Merv knew what to do with sheep, but this was different. Each birth of an Exmoor pony was a triumph after the herds had been decimated during World War II. His wife had anticipated this foal with as much excitement as the birth of her own daughters. Deep down he knew the mare could do this without a barn or his help. She was of Exmoor: strong, hardy, from ancient stock that had survived great adversity. Like himself, really. But surviving marriage was on his mind right now.

The mare grunted, tried to sit up, then rolled flat on her side again. One rock of the legs ... two rocks ... three. A white bubble appeared first, then a nose, head, and neck, quickly followed by tiny shrouded hooves. The soon-to-be mother rested briefly, then finished her job, sliding her newborn onto the grass. The farmer approached, reassuring and praising the mare. At least he could tell his wife he'd done that much. He grasped the white sack that gave the foal a ghostly silhouette in the dawn light. Tearing the membrane to free the head and body, he cleared the foal's nostrils and glanced back to check the gender.

Good. He hadn't wanted to shout his mother-in-law's name across a field. The mare nickered softly, then more urgently, as she scrambled up and spun around to meet her baby boy. She licked his nose and eyes, nudged his neck and belly, breathing in the scent of her descendant, the newborn doing the same of his ancestor.

Dunster had arrived.

Chapter One

Wisconsin, USA. 2016

"Oh, and you need to get US citizenship." A patriotic challenge, wrapped around a xenophobic hand grenade, pin pulled … five … four …

That first shot arced across the dining room table, rattling the Wedgwood tea set and sending the dogs scurrying for their beds in the kitchen. With horror, Samantha McClintock watched the fires of global domination flicker in her husband's eyes.

"Did you hear me, Sam? The committee felt it was in the best interests of the campaign." Brody stopped eating to look at his wife. Three … two … one …

Campaign? Campaign! Sam heard the words ricochet off the inside of her skull, refusing to quietly absorb themselves into a brain that, until now, had been fully capable of comprehending most of her husband's utterances. The campaign was supposed to involve her husband knocking on about three hundred doors. He'd be clutching a flyer sporting every icon from the free clipart program even remotely related to elections, or America. She'd assumed, with some fear, gastronomically challenged as she was, she would have to bake a few cookies. She'd been told there would be a couple of appearances at the local beer festivals and a doughnut-heavy meet and greet. Knowing Brody's proclivity for healthy eating, Sam was amazed he'd even agreed to have doughnuts on the agenda, though it should have been her first clue that political ambition trumped prior values. "There'll be no polling over how your dresses are playing with the voters, no deleting questionable e-mails, and no paying for the silence of long-lost college roommates," Brody had jokingly said. But nowhere in the discussion had there ever been mention of a change in citizenship status.

"You haven't said anything. Citizenship?" Brody stared into Sam's face like he'd never seen her before. Sam came to her senses and realised this conversation was really happening.

"Umm … what's to say?" she responded, trying to keep the incredulousness out of her voice. "We talk about me getting citizenship about once a decade. I say no, and we move on with our lives. You know my reasons. You always said it was up to me. I don't see what's changed."

"Everything's changed!" Brody's organic noodles infused with low-sodium soy sauce clung to ashen chunks of tofu. They fell from his chopsticks with a splat as he waved his arm to encompass the entire known universe. "I have a chance to influence the direction of our town! To introduce new concepts and present myself in a much bigger arena than the local banking world. This could lead from town to county to state politics!"

As if in response to this grandiose speech, a cheer broke out from the den. Some baseball game. Sam heard the crack of a willow cricket bat knocking a ball for six. *Where'd that come from?*

"Tell you what then," Sam said, still trying to shake the sounds of cricket from her head. "I'll wait to get citizenship until you run for president."

"They'll say you only did it to get to the White House."

"I was joking!" Sam spluttered, adding as the horrifying prospect sunk in, "Are you seriously thinking about the presidency?" *How could I have missed this one?*

"Well, no, but hypothetically … anyway, the point is,

the exploratory committee felt that you being a British citizen could lead to uncomfortable questions about why America still isn't good enough for you."

"What? Who said anything about America not being good enough?" Sam started to hear that screech in her voice that made her turn off any talk show with multiple female hosts. "Would I have married an American, spent twenty-six years here, raised my children here, and tolerated the accent and appalling grammar—well, strike that last one because I don't tolerate it—if America wasn't good enough? This has nothing to do with good enough and everything to do with me just wanting to remain British. Not a 'dual' anything. Just British. If your committee doesn't understand patriotism, loyalty, and acceptance, you might be on the wrong committee." Sam folded her arms and waited for another rousing cheer from the den. Nothing. Just a Jeep commercial.

"But, honey," Brody pleaded, "it's such a small thing. Just fill in a few forms, hold up your right hand, say a few words—you can even cross your fingers behind you back, if you like—and you're done. You'll feel no different, and nothing will change the big picture for you. But you not being a citizen may change *my* big picture. I want to be a greater part of things. Can you help me? Please?"

Sam chose to ignore the comment about crossing her fingers during a solemn oath, though if she'd been looking for a representative of her values, Brody at that moment wouldn't have fit the bill. And she knew that statement didn't fit Brody's ex-military moral code either. Well, usually. Second time her newly minted politician husband had compromised his values. *I hadn't realised all this compromising started so early in the process.*

"So tell me," Sam asked. "How does 'The Committee' feel about your name, Mr. I'm-So-Proud-of-My-Scottish-Heritage McClintock? Should I be calling you Buck or Buddy or John Wayne from now on?"

"You're being ridiculous," Brody said as he pushed

his unfinished plate away and threw his napkin on the table. "Everyone has a surname from Europe around here."

"Soooo, a European name is okay but an actual European wife is not? I'm confused." Sam felt at this point the battle was won. Apparently not.

"Look," Brody countered. "It's a small town, and I'm already an outsider. We've only been here ten years, and my competition, whoever that is, will have been here for at least three generations. The committee felt I was enough of a new concept. A non-citizen wife may be the tipping point." Brody pouted like a toddler at enforced naptime.

"Well, speaking of new concepts, why don't we start with differences and tolerance?" Sam shot back. "Not that this town needs introducing to them, or so I thought until a few seconds ago, because I've never been anything but graciously welcomed here." Sam's raised eyebrows dared Brody to disagree.

"Of course you're welcome here," Brody placated, carefully replacing his water glass on the table. "No one is suggesting you aren't welcome. The committee just wanted to ensure that there were no obstacles in the way. You know, for the voters."

"Oh, the voters." Sam leaned back, folded her arms, and nodded her head slowly. "You mean, my best friend Gail? Macy at the grocery store? Anne and John at the coffee shop? People we've known for the decade we've lived here who couldn't care less whether or not I have citizenship? Do you really think Dennis at the gas station is going to make a fuss about my heritage? This is all stupid." Sam tried to imagine Dennis, who doubled as the town's snowplough driver, starting an anti-British smear campaign. The man was the biggest Manchester United fan ever born the US side of the pond.

"Maybe they do care," Brody said softly. "More than one person on the committee brought it up."

Sam started, her jaw dropping open. She unfolded her arms and slumped in her chair.

"People have said as much?" *Et tu, Macy?* "People doubt my engagement in this community because I'm British? Wish I'd known *that* before I spent all those years with the PTO, volunteered at every fundraiser, and cleaned miles of American trash off the side of the town roads. Because chances are slim it's the Brits dumping garbage out of their car windows on the way to Heathrow—via Wisconsin!" Sam paused to draw breath before delivering her pièce de résistance. "Call me barmy, but a non-meat, non-dairy leader in the middle of Dairyland, USA, gives much bigger cause for suspicion than I do!" Brody's decision to lower his cholesterol a couple of years ago had rendered most of Sam's meat and two veg meal plans obsolete.

"There's no need to take names and cry traitor. This is standard practice in politics: try to head off any unpleasantness before the opposition can sink their teeth into any skele—" The panic on Brody's face was almost comical as he grasped the enormity of his error.

"So now I'm foreign, unpleasant, and a skeleton in your political closet?! What the hell, Brody!" Sam tried to bring her voice down an octave. She stared at the floor for a moment, allowing Brody to stammer a retraction. Ignoring his back-pedalling, Sam lifted her eyes to meet her husband's, then rose slowly to her feet, displaying what Brody had learned to call her "Dam Busters" look.

"You always loved the fact I was from somewhere else," she began slowly and deliberately. "Remember you only spoke to me on the ferry in New York Harbor because you heard my accent. You used to say in the old days— like yesterday—that my British accent actually opened doors for you, an icebreaker at banking conventions. You loved telling your friends about English beer and castles and tweed jackets. And, with the exception of that one party where you told the joke about the British Isles being a slow-moving US aircraft carrier, you fit right in in England. And you made me believe I fit right in here. But now, overnight, you're saying my heritage is a liability for you? That it's okay for me to *sound* British but not to *be* British? That *you* get to stand out only if *I* agree to blend in? Well, concept this, *Buck!*"

The gesture that followed wouldn't have looked good at any election rally.

Chapter Two

The night had started on the couch, despite entreaties to "Please explain why such a simple task is so hard" and Brody's final plea: "At least think about it."

"It's like we've never met!" Sam had fired back after spitting toothpaste into the sink with the velocity of bullets. "Like you've forgotten you agreed to work towards getting a job in England. Like you had no idea I'd never wanted US citizenship!" The old Brody had understood. Old Brody had promised to take her home.

The couch wasn't a new sleeping arrangement for Sam. Many a night of fantasizing about murdering with a pickaxe Mr. Snoring-Hard-Enough-to-Cause-Vibrating-Ripples-in-His-Bedside-Water ended with Sam choosing the couch over life without parole. But most days she didn't contemplate killing him. Brody was typically the most sensitive of men: kind, grateful, and caring. This current hiccup demonstrated a one-sidedness Sam wouldn't have believed possible in her husband of twenty-six years. But he had touched a nerve or, based on her current sleeping arrangement, hacked right through one.

"What kind of self respecting international crisis happens over a takeout dinner on a Thursday night? Seriously?" Sam spat at the ceiling. She lay on the lumpy cushions, trying to wrap her head around Dictator Brody's statement about it being a simple task to switch citizenship. "Let's see *you* switch from supporting the San Francisco 49ers to the Green Bay Packers just because I want to run the PTO," she muttered.

Tossing and turning on that midwestern sofa, miles and decades and memories from home, it took until 1:00 a.m. for Sam to remember that there were not one but two empty bedrooms upstairs that she could have used. And that was when the tears fell.

"We regret to inform you, Sam McClintock, you are no longer who you thought you were. Not a mother in the day-to-day sense. And not an accepted member of the community. Anymore."

∫∫

"So this is a midlife crisis," Sam muttered hours later, still awake. "Nah, can't be. That's ten years from now."

She'd always thought a midlife crisis would be more exciting somehow—all personal stylist consultations, start-up gelato businesses, wide-brimmed hats on exotic beaches. And who wasn't in crisis? Everyone Sam knew had woken up at the age of forty or fifty (or thirty-five in the case of one particularly irritating, overachieving co-worker) and asked that reflection in the mirror, "Who the heck is that?" Not for nothing was it the clichéd opening of every baby-boomer film.

Could first town administrator be Brody's equivalent to gelato and hair dye? Sam pulled the blanket tighter around her shoulders and pondered. Possibly, she had to admit. But from the day they'd meet all those years ago, if you put the word *first* in front of anything, Brody wanted it. So it shouldn't have been a complete surprise to Sam that when an exploratory committee asked Brody if he'd be interested in the first town administrator position, the bull just had to charge the red flag. The minor local position suddenly took on the importance of an ambassadorship to the United Nations.

Sam turned over, curling into a foetal position to protect her feet from the chilly air. Her last conscious thought was that if Brody had been offered the chance of a run at *second* town administrator, there would have been no crisis tonight. She'd have continued repainting the picket fence every year until she reached midlife, ten years from now, the seeds of discontent slumbering on, waiting for a less embarrassingly mundane reason to sprout.

❧∞❦

After a terse breakfast and even terser peck on the cheek from her work-bound husband, Sam sat at the kitchen counter trying to focus on the crossword puzzle. Her first patient of the day had cancelled so she was free to dawdle a bit. She'd scanned the front page; another immigration headline. The crossword puzzle seemed less threatening.

Three down: Cornish word for homesickness with a sense of loss.

Usually, for Sam, the word *Cornish* evoked pleasant thoughts of ice cream and clotted cream, preferably one on top of the other. But today, the word dredged up more, a dawning sense that something was askew. Sam googled "homesickness with a sense of loss." The search resulted in forays into websites for college counselling related to homesickness, which led to remedies, which led to families, which led to a brief encounter with an old Jerry Springer website (b*limey!*), then onto ancestors, which led to archaeology, which led to Druids, which led to the Cornish word *hireth*, with the Welsh version, *hiraeth.* Sam gazed, stunned at the meaning: homesickness for a home you cannot go back to, maybe a home that never was. She shivered. A six-letter word on top of a fight with her husband induced a sense that her expat existence was in jeopardy. Walls she didn't even remember erecting began to tumble. Scars across her heart tore open. Breathing hard, she found herself doing what she often did for comfort. She composed a letter in her head:

Dear Dunster,
I need your help …

Chapter Three

Sam had, up until dinner the previous night, enjoyed the attention her accent attracted in her adopted homeland. But that day at the hospital she felt she stood out like a lactose-intolerant tourist at a clotted cream festival.

"Mr. Locum? My name's Sam. I'm a speech-language pathologist, and your doctor would like me to evaluate your swallow, just to make sure you can eat okay after your stroke." Sam smiled at the lady sitting on the chair next to the bed. "And are you Mrs. Locum?"

"Well, that's sure a cute accent you got there," Mrs. Locum replied, sounding appropriately midwestern. "How'd you end up here?" Seeing as this was a pretty regular icebreaker as Sam entered a new patient's room, the comment should barely have registered. She'd always thought it was genuine interest. Before *hireth* and political ambition, that is.

"What do you mean, 'end up here'?" Sam's hackles rose under the ID lanyard she'd flipped around to her back to stop it dangling in the apple sauce. "I'm a legal resident of the United States, but I don't have to 'end up here' if I don't want to."

The nurse taking vitals gave Sam a wary look. Mrs. Locum added weakly, "Well, it's a cute accent," and retreated to the couch to look out the window. Sam was too busy wondering if Mrs. Locum's comment had been a veiled criticism of lax border control to notice any affront she herself had given. But she was to perceive every acknowledgement of her "not being from around here" as a slight for the rest of the day.

Sam sat on her swivel chair, eating lunch at her desk at 4:45 that Friday afternoon because that was lunchtime if you worked 8:00 a.m. to 4:00 p.m. in a hospital. Looking around the speech therapy office, she sighed and stared at the dried-out sandwich.

"I've evaluated three stoke patients younger than I am just this week," Sam suddenly emoted to her office mate, Christie. "Which should be a reminder to us all that none of us is too young or too healthy to lose in an instant our abilities to communicate, or travel, or decide our own destinies."

Christie raised her weary eyes briefly from the report she was writing. "That's a little heavy for a Friday afternoon, isn't it?"

"So when do you think midlife starts?" Segues were not Sam's forte. Christie looked ready to request clarification, but Sam cut her off.

"I think it's a moving target, at least ten years ahead of your current age," Sam ploughed on, stroking her chin. "But its symptoms can kick in early apparently, especially when the rug's pulled out from under your sensible hospital shoes."

"Trouble at home?" Christie raised an eyebrow and tried to look concerned.

"Maybe," Sam replied. Leaving Christie in the dark about that, she continued. "I think midlife is not so much a mathematical concept as a dawning revelation that you're out of sync with your husband, kids, car, job, house, dog, baggy eyes, cellulite, hot flashes, country of residence, or … whatever." Christie nodded in slightly perplexed agreement. "But here's the big clue that you're in early onset middle age: you wonder what happened to the life you pictured you'd have when you were developing your grand scheme as a child."

"I was going to work with dolphins …" Christie

began, resting her chin on her hands and looking dreamily into space.

"My scheme revolved around a stable full of horses and a farmhouse. And an immortal—yes, immortal—Exmoor pony," Sam said, ignoring the dolphins because Christie wasn't really part of this conversation. "That part was written in hard stone." In softer stone, more like soap as it turned out, she'd pictured a book deal, make that multiple book deals, and training at the Spanish Riding School in Vienna. "But a speech pathologist? In America? Never!"

"Well, how did we Yanks push you off track?" Christie was starting to get tetchy.

"Making me marry one of you was one spanner in the works." Sam glared at Christie as though she were the matchmaker. But even in that moment of anger, Sam knew multiple smaller cogs had led up to her giant matrimonial spoked wheel.

Nibbling at the curly crusted sandwich while staring at the report on her computer screen, Sam pondered her foreign status and the "what happened to my life?" question. "I just don't recognize one Iowa of the person I'd planned to be," Sam breathed quietly, stealing the turn of phrase her daughter started to use after the family moved from the East Coast to the Midwest. Life had ticked by, bearing no semblance to the only life she could have imagined in her younger years.

Sam could not deny her émigré status had been fulfilling and rewarding, even exciting. But on that Friday afternoon, twenty-six years after leaving England to become a lawful permanent resident of the United States of America, *hireth* was buzzing around her brain like a rogue torpedo, national identity confusion pulling at her sense of equilibrium. As she threw the last of her sandwich in the rubbish bin, she feared she was married to a complete stranger, her heritage was a detriment, and she had a disease called *hireth*. And she didn't even find her condition on WebMD, but on a Gaelic website devoted to Druids.

"So that's why Stonehenge has a weird kind of effect on me …"

"Oh, for God's sake!" Christie shot across the desk. "What's with the non sequiturs and the blame? Though how the Yanks are to blame for Stonehenge, I just can't fathom."

"Sorry," Sam mouthed. She hit the power switch and grabbed her coat. Let the IT guys work out why she'd crashed her computer.

Chapter Four

Brody would be gone all weekend, an event scheduled long before the chow mein meltdown. Sam tended to roll her eyes when she thought of grown men getting together to stare under the bonnets of vintage cars. Though she didn't get its therapeutic benefit, she had to admit Brody's need for it was probably wife-induced. She was high maintenance and her weekend to-do lists were legendary.

It had been chilly indeed since dinner last night, despite Brody's mid-morning text offer to stay home that weekend to talk things over. He'd also mentioned deadlines were approaching to file "Intent to Run" paperwork, so the elephant with the foreign accent couldn't remain incognito behind the Welsh dresser for long.

"I need to think this through myself before I can explain anything to you," Sam had texted back. She never used text speak or shorthand, as they didn't gel with her communication ethics. Seething and texting, a dangerous combination, she quietly mouthed as she typed, "I cannot quickly make a far-reaching decision like this just because you came home from school waving your political field trip permission slip."

"This is not all sorted but the signing," she added to the text.

"I never said it was all sorted out." Sam felt Brody emphasizing the "out" with his thumbs like suddenly its omission irritated him. "My British turn of phrase didn't bother you before," she muttered at the phone screen.

When Sam finally got home, Brody had already left, leaving his briefcase on the kitchen table, a pet peeve of hers. The note next to it didn't help: "I guess I just don't understand what would be so different if you got US citizenship. You've lived as one of us for decades now. Clotted cream would taste just the same, you know ☺. We'll talk Sunday afternoon."

"What do you know of clotted cream?" Sam snapped. Jason Bourne (JB to his friends) and Sherlock, Sam's two large rescue dogs of questionable parentage, padded over to her side. *"She must be talking to us,"* their tails said.

"I know. I know," Sam sighed to the upturned faces. "I'm a little irritable over all this. I've got to think about whether or not the plan we made to go back to England is still valid, about where my home is." At this, Sam's lower lip began to tremble.

The dogs stole a glance at each other. Good to know everything was sorted then.

❧

That Friday evening, cuddling a cup of tea and staring at her knees under the blanket she always kept on the couch for snoring emergencies, Sam determined to spend the weekend discovering the defining moments that brought her to this life as a foreigner.

"Sorry, Gail. Won't be able to make the bake sale tomorrow." Sam held the phone tightly to harden her resolve. Saying no to fundraising efforts wasn't easy for her, especially when her best friend was involved. "Got a little crisis I need to deal with at home."

"I thought Brody was going away?" Gail replied. "No husband at home, empty-nester. And I know you've got British biscuits stashed away. How big a crisis can you be having?"

"Oh, just have to determine why I made decisions that dragged my childhood grand scheme off track. And why

British citizenship is still so important to me; what still calls me to my ancestral lands when I've spent half my life elsewhere. Nothing major." Sam clutched the blanket to her cheek in an infantile effort to comfort herself.

"Sounds heavy. Can't wait to hear what brought this on. But you can think about all that while selling cookies. We'll talk it through tomorrow. Pick you up at ten."

"Look ... wait. Damn it!" Gail had hung up before Sam realised her first word should have been no. "Well, maybe I do need a sounding board." The dogs padded over for their chin-scratching reward for not barking at the squirrels during her phone call. Sam absentmindedly ran her fingers through Sherlock's hair.

"How's Gail supposed to help me decide whether to get US citizenship or go back to Queen and Country?" Looking at the dogs for an answer proved somewhat disappointing too. Drawing herself up with resolve, Sam took a deep breath. "Right, it's now or never. I've been unofficially subpoenaed to defend my choices and my heritage in the court of small-town politics. And defend myself, I will."

Luckily, Gail was right about the stash of English tea and biscuits in the house. These were her true and constant allies, bought in bulk from the United Brits website. As she walked over to get the box of biscuits from the kitchen, Sam was sure she could smell heather-tinged breezes, clotted cream, and horses. Oh, the horses ...

Minus Thirty-Three

Exmoor, England. 1970s

It was a shared passion for horses that drew Samantha Weston and Polly Dale together. That and the bright orange space hopper Sam had seen in Polly's garden when they were two-year-olds. Their families were long of Porlock, a small coastal village on the edge of Exmoor. As a child, Sam imagined the village to be wrapped in the protective arms of the hills that rose behind the church and the cricket pitch, shielding the whole vale and village from the expanse of farm and moorland that was Exmoor. Porlock needed that embrace, Sam's little mind rationalized, as it practically clung to the edge of the Somerset coastline, sliding down the steep wooded slopes into the waters of the Bristol Channel. The aroma of tea and coffee from the local tea merchant mingled with the crisp moor air, honey-scented heather, and the salty marshland that acted as gatekeeper between the village and the sea. Sam would grow to be thankful that Exmoor was somewhat off the beaten track; otherwise, six billion people would want to live in its spectacular scenery and the narrow lanes couldn't have handled the traffic. Nor could the cream tea shops.

During Sam's fifth birthday party game of hide-and-seek, she and Polly had found a battered, leather-bound copy of *Moorland Mousie* behind the attic door of Sam's house. Carrying it to the kitchen, Sam's mum took a look at the bookplate. "Better be careful with this one. It's an old copy, signed by the illustrator, Mr. Lionel Edwards, himself," Emma Weston told them. "Maybe one day someone will come looking for this book." She was right about that one.

Opening the musty-smelling cover slowly, Sam gasped. "Look! That must be Mousie!" The girls stared at the beautiful pencil illustration of an Exmoor pony on the first page, windswept mane and perky ears, looking right at them. The girls followed the picture trail through Mousie's foal-hood and first encounters watching the hunters whiz by, of ponies being rounded up on the moors or wading through streams. "Look how proud he is in the show ring!" Sam said as they flicked through the pages.

"But look how unhappy and thin he is by himself in that stable with the rats," Polly said. The friends spent many hours making up their own stories to go with those beautiful renderings. How they loved Mousie. When Emma read to them, they yelled at the spoiled child and the greengrocer who abused their ponies and cheered for the groomsmen and caring children who saved the day. The girls searched for the exact places they thought the ponies rested as foals or crossed the rivers. They studied real Exmoor ponies on their trips to the moors and marvelled at the way Mr. Edwards so perfectly captured the wind whipping through manes and tails.

"When I get a pony, I'll never sell it—especially to a greengrocer," Sam told Polly.

The first grand scheme was in place: get a pony, and never let it go.

ॐॐ

With Mousie in their hearts, two purposeful girls strode down muddy footpaths eating butter and sugar sandwiches. (Polly's mum's dire predictions in all else didn't run to tooth rot and diabetes.) They leaned over rickety gates in search of pony noses to stroke, first with a parent in tow, then on their own as the threat of danger seemed to decrease as parental boredom increased. When the girls came across a field full of ponies, they'd look for eyes like Mousie's. Once found, how could a child not ascribe dreams and storytelling to the owners of those eyes? Mousie was alive and well in a muddy field by the sea.

When the children could walk a bit farther, they discovered the fields of school horses at The Weir Equitation Centre, or WEC, as it was known in the area. Nobody called it a riding school. But what did seven-year-olds understand of international reputations or Olympic training grounds? They just knew all they needed was enough pocket money for the price of a lesson.

"Let's check the telephone box again for coins," Sam said as they counted their meagre savings in their money boxes.

"Better not walk past the sweetshop." Polly always seemed fearful of its magnetic pull.

School holiday and weekend mornings found Polly and Sam scampering down the bridle path that led from just outside their houses to the very gates of the equitation centre. "A sign we're meant to be here," Sam would say. There they would sit in their favourite position in the hedgerow and gaze at the grand country house surrounded by paddocks, lawns, and shrubbery. There were multiple stable blocks, the most prominent being the U-shaped main yard that matched the house with its whitewashed walls and moss-covered tile roof. The setting was bordered in front by Porlockford Combe that led up onto Porlock Hill with its glorious views out over the Bristol Channel. Behind the house, gently sloping lawns and paddocks opened out onto the arc of Porlock Bay, where man fought his King Canute-style battle against the tides with front-end loaders. They pushed the piles of pebbles upwards into banks to protect the low-lying fields, only to be laughed at by each storm tide. It was never a fair fight.

"Hurry up or we'll miss it!" Polly yelled to Sam as they ran down the bridle path. Panting and shifting the rucksack full of sandwiches from one shoulder to another, Sam struggled into the viewing gap in the hedgerow in time to catch the squeak of wheelbarrows and clatter of pitchforks, the slosh of water buckets and the rhythmic sweep of body brush against sleek equine coats.

"The bell's late," said Polly, studying her Mickey Mouse watch with enough concern on her face to suggest impending disaster. The bell was only supposed to give the students a fifteen-minute warning before each meal.

"Have a sandwich," Sam said, already an expert in distracting her friend from her predictions of doom. The pheasants watched two little girls as they ran quickly into the woods across the road to pee so as not to miss the main event.

Once breakfast was over, Sam and Polly's favourite sights unfolded. The messy students had transformed into Lionel Edwards drawings: shirts and ties, tweed jackets, cream-colored britches, and the shiniest black leather boots outside of a show ring.

"I hope someone's got Copper today," Sam said with her fingers crossed. "He's so beautiful!"

The sedate parade of horses and riders followed various instructors to either the indoor riding schools, the outdoor arena, the jumping grids, or— "Eeekkkk! Cross-country today!!" the girls squeaked in unison from the hedgerow. Joy of joys for the two viewers, riders sometimes headed to the cross-country fields. Terrifyingly solid wood jumps, water jumps, and drop fences turned many a rookie equestrian green in the face right in front of one's eyes. Nothing was more exciting than the cry of "Loose horse!" as another rider bit the dust.

"Heck, I could do better than that," Sam would say as the rookie riders, coming in at the beginning of their three-, or six-, or twelve-month courses, attempted smooth canter strike offs. From their privet hedge judging box, the girls actually sneered as wrong canter leads and misjudged strides into fences produced yells of derision from the instructors. Never having done more than pat an equine nose, the girls were rosette-winning experts. "I am absolutely going to be the first female rider at the Spanish Riding School in Vienna," Sam announced. She'd seen photos of the noble white Lipizzaner stallions in the library and had even made the pointed hats worn by the Viennese riders out of newspaper.

As they watched the WEC students, Polly and Sam were unaware of the endless, torturous hours without stirrups, the bleeding inner thighs (and worse!), and the muscles so weak at the end of a lesson that legs collapsed under the dismounting riders. And if they had known about all that, they'd have thought it glamorous and character building; a steppingstone to glory at the Badminton Three-Day Event or Goodwood Dressage competition.

જીન્જી

When five Lipizzaner stallions arrived at WEC for an extended stay with their trainer, Sam and Polly just about spat their teeth out.

"This is destiny!" Sam yelled, as she trotted on the spot with elevated knees. "And I know I could do piaffe if I had a pair of black riding boots." Polly nodded tentative agreement, like she was a little less sure of her abilities, with or without the boots.

Their Christmas presents that year were tickets to one of the Lipizzaner shows that brought dressage fans from near and far. In silent awe, perched on the edge of their seats in the viewing balcony of the indoor arena, two wide-eyed girls watched the stallions perform quadrilles. Stirring Viennese music played as the horses glided through space with the grace of ballet stars and the strength of equine warriors, which they had originally been bred to be. Through it all, the riders in top hats and tailcoats sat almost motionless, as though their very thoughts dictated the movements under them.

"Look at her dress! I love that veil!" Sam whispered to Polly as two riders, one a lady riding side-saddle, the other a gentleman in seventeenth-century costume, performed an elegant Pas de Deux on sleek, shiny stallions. The girls respectfully returned the riders' bow to the viewing box as the music ended.

Most exciting of all was the finale: a stunning demonstration of the Levade, a controlled rear, the Courbette, a bunny hop with malice, and Sam's personal favourite, the Capriole, a leap into the air with a backwards kick.

"These moves were designed to protect the rider in battle and inflict damage on the enemy," the commentator said.

"How thrilling!" Sam turned to Polly with her mouth open, imagining her own wished-for pony risking it all to save her from James Cuthbertson, the school bully.

"James would look so good with a horseshoe-shaped divot in his forehead," Polly whispered back, earning her a nudge in the ribs and a scowl from her mother.

Life after the show was even more trying for Sam's mother. "Oh, please, Mum! I only want one pony, not lots like Jack has," Sam pleaded for the umpteenth time. Emma rolled her eyes, also for the umpteenth time.

"Just like your father. You think money grows on trees." Emma slapped the bottom of the baked-bean tin, which released a disgusting belch as the beans plopped out into the saucepan. Larry winked at his daughter. He remained optimistic, Emma said, by never paying attention to what was going on around him. Emma had to constantly remind a jubilant daughter who'd been promised a hot air balloon ride or a back garden swimming pool that she, Emma, was a realist, who knew what was going on around her—a mix of financial insecurity and unrealistic expectations. Sam had worked out from a young age that her mother fell somewhere between her dad and Mrs. Dale, Polly's mum. Everyone called Helen Dale a pessimist. But the realist appeared pessimistic to the optimist, and the pessimist found optimists woefully lacking in forethought. Sam didn't care about labels.

Addition to Grand Scheme: train to be an expert rider at the Weir Equitation Centre. And ride side-saddle.

Oh, and put a divot or six in James Cuthbertson's forehead.

∂∽∾

"Under the bed! Ceiling collapse!" Sam slid under the bed to come face to face with a torch and a packet of Jaffa Cakes labelled "Emergency use only."

"Flood! The attic! Now!" Without batting an eye, Sam took the stairs two at a time. Obviously tonight's sleepover at Polly's house was going to be a double-driller.

Polly learned to plan for disasters while most children were learning to write cute little love letters to their mummies and daddies. Sam, quite used to the mayhem scenarios, made the mistake of musing once, "If we run into the woods behind your house" (emptying the contents of the fridge into a pillowcase first), "aren't we going to be hit by the car your mum says is going to come through your kitchen window?" The girls' houses backed up to Porlock Hill, the steepest road in Britain—not an ideal location for Helen Dale. A psychotherapist would have had a field day with Polly. And her mother. Luckily, there were no therapists in Porlock, or probably Somerset, in the 1970s. But neither financial insecurity nor fear of disaster stopped Sam and Polly petitioning for ponies. The girls bridled Rascal, Polly's dog, with skipping ropes and trotted him around the garden until he got sick of it and dragged them through the hedge.

"Rascal asked Mum and Dad if he could go and live on a farm somewhere," Polly announced one day as Sam arrived in her garden. "We can't ride him anymore."

"Oh," said Sam. "You be the horse today then." So Polly sucked on a baler twine bit as Sam flapped her arms to encourage more speed. Tongues clicked madly as the bamboo cane placed between the lawn mower and the deck chair approached, the makeshift jump substituting for the Puissance Wall at the Horse of the Year Show.

Polly didn't walk to school, she cantered. Sam didn't jump up steps, she steeple-chased them. The two friends didn't say hello to each other, they whinnied. Their very DNA screamed for infusions of horse. Finally, they convinced their parents of this, each getting slightly different results.

Chapter Five

Sam was roused from her couch reverie by a wet nose and a hairy kiss that left her pulling tan dog hair from her mouth. Hardly surprising, seeing as she was now an hour late feeding the dogs. They must have been sitting there staring at her for ages, but obviously this strategy hadn't been successful at getting food. Hence, JB's drastic action.

The kiss catapulted Sam through time and space forty-odd years and four thousand miles. The rapid transit was a jolt. She could still smell and hear and see her past so clearly as she trudged to the kitchen. Hands automatically emptied kibbles into dog dishes, filled the tea kettle, spooned fresh Typhoo into the pot, and waited for the whistle. Chuckles and silent head shakes, tutting and sighing, smiles and the prickle of tears. Sam caught herself laughing out loud and looked around the kitchen. If she'd been on camera right then, the viewers would have found her rather disturbing. But it was hard to stay in the present with all its looming issues and impending decisions, its foreignness and altered reality. The present felt like an intrusion.

An inkling of resentment stirred in Sam's belly, at first only about Brody running for office and pushing her to think about citizenship. Then it built to include not having a pony in the backyard. It was against the homeowners' association rules and something Sam hadn't considered getting, but its absence now was entirely Brody's fault. Then the resentment exploded. "He should have known asking me to say yes all those years ago was unfair!" she yelled at the kettle. "He should have known I was happy where I was! He forced me to make choices I never wanted to make! He stole my identity!"

Sam turned and leaned over the kitchen counter, breathing hard and gripping the granite. Stone. So much was written in stone. Stonehenge. The marker on Dunkery Beacon on Exmoor. Porlock Beach. The diamond on her finger. Her grand schemes. As the storm inside her peaked and began to recede, the truth spread: nothing was really written in stone. Not life then. Not life now.

Sherlock had finished his dinner and tiptoed over during the tirade to lean against Sam's leg. She loosened her grip on the granite and curled her fingers in his thick coat. Another time. Another handful of hair. Another world. Another scheme. She had to acknowledge that life hadn't been so perfect back when she and Brody met. She'd been running from the utopia she now craved. Brody had in fact offered her a lifeline of sorts. And she'd reached for it, being of sound mind, under no coercion, with the full knowledge that life was going to change. She just hadn't realised that it was going to change so much. And for so long.

She traipsed back to the couch with her teapot and flopped down, drained and confused, knowing she couldn't stop her mental blockbuster childhood screenplay now.

Minus Thirty-Two

"I got riding lessons for my birthday!" Polly yelled up to Sam's bedroom window, hopping from foot to foot in the road and wearing the faded velvet riding hat she'd just unwrapped. The professional rider look was somewhat diminished by the nightdress she was still wearing, and the glittery bow stuck on top of the hat.

Polly's eighth birthday, six weeks before her best friend's, found Sam watching with jealousy, though trying to smile and clap, as Polly proudly strutted around a muddy field on an even muddier pony. Mrs. Hurly, the instructor, was a jolly ex-gym teacher who owned three ponies, a donkey, and a retired hunter named Chaucer. Nobody had ever actually seen Mrs. Hurly ride, but she'd convinced generations of local parents that she was a worthy instructor. Her self-professed forte was introducing ponies to elaborate costumes for fancy dress competitions. She didn't quietly and gently add pieces of the outfit, making sure the pony was comfortable and confident before adding the next bit. She threw on the entire kit and caboodle: headdresses, feather boas, swinging caterpillar legs, and hand-drawn posters around necks (her costumes often needed explanatory comments). Then she plopped the terrified rider on top and allowed the pony to gallop, wide-eyed and foaming, around her field until tired enough to be declared "ready for the show." More than once, in fact weekly, a pony was found not ready for the show, as a poster impeded vision or a feather got inhaled into a nostril. Then the fancy dress class became a rodeo. All it needed was the theme music to the *Benny Hill Show* running in the background.

"Given Helen's paranoia in all else, it's somewhat surprising she chose Mrs. Hurly," Sam heard her mother tell her father. "Price and availability must have trumped safety and reputation." Besides, Mrs. Dale and Polly had probably spent hours devising a Plan B in the event of disaster.

"You don't look like the riders at the equitation centre," Sam said disappointedly before one lesson as Polly hauled her jeans and hand-me-down Jodhpur boots onto her pony.

"How do you stop it from eating?" Polly yelled over her shoulder as her mount headed over to a grass verge, pulling her practically over his head and then acting for all the world like he didn't realise "Stop it!" was directed at him. Grass breaks aside, Polly soon learned to walk, turn, and do a shuddering, jolting, up/down, timing-somewhat-off rising trot with flailing legs and flapping elbows. Her greying velvet riding cap nodded precariously on her head and crept down over her eyes with each trotted jolt until she could barely see.

"You did so too have your fingers hooked under the pommel!" Sam would comment every week on the walk home.

"Did not!" Polly would yell back.

స్~ఆ

Sam's eighth birthday. There was a pony in her backyard. A dark brown, shiny-coated, 12.2 hand, fourteen-year-old Exmoor pony. Mane as thick as the privet hedge Sam had become an expert rider over, hairy fetlocks, rotund tummy, and fountain-like tail, all preceded by soft brown eyes that stared into hers without blinking. Sam would remember forever that warm breath on her neck and shoulder as she cried into a patient cheek. The pony inhaled the scent of her, this new child to add to his collection.

Sam couldn't take him all in—the whorl on his forehead, the velvety, mealy-coloured muzzle, the little horseshoes, the wisdom that oozed out of him, the patient way he accepted her hug for as long as she wanted to hold him. The saddle and bridle were sitting on the doorstep, clearly second-hand to anyone without her rose-coloured blinkers. But to Sam that saddle looked like a royal throne of gleaming gold, all shiny on top from years of breeches-on-leather friction. It was ages before Sam got to the point where "Oh you! Oh you beautiful thing! Oh my! Oh ..." turned into needing an actual name. She turned to her parents, cheeks aflame.

"His name's Dunster," Larry said, beaming. "And he's a really good pony because of all the ones I looked at, he was the only one not to push me away with his nose."

Sam heard a "tut" from her mother and briefly racked her brain to see if she could remember the Lipizzaners pushing riders with their noses, or if that particular trait of a bad horse had been mentioned in the pony books she'd read. She couldn't recall anything.

"You're perfect in every way," Sam whispered, stroking Dunster's ears.

"Pony! Pony! Pony!" Sam screamed into the phone at a pitch only dogs and Polly could hear, then raced back into the garden from the kitchen just in time to catch the thunder of Polly's feet flying down the road and the bang of the gate as she hurtled into the back garden. And there was Dunster, cropping grass because Sam couldn't pull his head up to greet the gasping Polly in a more dignified stance. Sam noted with glee the slowing of Polly's gait and her slack jaw.

"Pony! Pony! Pony!" Polly echoed. "We have a pony!" Because she and Sam shared everything, didn't they? The joyous friends jumped up and down, hugging and screaming, which startled Dunster for a split second before the tranquillizing effect of more grass stilled his fears.

"Better check his legs," Polly stated, running her hands down his four stocky legs like the girls had seen the fancy riders do. Checking for what she had no idea. "We should get an emergency horse evacuation plan sorted too. You draw a shortcut map to the vet's. I'll make an antitheft collar for Dunster to wear. I've got some bells somewhere."

Emma rolled her eyes and, before the happy event spiralled into a horror show complete with zombies, she brought out some cut-up apple. The girls marvelled at the practiced way Dunster picked the pieces with gentle lips from their hands and then licked their fingers. He knew more about children than they would ever know about ponies, striving to avoid their toes, assessing instantly how determined they were to pull him away from the flowerpots, and politely listening to, but politely ignoring, their pleas to stop eating while they took a photo. The first pile of manure was a bit of a shock close up. From the hedgerow viewing position, the piles hadn't seemed so big or steamy and certainly not so ripe. Larry got a shovel and scooped the pile straight onto the rose bed while the girls held their noses and tried not to gag.

"That's the last time I'll be doing *that*," Larry said.

"Blah, blah, you must ... blah, blah, save your money ... blah, blah, I won't ..." Sam heard none of her mother's instructions. Finally, still in a dazed stupor, Sam was pushed towards the garden gate for the triumphant march twenty feet across the road to Dunster's new home at Seabreeze Farm. Actually it was less of a triumphant march than a ricocheting off one hedgerow after another, as Dunster sought sustenance for the long journey, zigzagging from tussock to tussock. Sam flitted behind like a kite on a purple lead rope.

Girl and pony finally got to the gate, trailed by Polly, where Geraldine met them. Her father, Mr. Winterbourne, owned the farm. "Right. You open and fasten the gate like this, get water here, and spread out the straw in the shelter like this," Geraldine instructed, Sam now paying full attention. The wooden shelter looked like a sway-backed pony itself. The slate roof sagged alarmingly in the middle, mirroring the slope of the combes behind. Polly looked at it with mistrust as she ducked her head to go inside.

"It's okay," Geraldine said. "The roof's been like that for the whole sixty years my family's owned this farm and probably for sixty years before that. Dunster's safe here." Sam knew Polly was already completing a risk assessment. The walls looked strong, though, and it was warm and dry inside, out of the wind.

Sam slept on the bay windowsill of her room for a week, checking in the moonlight every few minutes until she fell asleep to make sure her Dunster hadn't evaporated like some kind of mirage. She'd overlooked that paddock from her bedroom window since she was born, but never in all her wildest dreams of waltzing stallions had she ever thought she'd look over that gate and see her own pony.

Get a pony: check.

Never let him go: harder than she imagined.

Chapter Six

Sam couldn't stop smiling from her midwestern cinema. The teapot was long cold, the biscuit plate in need of a refill, and her neck stiff from the clasped hands behind it. The ceiling had been a perfect film screen, showing scenes with such detail that their appearance had shocked and thrilled her to the core. *Dunster. What a treasure*, she thought. How many horses had passed through her life? Hundreds, probably. And each one had left a mark, on heart or wallet or buttocks. But Dunster was the one, her equine soulmate.

She thought of her father, shaking her head. Dunster's impulsive purchase was just like him. Get the pony before the lessons. It was a good job she hadn't heard the conversation between her mother and father, as, once again, he had acted without consultation or forethought. She could only imagine her mother's incredulous "You did what?! She's never even been on a horse! Where will you be while I call the vet, schedule blacksmiths, and spend every weekend eating sandwiches out of the boot of my car at some windy gymkhana? And where'll the money come from?!" Sam pictured her father looking round the side of the newspaper while perusing the rugby results to give her mother that "What are you yelling about now?" look that so angered Emma. Emma knew about ponies. Larry's claim to equine fame had been watching *White Horses* on the telly.

Sam contemplated how she could possibly have missed the cues that this was a financial stretch for her family. As a child, she never noticed that her mum stopped going into the village for her weekly hair set. (Larry never mentioned it either.) Or that her dad's shoes were a little more worn down. But Sam had Dunster. Through eight-year-old eyes, what others had, or didn't have, was of no concern to her. Guilt shouldn't belong to a child anyway, but Sam cringed now to think of the hardships she'd caused.

Projecting forward through time, Sam felt the beginnings of a revelation: Dunster may have been as much responsible for her life choices as anything else. With the exception of Mrs. Althorp.

On a trip to see the Bayeux Tapestry in France years ago, Sam and Brody had discussed what would have been in the running border of their lives if a tapestry had ever been commissioned for them.

"Submarines, scuba gear, California sunshine, footballs, English girls," Brody said.

"Church bells, heather, cream teas, Dunster, Mrs. Althorp," Sam decided. The last two had been a trail that tied one historical scene to another, providing context and answering questions Sam didn't even know she'd asked.

It was late. A crime thriller set in New York lay on the bedside table, about a third complete. But that night it wouldn't do. Thirty minutes later, Sam's e-reader was loaded with Brontë sisters, Thomas Hardy, Jane Austen, Wilkie Collins, Anna Sewell, James Herriot, and Laurie Lee. As Sam scanned the titles, trying to decide which one to read first, though all read before, suddenly the Kindle didn't seem right. Too disconnected to the world she was trying to recapture. Too now. Too American. She got out of bed and reached up to the top shelf of the bookcase. *Moorland Mousie*, covered in dust and still smelling of slightly damp leather. Sam opened the pages carefully, pausing at each illustration. The tissue paper plate covers were even more yellow than she remembered them. But the memories were intact. She ran her fingers over a rendering of a windswept mane. Dunster was calling. And again the tears fell, leaving indentations in the tissue paper. Not dramatic tears. Just big, blotchy, quiet tears; the only sound the splat on the paper.

A midlife crisis should be louder.

Minus Thirty-One

Polly continued her lessons with Mrs. Hurly, but Emma signed Sam up for lessons with Geraldine, getting a discount as Dunster was a boarder, and because Geraldine appeared less likely to cause bodily harm in the fancy dress department. As Emma had predicted, Larry's involvement with the whole enterprise ended with the signing of the cheque.

Geraldine ran a revolving stable door of hunters, jumpers, and dressage horses. This constant coming and going at the farm made Sam sceptical of Geraldine. "How could she do it?" Sam had asked Polly after a lesson. "Hasn't she read *Moorland Mousie*? It would be like selling your best friend, wouldn't it?"

It never really registered with Sam that Dunster had been through a couple of homes before hers. In her mind, he had been "born" into her family, part of her forever. She had yet to experience the gut-wrenching realisation that you could actually outgrow a friend, equine or otherwise.

Polly helped with chores, and they took it in turns to hoist each other up on Dunster's back for a wander around the paddock before tucking him in for the night. The girls would put their docile charge in the three-sided shelter, fluff up the straw, and try to get him to lie down so they could stroke and sing him to sleep. He wasn't having any of it. As soon as they gave up and turned to go, he would amble out into the paddock to eat.

"Put that comforter back on your bed!" Emma had yelled across the road one night.

"But he's cold, Mum!" Sam had yelled back. Emma made Sam return the comforter and write a one-page essay on "The Exmoor Pony's Coat."

"It's all well and good him already having two natural coat layers," Sam had explained to Polly later, "but I'm still knitting him a warm blanket." She gave up the idea after realising it would have to be a hundred times bigger than the scarf she'd given up knitting the year before.

಄಄

Sam survived that first autumn and winter, getting up before school in the sparkly frost to feed Dunster and scoop any muck from the shelter into a bucket to place in the corner of the field. She tried to make her little muck-heap look like the perfectly rectangular one at the equitation centre, but it was hard with only one pony, a few frozen balls, and a little straw. Still, it was part of having a pony as she knew it, so she persevered, even after Mr. Winterbourne drove over her efforts in the tractor.

Weekly lessons for both girls led to the ability to prevent grass-eating excursions, steer, go from stand to walk to trot, make circles (well, if "pentagon" was in fact synonymous with "circle"), and rein-back to open a gate.

"He can't do canter," Sam had explained patiently to Geraldine during one lesson.

"Yes, he can," Geraldine, not so patiently, explained back. "It's getting him to agree to the additional expenditure of energy that's the trick." Sam watched in frustration as Geraldine got on Dunster and with the merest squeeze of her lower leg went from walk to canter. Dunster's eyes were practically out on stalks at the shock of the demand. Sam got back on, and Dunster's relief at not having to canter again was palpable.

"All the rein-flapping, leg-thumping, seat-gyrating, voice-growling in the world is not going to distract me from my calling of keeping Sam safe," Sam could just hear

Dunster telling his friends over the fence in the evenings.

The first time Sam got mad enough to bring both spindly legs crashing into Dunster's sides with the force to actually get canter, he rocketed off forward and she rocketed off backwards, ankles over arse, and riding hat over eyes with Polly smirking over the fence and Geraldine doubled over in hysterical laughter. But with humiliation came that light bulb moment: "So I *can* get you to canter!" A Christopher Lee-inspired cackle broke loose.

Jumping was not as glamorous as Sam had thought it would be. Having not slept for days in anticipation of her first aerial assault, she had pictured herself galloping up to the jump and hanging airborne in slow-motion flight for long enough to look at the sea over the hedge, smirk at Polly over the gate, and appreciate Geraldine's open-mouthed gape. The reality was somewhat different, except for the open-mouthed gape.

"Tchick tchick." Sam clicked Dunster into an energetic trot, "energetic" being a relative term for Dunster. The cross poles had been set up in the paddock for days, so Dunster really shouldn't have been surprised by their appearance on his radar. But surprised he was. The resulting head-down, knees-buckled, cat-like arched-back refusal followed by a half-hearted trip over the poles brought snorts of barely contained derision from Polly and rolling-eyed disbelief from Geraldine.

On the next approach, Geraldine added a little help. One stride out from the fence, she growled loudly and lunged from the side of the jump, clapping her hands. Dunster, who was unceremoniously woken from a deep slumber at this point, hurtled up and over the one-foot-high cross poles like a steeplechaser over Beeches Brook. Or that was how it seemed from on top. Sam's merest contact with the airborne pony consisted of two tiny seat bones for a brief second. Then nothing at all. Lower legs (actually now upper legs, as they were higher than her head), thighs, hands, seat, all imitated how Neil Armstrong would have looked if he'd fallen out of the Apollo 11 capsule onto the moon: gravitational pull non-existent, attachment to the mother ship consisting of a finger hooked under a loose-flapping rein, and limbs outreached for who knows what. The difference between Sam and Mr. Armstrong was the timing of the inevitable return to Earth: he after several days, and Sam after a few seconds, hitting Dunster's rump first, followed by hock followed by riding cap (why did anyone bother? Those hats never stayed on) followed by earth. And there was Geraldine's open-mouthed gape again. Polly was nowhere in sight. Sam learned years later Polly had wet herself laughing and gone home.

"You know," Larry said one evening at the tea table when Sam had complained about it taking ages to get ready for the Spanish Riding School, where she assumed show jumping just took a backseat, "Churchill said something about success consisting of going from failure to failure without loss of enthusiasm."

Well, Sam had to admit to loss of enthusiasm sometimes. She almost missed the days of riding from behind the hedgerow; it was so much prettier. And with regards to the Grand Scheme, Sam learned that there were in fact several steps between owning a pony and eating *Sachertorte* on horseback in Vienna. She accepted she may need to allow extra time. But those tiny steps forward taken through the winter and spring, the sitting trot that no longer shook her hat off, the quick strike off on the correct canter lead, the anticipation of the jump at the right time, all lead to the inevitable. "I think you're ready for your first horse show," Geraldine told her. "Let's sign you up for Bossington."

Sam beamed.

Chapter Seven

Bossington. A tiny hamlet in the shadow of North Hill, its winding lane leading to Allerford and then on to the walking paths to Selworthy. In Sam's mind, there had always been a full sense of perfection in this tiny bucolic corner of the universe. Except for the day of the horse show.

Sam lay in bed but soon realised she'd just switched one ceiling film screen for another. She pictured the moss-encrusted stone walls that guarded the thatch-roofed cottages, each home encircled by floral skirt gardens. Hollyhocks stood at attention beside carved wooden doorways, and unruly roses tumbled over window frames, snagging and trapping lace curtains that fluttered in the breeze. Sleepy cats and copper kettles shared the sunny sills. As she recalled that first horse show, Sam felt the colour rise in her cheeks and the blood begin to pound in her ears. How could such abject humiliation and chaos be associated with such quintessential English serenity?

The phone rang by the bed, making Sam jump. She looked at the clock. Tori. Her daughter was as time-zone challenged as her mother.

"Hello, Mum. How's sunny Wisconsin?"

"Well, not so sunny at, oh, let's see, half past eleven. That's at night, dear."

"Oops. Sorry. It's sunny in Sydney. I'm meeting friends later for dinner, and then we're having a bonfire on the beach."

"You won't be waving sparklers around in people's

faces, will you?" Sam would never be other than the mother of two three-year-olds.

"No, Mum. We're all behaving."

"What's your bonfire celebrating?"

"I have no idea. Just having a good time."

"Oh, those were the days. No 'why,' just 'where should we meet and who's bringing the wine?' Enjoy it while you can."

Sam smiled as visions of a bonfire triggered a memory of her and Polly joining the celebration on Dunkery Beacon. *Could that really have been 1981? So long ago!* "I remember the bonfire the night before Charles and Diana's wedding. The musical tendrils of a lone piper snaked through the air, welcoming the throng as we all hiked up the hill towards the fire beacon. Bet you won't have bagpipes."

"I hope not," said Tori. Her father's Scottish roots had never swayed her musical tastes.

"We never even thought of going to London to see history in the making. A four-hour drive seemed a long way. And here you are, on the other side of the world for no better reason than because you can be." Sam sighed and recalled the crowd straining their eyes east, looking for the first glimmer of the chain of lighted beacons that would radiate out from London through Berkshire, then Wiltshire, and on to Somerset. With a great shout in unison, the crowd had seen the speck of flame glow in the distance, and Dunkery's wooden beacon was lit in response, quickly relayed to another across the channel in Wales. From her perch at the top of the world on Exmoor in 1981, and from her perch on a midwestern bed in 2016, Sam wouldn't have traded her place under that twinkling dome for a chair at the altar of Saint Paul's Cathedral itself.

"Funny you should mention England. I was thinking about Exmoor today. Well, Bossington actually." Tori's words delighted Sam. She and her daughter were always on the same wavelength, no matter how far apart.

"Someone was feeding cake to some birds today, and it took me right back to Dad and the robins."

A fit of giggles shook Sam's body. "Ah, the robins!"

Despite all the glorious scenery, Bossington was most closely affiliated with teatime for young Sam. Hungry hikers made West Country pilgrimages to the Bossington Tearoom. The Welsh dresser opposite the kitchen door fairly groaned under the weight of cakes and scones, homemade jam in pots with cloth covers, and tiered silver cake stands for those hardy enough to attempt the World Famous High Tea. This particular treat was Larry's birthday present to Emma every year. It included a daunting array of miniature, crust-less sandwiches on the bottom tier, doorstop-sized slabs of fruit and sponge cakes on the second tier, with the whole monument crowned by scones, jam, and clotted cream. The Tower of Babel itself suddenly rising out of the Bristol Channel couldn't have produced more appreciative gasps as the feast was paraded to the table near the fireplace.

Sam's children had preferred to sit in the tea gardens to make their memories. Walking sticks, tired dogs, and dusty rucksacks were strewn beside wrought-iron tables dotted around the lawn at the back of the tearoom. The wooden trellises sagged under honeysuckle and roses while the hum of lazy bees lulled the visitors to numb contentment. In the intoxicating stupor induced by nature's best and the cook's treats, tourists planned early retirements.

"I'm going to live here and eat cream teas for breakfast," Tori, the ten-year-old, had announced one day. She wasn't the only one to fantasize. The cream-tea dreamers didn't see themselves as grockles, the slightly derogatory term used in Somerset for tourists; they were merely misplaced locals. Sam understood the sentiment now.

"Oh, those territorial robins, dive-bombing the tables for scone crumbs!" Sam could see Tori smile down the phone line. "Dad was taking photos of the 'cute little chappies' one minute and then flapping arms and menus the next, hiding plates under his armpits, and shooing robins out of his hair. Remember the tea sloshing into saucers and cake stands wavering?"

"He was so mad at that 'Don't Feed the Birds' sign," Tori giggled. "Said it suggested a choice he didn't feel he'd been offered." The phone line filled with silent reminiscence. "Well, I've got to go. Just checking in. Love you, Mum." And she was gone. Like the robins.

Beaches. Weddings. Robins. Sam stared through the darkness while memories floated and bobbed, ebbed and flowed, and skipped and jumped through time and space; one scene or scent or word or smile leading to a thousand other scenes, scents, words, or smiles.

A wave of appreciation for Brody unexpectedly washed over Sam. Picturing him in England through the years brought comfort. He *had* felt at home there. In fact, he'd been quite besotted with her homeland. He'd been an active participant in planning their first joint grand scheme: find a way to live in England. She knew he understood her love for it all. She knew he'd been telling the truth about wanting to live there.

"I didn't imagine it," Sam defended herself to the judgemental crack in the ceiling. "So why this change? Why commit himself to a four-year term in office just as we could think about relocating? Is he having his own panic response to the prospect of leaving native turf?" Sam racked her brain but couldn't recall openly discussing moving in ages, so why would this be an active concern of Brody's at this particular time? She felt a softening in her heart for her husband. She knew how hard it was to live a new life in a new world.

Sam rubbed her temples to clear her brain, but Bossington flooded in.

Minus Thirty

Despite Geraldine's protestations, Dunster and Squirt, Polly's loaner pony, set off on the hack to Bossington gymkhana sporting plaited tails looking like battered toilet brushes and enormous mane plaits.

"Bet you could pick up BBC Wales on those," Mr. Winterbourne chuckled as the girls mounted up. Squirt was supposedly named after his size, but the girls associated the name more with his sloppy diarrhoea that was impossible to scoop onto a shovel or brush out of a tail.

Emma planned to follow on to the show later with a picnic lunch and the camera, joined by Helen who was already predicting disaster with her "Don't hurt Squirt. We can't afford to fix him" like he was a battery-operated toy, which in fact he may have been based on his either full-stop or full-start mentality.

With Bossington in sight, Sam looked back over her shoulder across the fields and the bay, seeing in the distance the hamlet of Porlock Weir, known simply as The Weir to locals. Between her and the fishing boats and pubs of The Weir stood the equitation centre. "I'll make you proud," Sam promised quietly under her breath. Knowing it was there gave the nerve-wracked novice courage. Briefly.

The clattering of hoofs on the lane, the roar of horse box engines, and the excited nickering of pony friends greeting pony friends set copper kettles rattling on sills and sent sleepy cats diving for cover. Dunster and Squirt sidestepped and arched their necks as they spooked at the hollyhocks. Hikers turned to take photos before disappearing into the garden behind the tea shop for a well-earned cuppa. They sensed safety from the fray. Until they met the robins.

Riding through the gates of the show grounds, Sam fingered the plastic bag in her pocket that she'd brought to carry all the rosettes home in. Her pockets were so stuffed as to make Sam look like she had dual inflatable airbags under her hand-me-down waxed jacket. Sugar lumps took up a large amount of space, speaking of Sam's certainty that a great deal of bribery was going to be necessary. She also had chewing gum (to calm her nerves) and emergency phone numbers to be found by the St John Ambulance Society crew if she was "incapacitated," according to Polly's mum. Sam wasn't really sure what "incapacitated" meant, but it sounded ominous. And of course there was money for slices of cake from the Women's Institute stall.

Sam and Polly gasped as they passed the cake stall; white, lacy cloth-covered tables were laden with the entire contents of the *WI Bakery Cookbook*. You could tell the fairy cakes the younger children had helped to decorate by the uneven clumping of sprinkles, an inch thick in some areas. Little signs with 2p, 5p, or 10p were placed precisely in front of each cake plate. It was the best recruiting tool for the St John Ambulance Society there was. "Why else would otherwise normal people sign up?" Sam had heard Mrs. Dale say to Emma. "They can't enjoy watching out-of-control ponies career into fences, splattering blood from split lips and noses everywhere." Not exactly what Sam needed to hear.

Dunster and Squirt made it safely past the bunting, barking dogs, loudspeaker poles, judges' caravan, and screaming prams. The two pony friends knew how to be good ambassadors for their breed, despite their embarrassment at having to go out in public sporting the awful plaits. Only hollyhocks freaked them out.

"Why don't the other Exmoor ponies have plaits?"

Polly had asked out of the side of her mouth.

"Because their riders didn't train at WEC," Sam replied with distain.

"Oh, right then. Let's set up camp over there." Polly waved to a quiet spot by a fence. They dismounted, loosened girths, and unwrapped the head collars and lead ropes from around their waists. This cued Dunster and Squirt to graze. Polly looked sceptically at the forming green mouths.

"It's all right," Sam said cheerfully. "We've got our bit cloths if we need to clean off any green glop before our class."

"If?" said Polly.

The girls began to check out the competition. Louise Fotheringham was there, of course. Expensive pony tied to the back of the Range Rover, mother in heels setting up a four-course meal on the sturdy-looking folding table. Jack Sturgis, the butcher's son, was there on yet another pony the girls had never seen before. He seemed to have a new pony almost every week at lessons with Geraldine and was always a favourite to win on any one of them. Polly had wondered out loud one time if Jack's dad's line of work encouraged the ponies to do well. From then on, Sam tended to glare accusingly at Jack when he arrived for lessons on a new mount.

"What happened to Oliver?" Sam once asked Jack, having heard that Oliver had knocked down two fences at the Porlock Show. Jack cheerfully told of a buyer in Bristol, but Sam's accusatory, squinty-eyed look said she didn't buy it.

Wendy, Wanda, and William Waverly arrived in a hired commercial horse lorry with five ponies on board. Polly and Sam spent many a sleepover coming up with silly names beginning with W that would suit their ponies: Wally, Wobbly, Whoops, Weaver, Wavy. Oh, how the girls wished the Waverly's lived in one of the "W" villages—Wheddon Cross, Withypool, Wootton Courtney,

Watchet, Wiveliscombe—just so they could pretend to be the announcer at the show. "And next we have Wanda Waverly from Withypool on Wobbly. She's weaving up to the first fence. Whoops! She's whacked it, and wow! She wiped out! Wescue her, pwease." Well, it took the sting out of hearing about all the Waverly wosettes at school the next day.

Sam had time to acknowledge the envious glance of a little girl holding her mother's hand and peeking through the fence at all the commotion. Sam took Dunster up to the fence and let the girl stroke his nose, offering her a ride on the soon-to-be rosette-bedecked Dunster after the show. The little girl's look of stunned joy was lovely to see.

Sam and Polly had entered three events: the bending race, egg and spoon race, and the sack race. Emma had said this was enough for a first try, as she didn't want Sam jumping anything yet until she knew how Dunster would do in crowds. It was a chilly, windy June day in a muddy field, so expecting crowds may have been a little optimistic. Most spectators were sitting in their cars. Except for Louise's mum, who, having purchased at great expense the Fortnum and Mason wicker hamper with the famous F and M logo on the side when they first bought Ye Olde Vicarage, wanted to make sure that everyone knew her sandwiches and pâtés had been packed in the best. Therefore, the hamper was displayed prominently, guarded by a goose bump-covered, beautifully coiffed, short-skirted, nonsensible-shoed, scowling lady praying for the entire event to be rained off.

As Polly and Sam watched the other children tack up and swing into the saddle, they faced their first rookie show dilemma.

"Should we warm up and show how well trained we are, or keep it a surprise?" Polly asked. After all, they were an unknown entity to the other competitors, who had only heard about Sam and Polly's exploits at school, and a carefully edited version of them it was too. The two friends watched the Waverlys practise leaping on and off ponies, bend ponies at speed through imaginary poles, and flap Hessian sacks around to desensitise their mounts to this kind of shenanigans. Sam watched Jack charge along with his egg and spoon with his willing Connemara pony keeping pace at his side, neck arched and nicely extended forelegs in trot.

"Nah," Sam replied. "We practised at home." Truth be told, Squirt and Dunster looked to have no interest in more practice. They looked like conserving any modicum of energy they had left after the hack to the show might be important. Having eaten all he could reach, Dunster rested on three legs, looking like if he could rest another without tipping over he would. Squirt stood so close to Dunster with his eyes shut that if Dunster had tipped over, Squirt would have fallen like a domino. Sam opened three or four sticks of gum to settle the queasiness she felt. Chewing loudly, she heard her name called and turned to find her mum had arrived.

"Your mum won't be coming after all, due to … er … nerves," Emma apologized to Polly. Sam jammed on a hairnet to stop all her thick, red, curly hair from squirting out from under her hat like exploding ginger beer from a bottle. And because that's what the WEC riders wore.

"The gymkhana games will begin shortly, so everyone should make sure they have their numbers tied round their waists," the girls heard over the loudspeaker.

"Numbers?" Sam and Polly shrieked in unison. Throwing lead ropes at Emma, the girls raced to the show tent, grabbed their numbers, and flew back again. Sam was now chewing her gum frantically with enough force to crack walnuts. Emma hadn't seen that much of Sam's tonsils since she'd slammed Sam's toddler hand in a car door.

"You are not getting on that pony chewing gum," Emma dictated. "I've warned you a million times about choking while riding." Sam assumed Mrs. Dale had taught her mum that.

Sam spat the huge wad of gum over her shoulder and got ready to mount up. Both ponies sensed the increased fear in their riders and twirled in circles, showing more vim and vigour in the next thirty seconds than they had in the past week. While pulling on one rein to stop the circling, Sam saw the green ooze that was slithering out of Dunster's mouth, blowing bubbles through his bit ring, dripping down his chest, and splattering on his hooves.

"How could a bit of grass even begin to make that much mess?" Sam frantically asked no one in particular. There was nothing for it. She would have to get that bit rag and clean this up or she'd be the laughing stock of the show grounds. Sam grabbed the rag from the ground behind her and started rubbing bit, nose, lips, and eyes like those sweepers with the brooms in curling competitions. Looking over her shoulder to see Polly already walking away towards the ring, the rubbing increased until Sam noticed the rag wasn't moving very far. In fact, it wasn't moving at all. In confusion, she looked back at Dunster's head and to her horror saw chewing gum stuck over everything. *Note to self: Never spit gum over your shoulder if the bit rag's exact location is unknown.* A lesson to analyse later.

The bit rag adhered in goopy folds to the bit and noseband and every single whisker was coated with gum. Dunster was smacking his lips, trying to free whiskers from nostrils and teeth from the bit and bottom eyelashes from top eyelashes, nodding his head up and down in short bursts like something out of a cockatiel mating ritual. He attempted to lift his top lip but nothing budged except the ends of the rag that flapped in his eyes. With one final jerk, Dunster broke free of Sam and took off, neck bolt upright, nose in the air, trying to focus out of the tiny slits that were all that were left of his eyesight.

Show people were used to loose ponies. They knew to grab young children, turn an unfriendly pony's haunches away from the oncoming assault, and assemble a few grown-ups to jump in front of the free spirit with arms outstretched. This time was different, though. It was clear from the flapping cloth and the for-some-reason almost closed eyes that this particular escapee was essentially blind. Prospective pony catchers leapt for safety, car doors slammed shut, the St John Ambulance crew members went into crisis mode (meaning, they put down their cake plates), and the voice over the loudspeaker barked useful instructions like "Heads up!" and "Whoa!" Sam was in pursuit, and though this was her first experience hunting Exmoor pony, she was pretty convinced the situation was hopeless. Emma had already turned her back with her hand over her mouth. Larry's name was mentioned through clenched teeth. (Incidentally, Larry was in Minehead watching rugby that afternoon. Never would there have been a better time to have rugby players at a horse show, the only breed of human willing to launch themselves at the legs of a galloping pony. Opportunity missed to join the two cultures.)

The good news: Dunster missed the fancy dress parade that was currently in the ring. Little Indians, princesses, chocolate bars, and a wizard on a piebald broomstick turned to watch the galloping freak show as parents in the ring placed protective arms around the backsides of their mounted charges. More good news: Dunster missed the parking cones, loudspeaker pole, and the horse lorries. The bad news: the Women's Institute took the brunt of it.

Dunster must have seen the white flash of tablecloths appear in front of him, and maybe he thought he was running towards The Light. Anyway, at the last second, he tried to jump the table, but he'd only practised for the egg and spoon race, so his jumping skills were rusty. He made contact with outstretched forelegs that, rather than collapsing the table, sent it in an upward slow-motion spin, centrifugal force doing the rest of the damage. Cream and strawberries squirted from the centre of chocolate cakes and splattered the faces, aprons, and shoes of the stunned bakers. Pies catapulted from shiny tins, and biscuits hurtled through space like miniature meteor showers. Jam rolls unrolled, marzipan stuck in hair, and the breeze was filled with the aroma of almonds, lemon curd, ginger, and maraschino cherries. Clouds of icing sugar burst like tear gas over the riot beneath. Rock cakes came by their name honestly, as the flying projectiles cracked plates and lips alike. They were the only baked goods that retained shape well enough to be positively identified later. Sprinkles were found in pockets, socks, and ears for days after.

It was the vet who finally grabbed Dunster. The confused, panting little Exmoor looked more like a birthday cake caricature of a pony than a real one, as he was covered in jam and icing. Dr. Bates managed to pry open one eye enough to help Dunster see he was in fact still on planet Earth in the presence of friends. The rag was yanked from the bit ring, removing a few whiskers in the process, and as Sam came gasping up on the scene, she heard more than one person asking, "What the bloody hell is stuck all over his face?"

Beetroot to the hairline, Sam stood holding the sticky lead rope, unable to let it go. Dunster was checked for injuries, though no one could have identified blood through all that jam. The WI ladies were checked by the St John Ambulance crew. But no one checked on Sam. She thought she was possibly incapacitated, but if the medics had found the phone number in her pocket, she bet no one in her family would have answered the phone anyway.

కురా

Heading home in stunned silence, Sam knew her mother was right when she'd said it wasn't appropriate to expect Dunster to perform after all he'd been through.

"Sorry, Sam." Polly offered commiserations but appeared to be trying to distance herself from it all in front of the Waverlys.

Seriously? Sam thought. *The only girl on the planet to have a plan for evading rabid flocks of canaries and Polly hadn't anticipated chewing gum-induced equine blindness?*

Sam led Dunster back up the lane towards Porlock, as there was too much icing and jam all over the tack and dishevelled plaits to get a good grip for mounting. Dunster's nostrils were still stuck together, leaving him to breathe noisily through his mouth. His humiliated owner was grateful for the towering hedges during her disgraced exit, but the single *clip-clop* on the tarmac going in a different direction to all the other *clip-clops* sounded like an accusatory gong to her ears. Sam pulled Dunster into a lay-by to let a car go past. It was her mum, with a set jaw and a "Wait 'til I see your father" kind of expression. Sam dropped her eyes to the ground.

During her lonely walk home, Sam had time to wonder if the expression "caked" came from an incident like this. Caked in cake. Which came first, the noun or the verb? And would they have to cancel the rest of the show if the St John Ambulance Society abandoned the place now that there was no cake stall? Brushing against Dunster, Sam felt something sharp sticking out from under the saddle pad and found an unbroken gingersnap. Somewhat of a miracle. On seeing the biscuit, Sam cried for the first time, humiliation giving way to disappointment over all the wasted practice and the knowledge that Monday morning at school was going to be unbearable. But mostly she cried because she could have hurt Dunster. Unforgivable.

"I'm worse than the greengrocer in *Moorland Mousie,*" Sam sobbed out loud. Dunster didn't make eye contact, which made Sam sob harder.

The story had reached Seabreeze Farm long before Sam got back. Mr. Winterbourne silently took Dunster from her and gallantly began the unenviable task of de-caking and de-gumming a dejected-looking pony, joined by a furious-looking Emma. Larry, having just got back from the rugby match, saw Sam arrive in the farmyard across the road. He cheerfully shouted out the window, "The kettle's on. Would you like cake?"

The news hadn't reached Minehead yet then.

Chapter Eight

"Is this why I ended up leaving Exmoor?" Sam sat upright in bed. "Subconsciously holding onto abject humiliation?"

It was Saturday morning, so obviously she must have slept, though the film had played all night in her dreams: rock cake galaxies, a space-suited Dunster, Mission Control sounding a lot like her mother. She laid back down and took deep breaths. Forty-plus years later, that first show could still wake her in a sweat. She could feel the tiny drops on her upper lip and the flush of shame as that Dead Rider Walking scene played in her head. It was true: women held onto failure so much more tightly than success.

Dressed and heading to the kitchen, Sam opened the back door. There was no Brody to let the dogs out at 6:30 a.m., so their legs must have been crossed for a while now. She looked at her distorted face in the shiny surface of the stainless steel tea kettle as she waited for it to boil. She warmed the new Spode teapot over the sink. No microwaving teabags in a mug for her. She tried to imagine something happening to her now that would cause Bossington levels of humiliation. She couldn't come up with anything.

Finding she was out of milk, Sam turned off the kettle, called the dogs in, and grabbed her car keys. The realisation of how Americanised she'd become hit her as she thought surely she could walk to the store from here. Back in Porlock, she'd have walked, with both dogs, who would have been happy to be tied to a bus stop sign outside the shop while she chatted away inside. Simpler time. Simpler place. In the States in 2016, the police would have been called to check on the welfare of the animals and to assess the safety of citizens as they walked past potentially dangerous cuddly bears. Sam loaded the excited boys into the back of the car for the sixty-second ride.

"Morning, Macy!" Sam called towards the deli counter as she headed to the refrigerators at the back of the shop.

"Hi, Sam," replied Macy, as she wrapped up an order of roast beef. "Congrats on the big news!"

Sam stopped in her tracks, walked backwards, pirouetted on one foot to face Macy, and asked, "What big news?"

"The citizenship news, of course!" Macy beamed. "It's about time you became one of us!"

"Who said anything about citizenship? And since when haven't I been one of you?"

"Thomas told me," Macy continued brightly, referring to Thomas Sunby, the committee chairman. "You didn't think we'd pass up this opportunity for a party, did you? Of course, none of us has any idea what you do at a citizenship party, but if there's beer and brats, you can rest assured we'll all be there."

"Who's 'all'? And when was I to be invited?" Sam's brain raced to determine if Thomas was in a position to not only decide which citizenship she should have but also when the celebration should begin.

"Well, everyone on the committee's coming. The Board of Ed's coming, unofficially, of course, as I'm not sure the BOE is supposed to show favouritism, and Janice from the paper's coming to take photos. They thought it would be nice to do a write-up on you and Brody to get everyone excited about the election. Oh, and Thomas's daughter's making the cake. Have you met—?"

"Wait! Just wait!" Sam interrupted. "There's a cake?

A citizenship cake has been commissioned before I've filed one Iowa of paperwork? Before I've even decided whether I'm going to get citizenship?"

Sam's mouth hung open as her eyes prickled and her palms, upturned and shaking, itched to close around Brody's neck. She had just time enough to catch Macy's startled eyes before she bolted from the shop.

Humiliation was not confined to Somerset after all.

⋙⋘

It was a good job Brody's vintage car show was a three-hour drive away. Sam's first impulse had been to drive straight there, march up to the MG BGT tent, kick down the bonnet support, drag Brody to his knees, and beat him with an antique tire iron for two reasons: one, for assuming that he controlled her life enough to tell others her plans before she knew them herself, and two, no one told Sam what kind of cake to have at her own party. No one.

During the sixty-second trip home, Sam managed to calm herself enough to realise an arrest for aggravated assault, however justified, could take away her citizenship choices. Not that she was saying she'd get US citizenship, just that options should remain open. A saying Brody used sometimes (usually when in trouble) went something like "If you knew this was your last five minutes on Earth, would you remain angry? If the answer is yes, go ahead and be angry." Sam thought hard about that.

She sat, angry, on the couch, drinking her breakfast tea without milk. "Another American practice," she cursed through clenched teeth. "Amazing the damn Yanks got to the moon first based on such primitive behaviours."

Glaring accusingly at her black tea as though its deficiencies alone explained why she couldn't possibly become an American citizen, Sam's mind raced. How many people in town knew she'd been presumptively declared unfit for political consumption and sentenced to US citizenship? Well, the answer to that was, of course, everyone. If Thomas knew and Macy knew, it was chaff in the wind, settling on every roof in the county. Then another thought. It was Saturday now. The meeting was Thursday night, two hours before her chopstick fight with Brody. So all day Friday, Sam realised with horror, she was the only person in town not to know her predetermined fate!

"Bloody hell!" Sam yelled, forcing the dogs to tiptoe towards her, tails swaying infinitesimally.

"Did you set her off?" Sherlock looked accusingly at his brother.

"Not me. Bet it was Dad," suggested the much more astute JB.

Clutching her tea and narrowing her eyes, Sam had to concede it was a smart move on Brody's part. Now not only was she fighting him, she was a gang of one against a whole town. Standing up and pacing the sitting room, sloshing tea on the rug, Sam asked herself how she was going to explain to a whole community that she didn't want to be one of them. How could she offend her friends and colleagues by saying, "Look, I enjoy your company, but I really don't think I want to part of the clan. Are we good?" It would beg the question, "Why not?" And Sam found herself unable to fault that. She'd ask, wouldn't she? If she were celebrating the Queen's birthday at a tea party on British soil, and some foreigner announced over the cucumber sandwiches that he wouldn't consider British citizenship, she'd look at him strangely and wonder what was wrong with him, wouldn't she? She'd politely, though somewhat condescendingly, enquire, "Why do you feel being a citizen of Lichtenstein, or Turkey, or Peru, or the good ol' USA is preferable to being a fully-fledged, card-carrying member of the GNE—that's Greatest Nation on Earth?" Or words to that effect, asked with a belittling smile while peeking out from under her floppy tea party hat trimmed with a Union Jack on a stick.

But back to the issue at hand. "Brody agreed at the meeting that I'd get US citizenship! On the spot! No 'I'll get back to you.' No 'Let me talk to Sam about it.' He'd said yes straight away! And proceeded to order the cake!"

Despicable. On both counts.

Minus Twenty-Nine

"Who'd find a horse show fun after that?" Sam argued with Polly, sitting on the paddock fence after school on Monday. Louise, Jack, and the Waverlys had obviously been told not to tease her at school, so their lips were sealed, but their smirks spoke volumes. Some talented peer, as it turned out related to the humourous poet Pam Ayres, had put a poem in her desk entitled "Ode to Chewing Gum": "Covered in gum / Leaving Sam on her bum / Dunster set off hunting cake." Sam knew this episode of her life would go down in the history of the village permanently, like Olympic training grounds, Porlock Hill, famous poets, and smuggler pubs. Only not so likely to attract grockles.

Despite encouragement from Geraldine, there were no more horse shows that summer for Sam. Dunster was, for some reason, head-shy. Bit rags were spotted a mile off. In all his fifteen years, no one had ever seen this side of him. "*Even a steadfast Exmoor pony can only tolerate so much*," his wary eyes suggested. Sam wasn't allowed to groom his head until Geraldine had worked the kinks out.

But each time Sam slept over at Polly's, she saw an ever-increasing display of rosettes. Fancy dress competitions were fast becoming Polly's passion. She and her mum had made a skirt of brown fabric that hung down over Squirt's body and legs, with a puffy topping of white fabric draped around Polly, the whole thing dotted with brightly coloured sprinkles. Polly wore a cherry-red cap on top. Her "Chocolate Fairy Cake" came in second at the

Huntscott show a few weeks following "The Disaster."

"It's a tribute to the Women's Institute," Polly placated.

"It's treason," an unplacated Sam muttered back.

Polly had the nerve to ask Sam to show again late that summer. She needed a second pony to complete her idea for a Spanish Riding School-inspired fancy dress entry. She showed Sam how she had made hats, and she got Squirt to demonstrate the one-legged wave she'd taught him that was supposed to represent the Levade. It looked more like a drunken attempt to hail an equine taxi. "Not in my lifetime!" Sam had snapped.

Once Dunster had forgiven his owner (sugar lumps were involved), and Sam had forgiven Polly (sugary treats were involved), the girls spent most of the summer holidays hacking through the combes and hills around Porlock village. They were a familiar sight at the thatched Worthy toll gate, heading up the bridle path and through the tunnels that led to Culbone Church. Ley Hill saw them fleeing imaginary Welsh marauders, a skill they'd have done well to hone, as it turned out. North Hill left them panting for breath as they gazed out over the foreign world beyond Porlock Vale. Sam saw the little girl a few weeks after the Bossington mishap, the one who had looked through the fence at her. She was being led through the village on a tiny skewbald pony. When she saw Sam, her back got straighter, her reins higher, her heels lower. She seemed to be the only one in Somerset who thought Sam was still worthy of any respect as a rider. Equestrian life, though at times humiliating, was indeed still inherently good.

అ∽అ

Sam's self-imposed show ban was lifted the following summer. She went to Luccombe Show in June, just before her tenth birthday. Polly and Sam set off early through the narrow winding lanes of Doverhay, through the sleepy hamlet of Horner, edged by Horner Water, the crystal-clear stream chasing leaves and dragonflies down from the moors. No plaits this time.

"Did you know Exmoor covers two hundred and sixty-seven square miles?" Polly asked through a mouthful of butter and sugar sandwich.

"I did not," replied an equally stuffed mouth. Sam tried to picture anything square about Exmoor. Streams meandered, ponies ambled, lanes wobbled, winds gyrated, earth undulated. No, nothing square about it. "But shouldn't we be focusing on winning rosettes?"

Without responding, Polly ploughed on. "Do you ever feel bad that Dunster and Squirt aren't able to wander with their ancestor's descendants? I wonder if they dream about ambling through the heather, lifting their unbridled heads, sniffing the free winds that frolic through the woods and valleys, playfully catching manes and tails." Sam looked over at her friend, then down at the sandwiches, wondering if they were responsible for the depth of this conversation.

Oh, I get it, Sam twigged. Polly had just entered her first poetry competition.

"I think Dunster would love stealing picnic lunches and being part of a gang ... er ... following paths carved out by ancient ponies ... long ago." Sam had decided not to enter the poetry competition. "But something tells me Dunster would like to be a part-time free-living pony," Sam continued, because free-living is what the Exmoor pony herds were. They were not truly wild, as they did in fact belong to someone and were rounded up, bred judiciously, and at times sold on to form other herds or to find employment as riding ponies. "Dunster would like to be free between meals but captive for sugar lumps, bran mashes, and apple cores served in a nice shelter with fluffy straw. He's a smart old boy."

಄

Some things at the Luccombe Show looked the same to Sam as that fateful first attempt: the bunting, the horse lorries, and the cake stall. Sam swore she detected a minuscule motion of bakers' hands reaching to move the table a little farther back as she passed. But some things were different: no chewing gum and more oversight from Emma, for which Sam was quietly grateful, though would never say so.

Today, Sam was trading the gymkhana games for show jumping. She and Dunster had actually become quite good over the last several months. "Steer to the centre of the jump, anticipate the take-off, look for the next jump, and change your canter lead or you'll fall over during a tight turn! Good job!" Geraldine's instructions flooded her brain. Sam never needed reminding to knot her fingers in the mane if things got hairy, so to speak.

"That sandwich feels like it's churning a bit," Sam complained to Polly, holding her nervous stomach while standing outside the show-jumping ring. The small jumps appeared to increase in size from embarrassingly tiny to humongous proportions the closer it came to her turn. Surely there was some mistake and she'd accidentally entered the Hickstead Grand Prix! Her fear increased as the previous pony was caught, rider scooped up by the jump crew, and the fence rebuilt as she heard the consoling remarks by the announcer: "Wanda Waverly is alwight and weady to twy again next week." Well, that's what Sam heard, anyway. Dunster didn't seem too traumatized by the events. A twitching ear and a sniff of the breeze explained all to him. Wanda gave Sam a grim, teary glance as she walked from the ring to gentle applause.

It was a few seconds before Sam realised that the voices in her head were in fact coming from her mother. "They've announced your name twice! Wake up! Into the ring at a strong trot, now." And Dunster did just that, not just a relatively strong trot, but a *real* strong trot. He hadn't competed since Sam had owned him, and it occurred to her during the easy transition into canter that maybe he'd missed the bright lights and the opportunity for a celebratory buck as he sped through the finish line.

With his neck arched and a spring in his step, Dunster cantered once around the ring, and on hearing the start bell, he acted like he knew just what to do. Just not the course. He attempted to swing towards the first jump in sight, which led to some barely contained gasps from the sparse spectator section. "Here we go again," the gasp insinuated. But Sam steered away and around to the start gates, and from there, she remembered absolutely nothing until standing outside the ring. With her smiling mum on one side and Polly on the other, Dunster was enjoying exuberant patting. Polly looked happy, so Sam assumed she'd not only survived but had done nothing to embarrass anyone. When Geraldine ran up smiling, Sam plucked up the courage to speak.

"Did I knock down any fences?"

"No!" replied a relieved Geraldine. "You're in the jump-off against Jack and William. Only three clear rounds in the whole class!"

Sam knew both Jack and William were riding young ponies in their mounts' jumping debuts, the only reason they were tackling such a small course. And for her, at her age on a well-seasoned Exmoor statesman, it probably should have felt a little embarrassing. But she'd known true humiliation, so this didn't sting at all. And Dunster didn't look like this was all beneath him either; in fact, he looked quite chuffed with himself, huffing a little, but all four legs firmly on the ground rather than one instantly resting after any kind of exercise. Sam was used to the feeling of sliding off his side, like an egg from a frying pan, due to his dipped hip, so standing at a square halt had Sam looking underneath him to see if the landing gear was all right.

As the initial joy of a clear round abated, Sam began to process the implications.

"I don't know the jump-off course!" she wailed. "I never thought I'd need to!" The surprise seemed universal in her small entourage. For a moment, all stood silently nodding. Then they snapped to it. It seemed unfair to rely on Dunster to learn the course, so Emma grabbed the reins, Polly offered to clean Dunster, and Geraldine took Sam to the board displaying the jump-off course.

"Right, start here, over one and two, tight turn here, over the double ..." Geraldine made it all sound straightforward, like all the jumps were stationary and in a logical order. To Sam, in her panic, the jumps kept moving around the paper like manic ants.

"Breathe. Focus," Geraldine said in Sam's ear, praying for redemption.

Several minutes later, with the course now prepared for the jump-off, Sam was ready. She briefly thought of that first show and the disappointment and the Monday after at school. There was no way that was happening again.

Sam was the last to go. She watched Jack, then William, fly around the course, laying low on their ponies' necks, booting hard to cut corners, both going clear like blurred streaks full pelt through the finish gates. *No pressure then.*

Once in the ring, everything seemed to go quiet, just the wind rushing past Sam's ears, the thud of Dunster's hooves, the tap of horseshoes on wooden poles, and the sensation of being on a wind-up toy that was close to spent. It seemed to take longer and longer to get to the next fence. Sam felt she had to hold her jump position for longer and longer too. The rushing wind noises disappeared and were replaced by frantic tongue clicking, which Sam realised were coming from her. The pair didn't exactly streak through the finish gates, but at least they didn't break into a trot before going through them. *"Well, I've already hacked from Porlock to Luccombe with very little sustenance,"* Dunster seemed to pant.

Once outside the ring, someone turned up the volume again, and Sam could hear Polly shouting, "Well done!," and some tinkling clapping. Not exactly the deafening applause Sam had imagined, but music to her ears anyway.

"Did I knock down any fences?" she gasped, holding her side.

"No. Just a few time faults, but very well done," Geraldine said, patting Sam's leg and Dunster's neck. Sam didn't even know what a time fault was, so hearing she'd had a few, quite a few actually, didn't bother her. All she knew was she'd won third place.

"I won third place, Mum!" Sam yelled over her shoulder at her grinning (read "not embarrassed") mother. "Over real fences!" Sam collapsed on Dunster's neck, hugging and patting him gleefully.

Both Jack and William were mounted near the gate ready to get their rosettes. Jack gave Sam a cheery thumbs up as they marched to the judges for their prizes and a photo for the paper. Sam was on cloud nine. Dunster was on dinner time. The apple offered by Mrs. Peal, the vicar's wife, who clipped the rosette to Dunster's brow band, was wolfed down with gusto, and he nearly knocked Mrs. Peal over, rooting for a repeat.

Outside the ring, there was a hero's welcome from the little girl on the skewbald pony who was there competing in her first show. She asked if she could pat Dunster, and Sam finally asked her name.

"Charlotte," whispered a shy voice. Sam began writing, "To Charlotte: Keep practicing and you will achieve our level of success. Love, Sam and Dunster," on the outstretched show program. This didn't actually happen, but it was just a matter of time now, Sam felt. In years to come, Sam would remember Charlotte.

Miraculously, Larry had appeared from somewhere, beaming and nodding to the other parents. Must be a rugby match close by.

"Don't know what all the fuss was about," he said to

Emma. "Windy hillsides and chaos indeed! You're all having a great time today, winning in the sunshine." Emma folded her arms, a "you have no idea" glare in her eyes.

"Here's some money for cake," Larry said. Sam was so euphoric she forgot to be embarrassed at the WI table.

Dunster was settled under a shady oak with lunch. Tack off, brushed down like the champion he was, he was soon in his three-legged, closed-eyed position with floppy lower lip, which was just how Sam assumed Stroller, the real life wonder pony, looked after the Olympics. Sam spent the afternoon helping Polly with her Boadicea fancy dress costume and watching the big horses compete, those long-legged teenaged riders jumping impossible high fences at the speed of light.

"Oh, yes, I could do that," Sam said to herself, wiping cake from her mouth. "Move over, Mousie. Long live Dunster, king of the ponies!"

∂∽∾

At school, creative writing was Sam's thing. Her teacher taught her two rules: never use the word *thing* and write about what you know. Sam knew about cream teas, so early literary endeavours included superhero stories about Skippy the Super Scone, loosely based on the popular Australian television show *Skippy the Bush Kangaroo*. Only in England. With Skippy in constant peril of being eaten by Evil Grockles. Murdering jam pots and owners of contaminated clotted cream factories intent on global domination kept Skippy busy. Mrs. Dale would have been proud. Surprisingly, the novice author was underappreciated by her English teacher. Her art teacher was guilty of same when Sam tried to illustrate the novels for publication.

"I admit that an accurate depiction of a terrified scone is difficult," a paint-splattered Mrs. Mona said. But she gave little credit for trying. So Skippy the Super Scone remained unpublished. Sam would watch *SpongeBob SquarePants* in later decades and quietly rage.

Unfulfilled literary dreams aside, Sam's and Polly's lives followed the rhythms of the marvellous gift that was life on Exmoor. School, horses, Brownies. Horses and school. Horses, school, and, occasionally, boys. It seemed this idyllic existence would go on forever.

Minus Twenty-Eight

Exmoor, England. 1980s

"What the heck?" said Sam as she turned sideways in the bathroom mirror to assess the growing mounds on her chest.

"What the heck?" said Emma as she stared at the newly bought jeans swinging above ankle level on Sam's legs.

"*What the heck?*" said Dunster's stumbling gait as Sam's boots almost dragged along the ground during rides.

And so Equine Paradise was lost due to an inconvenient growth spurt. While Sam had given up on competing against Stroller for the smallest pony/rider international jumping sensation, she had assumed that she and Dunster would continue their domination of the Prix Caprilli. They were rarely out of the medals when the Waverlys were on vacation, Jack was sick, and when Louise's family moved back to London permanently after a messy divorce involving a scandal with a greengrocer from Fortnum and Mason.

For Polly, Squirt had been replaced by a new loaner, Eccles. The dark spots on his white coat obviously reminded someone of the dried fruit in an Eccles cake. Eccles was an actual horse at sixteen-hands high. Polly needed an actual leg up rather than just folding at the waist to lay across Squirt's saddle. This transition happened earlier in the year when, overnight, Polly's legs took on the proportions of an Olympic high jumper. Riding beside her on hacks since then had involved a certain amount of neck craning to talk, and Dunster had to break into begrudging trots to keep up. But this sign of things to come hadn't really registered with Sam until her boots started to trip Dunster as they cantered along.

Unbeknownst to Sam, Geraldine had started the conversation with the Westons about what they would do when Dunster was outgrown.

"My job's more secure these days," Larry said to Emma over lunch. He was now manager of a hotel on the Minehead seafront and had brought in lots of visiting rugby club business. Emma had, unnoticed by all, started going to the hairdressers again. "With what we could sell Dunster for, combined with a bit extra, we could get an upgraded model."

Emma, being more in tune with … well … everything, said, "This won't be a straightforward swap, you know."

When the issue of an upgrade was raised over sausages one night, Sam assumed they were talking about getting a more comprehensive French dictionary for her O level class. As "sell Dunster for an upgraded model" floated into her consciousness, visions of her bedroom mixed with the mashed potatoes and beans: Framed photos of Dunster at every show and a notice board three-deep in photos of him in fancy dress, covered in mud, lying down in his shelter with Sam curled up under his chin, bath time, and wading in streams. Albums on shelves were full of Dunster eating watermelon with his top lip in the air, helping Sam blow out birthday candles, in his paddock covered in snow, and dressed in tinsel and a Christmas cracker hat for carolling. It was all there. Irrefutable documentation that when Dunster joined the Weston family, his days on the open market were over.

Sam sat at the dinner table, food halfway to her mouth, trying to unscramble the meaning of the sounds she was hearing, actions she would repeat on a future Thursday night. What were they talking about? Dunster was as big a part of her as anything she'd ever known. He knew more about her than Polly or anyone ever would. He knew about secret crushes, Sam's song-writing attempts, and how much Polly's acne grossed Sam out. And he even knew about that time Sam had sneaked a glass of vodka at the family Christmas party and immediately thrown up. It was easy for a teenager to feel no one but her pony could have known all this and loved her anyway. Forget the new boobs, longer legs, and wolf whistles. She'd have traded those new appendages and experiences for Dunster any day. Larry learned this with ear-splitting clarity at the dinner table.

"Overmydeadbody! IwillleavethishousewithDunsterandnevercomeback!"   The tirade echoed off the walls, followed by running feet from the dining room, slamming door, and floods of tears. Then the even more rapid exit from the bedroom, dragging her comforter to sleep with Dunster in the shelter in case of abduction during the night. Larry's open mouth didn't close until Sam had her arms around Dunster's neck.

"Has no one read *Moorland Mousie*?!" Sam screamed into the still air. "Does no one remember how Mousie ended up with Mr. Greengrocer, sick, starved, and exhausted? No one's doing that to Dunster. Ever!" Dunster's ears twitched in agreement. Sam pictured the young Olympic rider, Marion Coates, having this exact same reaction when her father suggested she exchange Stroller for some inferior specimen just because it was taller. Miss Coates had stuck to her guns and got to the Olympics. "Doesn't anyone study history around here?" Sam demanded. She looked around at all the horses staring at her but saw not a single hoof raised.

"We won't do anything without your permission," Emma had to promise before Sam would return to the house that night. A thunderstorm, no torch, and a forgotten food supply also assisted in the return. Sam shuffled across the road from the paddock to the house, trailing an angry mother and chastened father. She determined to sleep sentinel on her windowsill. Larry started to protest about the sleeping arrangement, but Emma silenced him with a look and brought Sam an extra pillow.

"I can't believe Dad thinks ownership is about writing a cheque," Sam said to her mother. "It's nothing to do with a cheque."

"Maybe you'd feel differently if you had to write the flippin' cheque," Emma said, as she took yet another deep breath and closed the bedroom door.

Sitting on the windowsill, Sam watched Dunster amble along in the moonlight once the thunderclouds had taken their anger to Wales. Head down, eating grass, he had no inkling that his life there was on the line. It had never occurred to Sam either.

Chapter Nine

Breakfast was cereal with Brody's rice milk. Not that Sam liked rice milk; it was just there was no way she was going back to the shop. She'd barely noticed anything she'd eaten anyway, and when Gail knocked on the door to take her to the Humane Society bake sale, Sam was shocked to find herself in her present-day kitchen.

"Why are we so besotted with our pets?" Sam asked as Gail drove them over to the kennels, the back seat loaded with trays of cookies, two pouting hounds left behind. "It's funny," Sam continued, without waiting for an answer. "When you first meet your animal friend, you know all the deep stuff instantly. The humility, the gentle spirit, the honesty, the kindness. The humanity—or should that be equin-ity, or felin-ity, or canin-ity? In contrast, it's weeks or months or even years after meeting a new human before all the important stuff struggles to the surface, through all the 'OMG, look at her shoes,' or the bravado, the posturing. The lies."

"Oh, I agree," said Gail. "When was the last time a dog told a lie?"

Sam pictured the look Sherlock had given JB to remind him to zip it about the missing flip-flop. She conceded pets could possibly be neglectful of the whole truth at times. But not about the big stuff.

Sam knew all about neglect. Working in the reception area of the Humane Society introduced a person to the very worst of human nature. "Maybe I'm just a bit jaded today, and I know Moorland Mousie's been on my mind, but the stupidity, cruelty, and neglect humans inflict on their animals can be mind-boggling, can't it?" Gail opened her mouth to ask who Moorland Mousie was, but Sam continued as she stared out of the window. "Intentional or unintentional, I struggle to accept ignorance as an excuse for some of the sorry cases that are carried through the door. The impact on the animal is the same."

"Yet through the whole ordeal the animals are so forgiving." Gail finally got a word in. "Afraid, yes. Sad, yes. But uncomplaining and patient, willing in an amazingly short time to reach out again to a kind hand or a gentle word. With surprisingly few exceptions, they never give up on humans, do they? But may I remind you that we also see the best of humanity in our work here too?"

"True," Sam said. The passer-by who stopped to help an injured animal, even though it would make them late for work. The minimum-wage earner who insisted on paying for medical attention for their unknown friend at the expense of their human healthcare needs, or even their own food. The physician who, after a twelve-hour shift, came to walk a couple of dogs to introduce them again to kindness and respect. Sam witnessed the countless hours volunteers invested in rehabilitating their broken, helpless charges for no more payment than a lick or a wagging tail. Or the joy of a purring little body curled up in their laps, slowly filling out with good food.

"I fell in love with Dunster during the first exchange of glances. In love long before in like." Sam sighed. "That first breath on my cheek. That first conversation we had." And yes, Dunster did talk. To Sam, he did.

"It's all about how they make you feel," Gail said. "Places can be like that too, can't they?" Having been filled in on the diplomatic crisis playing out in the McClintock household, she wasn't surprised to be caught in this Trans-Atlantic tug-of-reminiscence.

Sam laid her head back on the seat rest and closed her eyes. Dunster had made her feel better about herself than almost anyone else ever had with nothing more than a nicker and a nuzzle. So why had she left him? And Exmoor had soothed her soul with nothing more than the scent of heather and a breeze. So why had she left it?

Minus Twenty-Seven

There were some minor attempts by Geraldine, Larry, and Polly to encourage Sam to at least look at some bigger horses. Emma was conspicuously absent from the conversation. Sam noted a copy of *Horse and Hound* on the kitchen table, left open to the For Sale pages. She wasn't fooled at all by a certain sixteen-hand-high addition to Seabreeze Farm that Geraldine just happened to be riding around the paddock every time Sam was about. Sam wouldn't deny secretly scanning a few photos on the sale page, or watching the pretty palomino out of the corner of her eye as he arched his neck and strutted his stuff.

"Look at that plonker," Sam whispered in Dunster's ear one day as the new arrival did a rather impressive extended trot across the paddock, only to spook at a robin in the hedgerow. "What a show-off. And let's see him all tinselled up for Christmas carolling. He'd have a heart attack if that's how he does with a robin." Dunster huffed condescendingly. "But then, I seem to remember you having a bit of a phobia of hollyhocks ..." Dunster's ears flopped outward. "*That's different,*" they said, as he lifted his chin haughtily. Sam looked at Dunster, and Dunster looked back at Sam. Any discussion about a new horse was over.

She wouldn't be like Geraldine or Jack. Sam would never have multiple ponies or horses at one time. Her family simply couldn't afford it, despite Larry's work advancements. So this was the end of Sam's show dreams, career dreams, life dreams. And she had no other dreams—

except for the one about George Michael driving her around London in his car. Which wasn't going to happen for so many reasons. Even Dunster rolled his eyes when Sam told him that one.

What on earth am I to do? Sam thought one night as she sat on her windowsill, watching Dunster's silhouette. He was twenty-one, and she was almost sixteen. Both of them had a grand scheme mapped out. Dunster would live with Sam and eat. Sam would leave school after O level exams and go to the Weir Equitation Centre. She'd train to be a riding instructor. She'd compete. She'd go to the Spanish Riding School (a month or two should be enough surely?), and then return to co-own a livery stable with Polly. They even had a name picked out: Polsam Stables. They both knew Dunster would have the best stall. There was no other life but a life on Exmoor with horses. But Larry had made it quite clear about the grand scheme and his part in it: they were a one-horse family and there were no funds for the Weir Equitation Centre.

With the light turned back on, Sam settled in to map a new direction, blanket over her knees, chewing a pencil with a notepad on her lap.

"Let's start with what we have," she whispered quietly, taking notes. "Get a pony; check. Never let it go. So far, so good, but not out of the woods yet on that one. Train at the equitation centre; working on it. Be first female rider at the Spanish Riding School. Probably should delete this one because I can't take Dunster to Vienna. But I do so love *Sachertorte*. Okay, leave it on the list. All in all, not many checked boxes to show for my first fifteen years on Earth. May have to pick up the pace a bit to fit everything in before I'm seventy-five."

In looking for patterns, it seemed to Sam like the grand scheme was missing one main ingredient: money. "Soooo … I need to increase the money coming in and decrease the money going out. Brilliant!" she said to her notepad. "Wonder if anyone else ever thought of this?

Now, what are my marketable skills?" Pencil poised. "Good with a pitchfork and muck-heap sculpting," Sam wrote as she spoke. "Good with dogs and children" (based solely on limited interactions with Rascal and Charlotte). "Good eater/doer. Good friend. Good with chores. *Good* may be a relative term here. Strong writing skills." Sam's English grades had improved once she'd discovered alliteration was a real concept, and she'd received a prize for her piece entitled "Humiliation and the Road Back," based on a true story.

"Writers earn tons of money, don't they?" Sam mused. "Maybe I could write about Mousie's great-great-great-great-grandson?" However, she knew illustrations may be harder to come by with no Lionel Edwards in her Rolodex of go-to illustrators and only her Skippy the Super Scone attempts to endear her to publishers. This was going to be tougher than she thought. If only there was someone she could ask for advice, someone who would understand her problems. Someone …

"An agony aunt! I'll be an agony aunt!" Sam proclaimed loudly enough to make her mother bang on the bedroom wall. Well, she'd had as much experience with agony as any other fifteen-year-old living in a beautiful village in glorious countryside with a loving family, a great friend, good health, and a pony, hadn't she?

❧❧

Sam ran the idea past Dunster as she fed him the next morning. "I see the potential," his lower lip suggested.

"You can offer advice to the ponies, and I'll offer advice to the riders!" Sam said as she fluffed straw. "Brilliant idea number two!" she said, on a roll after the impressive "save more/spend less/get a job" revelation. Polly climbed over the fence and kissed Dunster good morning. Sam filled her in on the wealthy-author plan.

"Being an agony aunt could be very lucrative," Sam

said, Polly and Dunster all ears. "We could sell this a
dozen ways. What about an agony column in the papers?"
Sam immediately had visions of herself bent over a
typewriter, drumming out sage judgements that would be
discussed in homes and stables all over the country. She'd
outwit deadlines for the next day's edition of the *Exmoor
Gazette*, which in her head for some reason was
headquartered in London. And involved meeting secret
sources in dark alleys in Istanbul. On second thoughts, the
travel part seemed a little daunting.

"Or what about going straight to book format? An
equine agony book?" Not to be confused with an
"agonizing book," as Skippy the Super Sconc had been
described by that unimaginative English teacher. "Oh yes!"
Sam pictured the shiny hardcover, with a photo of her and
Dunster standing on Dunkery Beacon looking thoughtful
as though receiving knowledgeable, ancient vibes from
somewhere over the rolling hills. "I could get a review
from Marion Coates; her raving about my 'rare ability to
get to the meat of a matter with tact and astuteness well
beyond her years. A must-read for all who need advice on
anything.'"

As all the ways this could fail raced across Polly's
face, she remained silent for a change. There was
pessimism and then there was just plain unkind.

"Dunster can teach other ponies how to know their
human's feelings by looking at them and sniffing the air."
Sam had always marvelled at how Dunster seemed to
know exactly when to push at her hands in a cheeky
attempt to get food, or to quietly stand, gently breathing
into her outstretched palms as she lamented a poor test
result or rebuke from that dishy-looking boy at school.

"Well, Dunster sounds very clever in the book,
anyway," Polly encouraged.

New addition to Grand Scheme: Become famous
writer. Earn lots of money. Use money to check off all
other items on Grand Scheme list.

Chapter Ten

Five hundred cookies sold, a dozen doggy heads patted, three kittens cuddled, and one rebuke for the idiot who'd been stupid enough to congratulate Sam on her new citizenship status. He'd continued even as Gail made slashing gestures across her throat behind Sam's back.

Back home again, Sam was brushing her own dogs to assuage the guilt of leaving them for others. Sherlock and JB sniffed accusingly at the scent of treachery on her jeans.

She had almost forgotten how she'd come up with the idea of an agony book. She supposed it was just another example of being ahead of her time. Millions of self-help books were now sold to get the reader through nappy rash, adolescence (apparently anyone under forty), crazy bosses, or addiction to electronic devices. Sam had even seen a paperback entitled *Hope for Hoarders* at Barnes and Noble the week before. Back in the day you were just slovenly. That's what her mother called her father's shed, anyway.

Pulling clumps of white hair out of the brush bristles, Sam wondered what she did with that copy of her first attempt at writing a book. Well, second attempt, if you counted the Skippy the Super Scone epic. "How easy I'd thought it would be," Sam said to a wriggling Sherlock. "Grab a pencil and paper, find a quiet corner, write for a week or two, and watch the money roll in." She racked her brain for a moment and then realised those priceless yet worthless pages must be in the attic.

Sam padded across the floor and climbed the stairs. She felt a sense of imminent discovery, a little thrill at going to meet an old friend she hadn't seen in a long time. That book had meant so much in her youth it was hard to imagine how she'd ever decided to tuck it away in the attic. What else had she tucked away during her journey to middle age minus ten? What else meant so much to her that she'd had to bury it in dust and cobwebs and old furniture? *Hireth* buried deep.

The attic was a typical monument to a shop-to-excess culture. Western civilization's hunter-gatherers had morphed into storage-lockerers. Sam scanned all the stuff that was supposed to be useful or worth something one day. It would not be useful or worth anything. Ever. Looking through the dust, she couldn't help but see again her father's shed in Porlock.

"One day I'll find something that will make our fortunes," Larry had said as he'd proudly surveyed the mouldering treasures found at various auctions in his own shed. And as a child, Sam believed. After large purchases, Emma would stop her hair appointments again, stoically taking up the slack. Because that was what wives and mothers did. What they still do. When the shed burned down, Larry couldn't describe even a single heirloom, as he called the junk, to the insurance man.

Looking around the attic, Sam shook her head at the empty picture frames, bags of clothing, old files from grad school, wonky swivel chairs, and mountains of toys. "They're for the grandkids!" she'd yell each time Brody suggested Ben and Tori may have outgrown the rocking horse and the Barbie kitchen. But every woman knew it wasn't for the grandkids. How could men not know that?

Sam perused the stamp collection. If only Grandma had sent her birthday cards with a Penny Black on the envelope. Her Noddy Club certificate, priceless to the six-year-old Sam, as anything you had to send off five cereal box tops and postage for and then wait six weeks to receive must increase in value exponentially, surely? The Skippy the Super Scone illustrations. "Oh, good grief," Sam fumed for the umpteenth time. "He looks just like SpongeBob SquarePants." Only with a blob of clotted cream in place of the Krusty Krab employee hat.

In a box on a bookshelf, Sam found her manuscript. Blowing dust from the lid, she carried it carefully downstairs. That book was supposed to have changed her life. And in fact it had. Just not in a rich, famous-author kind of way.

Minus Twenty-Six

So Sam got down to writing; actually, more like acquiring the accoutrements of writing. She found *Moorland Mousie* and a dictionary and put them in a box. Put *Moorland Mousie* back on the shelf, as the illustrations were too intimidating. Bought a journal she found in the newsagents, with a faux red leather cover and an inbuilt elastic band to keep all the notes, pearls of wisdom, and scraps of genius together. Found some English grammar books, flicked through the pages, and instantly knew she'd never read them. She thought nevertheless that they'd look smashing on the shelf above her writing desk. Not that she had a writing desk. "The true writer must visualize first," said Sam, holding the grammar book out in front of her like Yorick's skull.

With the basic tools of the trade in hand, or rather in a box in the kitchen, the next famous-author essential was a writing space, a safe haven for creative ideas to flow. With a view of the water. Preferably with easy access to the bakery for sugar-related inspiration. And a kettle. And a fireplace for leaning on with head in hand when writer's block hit hardest. Sam found herself surprised that she had such a clear vision of what a writer looked like, acted like, felt like. She thought this a clue that she was destined to be one. She also thought maybe she was getting a little off track. Maybe she should focus on the actual writing. Now, what did a writer wear?

∽∾

"Mrs. Althorp has a little sunroom in her garden," Polly said, sitting up straighter and beaming like someone who'd just saved the day. The more Sam told her about the promise of literary gold, the more excited about the book Polly seemed to get. Rich people still needed friends after all. "I've never actually seen it," Polly continued. "But Mum says it has huge windows on one side looking out over the water, and you could easily fit a desk in it surely if it's got a huge window. Apparently, Mrs. Althorp's never used it since Mr. Althorp died." This last tidbit had to be rumour, as Mrs. Althorp and Helen weren't exactly bosom buddies. Somewhat different outlooks on life.

Sam and Polly were sitting on one of the pillboxes on the beach at Porlock Weir. Originally World War II gun posts built to protect shipping in the Bristol Channel, the pillboxes were now slowly tilting over onto the shingle beach. This made their flat, slanted roofs a great spot for sunbathing and writing lists. From their perch, the girls watched children running from the tiny marine supply shop, ice creams in hand, across the closed harbour gate walkway towards the row of beach cottages. The wind caught the rigging on the sailboats lying practically on their sides at low tide in the harbour. The sound of clanging rigging, no matter where in the world it was, would forever conjure up visions for Sam of the ancient port of Porlock Weir.

"Okay. We'll take a look at it, if Mrs. Althorp allows," Sam stated while secretly trying to imagine writing with Mrs. Althorp's four King Charles Spaniels snapping around the door. No one managed to get past the wooden gate on a walk down the bridle path access to the cottage without dodging the dogs. Snotty snouts attached to sets of snapping teeth attached to a blur of digging feet, and the occasional pirate eye (either the wide-open one or the squinty one) greeted marauders from under the gate. Sam had to confess to kicking dirt at the snouts on occasion. She'd come off Dunster twice as he spooked at the canine assault, so surely retaliation was warranted. But she wondered if Mrs. Althorp would loan out her sunroom if she knew that. "Right, we have two contenders," Sam concluded. "My bedroom and Mrs. Althorp's sunroom. Let's go over pros and cons."

Polly looked thoughtful and said, "Your bedroom. It's comfortable, water view, close to the bakery. Checks a lot of your boxes, doesn't it?"

"Yes, but Mum would always be banging around in the kitchen downstairs and Dad would be calling up the stairs offering tea and asking how the writing was going," Sam countered. She'd started to think her dad was secretly hinging his retirement on her book. He'd made comments about "blockbuster debuts," which was adding a certain amount of pressure.

"So we're down to Mrs. Althorp's sunroom. Better go and talk to her then," Sam concluded with the uneasy feeling that they'd only added it to the list because it was reportedly a structure with a view. A bit like adding Westminster Abbey to your list of potential wedding venues because you'd heard it had an altar.

Back at the house, Emma tried to be supportive of another far-fetched venture and phoned Mrs. Althorp. "She's delighted a writer would be interested in her potting shed," Emma said as she hung up the phone.

Sam turned from her mother to look at Polly with widening eyes, mouthing, "Potting shed?"

Polly shrugged her shoulders and mouthed back, "Mum said it was a sunroom."

After lunch, Sam and Polly set off down the bridle path that ran parallel to the road to Porlock Weir for the short walk to Mrs. Althorp's. Sam carried a written list of questions—a writer should have everything in writing. However, the words *potting shed* kept circling Sam's brain and clashing terribly with the vision she had of a writer's retreat.

The girls knew the cottage well, passing it on so many

rides and walks. They enjoyed the view of the beautiful garden over the hedge. They also knew Mrs. Althorp, who was their Brownie troop leader years ago.

"Do you think she'll recognize us?" Sam asked as they ambled along.

"If she remembers the incident with the Boy Scouts, she will," Polly replied. "Remember throwing sticks up at that Scout stuck in a tree? It was so unfair that Mrs. Althorp singled us out just because we inflicted the most direct hits." More likely it was because they didn't see Mrs. Althorp rounding the corner and were caught in mid-throw, unlike the other Brownies who had suddenly become very interested in the flora and fauna.

"Ah yes," winced Sam. Mrs. Althorp would probably recognize them.

As they approached the cottage, the two friends peered over the hedge to try to locate the sunroom, or greenhouse, or potting shed, or whatever it was. Seeing nothing that looked like an outbuilding of any kind, they prepared for the attack of the spaniels. Surprisingly, there was no barking or snout-pushing or pirate-eyed squints under the gate, so Sam pushed it open and headed for the front door.

A more delightful English cottage couldn't be found on all of Exmoor, with its whitewashed stone walls under a thatched roof and a bay window overlooking the channel. It was surrounded by the quintessential chocolate box country garden. This cottage haunted the dreams of many misplaced residents as they, not realizing they were grockles, pictured living in it. A rich, dark carved oak stable door with iron hinges and rivets was tucked inside a small sheltered alcove. Built-in roughhewn wooden benches framed each side. Log supports held up a slate roof, and eye-level ripples of moss dripped off the tiles, slithering like furry caterpillars to meet the walls. The alcove was surrounded by roses, hollyhocks, and lavender. The small, round glass porthole in the top section of the stable door allowed a distorted view of the person on the other side, like looking through a fishbowl or glass Christmas ornament.

When Mrs. Althorp appeared on the other side of the door, Sam was reminded of faces in the mirror house at a fairground. There was that pirate eye, the one closest to the glass orb, looking wide and startled while the other looked slit and mistrustful. Mrs. Althorp threw the top half of the stable door open, surrounded by a living, breathing skirt of prancing, screaming spaniels. She proceeded to welcome the girls, or so they assumed based on the movement of her lips. But all words were drowned out by the raving dogs. Their mistress only appeared to notice the cacophony when she asked a couple of questions for which she got no reply. Then she slammed the door shut, and the girls watched the distorted shapes of flapping arms as animals were shooed into the kitchen. Finally, Mrs. Althorp returned, her jovial face surrounded by a cloud of grey hair that topped a trim body. Her fluid movements and twinkling eyes were indicative of one who still hiked all over Exmoor.

"Welcome, welcome!" The kind voice ushered the girls into the sitting room. Sam took in the dark wooden ceiling beams, horse brasses, floral prints on the walls, a jigsaw puzzle on a little side table, a copper coal scuttle, and chintz curtains. With it being spring, the fireplace was filled with a vase of flowers from the garden, but it was easy to imagine the little winter blaze casting warmth and flickering light around the room. A French door framed by curtains led out to a small flagstone patio. A brass bucket held a selection of *Country Life* magazines. Sam was drawn to the bay window, a fitted cushion on the window seat matching the floral curtains. She caught her breath. Hurlstone Point was framed in early rosebuds with the sun sparkling off the channel, white puffy clouds chasing each other in and out of the swaying holly tree branches that could just be seen to one side of the garden.

Oh, I could write a book in here, Sam thought. *Please say this is the potting shed!*

"Do you still have the stick-throwing badge from the Brownies?" Mrs. Althorp's eyes twinkled again, and she chuckled at the awkward silence. On her return from the kitchen with a tea tray, she was trailed by a flurry of stray dog hairs that caught in the sunbeams streaming through the window. As tea was served, Sam gamely parried back when peppered with questions about her book's theme (*Note to self, find out what a theme is*), the plot, the characters, and Polly's involvement with the project. Finding she hadn't even begun to formulate a literary pitch, or whatever the heck it was you did to explain a book, Sam began to panic a bit. Brain doing loop the loops, she wondered if she needed all the answers to these questions before even getting to look at the location for the book's birth. Surely she needed the writer's haven sorted before coming up with specific ideas? And why exactly was Polly there? Did finding the potting shed really entitle her to 50 percent of the book's royalties?

Soldiering on, Sam started to talk about Dunster and his part in her "possible agony aunt-type equestrian thingy" book, when she was silenced by the at first startled and then softening look in Mrs. Althorp's eyes at the mention of a pony.

"I didn't know you were a rider!" Mrs. Althorp exclaimed. "Oh, how lovely to write about a pony!"

Sam realised she'd never discussed Dunster with Mrs. Althorp at the Brownie meetings. Her pony was the reason Sam didn't go on to join the Girl Guides, but she probably failed to tell Mrs. Althorp this. Sam's second thought was amazed gratitude that maybe, just maybe, she was wrong in thinking the whole world knew about her fiasco at the Bossington Horse Show seven years earlier.

Sam watched Mrs. Althorp's eyes stealing around the room to focus on objects Sam hadn't noticed before: a china plough horse on the mantle, an old frame with a yellowing photo of an adorable foal, another photo of a child with a sweet grin leading a pony and waving a rosette at the camera, the horse prints on the wall, the encyclopaedia of horses on the bookshelf. On the mantle over the fireplace were several aging photos of a distinguished-looking gentleman on various horses and a lady riding side-saddle, leading a beaming young child on an Exmoor pony.

"So you're a horse rider too!" Sam blurted out.

"Oh, years ago," replied Mrs. Althorp. "Soooo many years ago. But tell me about your ponies."

The girls regaled Mrs. Althorp with stories of Dunster, Squirt, and Eccles and their exploits, carefully censored to make Sam look capable of writing a book about horses. As Polly jumped in here and there with her tales of showing mishaps and victories, Sam held her breath, but she needn't have worried. Polly had a vested interest in this going well after all. Mrs. Althorp listened intently, nodding and chuckling, shaking and commiserating as the tales warranted. She looked as though she could have listened all day. Then with a puzzled look, she posed her final question.

"So tell me, dear," she asked, looking squarely at Sam. "Why do you want to take time away from your beloved Dunster to sit in my garden writing a book?"

The question caught Sam completely off guard. The reason for writing suddenly seemed so petty, yet at the same time so monumental. A growth spurt seemed ridiculous, the monetary rationale tawdry, when spoken out loud to this sympathetic, horse-loving lady in this glorious writer's paradise. Sam felt with horror the tears start to itch in the corners of her eyes, the uncontrollable gyrations of her chin, and the intake of breath as once more the thought of losing Dunster overwhelmed her. The dream of wearing a tweed jacket on the school horses in that spectacular driveway suddenly seemed so unattainable.

What was I thinking? How could I be so stupid as to assume I could save Dunster and my future by writing a book? The thoughts burned in Sam's head as she looked away from Mrs. Althorp, who, Sam assumed, had seen right through her. *I'm a fraud, and I'm going to lose everything.*

Composure turned out to be first thing to go. It all poured out between sobs and gulps, with Polly, looking a bit embarrassed, rubbing Sam's back and Mrs. Althorp offering quiet encouragement to continue or take a break as necessary. Chocolate biscuits appeared from nowhere (well, obviously from the kitchen, as Sam had to pull dog hairs from her mouth every other bite). Sam realised she didn't have advice for anyone. She couldn't fix anyone's problems. All she had was a need. A need for money. Hardly a grandiose reason for putting pen to paper. Surely Shakespeare had found a better muse than coinage?

So thanks for the tea. We'll be going now. Sorry to have wasted your time.

As Sam stood up to leave, Mrs. Althorp gathered up her cardigan from the back of her armchair and said, "Ah yes. You're right. It's time to see your writing cabin."

Wait, Sam thought. *Did she not hear a word I just said? Why does she still think I need to see the potting shed, or whatever it is? And why is she calling it a writing cabin?*

Sam looked at Polly, who gave her a thumbs up with a grin. In a daze, Sam followed Mrs. Althorp and Polly out past the kitchen with its cream-coloured AGA and rows of potted plants on the windowsill, through the mudroom full of gardening shoes, vegetable baskets, doggie toys, and water dishes, and then past four sleepy spaniels in thick doggie beds who had obviously decided that these two rather emotionally needy visitors were not worth barking at anymore. Once the back door was opened, the dogs roused themselves, stretched luxuriously with four bottoms in the air, and waddled out into the sheltered garden behind the cottage.

"Watch your step," said Mrs. Althorp, as Sam tripped over a stepping-stone. The trio was on a gravel walkway traversing the slope behind the cottage, their arms brushed by the branches of twenty-foot-high rhododendron trees dipping under the weight of blooms in red, pink, and white. Tiny forget-me-nots and primrose leaves poked through the gravel. The garden behind the cottage was a contrast to the order of the flower borders on each side of the front door. Back here, one got a sense of wilderness. Bamboo, laurel, bent and gnarled apple trees, arborvitae, and moss- and ivy-covered stone walls formed the bones of the space. Ferns added ground cover, and an old ornamental well partially obscured by trailing brambles provided a delightful accent in one corner. Ancient-looking holly bushes and holm oaks screened the garden from the quiet road threading up the combe behind the fence. Few cars needed to bypass the steepness of Porlock Hill now, so the Toll Road remained hushed.

The girls and Mrs. Althorp took a zig and then a zag to follow the path upwards until they were slightly above the level of the roof on the little cottage below. There was a compost pile and a wheelbarrow tipped up on end to the side of the pathway. Once past that, her nose distinctly aware of the warm, musty odour of rotting grass, Sam saw it. A small wooden hut, made to stand level on the hillside by wooden support struts underneath the front corners, the back edge dug slightly into the mossy hillside. She was looking at the side of it, staring at a door with a large brass knob. Mrs. Althorp brushed a cobweb off the frame and pushed the door open. For a split second she hesitated to enter. Sam hung back for a moment, wondering if she should call the whole thing off to spare feelings, but the moment was gone as fast as it arrived, and Mrs. Althorp was inside.

Well, Polly's mum was right. There was a huge window. In fact, the whole of the front side was comprised of glass, dirty glass, cobwebby glass, partially obscured by tree branches, but glass nevertheless. Sam stared around the space, looking at the abandoned pots, hand trowels, bags of potting soil, hanging string baskets, and dead leaves in all the corners. She inhaled the earthy odour and looked at the old leather armchair in the corner, mildewed and faded.

Right. My bedroom it is. Then she turned to look out the window.

The thatch and the little chimney of the cottage provided a lower border, and a towering evergreen to the left and an old holly tree to the right blocked about half of the window. But this did little to detract from the view. Sam gasped as her eye was drawn slowly upwards over the rooftop and across the distant fields of sheep, skipping across the sparkling water of the Bristol Channel to rest on Hurlstone Point and the coast of Wales. Though tree branches obscured parts, the arc of Porlock Bay spread before the window. It was glorious.

Anyone could write a book here. Anyone.

Both Polly and Mrs. Althorp were looking at Sam expectantly. She had no idea how long she'd been staring out the window, but obviously she was supposed to have said something by now. She looked from Polly to Mrs. Althorp, then back at the view, and then tried to move her mouth. She swallowed and tried again.

"It's perfect!" Sam breathed. She saw in Mrs. Althorp's eyes a flash of excitement, or maybe it was relief, as though it had really mattered to her that Sam would like this place.

"So that was why we hadn't seen the potting shed from the bridle path," Polly piped up. "It was wrapped in trees."

Sam gave Polly a silencing glare. "It's lovely, Mrs. Althorp. Just lovely." She didn't ask a single question off her list. Being a famous author took one step forward based entirely on a glorious view. And a good feeling about a person. Having a cottage just like Mrs. Althorp's was added to the Grand Scheme.

Chapter Eleven

A contemporary American midwestern house. Never in a million years would Sam have seen herself living in a home like this. She looked around her sitting area as she set the dusty manuscript on the coffee table, afraid to open it yet. She could still picture every detail of Mrs. Althorp's cottage. After all, she'd tried to emulate it in every home she'd lived in. Her rooms had never quite come to life the way she wanted them to, though.

Her current abode couldn't be less like that cottage if she'd tried: modern, open-plan layout, floor-to-ceiling windows, the stainless steel, all fighting with her attempts to replicate the overstuffed, chintzy cottage comfort of a home she'd dreamily inhabited for over thirty years. She pictured lace-curtained windows with potted herbs on the sill, carved wooden armoires instead of walk-in closets, bear-claw tubs, and uneven, wide-plank floors. Which came with questionable plumbing, drafty doors, rising damp, thumping furnace, and mice in the thatched roof. Hey, nothing's perfect in the light of day.

Sam did like this hilltop house, though. The huge, floor-to-ceiling windows and the sweeping views down over the valley to the small town below gave a sense of being on board a ship, of open seas and wind-tossed birds. Wind through cornfields could produce rippling waves, after all. Summer storms were powerful, with vertical and horizontal bolts of lightning, clouds boiling and bubbling overhead. There were times it rained so hard against the windows it was like sitting inside a car wash. Sam dreaded the eerie fade-in, fade-out of the tornado sirens as the wind buffeted the warning around. Then everything would stop as quickly as it started, followed by the appearance of a rainbow, like a "Just kidding!" sign from above. In the winter, blizzards would sweep down from Canada, with no regard for customs and immigration. Snow obliterated the town in a swirling shroud, eventually forming snow sculptures around the foundations.

Polly would have a field day living in the Midwest. The weather required constant vigilance, with emergency supply kits in the basement and evacuation plans. It was surprising the Dales hadn't tried to install a tornado siren in Porlock after Sam had filled them in on the dangers during one visit home. Helen Dale said, "American weather is murderous. English weather just induces suicidal tendencies after sixty or seventy years." But then Helen had only ever seen the rain, never the rainbow.

Seeing the garden shed through the window, Sam wondered if she could make it look like her Exmoor writer's cabin inside.

"If I'd stayed on Exmoor I'd have been a writer," she'd told Gail, while passing out cookies that morning after describing Skippy the Super Scone and her epistle money-raising attempts. Gail hadn't appeared impressed on either count. "I had the writer's cabin, the writing table, the tea and biscuits. Everything I needed."

"Don't we have all those things in America?" Gail's enquiry seemed rather half-hearted, as though she wasn't sure she wanted to encourage her friend in this direction.

"Okay, so maybe it was the view I needed," Sam shot back, not sure she really wanted encouraging in this direction either.

To stop herself looking at the manuscript, Sam grabbed a dust mop and attempted to harvest the dog hair tumbleweed collecting against the desk legs in the office. She stopped in front of her speech-language pathologist certificate hanging on the wall.

"Who saw that coming?" her reflection said from the glass frame. Speech-language pathology was a good profession, both rewarding and humbling. Working with a stroke patient in those scary first few days, Sam comforted the families and provided basic communication tools to help ask for the bathroom, give a greeting, and request the food the patient wanted rather than the food their spouse thought they wanted. In later sessions, as the healing began, hopefully, Sam worked to improve clear speech and taught new writing skills with non-dominant hands. Or, after the realisation of an altered lifelong trajectory emerged, devastatingly, Sam provided hope in the form of support groups or introducing speech-generating devices to restore, at least partially, the gift of sharing thoughts. Communication: spoken, heard, written, read. So taken for granted until taken away. No, Sam couldn't say she regretted her career choice.

"But where are the horses in my life?" Her eyes rested on a photo of Dunster standing in his paddock, a daisy chain looped over his ears. Where was the livery yard? The show ring? The only things Sam thought were written in stone? Her stroke patients had also thought many things were written in stone.

A rising sense of panic enveloped her. She had a vision of time running through an hourglass, but instead of sand, little bits of her were squeezing through the gap from the "Not Happened Yet" upper chamber to the "It's All Over" lower chamber. "What do you really want, Sam? Today? Now?" she asked herself under her breath. But the dogs heard anyway and dutifully shuffled over, shedding more hair.

"What I appear to want," she answered herself, leaning against her mop, "is what I already have: my husband, children, health, friends, career. Just in a different setting." Sam's voice got louder. "Are you going to do this, or what?"

At that moment, Sam identified completely with a storm-tossed sailor standing in her ocean-liner house, searching the horizon for a life boat and sending up a distress flare. She pushed the four-legged sounding boards out of the way, good sports that they were, and found her laptop. Ignoring the manuscript on the table, still afraid to open it, she typed in her distress signal: "Speech Pathology Jobs. Somerset."

Minus Twenty-Five

"Wonderful!" exclaimed Mrs. Althorp. Looking around the space, she seemed to notice for the first time the cobwebs and remnants of garden projects of old.

"Now, we'll have to clean it up a bit, of course." Mrs. Althorp became all business, rubbing her hands together as though plotting a daring escapade. "There's no electricity, so you'll have to bring a torch if you plan to write all night. You'll need a desk or table. A chair, high-backed and hard so you don't fall asleep. Or could we just clean up Mr. Althorp's old leather armchair there and have you write on your lap?" A smile of remembrance broke across her lips. "I often wondered how much time he spent asleep in that old thing. Sometimes it took him days to pot a few geraniums."

The crew made a list of needed equipment and supplies. Finding an old broom leaning against the outside of the shed—because that's what it really was, a glass-sided shed—Sam swept down some of the cobwebs from the ceiling and window and scooted them out the door along with the dead leaves, piles of potting soil, and more than a few disgruntled spiders and cockroaches. She had time to think of the criteria she thought she required for her writer's haven and how many boxes had not been checked here. But that shelf would do instead of a fireplace, she could bring a thermos of tea instead of a kettle, and who really cared about the bakery? How much inspiration did one really get from a cake anyway?

It was supper time before they knew it, so Sam and Polly took their leave of the writer's cabin, all coming to the agreement that that was what the tiny sanctuary would be called. Mrs. Althorp hustled the dogs into the mudroom and turned to give Polly and Sam a hug in parting. It was a happy walk home, though Sam was still a little embarrassed by her breakdown over tea.

"This means so much to you, doesn't it?" said Polly, her arm linked through Sam's.

"More than anything," Sam replied. She got the distinct impression Mrs. Althorp knew that too.

ॐ

The girls returned to the cabin after breakfast the next day with arms full of glass cleaner, wood polish, rags, and dusters in a bucket.

"We didn't ask Mrs. Althorp if we should go straight to the cabin or knock at the cottage door first," Polly said.

"That's not the worst of it," Sam added. "I didn't discuss any kind of payment with her. What if Mrs. Althorp's expecting me to supplement her retirement with a monthly cheque? What if she wants an editorial position on the book committee? What if I've just signed away a part share in Dunster in return for use of the cabin?"

"I think all that sounds a bit paranoid." Polly rolled her eyes.

"You would know."

The girls started for the cottage door but were redirected by the sound of dogs rummaging through leaves on the hillside and the sudden crack of a falling branch. They started running, fearful that a King Charles Spaniel had somehow got lodged in a tree and come crashing back to earth on top of the others, a surprising visual based on their knowledge of the four elder statesmen. Not surprising based on the lifelong influence of Mrs. Dale.

The girls skidded to a halt as Mrs. Althorp appeared at

the top of the path. She greeted them wearing what looked like old-fashioned leather pilot's goggles, thick canvas gloves, and a sawdust-covered apron over a floral dress and rubber boots. In her hand was a lethal-looking handsaw. She smiled at the girls' surprise and stepped to one side so they could see her handiwork. She had cleared several branches away from the glass window. The startled friends stared at the ladder wobbling in the breeze and marvelled at how much work it must have taken to cut through those branches with a handsaw.

"I see you think I'm such an old relic that I shouldn't be doing anything but waiting for the postman in my rocking chair," Mrs. Althorp said with a stern scowl.

Polly and Sam looked at the ground for a moment until they heard the chuckle.

"You're right about one thing, though. I'm far too old to wash windows, so you'd better get cracking on that!" She grinned and led them into the cabin to assess the newly enlarged view of Porlock Bay.

"That's better," Mrs. Althorp said. Sam looked at the resolute lady, hands on hips, face covered in sawdust, goggles perched on top of her head. Something Sam's grandfather always said sprung to mind, still repeated long after his death. "Great Britain could not possibly have lost the war."

"Thought you were after the view more than the trees," Mrs. Althorp stated.

"It's wonderful!" Sam exclaimed. "Just wonderful!" They could now see from Bossington to Porlock Weir and the entirety of Mrs. Althorp's garden, which was spread in front of them like a brightly coloured quilt. Just a hint of leaves bordered the window now, making it feel like looking into a framed picture postcard of someone else's holiday. Thank you hugs didn't seem enough.

As Mrs. Althorp trudged away with the ladder under one arm, the girls began the task of washing windows inside and out. This took several goes, as the dirt first turned to thick smears that blocked the new view completely, then to smudges, then to cloudy streaks, before finally clearing to allow the light to shine through. It was amazing how bright the cabin became once the grime had cleared—and how much the cobwebs now glistened in the corners and the dust sparkled on every surface.

"Maybe we should have left the dirt on the windows," Polly whispered out of the corner of her mouth. However, Sam was busy thinking how lovely the light was as it bounced around the cabin, warm and inviting.

Considering how much Sam hated housework, the morning passed surprisingly cheerfully. The girls dusted and swept, polished and swept again, shook cobwebs out of their hair and swept again, then washed the floor and walls with soap and warm water, sloshing buckets up the pathway from the mudroom, until the warmth of the woodgrain shone through. The leather chair had been taken outside earlier, swept clean of cobwebs and wiped down with saddle soap several times, then left in the shade to dry. The mildew hadn't been fully removed and a musty odour permeated the nostrils each time someone plonked down onto the sunken cushions, but there was now a slight return of the suppleness and sheen to the leather. Sam decided that a throw blanket over the top would work well to hide imperfections. Surveying the interior of the cabin, it now looked more like a wood-panelled sauna than a potting shed. Not quite a writer's retreat yet.

Sam and Polly had planned to leave for lunch, but as though reading their minds or hearing their hungry stomachs, Mrs. Althorp appeared with a plate full of cheese and pickle sandwiches on chunky whole grain bread with mugs of tea. The girls squished into the leather armchair together, having been turned down when they offered it to Mrs. Althorp. Their new friend pulled up a wooden stool. They all munched on the sandwiches while the distant seagulls plunged and climbed again, the whitecaps danced, and the cloudy shadows chased across

Hurlstone. Sam plucked up the courage to ask about payment for the cabin, but Mrs. Althorp waved her query away with her hand, laughing at the very notion.

After that, conversation was light and funny, with Mrs. Althorp telling horse stories from her childhood. She spoke of carriages pulling guests to dinner parties. She recalled being taken down to the stables by the nanny to see a new pony and, if very lucky, a glimpse of the Colonel, her father, as he mounted his hunter in his gleaming black boots and jodhpurs that billowed out at the thighs like sails. She spoke of the elegance of the side-saddle habit her mother wore and her poker-straight back, buttoning black leather gloves, lowering the veil over her face from the bowler hat, and giving a charming nod to the groom in thanks. Not a hair out of place on rider or horse. Polly and Sam listened, enraptured.

"Oh, look at the time!" Mrs. Althorp yelped with a look at her watch. "You've got things to do." After begging entreaties, she promised to tell more tales another day, but for now she headed off down the zigzag path with the tray of empty plates, dogs waddling behind.

It was time to start moving in the furniture.

"If you call it the 'accoutrements of the writer' one more time, I'm going home," said Polly.

Emma had given Sam an old rug from her grandmother's house, and the girls grappled it into a roll and marched it down the bridle path. At one point they had to stop, doubled over with laughter. "We must look like Mafia gangsters carrying a body wrapped in a blanket," Polly chortled.

"James Cuthbertson comes to mind," Sam replied, and the girls passed the fifteen minutes it took to wrestle the rug from the garage to the cabin dredging up all his past wrongs.

Next came an old sewing machine table that had been stored in the pre-fire groaning shed for years but was moved to the sitting room just prior to the fatal spark.

Larry helped get the table to the cabin by backing his Vauxhall estate car slowly down the bridle path with Polly and Sam leaning over the front seat trying to hold the table upright over the bumps. Once Larry got to the cottage and saw the climb to the cabin, he claimed he had done enough for the day. He abandoned the girls to the job of heaving the iron lump up the path, resting every few steps and skinning shins on the scrollwork. A friendship was nearly ended when Sam forgot to roll the rug down before humping the table into position and they had to hump the table back out again to put the rug down.

"My percentage of the royalties just went up," Polly muttered.

The leather chair was replaced at an angle across the back corner with the throw rug from Sam's bedroom draped across it and tucked in at the sides to cover the mildew. It didn't cover the smell, but the bright sunflower motif brought a lovely cheerful element to the cabin. Next came a straight-backed chair in front of the desk, a find from Polly's garage that, despite it's obvious wobble and loose joints, was the perfect height for the sewing table. On the shelf, Sam placed a framed photo of Dunster, *Moorland Mousie*, the dictionary, and the grammar books. Finishing touches included a small pottery vase Sam had made at school containing pens and pencils and a wastepaper bin for out-takes from the book. An upturned wooden crate served as a side table for the leather chair for teacups and the like.

Sam looked around the room with barely contained glee.

"I think you'll be very productive here," said a grimy Polly, hands on hips. "I actually wish I was going to write a book too. 'Author' sounds so much better than, say, 'O level student' when talking to dishy-looking boys." Polly had a point, but boyfriends were not going to pay the bills so were not part of Sam's Grand Scheme. Polly, on the other hand, was embracing the new challenge of snagging a partner for the village dance. She practised in front of her mirror, twirling her hair, head on one side, looking up through her lashes. Sam discussed this turn of events with Dunster, and he didn't appear able to fathom the point either. But Sam knew he had a vested interest in her remaining focused on the book. So he may not have been the best one to ask.

Chapter Twelve

Sam should have known better than to search anything England-related in her current state. Speech pathology jobs quickly turned to websites full of Exmoor ponies, scone recipes, *Lorna Doone,* National Trust properties, and houses for sale in Porlock. Expat blogs came next, an interesting mix of those so happy to be living a new life elsewhere and those pining sorrowfully for home. The images and comments left Sam feeling not so alone. She pushed the laptop aside and picked up the manuscript. She'd thought it was the dusty paper she could smell, but now she was sure it was the old leather chair in the writer's cabin that had stimulated her mind's nose. From the mouldy chair, her olfactory memory moved to the lavender and roses in the garden, then to the smell of cake baking in Mrs. Althorp's kitchen. Her ocular memory recalled clearly the light streaming through the cabin window, making the dust look like glitter floating in air before settling on the picture frame on the shelf. Her audiological memory added birdsong, soft equine nickers, and rustling leaves to the jumpy film footage. A sigh and a pounding in her chest. The heartbeat she felt today was the same one she'd felt pulsing in that cabin. Only sadder now. Lost now.

Dialling Gail's number and dispensing with pleasantries and segues, Sam jumped straight in. "Does everyone feel this way? Does everyone have a small corner of the world that means so much to them nowhere else ever fills the void? And if they do, is it always the place they were born? Because I've been gone a long time but can't seem to leave my first home behind."

"Well, there've been world travellers who could never settle in one place," Gail replied, ignoring the lack of pleasantries and segues. "And others, writers and artists particularly, who seem to discover home later in life. That place speaks to them in words or colours that makes it impossible for them to leave. Everyone's different, Sam. You're allowed to feel what you feel."

Sam thought of her grandparents. They had never left Exmoor during their mortal lives. She wished she'd known them at an age when she'd thought to ask them why. But maybe she knew already. That tiny village in that small national park in that little country truly was the centre of the universe to them. Sam heard their long-silenced rationale through time: because it was home.

"My kin built Porlock High Street, fed the soldiers on duty in the gun pillboxes on the beach, and knew the equitation centre before it was even born. It's all my history too, like the Celts and Doomsday and wild ponies. I want it back." Her voice wobbled down the phone line.

"Look," Gail cooed softly. "Why don't we do something tonight? Movie? Dinner? Or should I be saying, 'film and high tea'?"

Sam managed a watery smile.

"How about we meet at Bernie's at seven?"

Sam sniffed and wiped her eyes. "Thanks, Gail."

Hanging up the phone, Sam caught a glimpse of a ghostly image in the glass of Dunster's photo of an immaculately turned-out lady with a top hat and veil, wearing a tiny-waisted side-saddle habit. Her horse gleamed. Outward appearance was everything back in those days. Stifled emotion constrained by corsets, restricted by protocol, mandated by class. But what was constraining Sam? Surely the world wasn't so stifled now? But outward appearance never really gave much clue to internal status, not then, not now. Ripped jeans adorned billionaires, Armani suits hid extraordinary debt, day-to-day normalcy hid chaos. Midwestern walls hid English hearts.

Minus Twenty-Four

It was July. Sam had just finished her last O level exam and life was full of promise as she awaited results. She took care of Dunster, told him she was off to make their fortunes, then headed down to the cabin for her first day of writing. "Better take the newspaper with you—to look for jobs," her father had shouted out the door after her.

Sam had frequented the cabin before this but only to study in peace for O levels. Now it was author time. Mrs. Althorp was watering plants in the garden when Sam arrived, so they walked up to the cabin together.

"Can I take a look inside?" Mrs. Althorp asked. Sam flinched. Had she really not invited her friend in before this?

As they entered the cabin, Mrs. Althorp's reaction was one of pure joy. She exclaimed and clasped her hands together as Sam showed her each new addition to the furniture, the books on the shelf, the paper and pens. A miniscule shadow crossed her face as Mrs. Althorp looked at the leather chair. She gently rubbed the sunflower throw rug between her fingers.

"You've done a lovely job, Sam. My husband would be so happy his favourite spot is getting a new lease on life. We both hope you are inspired to great success by the beauty and tranquillity of this place. And who knows, maybe one day they'll be bringing tourists here to see where it all started, like they do Thomas Hardy's cottage in Dorset." Mrs. Althorp chuckled at Sam's incredulous reaction. "Never say never," she said, pointing her finger at

Sam. "Never say never."

"Speaking of never," Sam said. "You know you never have to ask if you can come in here. It's your cabin, and you won't even let me pay rent, so please come in anytime. I'm so grateful to you for this special place."

Mrs. Althorp smiled and said, "Writers need a dedicated space full of peace and calm where only their thoughts and characters inhabit the air. Other bodies are intrusions and likely to cause a block in the flow of creative juices."

Sam didn't really know what creative juices were or how she would know if she had some, and she couldn't help feeling Mrs. Althorp had put more thought into writing than her protégé had. But she nodded thoughtfully, wishing Polly had been this understanding. "No, you can't come and watch me write" hadn't been taken well.

"I certainly don't want to be your 'Person from Porlock,' do I?" Mrs. Althorp chuckled.

Sam smiled, knowing full well she would never fall victim to the poet Samuel Taylor Coleridge's infamous stealer of creative juices.

As Mrs. Althorp walked away down the gravel path, Sam took a deep breath and stepped back into the cabin, softly closing the door. After the planning, the cleaning, the finding furniture, the making sure everything was in its right place, there was just one small thing left to do. Sam strode purposely over to the desk and lowered herself into the creaking wooden chair, less confident in her mission with each lowered inch. Her eyes raked the view from left to right, taking in the sparkling sunlight on the smooth waters of the channel and distant outline of the Gower Peninsula. Suddenly, the enormity of what she'd taken on engulfed her. As she looked at the fresh stack of loose-leaf paper on the table and the sharp pencils, the objects seemed to take on an expectant air, waiting for her first glorious words, sowing seeds of doubt with their silence. Echoing Sam's. She couldn't think of a single thing to write. She couldn't even think of a topic, let alone jot down a first sentence. It had seemed amazingly simple in concept: Write book. Make money. Keep Dunster. Go to the Weir Equitation Centre. Bob's your uncle. The warning bells sounded.

"Okay," Sam barked at her pencil. "Focus!" She remembered reading somewhere that just visualizing the outcome you wanted could lead you to the goal, so for a minute she closed her eyes and pictured herself in a tweed jacket. She was being congratulated by other students on her perfect position during canter pirouettes. She then pictured herself standing in the middle of the cross-country course as a fully qualified riding instructor, bellowing directions at her own international students. And most importantly, she pictured herself an elderly lady, maybe thirty-five or so, leading a creaky but still mobile Dunster across a paddock to his very own custom-built stable.

"Mission accomplished." She now remembered why she was here.

৵৽

Two hours later, Sam was in the same chair, holding the same pencil, leaning on the same spot of the table. The only difference was that there was now one sheet of crumpled white paper in the wastepaper bin. Not because the words for her grand opening paragraph hadn't quite caught the imagination the way she'd pictured, but because there was room for not one more single doodle. Spirally circles, boxes inside boxes, holly leaves, chequered squares, bug eyes, Kilroy, even a Skippy the Super Scone. (Sam didn't remember drawing him at all, but looking at his face, she saw perhaps for the first time what her art teacher had seen.) But not a single word had been written.

Sam entertained the notion that she may not have so much as a rudimentary grasp on how to write a book or even what the heck it was she wanted to write about. An elongated agony column thingy? A horse manual? A horse story? What? And then there was that whole "audience" thing.

"How many times have I used the word *thing*?" Sam asked the listening spiders. "Surely this is an indication that I shouldn't be charged with writing anything. Does 'anything' count as a 'thing' too? Oh just stop, for crying out loud!" Sam held her head in her hands until her last words finished echoing around the cabin.

But really, audience, apparently, was an important component of writing. Who was she writing for? Apart from someone with enough money to cough up the price of the book.

Sam decided to switch seats to the armchair, where she opened her lunch box. Maybe she just needed food after the walk to the cabin and all that doodling. "Who cares that it's only quarter past ten?" Sam announced to the walls with gusto. "Writers aren't known for sticking to pre-planned schedules. They write when the mood strikes, ready at a moment's notice to leave a dinner party, drop the frying pan, pull the car over, break off a conversation." Sam unwrapped her sandwich, picturing the strange stares she would get from others as she gazed off into the distance, seeing characters, hearing dialogue, plotting plot. She knew all she had to do was eat her sandwich and wait for the juices to drip.

Hours later, lying upside down on the leather chair, her legs thrown up over the back, Sam swished her hair from side to side across the floor because she liked the way it sounded. The sandwich was long gone, the thermos of tea empty, and not a word written. "If Dunster were on death row, I couldn't save him now," Sam lamented as she spun herself upright. She called it a day at one o'clock, sneaking out the garden gate, and staying away from Polly's house.

"It's not writer's block if you haven't written anything yet," Polly had said during a discussion while they were cleaning the cabin. "That's just laziness."

࿇

The next morning, Sam spent longer taking care of Dunster and walked more slowly to the cabin. Mrs. Althorp was in her sitting room as Sam entered the gate, the windows thrown wide open to let in the sunshine, the birdsong, and the glorious floral scents. She was dusting the china ornaments that delightfully cluttered a shelf by the window seat. Sam waved cheerfully, though avoided eye contact, and strode purposefully towards the cabin, telling herself today couldn't possibly be as bad as yesterday. Just beginner's nerves. Charles Dickens had them too.

Sam spent some time analysing the theme of the book. Or rather, trying to learn what a theme was from the dictionary. Apparently it was something to do with the underlying message of the book. What did she want her message to be?

Tick-tock, tick-tock ...

"Something about perseverance would be good. I persevered through cabin cleaning. I carried around that, admittedly empty, journal all day every day, ready to jot down snippets of wisdom and clever repartee at a moment's notice. I even read a few pages of my grammar books over the past few days. Now that's the epitome of perseverance." Sam congratulated herself, then second guessed her choice. "Or perhaps the theme should be something related to holding onto one's dreams. After all, I'm jumping through hoops here to keep my dreams alive of having my pony and equine training too. Oh yes! I can work with this!"

Sam put pencil to paper at 9:45, marking the time on her watch for posterity. "My advice to you ..."

At 9:45 and fifteen seconds, there was a loud *crack!* as the wobbly wooden chair split in two. Sam's lip hit the edge of the table. Four words were obliterated by blood while the pencil rolled forlornly across floor.

So actually today *could* be worse than yesterday.

ॐ∾ॐ

In Mrs. Althorp's kitchen, leaning over the sink holding several ice cubes wrapped in a tea towel against her swollen lip, Sam reflected on what she had learned so far about writing: writing was not for sissies. She had now spilled more blood during her tenure as a writer than she had in all her years of riding horses. Of course, there had been many minor cuts and scrapes from various falls, and more than a little bruising of arse and ego, but she'd never actually bled profusely. Maybe the creative type truly had to suffer for her art. Like with Van Gogh's lost ear. *Hey, this divot in my lip could actually be a good sign!* Sam smiled to herself.

"How are you feeling, dear?" Sam jumped as Mrs. Althorp entered the kitchen, carrying a red-tinged cloth from cleaning up the blood-splattered scene in the cabin. "May I assume you were setting the scene for a detective novel up there? All it needed was the taped outline of a body."

Sam giggled as she looked up at those twinkling eyes. She knew her secret was safe with Mrs. Althorp. There would be no anonymous poem circulating in the village about this catastrophe. So maybe it was safe to share another secret. The giggle died.

"I have no idea what I'm doing," Sam blurted out, pulling the ice away from her lip with a wince, once more experiencing that prickling sensation in the corner of her eyes. *What is it about Mrs. Althorp that reduces me to tears?*

"I thought I could quickly knock out this book about who-knows-what for who-knows-whom, but now it has come to it, I don't even know how to start!" Sam spluttered. "I don't know if I'm writing fact or fiction. All I know is there's a horse in it. And I'm supposed to be top of my class in writing. Pathetic, really." Sam hung her head over the sink and watched the edges of the droplets of blood feathering as they mixed with the salty tears.

Mrs. Althorp sighed quietly and pulled up a kitchen stool. She patted Sam's hand gently and said, "Well, you just used 'whom.' That's a good sign for a writer. So let's think what else you have in your favour. Based on what you've told me, you have a topic, *the* horse, if it's factual. You have factual knowledge about horses, as you've been taking care of one for years now. Or you have a character, *a* horse, if it's fictional, and you have knowledge about horses as characters. Think about Dunster. He's got character galore that you could make into a hilarious story. Don't you think others may find him funny and interesting too?"

Sam thought about all the photos on her notice board with Dunster in all kinds of costumes. She thought about her hilariously unsuccessful attempts to teach him how to bow. She'd given up placing treats on the floor in front of his nose, then given up trying to pick his front hoof up and place it out in front of him. She had finally resorted to getting up on Dunster's back and slowly creeping up his neck, thinking the weight would finally make him assume some kind of bow-like position. Of course, Dunster was smarter than that, and a small buck was all it took to send Sam into a face plant in front of him. The first jumping lesson sprung to mind too, funnier now than it had been at the time. (Now Sam knew why Polly had left the scene in a hurry. It was frankly hysterical, but better not include that in the book.) None of this made Sam look particularly competent, though, and she wasn't sure she wanted to risk enlightening a worldwide audience about her antics at the Equine School of Hard Knocks.

"Or what about this?" queried Mrs. Althorp, sitting up a little straighter. "What do you think Dunster would want others to know about him? Would he want them to know about his history? Or his little jokes on people? Or what he discusses over the fence with his friends?"

"He would want people to know where his sugar lumps are kept," Sam said, rolling her eyes.

Mrs. Althorp threw her head back and laughed so hard little tears appeared. She raised her apron to her eyes and dabbed at the corners delicately, shaking her head until her laughter subsided.

"That's true, he would, wouldn't he?" she responded, then continued on. "And what else would Dunster want to share?"

Sam slowly pulled the ice away from her lip again as she gazed out of the kitchen window. She wondered if Dunster ever felt the urge to tell others what he liked, what he needed, what he feared. Probably not. He was comfortable in the knowledge that he knew what he was doing in the present, knew his surroundings as being a place he belonged, and was with people and horses who were kind to him. He didn't suffer from the human curse of worrying about the future, well, beyond whether or not teatime would happen punctually. But it wouldn't hurt humans to think about these things with regards to their equine charges. Ann Sewell and Golden Gorse had been onto something.

"I for one would like to hear more about Dunster," Mrs. Althorp said, and Sam knew she meant it sincerely. Mrs. Althorp stood up expectantly. "Are you ready to write?"

Back in the cabin, with lemonade and some bourbon biscuits on a flowery plate, Sam sat down on a new chair from Mrs. Althorp's spare bedroom. She had a fat lip, renewed courage, and an idea that didn't involve agony. A writer once more, bruised, battered, but back on her literary horse.

అ౨ఛ

"I'm going to write a letter from Dunster, or rather a series of letters," Sam told the Bristol Channel. The book would be shaped as letters between Dunster and herself. "Write what you know. Thank you, stupid English teacher. And Mum." Sam knew how to write a letter. She'd been forced to write thank-you letters for every birthday and Christmas present since she could clasp a crayon. Letters seemed a little less daunting than a tome to perseverance and following your dreams. "I wonder if anyone else has ever thought of this?" Sam would be so disappointed later when her mother said, "Oh, so you're writing an epistle." Like it had been done before.

Anyway, Sam knew she had plenty to thank Dunster for, enough to fill many books: this cabin, Mrs. Althorp, the deer herds and the roaming Exmoor ponies that didn't scatter when she rode past. Branches coated with neon green lichen that she could reach from horseback and squeeze with her fingers. The cake stall at horse shows—usually. Warm breath down her neck, a furry covering for her frozen fingers. The gentle nicker as she climbed over the fence on a summer evening, those all-knowing eyes. And the patience, oh, the patience, as she unburdened herself on her pony though all the traumas of childhood and adolescence, perceived or real. She loved each one of these reasons with a passion that made her heart both ache and sing.

But what did Dunster have to thank her for? Did he enjoy sharing Exmoor with her? Was he glad he could show her this magical world from the back of a native speaker, a home-grown guide with all the knowledge of the moors intuitively ingrained? With each expedition, with each gallop across Ley Hill, with each trip under the arch of the Worthy toll gate, Dunster had helped make Sam part of Exmoor, though really, compared to him, she was nothing more than a grateful grockle. Sam couldn't help but feel she had more to thank him for than the other way around. "So should my working title be *Dear Sam* or *Dear*

Dunster?"

Tick-tock, tick-tock …

Then clarity. Sam just wanted Dunster to know how much he was loved. In that moment, it didn't matter to her what anyone else knew. "I'll write this book for him! *Dear Dunster* it is!"

"But wait!" A worried voice in Sam's head tried to apply the brakes. *"According to the Grand Scheme, the audience was supposed to be global. And number in the millions. And be able to pay for the book. And not be a horse."*

All true. All ignored.

As it turned out, learning to say what she needed to say would become a far greater asset than saying what she thought others wanted to hear.

Shame about the money, though.

Minus Twenty-Three

Post haemorrhage, things went quite well. No blood, no meltdowns, and a few words actually made it onto paper.

Sam jotted down the outlines of several experiences she was grateful for. Like the time Dunster had refused to exit a bridle path onto the road to Horner despite Sam's furious kicking and yelling. But Dunster had heard the lone cyclist heading their way at great speed. He saved bikes, bones, and possibly lives that day. Then there was the time he had to self-navigate his way down Porlock High Street during a May Day parade with a huge sombrero on his head. Unbeknownst to Sam, despite carefully cutting holes for his ears that she thought would hold the hat in place, it had slowly slipped farther and farther over his eyes until he was essentially blind. Being blind didn't have happy memories for Dunster, yet he refused to let a bad experience from the past taint the enjoyment of that day. So Sam, oblivious, waved to the spectators while Dunster took care of her. It seemed appropriate that her first letter would be thanking him for his forbearance as she learned the ropes.

> Dear Dunster,
>
> It seems like only yesterday you arrived in my back garden. I knew nothing about horses I hadn't learned by sitting in a hedge, and you seemed to know everything about me, or my kind at least: the child. The horse-mad child, the "determined to gallop

before I could walk" child, the "expect a Courbette while training for the egg and spoon race" child. Besotted but ignorant, my love for you put you in harm's way as I climbed underneath you, frightened you with chewing gum, and placed toxic Christmas decorations within munching reach. It's amazing that you survived at all really. Maybe a less intelligent pony wouldn't have. But you, Dunster, knew it all, especially when to say no. "No, I won't jump that ditch because it's too big for you." "No, I won't eat that suet pudding and custard." "No, I won't stand still so you and three of your friends can attempt that circus act." "No, I won't try to squeeze between those two parked cars because your legs will get squashed." "Just ... no."

Looking back, I thought you were stubborn. All right, you were stubborn. But now I know you were stubborn mostly in a good way, a protective way. You knew you could hurt me if you wanted to. And you knew I could hurt myself with my high-flying dreams and sense of invincibility. You taught me my limits as you imposed yours, gently, quietly, always with restraint and kindness. You knew it all. And I am so grateful for the way you shared your knowledge with me.

Thank you.

Love,

Sam

Brushing the tears from her eyes with the back of her hand, Sam reread the first page of her book, if that's what it was. She imagined herself reading this letter to Dunster. Then, of course, she wondered why she was imagining reading it to him. She leapt up, page one in hand, and hightailed it to the farm, the cabin door banging behind her.

Dunster nodded appreciatively after the reading, nudged Sam's pocket gently, then lifted his head slowly and rested his chin on his little girl's shoulder. Sam wrapped her arms around his neck and whispered, "Thank you, thank you, thank you."

≈≪

Dear Sam,

I remember that first meeting too. I was confused after the lorry ride. I was sad when they opened the ramp and led me into a strange place. I couldn't smell my friends. I didn't know I was supposed to say goodbye. But when I smelled you and your tears, I knew I would be all right. You were gentle and kind and so excited when you saw me that I was happy for you. I liked the feel of your hands when they stroked me and your little cheeks that snuggled against my neck. I liked the apples and the grass in your garden. Oh, and the day lilies too. I only knew they were called day lilies when I heard your mum yell, "What the heck happened to the day lilies?" I like your mum. She brings me treats while you're at school.

I agree. I am stubborn. It's part of being an Exmoor pony, along with the mealy muzzle and the toad eye. But thank you for sometimes asking yourself why I was being stubborn. Was the task too much for me, or too much for you? Sometimes being stubborn is simply the way I tell how serious you are about accomplishing a task. And you always seem more pleased with yourself when you finally get me to do something after several attempts than if I do it straightaway. But sometimes I just said no because it was the right thing to do. I knew I wasn't supposed to be in your mum's kitchen.

So thank you for remembering lorries can seem dark and noisy, ponies have friends they'd like to see sometimes, and I don't know the difference between plant pots and weed patches. And thank you for the sugar lumps.

Your friend,

Dunster

"It sounds like Dunster," Sam said, as she finished writing. Geraldine had told Sam about seeing her mother bring treats across the road when she thought no one was looking. Sam imagined James Cuthbertson sniggering as he read her book, ridiculing the idea of talking to your horse and your horse talking back. "But what does he know? He's not my audience," Sam huffed.

Chapter Thirteen

Sam gazed at the collection of letters on the table, finally finding the courage to stop calling it a manuscript. She scooped the yellowing papers into her lap with the hand that wasn't holding a chocolate biscuit. The mud was still visible on every sheet, the Wellington boot prints on pages ten through twenty. The tear stains weren't so obvious, but Sam knew they were there, absorbed into the fibres of the paper, adding to the backstory.

Brushing her fingers across the pages, Sam felt the crinkly paper that never dried flat after the storm. The pencil marks had faded somewhat (*so that's why the Magna Carta and the US Constitution were written in ink?*), but each word looked familiar. Each one was the memory of a lesson learned, a friendship cemented, or a dream either achieved or unfulfilled. Those letters would never see the light of published day, but they had provided hope for future happiness at the time. As Sam sat, four thousand miles and decades from the writer's cabin, she didn't feel much different from the teenager who dreamed and wrote thank-you letters to her pony. Still the same person, but now with a dose of *hireth* added to the mix.

How could Mrs. Althorp ever have found encouraging words to say? As Sam read, she struggled to believe that a single other person would have wanted to read those letters, let alone enough people to elevate her to diamonds and castles à la Barbara Cartland. The letters were sappy, overrun with clichés and primitive attempts to sum up in teenage words the feelings she couldn't then explain. And perhaps still couldn't. But as she read on, the intent began to shine through. Each treasured memory shone light on why she'd wanted to keep Dunster so badly, why she'd wanted to go to the Weir Equitation Centre, and why Exmoor was now pulling her back so hard she could practically hear the winch wheel winding the chain that wrapped around her heart.

"Oh, good grief. Talk about teenage sappiness, Sam. Get a grip!" Her voice echoed off the silent walls.

But she had a grip. On the intent of the writing. On the message it was still sending her, all those literary miles later. Those once-powerless letters were gaining strength with each passing moment.

Mrs. Althorp had seen the intent too. And had taken action.

Minus Twenty-Two

Over the next few weeks, the letters flew from Sam's pencil. But even to her inexperienced author eye, she knew the themes and ideas were disjointed and choppy, more like splattered paint on a Jackson Pollock canvas than the cohesive Monet image she'd imagined verbally painting at her first book reading. She tried to find a rhythm of asking and answering, thanking and you're welcoming, teaching and learning. She still thought this conversation through inter-species letters was a good concept, but just couldn't put it down on paper like it sounded in her head. She finally realised that was because in her head she was actually talking to Dunster as they ambled over Dunkery or snuggled in the straw. Dunster seemed to be her only audience, and she couldn't imagine letting anyone else read the words. It was too personal. And unmarketable.

One afternoon, Sam sat down in the leather chair to give herself a stern talking to. "Money is your Person from Porlock," she chided. Her financial need made every word a failure that wouldn't make money. Which meant *every* word. "Maybe you need to change things around. Just focus on thanking Dunster and reminding yourself about all you've learned. Forget other people." This would certainly make for much happier writing. But obviously the job search was going to have to start taking priority.

Sam heard a noise outside the cabin, and assuming it was Mrs. Althorp, she opened the door. She found a stranger shovelling compost from the pile into a wheelbarrow. He was a tall fellow, several years older than Sam, with red hair like hers and a sprinkling of freckles over his nose and cheekbones. He looked up briefly but focused quickly back on the musty compost.

"You'll be the writer then," he stated with that soft West Country accent that made "writer" sound more like "wroi-er." "Don't worry about me," he continued. "I've been told to leave you alone, and I like quiet meself so it should work out fine." With that, he thrust his fork into the steaming pile of compost in the barrow and ambled off down the path.

Sam went back inside the cabin and shut the door without even having the chance to ask the stranger's name. But as she sat down to begin the day's writing, a grin slowly spread across her face. Mr. Gardener had referred to her as a writer. And he hadn't said it with a smirk. No hint of sarcasm. Mrs. Althorp thought she was one too. Now maybe it was time for Sam to accept that role for herself. And Mrs. Althorp was right about something else: that darned Person from Porlock. For some reason, Dunster was talking about how much he liked freckles.

≈∽≈

Sam had more to worry about than freckles. O level exam results were in, and she'd passed English, geography, social studies, and also French, but the future would find this to be of limited value. No one had expected much from her maths and history results, so no one was disappointed.

"My dream of being an accountant for the Natural History Museum is in ruins," she'd joked at the dinner table.

"Based on these results, your ability to provide correct change or recall your own birth date might be questionable too." Her irritated father could recall every England Rugby Club statistic going back to 1946. "Hopefully you have job plans that don't require those skills?"

"I don't want you mucking out stables for the rest of your life. You need to broaden your horizons," Emma the Unbroadened said, though one day she would have to acknowledge that mucking out stables had broadened Sam's horizons considerably.

"An office-type position, I suppose then," said Sam, unenthused. But that could pay her enough to keep Dunster if she lived at home. Polly was training to be a bank teller, somewhat surprising given her better-than-Sam's-but-not-great maths results. Polly believed her mother about never being able to afford to train at the Weir Equitation Centre.

"But how does an office job broaden my horizons?" Sam rested her chin on her hands and looked at her mother. "You know, there are jobs in *Horse and Hound* for grooms all over Europe: show jumping stables in Holland, dressage stables in Germany, racing stables in Ireland. Sound like broadening opportunities, don't they? Albeit still involving a pitchfork."

Emma gave a little harrumph, like foreign travel was ever going to happen to her little person from Porlock. But for Sam, a tiny bite from a travel bug began to itch.

A surprising new addition to the Grand Scheme: global traveller.

Chapter Fourteen

A startled jolt threw Sam upright, sprinkling biscuit crumbs everywhere to the delight of the dogs.

"That's it! The big moment!" Sam cried, forcing the dogs to abandon their vacuuming duties to run to the window to see what exactly "it" was. "The moment everything went off kilter!" From the adoration of a single location and no expectation or desire to be elsewhere, the teenage Sam was considering other options. Middle-Age-Minus-Ten Sam jumped up from the couch and screamed through time, "Don't do it! Don't look into that British Airways light! Step away from the Greyhound Bus! Feast on the views you already have, drown in clotted cream! You'll never have it so good again!"

Sam's dire warnings were interrupted by inhaled biscuit. Through the coughing and spluttering, her perceived influence on Young Sam slipped away. It was too late to save her. If only Young Sam had known then of *hireth* and had any frame of reference on which to assess its meaning. If only she'd spoken to someone who longed for home. If only there had been those expat Facebook pages full of pleading for information on how best to retrace steps. If Young Sam could have seen Exmoor at that moment through the parched eyes of one who hadn't lived there in years, she'd have closed the *Horse and Hound* and turned off the television travel shows. But Pandora's box was open. And putting the lid back on would take decades.

Sam had found the moment she had set out to find that

weekend, the moment that changed everything. And there was some comfort in that because she knew she would now be better prepared to recognize a life-changing moment if one ever appeared again.

Sherlock and JB returned disappointedly from the "it"-less window and sat at Sam's feet.

"Well? Has she recognised it yet?" Sherlock panted.

JB just rolled his eyes at the sheer scale of human ignorance.

Minus Twenty-One

As Sam sat on the paddock gate considering foreign travel, Dunster's head in her lap, a shiver ran down her spine, like someone had walked over her grave or was trying to warn her of something. Or maybe it was just excitement at the possibilities.

"What would you say if I went away, Dunster?" Sam lifted the heavy head to look her pony in the eyes, searching for guidance. "Would you understand it was to just to earn more money for you and WEC?" Dunster blinked. It was hard to tell if it was an affirmative. "But what comes first? The training in order to get the job, or the job to earn the money to train?"

As Sam kissed Dunster goodbye and set off down the bridle path to Mrs. Althorp's, she tried to push all the chatter in her head aside so she could focus on the day's writing. The topic was something to do with being prepared to find dock leaves after having being bucked off into stinging nettles. True story. Not so much a thank you to Dunster as it was praise of the Brownie readiness that armed her with knowledge of the local flora and fauna. Surely that insight alone was worth the price of the book? And would it hurt Dunster to apologize once in a while?

As the afternoon wore on, Sam became increasingly aware of the rising temperature in the cabin. The sweat began to trickle down her nose and splosh on the paper. Her mind finally twigged that it was altogether possible a storm was brewing. She tried to ignore the discomfort, but it slowly sapped her creative energy, and she was forced to throw her body back in the chair, wiping her brow.

Seemingly from nowhere, a mighty gust of wind whipped around the rhododendron bushes and slammed into the cabin. The skies darkened ominously, and Sam found herself peering through the window, only to be blinded by a bolt of lightning out over the channel. Branches creaked and dry summer leaves crackled against each other, sounding like a papery electrical current. Another bolt of lightning, closer this time, with the accompanying rain falling in sheets. The wind fought to lift the cabin from its foundations. Sam had a brief vision of Dorothy arriving in Oz in a shed. She had just enough time to wonder if the Wizard would give her fare to the Weir Equitation Centre.

It was the door bursting open with a crash that brought Sam back to Kansas. The cabin's contents became a swirling, wet vortex of paper and pencils and sandwich bags and books and sunflower throw blankets, lit up by flashes of lightning and shaken by thunder. With hair and rain in her eyes, Sam struggled across the cabin with outstretched hands, groping for the door. She threw her weight behind it, but instead of a satisfying bang of door on doorframe, she felt a squishy sensation and heard a muffled, "Goruff!" Her blurred vision picked out a tinge of red with intermittent freckles. Gardener appeared through the vortex, unhappy at playing the part of doorframe. With a horrified squeak, Sam eased up on the door, letting said gardener in. He then leaned on the door hard to seal it shut, shaking the rain out of his hair as he staggered forward. Breathing hard, wiping pencil sharpenings and bits of digestive biscuits out of her eyes, Sam stared at Gardener, who stared back with the beginning of a bump on his forehead. The storm was already racing up the combes behind the cottage, heading upwards to rip the plastic Macintoshes off the tourists taking pictures on top of Porlock Hill. The rumbles faded. The light began to brighten. And Sam stared around the cabin.

Weeks' worth of writing hadn't looked that much in a tidy pile on the sewing table. Sam had worried that she would ever gather enough information to justify her use of the cabin to Mrs. Althorp. But viewing her writings now, sprayed around the space like the vomited contents of a loose-leaf blender, all that paper seemed enough to fill the British Library. A rather dazed redhead stood in the middle of it all. Clutching sheets of blowing paper to his stomach and standing with muddy wellies on about ten others, Gardener looked at Sam with a mix of apology and anger. Sam knew her next words were going to be important in helping him to decide which expression to accentuate.

"I'm so sorry about crushing you in the door. I couldn't see anything!" she blurted out with embarrassment. "I didn't hurt you, did I?"

Gardener appeared to take mental stock of his various body parts as he scanned his person. Seeing no blood and feeling only a dull ache in his forehead, he managed a weak smile. "Sorry meself. I was just trying to find a safe place to weather the storm. Reckon this weren't it." He gave Sam a shy, lopsided grin, and for the first time since the door crashed open, Sam's shoulders relaxed. She gave a breathy laugh.

"And I suppose this wasn't the safe writer's haven I thought it to be either," Sam said. "Who knew such a tucked-away corner could be so vulnerable to the weather?"

"Surprisin' innit?" Gardener said, starting to take a step forward.

"Don't move!" Sam yelled, making the already-jumpy chap leap upwards and clutch the papers in his hands against his stomach again. "You've got half my book stuck to your wellies!"

"Oh! So sorry!" he said, twisting to each side to survey his paper snowshoes. "Here. Let me pull 'em off and we'll 'ope you can still read the words."

He gently peeled each muddy sheet off his boots and

handed them to Sam with deference. She would never forget this act of kind respect for her work. No one else would ever show such delicate sensitivity to her words, written or otherwise. *He should be an English teacher*, she thought.

Once he was standing on rubber again, and Sam had placed the soggy mess he'd handed her on the table, Gardener swept the hair out of his eyes and said, "I'm Sidney. Just 'elping out in the garden for a few weeks. Certainly didn't mean to break me promise to Mrs. Althorp by barging in on your like this. She made me take an oath not to disturb you, 'and on heart and everything."

"Well, it's a good job she didn't make me promise not to slam you in the door then," Sam replied with an impish grin and a slight blush.

Sidney laughed. Then there came the awkward silence as they both tried to find something else to say.

"I s'pose I'd better be going. There's bound to be some damage to the garden, so I'll need to clear it up before leaving," Sidney said. "I'd offer to 'elp fix this mess, but I'm not sure I'm qualified."

"Not sure I am either," Sam stated, hand on forehead. "I don't know where to start."

"Well, start looking for page one and go from there," Sidney stated matter-of-factly. "Happy wroi-ing." He left the cabin, closing the door gently behind him.

And there it was. The moment Sam learned the importance of page numbering.

ॐ∞ॐ

Eighty-seven. That's how many unnumbered pages there were. And it took about three days to get them back in order. The first two hours after the storm were spent gently pulling sheets of paper off the soaking wet window, ceiling, leather chair, and lunch box. A mop and some old newspapers were found in Mrs. Althorp's mudroom, and

Sam got to work sopping up the water from the interior surfaces of the cabin. Then each written sheet had to be pulled apart from the others and spread out in a single layer to dry on the newspaper-covered floor. The next day, Sam sorted the crinkly, mud-splattered letters into two piles: those she'd written to Dunster in one, and his answers to her in another. She then tried to match the letters up.

While sorting and sequencing, Sam got to relive each episode, each laugh, each tear. And once again, she thanked her lucky stars for the gifts of Dunster and Exmoor. But at the same time, she finally stopped hoping that anyone else would find this very personal journey worth paying for. It would take more than Lionel Edwards to save this mess. Sam felt she should apologize to the mud-caked pages. Not exactly a ringing endorsement. Wasted effort, wasted time.

Move on.

੨੦ੴ

Mrs. Althorp was a great sounding board during the job hunt; non-judgemental with no ulterior motives. Sam's parents were sick of discussing the issue and had made their choice well known: anything that paid the bills. Sam had sneaked a sideways look at her mum's hair, finally working out it was a barometer of the family's financial status. The fringe needed a trim and the grey sprinkles that caught in the sunlight suggested Sam getting a job may be somewhat of a necessity.

Sam actually felt rather grown-up looking for work, searching through the *Exmoor Gazette*, looking through *Horse and Hound, The Lady,* and the listings on the wall at the post office, and with confusion at Polly across the teacups.

"We could open a magazine together!" Polly exclaimed over scones and Earl Grey at The Battlements Tea Shop in Dunster. The girls had taken the bus for an afternoon out in the ancient market town on the edge of Exmoor. Sometimes Sam forgot that her Dunster was named after the town. To Sam, Dunster, the pony, seemed timeless, as much a part of ancient history as Stonehenge or Druids or Cadburys. Then Sam would walk Dunster High Street, looking at the old Yarn Market and the cottages, all presided over by the castle dating back a thousand years, and she'd remember Dunster the town did in fact predate Dunster the pony.

"I got that camera for Christmas, so I can be the photographer," Polly continued. "And you'll be a published author soon, so you could write the articles. We'll get advertisers and people will put—"

"Hold on. Hold on," Sam interrupted. "A magazine? You've never shown any interest in this line of work before." In fact, Polly's job at the bank couldn't be further from a creative endeavour, based on the job description. All very strictly by the book apparently: vaults opened at exactly the same time, money drawers ready for inspection, paper slips filed on the dot. "And a magazine about what?"

"Well, I don't know specifics yet," Polly answered. "Maybe Exmoor, or Exmoor ponies, or horse showing, or … or … writing books!" If Sam found the first few topics far-fetched, as they had been covered so well by others, the last one seemed positively outlandish given the girls' combined success in writing so far.

"So let me get this straight," Sam said, her attempts to scrape the last of the clotted cream out of the flower-dotted ramekin momentarily forgotten. "We finished school in July, you took a week off, and then started at the bank. It's now August and you want a career change? A career change to something you have no clue about?"

"That about sums it up," said Polly quietly, head down, chin wobbling, eyes welling up. The first audible sob seemed to echo off the walls. Sam's first reaction was to look around the tea shop to see if anyone else had noticed the breakdown occurring at table six. Seemed safe. The other customers were all too wrapped up in the cake trolley to notice a full-blown crisis in the corner. Sam's second reaction was of complete guilt. She'd been wrapped up in her writing crisis, her own decision dilemma. And page numbering.

Sam quickly unfolded her arms, leaned forward in her chair, and pushed the teapot with the crocheted cover aside. She took Polly's hands in hers. "What's going on, Polly? You'd been so excited about the bank! So many people from school wanted that job, and you were proud of yourself for getting it. Are they mean to you there? What?"

"It just hit me one day," Polly wailed quietly. "I looked around the bank, saw all the same people I'd been seeing all my life, doing the same things they'd been doing all their lives. They put money in. They take money out. They borrow money, and they pay it off. They save up for this, and they sell that. And suddenly, the exciting life I thought I'd left school for was condensed into one long, boring string of monetary transactions. One long nine-to-five. One long yawn. Just the fact that I wasn't even good at maths at school but I'd already learned my job in about five days should have told me that I'd never be able to hack the minutia of my new life. No matter how good I was, or how soon I became branch manager, it would never change the fact I was repeating the same experiences over and over again, watching others repeat the same experiences over and over again. I almost hyperventilated when I thought of doing it for another month, let alone another year, another lifetime! Oh, Sam, you're doing something interesting! You're a writer! Get me out of here!"

"So *you* are relying on my writing too?" Sam panicked. She needed to come clean about what was really going on in that writer's cabin. But first, she had to find something encouraging to say about banking. She knew her dad would have stopped Polly right there in her tracks.

"Gods, I tell you!" Larry would pontificate over breakfast with a pile of bills beside his plate. "In total control over where people live, how they live, whether or not they can eat *and* write a book at the same time. Walk or drive. Sleep or toss and turn." But Sam couldn't expect Polly to know in her seventeenth year that a visit to the bank manager was like a visit to the Wizard of Oz.

Sam finally managed a lame "But banking is important." Polly just rolled her eyes.

Sam couldn't wrap her head around the fact that their lives were over so soon. They were barely old enough to drive! And here Sam was, trying to do exactly what Polly was doing. Conforming. Settling. Numbing the ambition. Where were those two girls who planned to take the Spanish Riding School by storm? The girls rescuing Mousie? Writing a book that would change the way people all over the world thought about Dunster. The pony, not the town.

"What happened to us?" Sam asked quietly. The girls looked at each other. Then Sam smacked her forehead and said, "Oh my gosh, Polly! I think you may have just saved me from making the biggest mistake of my life."

During the rest of the conversation that afternoon, which was spent plotting escape, it became clear that Polly may have something unique to bring to their collective escape plan. She'd never have used words like *monetary transactions* a few weeks earlier. So her banking experience, however brief, may prove to be a vital asset because to break out of there, the co-conspirators would definitely need a monetary transaction.

"Right," Sam said, taking charge of the still-weepy Polly. "It's obvious we're going to have to leave the country."

Minus Twenty

"Wait. Tell me why we have to leave the country again?" Polly asked with a pained expression. This less-than-exuberant reaction took Sam a little by surprise. Not an hour ago, Polly had begged to be transported to a life of daring originality, no matter the risk or the cost. But now she wanted reasons and rationales?

"Oh, you'll be asking for a Plan B next. Typical!" spat Sam.

The girls were sitting on the floor in Polly's bathroom, having survived the stares on the bus ride back from Dunster. They'd gone into hiding without Helen noticing Sam's presence or Polly's swollen eyes and red, blotchy face, the result of the "Clotted Cream Breakdown" as Polly had called the episode. She had regained some composure as they'd sneaked into the house, but the occasional sob caught in her throat still. Sam was only just beginning to fathom the depths of her friend's despair. She recalled a similar time, with roles reversed.

"Look at it this way," Sam explained more patiently. "Everyone has certain expectations of us. You're expected to turn up at the bank on Monday, and I'm expected to release a best-selling book in the near future. The book's very unlikely to happen, based on ... er ... editorial review, and quite frankly, you've made the local job angle seem less than appealing. Your parents aren't going to understand you being home in your pyjamas on Monday, and mine aren't going to understand the muddy, crinkly mess that, instead of a book of universal interest, has turned into a letter to a pony who can't pay a single penny for it. Nothing I set out to do has been accomplished. I can't stick around to hear the snide comments. And you'll be on a dozen hit lists when those who applied for the bank job find out you quit in four weeks. I see no way out but to leave the country." An immature response to a problem, looking back, but Sam would live to use the strategy on more than one occasion to great effect. Never knock the power of refusing to meet your problems head-on.

"I see your point, Sam. I really do," said Polly, chewing her fingernail. "But we have little money and no idea where to go. I really think we're going to have to deal with it for a bit and plan things out more."

"Well, that's a quick turnaround from the Moorland Bank damsel in distress!" Sam fired back, though she could hear the voice in her head saying, "Told you so." "From 'not another single minute' to 'let's get all our ducks in a row first'! Are you serious about this prison break or not?"

"Of course I am! I've never been more serious about anything in my life. But if I've learned one thing since I left school it's that reality doesn't match the dream." Polly sounded at that moment like a jaded housewife from *Coronation Street*.

Could one month really suck the life out of a person? Sam wondered. Looking across the bathroom floor at Polly, apparently so.

"And the reality is," Polly continued, "we need a plan. Or a rich, conveniently dead uncle. Or an alien abduction, complete with spaceship transportation, making stops in Calais and Dusseldorf."

The girls sat morosely on the hard tile, hands wrapped around knees, each lost in their own thoughts. The telephone rang somewhere in the background, followed by the sound of Mrs. Dale's footsteps coming up the stairs. She knocked on Polly's bedroom door.

"What?" Polly's voice came from across the hall in the

bathroom.

"Have you seen Sam?" Mrs. Dale asked through the door. "Her mother's looking for her."

"Er ... no. But I'll go and find her." Polly pushed her fingers against the door to prevent entry. "She's probably with Dunster."

The girls waited for the footsteps to recede and then tiptoed out of the bathroom and escaped to the road.

"Let's think hard about all this. There's got to be a way out," Sam said as they parted. "Ring me with any ideas."

"Righty ho," replied Polly, sounding defeated already. She walked slowly back to her house.

Emma was ironing in the kitchen when Sam walked in. "Mrs. Althorp rang," she said. "Wants you to go see her as soon as you can."

"What about?" Sam said, racking her brain to see if she could think of a reason Mrs. Althorp might be upset with her. Had she let the dogs out accidentally? Or had Mrs. Althorp read her book and decided to end the agony for them both? Sam didn't think so, not because her book wasn't agonizing but because she believed Mrs. Althorp would never have read it without permission. Sam supposed she'd just have to go and find out.

☙❧

It was a beautiful summer evening as Sam ambled down the bridle path after supper. The birds were chirping their final night-nights, and the sun was nodding off, leaving a trail of reds, oranges, and yellows as both a farewell and a teaser of what was in store for sunrise the next day. Sam looked at the slightly faded flowers in Mrs. Althorp's garden and was reminded of the passing of time.

Sam missed walking up to the magical front door of the cottage to knock gently and watch the colours change behind the glass orb. But she was family now, so Mrs.

Althorp said, and having her say that more than compensated for the loss of the main cottage entry. Sam headed for the back door and pushed it open, calling out, "It's me! Can I come in?"

Mrs. Althorp appeared in the sitting room doorway and beckoned Sam through with a wide grin. Her walk seemed full of pent-up energy, with her shoulders slightly hunched as though stifling a giggle. Once in the sitting room, she told Sam to sit down. Sam braced herself, an excuse ready: *But the book was rubbish long before Sidney distracted me.*

"I'm so glad you could come," Mrs. Althorp said. "I've been just bursting to share this with you since I got the letter this morning. How do you feel about Provence?"

"Um ..." was the only response Sam could produce out loud. Internally, she scanned her mind's atlas to locate Provence, came up with nothing, and wondered how she'd passed her geography exam.

"Provence!" Mrs. Althorp exclaimed again. Additional enthusiasm didn't equal comprehension. "How do you feel about going to Provence in France to work with horses?" Mrs. Althorp brought her hands to her mouth in tightened fists, barely able to contain herself.

Sam looked back at Mrs. Althorp in stunned silence, which Mrs. Althorp seemed to interpret as less than enthusiastic. She slowly dropped her hands to her lap, her eyes clouding over slightly. Sam, on the other hand, was wondering at that exact moment if Mrs. Althorp was some kind of witch.

❧

Over the next half hour, Mrs. Althorp laid out the most fantastic story. Sam had known from all the reminiscence sessions that Mrs. Althorp had been involved with horses as a child. She just hadn't known where. She was shown a photo album: a child, then a teenager, then a young woman, posing in riding gear, seated on various ponies and horses, alone or with groups of other riders. They were all of Mrs. Althorp. In a very familiar setting.

"I knew you rode, but you never said anything about this!" Sam stammered. She was looking at the very same country house and fields and stable yards she had dreamed about every night.

"My father ran the estate before it became the Weir Equitation Centre," Mrs. Althorp said almost apologetically, moving on quickly. "Those years, growing up in that home with the horses and the people, were the happiest, most magical years of my life." Mrs. Althorp sighed with a faraway look in her eyes. Bringing her attention back to Sam, she said, "I sensed how desperate you were to be part of it all. It seemed almost unkind to regale you with stories about living in a place you were so anxious to live in yourself. I've been rooting for you to find a way to make it happen for you too. You're a good writer, Sam, and I think you should continue with your ideas. But I also think it may be hard to make enough as a teenaged author to meet your immediate needs. Maybe we have to look at other ways to make your dreams happen. Just for now. Then you could return to writing to support yourself financially when you're more ... settled."

Sam sighed audibly. Mrs. Althorp was being so much kinder than that English teacher.

But she was being truthful too. For every Mary Shelley or Joyce Maynard, there were tens of thousands of teenagers sitting in garden sheds trying unsuccessfully to make their fortunes. Well, maybe not tens of thousands. And maybe not all in garden sheds. But still.

Sam switched her focus back to Mrs. Althorp's opening line. "Thank you for thinking of me, but what has all this got to do with Provence?"

"Oh yes, well!" Mrs. Althorp clapped her hands together. "I made so many friends over the years in the horse community. They've scattered to the winds and live all over the world now. Funny how they still feel the magical pull of Exmoor, though, and how lucky they think I am to have stayed here. As do I. Anyway, these friends now have children and grandchildren, of course. My dearest friend, Shirley Burrough, now Shirley Bisset, lives in France. She was from Exford originally, but she found herself swept off her feet and married to a Frenchman she met before the war. Well, her daughter, Annabelle Mucharde, has a stable full of horses in the Provence area of the South of France. And Annabelle needs help because her own daughter, Nicole, who's horse mad, has decided to go to America for eight months to train with a show-jumping rider there. This leaves six horses, two ponies, a goat, ten rabbits, two dogs, and a parrot in need of a groom for eight months. It pays well, as Annabelle needs someone straightaway, and there's a lovely little cottage that comes with the placement. All your food would be provided, so there'd be no expenses. I've stayed with Shirley and Annabelle many times, and it's so beautiful. I'd go myself if I were, oh, let's say, fifty years younger! But unable to fulfil the duties myself, I thought of you. Is this the answer to your problems?" Mrs. Althorp rocked back in her chair and regarded Sam through smiling eyes as she chuckled. "Or perhaps your local job search is going better than when we last spoke?"

Sam collapsed back on the couch, unable to hold her spine straight anymore, her hands limp in her lap and her head spinning. Her first thought was that this was the second best thing that had ever happened to her. Well, knowing Mrs. Althorp was up there too. So maybe the joint second best thing. Her next thought was it was only for eight months. Dunster would understand. Would it be possible to save enough to go to the Weir as well in eight months? Questions on top of excitement on top of ecstasy! Sam's mouth was already forming the words "Yes! Yes! Yes!" Then a screeching mental halt. A vision of Polly. So desperate. So trapped.

Sam looked up at Mrs. Althorp, who was scanning the letter from Annabelle again. Sam breathed hard, watching her dream deflate like a balloon. She swallowed twice. But there was no real choice to be made. Sam began with a heavy heart but great resolve to formulate the question "Could Polly go in my place?" She pursed her lips and exhaled slowly, steadying her voice to give away this opportunity. Just as she inhaled to speak, Mrs. Althorp jumped and exclaimed, "Oh my! It looks like Annabelle needs *two* grooms, not one! Whatever shall we do about that?"

"Polly!" Sam shrieked, leaping off the sofa with her arms outstretched towards a startled Mrs. Althorp. Once more blubbering out of control, Sam pulled Mrs. Althorp from her chair to hug her, pumping her shoulders up and down in a most inconsiderate-of-osteoporosis way. It was amazing to her that Mrs. Althorp would even consider recommending her to anyone for anything as emotionally unstable as she was. This time, though, Mrs. Althorp didn't seem to think Sam needed comforting.

Chapter Fifteen

"Oh, the joy! Remember how excited we were, Mum?" Sam grabbed the telephone as it slipped from the niche between her ear and her shoulder. Trying to iron her dress for that night's dinner outing while talking to her mother required a lot of coordination. "How often do things come together like that? Filling so many voids and checking so many boxes in the grand scheme of life? I was only sixteen and I'd just won the lottery."

"If you'd heard of *hireth* at that teenage moment, or known that you'd spend so much time away, would it have stopped you going?" Emma had never lived anywhere but Porlock, so she may not have been the best one for Sam to call about her current dilemma. But she'd listened patiently while Sam filled her in. And it was a valid question.

"Of course not," Sam conceded. "But I hadn't been diagnosed then, and besides, *hireth* has to be earned. You aren't born with it. Blood, sweat, tears, time, loss, age, victory, defeat, love, and slog all play a part. Along with the cataclysmic spark of an infuriating husband."

"Oh, he's not bad—for a foreigner." Emma had forgiven Brody years ago for stealing her grandkids away to distant shores. Forgiving Sam would take a little longer. "But I reckon if the very Queen herself had sat you down and told you about the Pandora's box you were about to open, you'd have happily unleashed the chaos anyway."

She was right. A "You'll regret this" to Sam at that time would have been right up there with telling Polly a few years later, "That boy's no good for you." Sam's and Polly's responses would have been identical: "All very nice, and thanks for the warning, but I've got this." They never thought there would be payback for national desertion.

"God, teenagers are daft," Sam said with a half-hearted chuckle.

A harsh rap on the front door startled Sam into dropping the phone, then the iron. Retrieving both, she peered around the kitchen wall to view the door. Through the glass panel, she spied the familiar profile of a rotund tummy and a walking cane. If it wasn't Alfred Hitchcock …

"Oh, bother!" Sam exclaimed, speaking first into the iron, then the phone. "Got to go, Mum."

Thomas Sunby had come to call.

಄ඏ

"Sammy! Lovely to see you, dear." Thomas leaned in for a peck on the cheek, his due as a long-standing colleague of Brody's from the bank's board of directors and now as the committee chairman of "Brody McClintock for First Town Administrator."

Sam shooed the dogs into the kitchen, not for the first time wondering why they felt she needed vocal protection from a squirrel but allowed the likes of Mr. Sunby in without complaint.

"Last time I saw you, you were well into your second glass of something bubbly, ha ha!"

Banking dinners could be somewhat dry, and Sam challenged anyone to sit through a discussion about the dollar/euro exchange rate and its impact on the timber industry before judging. *And it was my fourth, by the way.*

Thomas took himself in to the sitting room and headed for the recliner. He grabbed the lever with familiar hands and settled in for the long haul. Eyeing the coffee table and the half-finished tube of Britain's greatest biscuit export, he chuckled.

"I see I've missed a Brody-less snack. Well, we can't all have his abs, can we?" Thomas slapped his Santa belly, though Sam wasn't sure if this was to compare his physique favourably with Brody's or not. Surely not. Sam chose to smile and politely ask if he was staying long enough for coffee. Apparently he was.

"No milk for me," Thomas shouted into the kitchen.

"Just as well," Sam muttered back.

Once Mrs. Sunby's hip replacement had been discussed and the cups were placed in front of them, Thomas got down to business. No points for guessing the reason for this visit. Sam held her breath.

"So, dear," Thomas began with the confident air of one who leads the troops. "We haven't had a chance, you and I, to discuss Brody's upcoming run for office. I hoped you'd be as excited as we are, but Macy mentioned you may have concerns. You know it's an honour. Many ladies have lived in this town all their lives, as had their mother's before them, and never had the opportunity to light the official Christmas tree lights, ha ha."

For most, "ha ha" would have denoted the speaker's awareness that the opportunity to light the official tree lights was a little inside joke. But Thomas said "ha ha" after almost every utterance, so it was hard to guess how he felt about the honour he'd just bestowed on Sam. Not that it wouldn't be an honour. Just not enough of an honour to renounce allegiance to the Queen and forsake the right to British protection in the event of Anglo-American relations heading south. Which they were certainly about to do.

"It's not that *I* have a problem with your citizenship," Thomas continued. "Hey, I insisted that Michael take the grandkids to Epcot as well as Disney World last spring … you know, to introduce them to other cultures, ha ha. They saw all of Europe, and little Jackson loved the United

Kingdom the best. Insisted on bangers and mash for a week after they got home, ha ha!"

Oh well, you're practically one of us then, Thomas. A veritable ambassador to the UN. So knowledgeable about British ... cuisine. And on top of being unpleasant, a skeleton, and a liability, I've now been Disney-fied. Perfect!

"So, Sam ..." Thomas paused, looking hopeful that Sam might leap up and start singing "Yankee Doodle Dandy." "So, Sam," he tried again. "I hear you have some reservations about jumping into the USA swimming pool, ha ha. You understand it would help your husband a great deal if you could call yourself a US citizen?" Thomas cocked his head to one side and raised his eyebrows, no mean feat given their weight. "Brody seemed to think you'd be wholeheartedly on board with his decision to run. Do you have any reservations about all this that I can smooth out for you?"

Oh, Thomas. Where to begin? "Well, I have reservations about everyone making major life decisions for me," Sam began. "I have reservations about everyone thinking citizenship is as easy to change as the bed sheets. And I have reservations about the committee thinking that the residents of this town are so closed-minded that they would vote either for or against my husband based on one criteria—my citizenship. I'd like to think that other issues were important to them, like taxes, education, and crime. I pay them. I have one. I don't participate in. There are many with the 'correct' pedigree to suit your First Wife criteria who don't, haven't got, and would commit in a heartbeat. There's more to my worthiness than whether or not I sing the national anthem or simply stand respectfully while others do. I'm not a threat. And I'd like to be allowed to make important emotional decisions myself. Cake or no cake."

That last bit prompted a slightly confused knitting of the mighty brows. But shaking his head slightly, Thomas battled on. "But doesn't it worry you that you can't even vote for your own husband?"

"But I can pay the taxes he'll spend in office."

"Don't you want a say in what happens in your town, to your children, to your life?"

"Don't you feel my actions give me a say?" Sam felt her hands shaking as she fought to control her voice. "I participate fully in society. I work, I fundraise, I nurture smart kids, I care, I appreciate, and I'm home in bed long before the bars close. My actions shape the town I live in and the life I lead, not my title. There are plenty of born-and-bred citizens of this country who take without giving, complain without providing solutions, and actively make life harder for others. Yet if I follow your meaning, they are better suited to your needs than I am. I think it's the committee that needs some time to rethink its position. Not me. More coffee?" That last one just slipped out. Classic female attempt to soften the edges of an argument she had totally won but now felt the need to apologize for. *Not sure politics is going to work for me.*

Only the dogs' panting could be heard through the rest of the coffee and Thomas's retreat out the front door.

Minus Nineteen

"I'd better get Polly!" Sam hurtled up the bridle path and shot thought Polly's back door, her tailwind scattering all the post off the kitchen table.

Polly was lying on the sofa in the sitting room watching *Minder* with a sullen expression and a mug of tea clasped to her chest. Sam belatedly remembered to shout over her shoulder, "Hello, Mr. Dale!" He appeared frozen in time, holding up his paper with his pipe barely balanced on his lower lip, as his mouth opened in surprise. Sam threw herself on the sofa, spilling tea everywhere, and blurted out a few nonsense words about prison breaks and baguettes.

Dragging Polly out the door in her slippers, Sam hustled Polly down to Mrs. Althorp's cottage, filling in some blanks as they ran to form a better segue between prison breaks and baguettes. By the time the girls burst through the cottage's back door, they were both squealing, watched by a delighted Mrs. Althorp. She had put the kettle on and placed some little Bakewell tarts on a plate, even though it was late in the evening. She didn't remark about the tea already splattered down the front of Polly's shirt. Or the muddy slippers. They all sat down to go through the details and to formulate a sales pitch to give to their parents. The next hour was as exhilarating as almost any gallop across Ley Hill had ever been. It became very clear that there was only really one question left to be asked: When?

ৡৎ৯

The girls made a whirlwind entrance back at Polly's house to grab items they needed for an emergency sleepover at Sam's, slamming the door behind them as they left.

"Goodness!" said Frank Dale. Helen looked shocked, as her husband so rarely displayed any sign of surprise. Was the world ending? Frank quickly settled back into his paper and his pipe, appearing certain his wife would have a plan to deal with the world if, in fact, it was ending.

It was a night of excruciating suspense. The girls practised their sales pitches, wondering what roadblocks their parents could put in their way, and discussed whether or not they had enough experience to look after show horses. They'd both been helping Geraldine more and more at the farm. Sam thought Geraldine was still trying to get her to fall in love with a more suitably sized horse. Sam didn't. But she enjoyed turning the big boys out in the paddock, tacking them up for rides, and riding a few herself on occasion along the lanes for exercise. She felt she could hold her own. Mrs. Althorp obviously thought the girls could do it.

Surprisingly, their parents didn't really take any convincing at all the next morning.

"Does it pay?" Larry asked. Even Emma seemed excited at the thought Sam was going to experience something new, even though it involved mucking out.

Helen had her usual panic attack. "Mum just researched the entire history of the French police force in the *Encyclopaedia Britannica*, pondered the possibility of another French Revolution happening in the next eight months, calculated the exact mileage between Provence and the Mafia-controlled island of Sicily, and finally agreed it was a frightening, but good, opportunity," Polly puffed as she flew in the door to tell the Westons her news.

"What about your dad?" Larry asked.

"He lit his pipe," Polly answered, which everyone knew denoted agreement.

"We're actually going abroad! Together!" Sam yelled.

"Where no one knows of our failures!" Polly yelled back.

Small details needed sorting. Polly had to go to the bank and hand in two weeks' notice. She was nervous but came home on Monday with a cheerful "They took it very well!" A quick look was exchanged between parents.

For Sam's part, Emma had made it quite clear that she was not taking care of Dunster for eight months. Larry, well, he was never an option. So Sam and Dunster racked their brains to think of how best to approach the problem. Dunster was completely on board with the adventure as long as the sugar lump supply chain wasn't disrupted. Non-negotiable. He seemed to suggest that he'd actually quite like to be ridden again, maybe show a little again, hack along the bridle paths again. He was twenty-two years old but had a willing heart still. Well, a stubborn heart, but certainly willing enough to take care of a young rider again. Sam agreed. "I should find you a loaner child."

"So who do I know who looks like me when I first got Dunster?" Sam mumbled at breakfast the next day, stroking her chin. "Who would love him almost as much as I do but would be about five years younger than me now? And a lot shorter." A vision of a little girl staring over a fence …

"Charlotte!" Sam yelled across the table, causing a second tea spill in less than forty-eight hours. Larry wasn't as forgiving as Polly. Maybe because the tea was hotter.

Sam tracked down the now eleven-year-old Charlotte. She and her family were delighted to have Dunster as a loaner pony for eight months. Her family lived in the village, so Charlotte could walk to the paddock and Dunster wouldn't have to relocate.

"You understand this is only temporary and Dunster is still a Weston and always will be a Weston. Agreed?" Sam must have repeated this a hundred times during her discussions with Dunster's new host family.

"Agreed," Charlotte said, a hundred and one times, hopping from one foot to the other, all the while her mind screaming, Pony! Pony! Pony!

⋞⋙

The next two weeks were a blur. Polly had to work only a five-day notice, which led to more furtive glances around dinner tables. Sam was free to work on the logistics of transferring Dunster's care to Charlotte. The excited and, just as importantly, short little girl came every day for instruction and to be watched by Sam's exacting eye as she groomed, tacked, rode, fed, and loved. When Charlotte offered to bring her grandmother's quilt from her bed for Dunster when it got cold, Sam knew she was leaving him in good hands. But she suggested Charlotte ask her grandmother first, and that she learn the composition of an Exmoor pony's coat.

Sam had never been abroad before. Polly had. Once. Amsterdam. The trip turned out to be a disaster when Mrs. Dale discovered on arrival that much of Holland was below sea level. This must have been mentioned in her *Encyclopaedia Britannica,* as the below-sea-level bit predated the ten-year-old information she had. Anyway, the shocking news necessitated moving to a higher room at the hotel and led to Mrs. Dale's constant apprehensive looks at the dikes and canals while clutching her handbag to her chest. Hence only one stamp in Polly's passport. Sam and her mum spent an exciting time in London getting an expedited passport application taken care of. They both left the city rather glad they didn't live closer to the bright lights. Nice to visit, but …

Tickets from Dover to Calais on the ferry and then train tickets from Calais through Paris to Avignon were purchased under the advice of Mrs. Althorp. She had made the trip many times and reassured both families that anyone could do it. Helen had told her doctor otherwise during a hysterical outbreak, so took medication for it. Madame Mucharde would meet them off the train and take the girls on to Les Baux en Provence, where they'd spend the next eight months. Parents had paid for the tickets with the agreement they would be paid back once the girls received wages.

"Wages!" Sam exclaimed to Polly. "I'm going to get real wages! To pay for … everything!" Though maybe she should see how much the wages actually were before getting too carried away. She had no idea how much a franc was worth. But it didn't really matter because she didn't have any idea what keeping a pony or equine training cost. As an afterthought, Sam had sent off for a brochure for WEC, enquiring about the Working Pupil course. This course lasted a full year and was cheaper than the three- or six-month equitation courses. The working pupil rode fewer times a day and did more yard work. Sam personally thought that spending a year in that gorgeous place was a far better deal than only three months, more work or not. Anyway, the brochure hadn't arrived yet, so she would be setting out on her adventure without a monetary goal as such.

The evening before leaving, Sam and Polly ran down to Mrs. Althorp's cottage to hug her goodbye. She was just as excited as the girls, but Sam wondered if she saw a twinge of sadness. Mrs. Althorp had the dogs for company, of course, but Sam knew how much she enjoyed their human chats. Actually, Sam couldn't imagine how she was going to get on without Mrs. Althorp's almost daily encouragement. The girls promised to write regularly, and Mrs. Althorp smiled at the promise. "Of course you will," she said, slipping fifty francs into their hands. "A leftover from my last visit to Provence. To a new independent you!" Mrs. Althorp exclaimed, refusing the girls' attempts to give the money back. "Spend it on something very French, and very frivolous," she dictated with a stern knitting of her brows, followed by a chuckle and a gentle push in the small of Sam's back to get her out the door, two sets of eyes watering.

Sam met Charlotte one more time in Dunster's paddock. She'd felt a twinge of jealousy as Dunster rooted in Charlotte's pocket for the expected carrot, but this was overridden by her gratitude at finding someone to love Dunster while she was gone. Dunster and Charlotte were perfect for each other. They would so enjoy riding together across the glorious autumn moors.

Autumn was Sam's favourite time of year on Exmoor. She thought wistfully of the purple heather out in all its glory, the whortleberries, and the young partridge and pheasant poults that constantly startled the ponies by shooting from their cover with that screeched "arrg arrg arrg" as they flew off. She thought of the first frosts, adding sparkle to the last of the berries and decorating the fallen leaves like a child's glitter-paint project. The frosty condensation from Dunster's nostrils would drift back into Sam's face in dual plumes, giving the world a misty hue that softened the edges. Then there was the joy of being the first to leave hoof prints across a hillside covered in a rare snowfall, singing, "Have a Holly, Jolly Christmas" at great volume all the way home. She'd miss the first snowdrops in Snowdrop Valley and the daffodils as they began to shake the moist soil off their sleepy heads and bob around dazedly in the spring breeze. The streams, fringed with icy lace and swollen with rain, would careen recklessly against the banks, waking up the primroses sleeping there. Later, sparkly dewdrops would fall like diamonds from unfurling bracken leaves. Wistful. Sam was already wistful. Just wait thirty years.

After Charlotte left the paddock, Sam stayed with Dunster until it got dark, rubbing his soft nose and explaining for the thousandth time that she was going to make their fortunes and that she'd be back soon. She'd made copies of some of the thank-you letters she'd written for the book. Feeling a little silly, she tucked them up in the rafters of Dunster's shelter. He was the only one who knew they were there.

Minus Eighteen

A hyperventilating Helen Dale was left behind as the Westons and Polly set out before daybreak for Dover. Sam craned her neck to greedily grab a last glimpse of Dunster over the fence as they drove off. He'd lifted his head at the unexpectedly early sound of a car, but he didn't seem too upset to see Sam go. Or upset at all, actually.

"He's just being brave," Sam told Polly as she brushed her eyes.

The journey was a strange juxtaposition of excited laughter and subdued thoughtfulness. Were they crazy to do this? It wasn't as though they hated the nest; they'd just leaned out a little too far to stop themselves from falling, pushed by an inappropriate career choice and a brag about being an author.

Dover was a seething mass of humanity, like something out of those old black-and-white war-time films of mass deployments of troops. Sam expected to see teary-eyed starlets standing on the dockside, beautifully coiffed, waving dramatically with upturned faces as the ship's horn blared. Neither Polly nor Sam looked like starlets.

"Innit hot?" Sam panted, looking at Polly. "Are you sure we need all this?" She pulled at the three sweaters and the puffy vest she was wearing. "I thought you'd researched Dover and Provençal climates."

Cases were counted, with an audible "tut" from Larry, hugs hugged, and final advice given. "Write. Be polite. Work hard. Save money. Look after each other. Practise your French. Don't be stupid."

Sam felt momentarily guilty she hadn't teared up saying goodbye to her mum and dad the way she had with Mrs. Althorp or Dunster. It wasn't that she wouldn't miss her parents. It was just time to leave their influence in a way it wasn't time to leave the influences of those other two beings in her life. Dunster and Mrs. Althorp provided loving care without the claustrophobia. Participation without expectation.

Having found a table in the buffet cabin, the now-sweaty girls plonked their bags and cases down and stripped off a few layers. They headed on deck to wait for France to appear, already forgetting the warnings about pickpockets and kidnappers from Mrs. Dale. The trip was so fast—only ninety minutes to Calais—that no sooner had they yelled and waved goodbye on one side of the boat, they were yelling, "There's France!" on the other and applying layers of clothing and grabbing suitcases to disembark.

The girls had to stand all the way to Paris on the train. By the time they collapsed in their seats on the train to Avignon, they were a mess of sweat and muscle exhaustion.

"French porters aren't very smart, are they?" Sam harrumphed after a shouted Froglish exchange regarding the correct train platform. Hand and arm gestures, despite what their French teacher had told them, didn't help at all. Once on the right train, more luck than skill, the girls found seats, stacked baggage, and dug out the flattened ham and cheese sandwiches, the bottles of bitter lemon, and the packet of Jammie Dodger biscuits Helen had packed for them. It would be the last time they considered this type of cuisine glorious. Or even considered it cuisine.

"It looks a lot like Kent, doesn't it?" Polly said disappointedly as she chomped on her sandwich.

"What did you expect? Mini Eiffel Towers and French mimes lining the route?" said the oh-so-culturally sophisticated Sam. Watching *Monty Python and the Holy*

Grail before leaving hadn't helped.

As Avignon got closer, vistas and colours changed to definitely not English-like. The soil appeared to dry up and lose its hue variation in reverse correlation with the increase in colours of the houses. The yellows, blues, and oranges of the walls and shutters vied for attention with the blue sky and silver-green groves of olive trees. At any one time, several vineyard chateaux could be seen dotting horizons and tucked into valleys, surrounded by skirts of sloping grapevines. If the cottages in Bossington wore skirts of English flowers, colourful, dense, and chaotic, these French chateaux twirled skirts of such size it was breathtaking. The ordered vines radiated out from the warm stone of the chateaux like pinstripes on a voluminous, billowing ball gown. It was all overwhelming for two girls from Porlock. *Heaven is heading to a new world,* Sam thought. Time would reverse the sentiment.

Sam had received a brief description of Annabelle Mucharde from Mrs. Althorp. One look at the chic lady standing on the platform with her eyebrows raised at the sight of all the suitcases told Sam this was the one.

"Bonjour! Bonjour! Bienvenue en Provence, Mademoiselles Sam et Polly!"

Watching the girls' brains and mouths frantically trying to translate these first basic tenets of French after five years of classes, Madame Mucharde switched to English. Somewhere in a Minehead classroom, Monsieur Nigel was slapping his hand to his forehead and contemplating, not for the first time, leaving the teaching profession.

They all shook hands, Sam so relieved that Mme Mucharde hadn't tried kissing both her cheeks, and staggered to the car with the luggage. The cream-coloured Citroen wound through tiny villages. Sam thought them so quintessentially French, based on her knowledge from the posters in the travel agent's window and a smattering of the *Astrix the Gaul* television cartoon. Awnings shaded pavement cafes, and villagers weaved in and out of displays of fruit and vegetables set out in wooden trays on the pavement. Small groups of men were drinking from shot glasses and using expressive hand gestures more successfully than the girls had. The patisseries looked amazing. Row after row of croissants, pastries, cakes, and pies.

"L'Institute de les Women has serious competition out here," Sam whispered to Polly.

Polly chuckled and poked Sam in the ribs. "Almost every person walking down the road has a baguette under their arm," she whispered. The girls saw, through the open door of a post office, three unwrapped baguettes sitting on the counter while their new owner bought stamps.

"I can just hear your mum screaming, 'Don't eat the bread!'" Sam laughed.

Mme Mucharde narrated their journey over the Alpilles, a small mountain range. On reaching one crest, it seemed the whole European continent appeared below the little Citroen That Could. Olive groves reached out as far as the horizon, interspersed with craggy rock features and solitary farms, the waters of the Camargue just out of view. The first glimpse of the fortress at Les Baux en Provence was stunning, though it actually had been pointed out by Mme Mucharde. The white rock of the ruined fortress with its undulating silhouette blended in so well with the craggy surroundings it was easy to lose its profile.

Mme Mucharde began to point out neighbours' homes and the beginnings of trails that the girls would be able to ride the horses along. The girls gave each other excited grins. Then Mme Mucharde turned into a long driveway between two stone fence posts. The driveway twisted and turned a few times before emptying out into the oval courtyard of a long stone farmhouse.

"Oh look!" Sam gasped, noticing the shutters first. They were that special Provencal blue, contrasting so perfectly with the lightly yellowed hue of the stone building itself. The rust-coloured tile roof completed the classic Mediterranean farmhouse.

Everyone got out of the car and crunched across the gravel of the courtyard with phase one of the luggage, following Mme Mucharde along a flagstone path behind the main house, across another little courtyard, to the guest cottage.

"What a treasure," Polly breathed. Same stone as the main house, same blue shutters, same tile roof, but in miniature. A little tiled porch roof threatened to catch Polly's forehead as she ducked to get under it. Inside, it was dark and cool. Mme Mucharde opened a French door ("Oh, so *that's* where the name comes from!" Polly blurted out), letting in the light and a breeze, which sent the lace curtains into gentle undulations. The light exposed the tiled floor, wooden furniture, and linen lampshades in the living area and the tiny kitchen with a stone sink and ancient-looking refrigerator. The bathroom opened out from the kitchen, a tiny shower stall but room for two toothbrushes on the tiled sink counter and cheerful sun-coloured towels on the rail. Back in the living room, a wooden staircase set against the back wall led up to the two bedrooms with no handrail and another opportunity to knock the sense out of a head on a beam. Each wooden-floored room held a bed, a dresser, and a small armoire with a mirror in the door. The view from each window was an enchanting mix of olive trees, stone walls, and paddocks.

The girls cooed over everything, thanking Mme Mucharde so much for the opportunity to come, and remembering finally to pass on Mrs. Althorp's best wishes.

"Ah, what a lovely lady she is!" Mme Mucharde gushed. "We adored her husband, Langdon, too. Did you know him?"

"No," Sam said, rather sorry for it, imagining him sleeping in his potting shed chair or reading in the cosy sitting room.

"We tried to get Hattie to come and stay after he

died," continued Mme Mucharde with a sigh. "But she refused. Maybe now we should try again. She loves it here."

Sam tried to reconcile the name Hattie with Mrs. Althorp. She conjured up a picture of the beloved comedienne Hattie Jacques, who seemed to portray rather dim-witted characters, hilarious and lovable, but in no way reflective of Mrs. Althorp's demeanour.

"I'll encourage her to come when I write to her," Sam said, promptly forgetting to do so in her first, well, only letter.

Chapter Sixteen

Still shaking, Sam put Thomas's coffee cup in the dishwasher and leaned over the sink. Staring down into the garbage disposal, she was reminded of another sink, blood and tears mingling, as she'd struggled to make sense of life. *Nothing changes, does it?*

"Can't wait to share this tale with Brody when he gets home tomorrow night." The sheer audacity of the visit would make Brody laugh. As they'd done many times before, they'd joke about Thomas's "ha ha" and make fun of his arrogance and …

But it would be different this time, wouldn't it? Brody would be on Thomas's side. Who knows? Maybe Brody even sent Thomas on this mission. Sam shook her head, feeling so alone and more foreign than she'd ever before felt.

Another knock on the door. "What could he possibly want now?" Sam cursed. Telling the worthless guard dogs to stay in the kitchen, she strode down the hallway to resume battle.

Throwing the door open and seeing nothing, Sam's confused eyes darted left and right. Then a couple of small voices squeaked in unison from about waist level, "Please buy some pies for our fundraiser, Mrs. McClintock!"

"Oh, hello, Beth. Hi, Abbie. I didn't see you down there. Of course I will! Why? Because I'm an actively involved, upstanding member of this community, that's why. Hi, Joan." The twins' mother was standing just out of sight behind the burning bush that flanked the steps to the porch.

"I didn't know we had to have such lofty goals for buying pies," Joan said. "Thought we just had to like a sugar rush."

"Yes, well …" Sam blushed. "Come on up. In fact, you've arrived at the perfect time."

The ladies sat on the porch bench while the girls laid countless glossy photos of pies, cakes, cookies, and chocolates in Sam's lap. "It'll take me a week to decide, so you'd better go inside and play with the dogs." The girls dropped to all fours and, wagging backsides in unison, took off down the hallway to find the dogs they adored. JB and Sherlock would have to tolerate being barked at. "You really should get them a dog, Joan. They're besotted with them."

"I know, I know. But six years of raising twins leaves one a little frazzled for small creatures."

"I can imagine," Sam replied. "Speaking of frazzled, do you ever question why you moved to this country?" Sam hated to admit she struggled to distinguish Joan's Canadian accent from all the others around her. But they'd become friends after meeting at yoga and now shared coffee each year to celebrate The Trooping of the Colour. Distance was no excuse for forgetting the Queen's birthday.

"Not really," Joan replied. "Jason likes his work, the kids are happy, nice house, big cars, the weather's better." Sam couldn't help feeling Joan must have once lived way too far north if she thought Wisconsin's weather was better. "I don't have to deal with Thomas like you do, though."

Sam looked surprised for a moment. "How did you know about Thomas?"

"Saw him leaving just now. And heard all about the citizenship party at the coffee shop this morning. I thought there may be fireworks about it. You'd always told me you wouldn't change citizenship."

"Does that make me so bad?" Sam almost wailed. "Can't I just be me, regardless of my Kennel Club papers?"

"Of course you can," Joan said, patting Sam's arm.

"Do you feel foreign still?" Sam needed an ally.

"Only on special occasions, like … hockey games," Joan replied. Sam grinned at her young friend, who hated the fact that as soon as someone heard she was Canadian he or she assumed Joan loved ice hockey.

"Ah, got to love stereotypes," Sam laughed. "I remember when my friend Polly's mother was introduced to Brody for the first time. He looked nothing like the Stetson-wearing, convertible-driving, camera-bedecked loudmouth she'd expected." Polly had recounted the dinner conversation to Sam later, to mutual tears of laughter. "But I think I'd take the hockey over the pip-pipping, tally-hoeing, and references to my supposed time at the palace." Sam was constantly reminding people she bought admission tickets to palaces like everyone else, adding, rather peevishly, that she had never known anyone who "pip-pipped" or "tally-hoed" in her life.

"It's probably easier being British in America than it is if you come from some other places," Sam mused. "Like it or not, the British accent's a status symbol. But I hate the way people look at me in every crisis and tell me to 'carry on.'"

"Then you shouldn't have done so well through wars and rain and soccer hooliganism," Joan laughed.

"Speaking of stereotypes …" Sam nudged Joan good-heartedly.

"Can you imagine what it's like for the Queen?" Joan asked. "If she ever watches TV when she's in America, she gets to look at herself and her corgis hawking teabags, vacuum cleaners, and toilet paper. She must wonder if she really sounds like that."

"I've never quite understood it: the American fascination with, and reverence for, an iconic institution they supposedly despise. Well, Brody certainly despised it when I first met him. To the point where he'd nearly been thrown off a tour of Windsor Castle on one of his first visits to England. 'Well, this begs the question,' Sam mimicked her husband's accent. '"Do my First Amendment rights protect me in the UK?' said to shushing from the other tourists who heard his comment about how I should be allowed to sit on the castle furniture. After all, according to Brody, 'It belongs to you too because the commoners paid for it all.'"

Joan threw her head back and laughed. "Well, did his rights protect him?"

"'Those rights won't even protect you in the hotel room if you don't shut up.' That's what I told him." Sam had to grin at the memory. To Brody's credit, he'd accepted Sam's deference to the royal institution over the years. He'd come to see it was part of the makeup of his wife's character, part of what made her proud to be British. If he were allowed to be proud of the Second Amendment and baseball, concepts that made little sense to other nations, waking up at 3:00 a.m. to watch royal weddings was a small price to pay. He'd actually grown to love castle tours and stately home gardens. The sense of continuity and the sheer scale of social time they encompassed felt somewhat humbling. Would the White House last fourteen hundred years? Would Las Vegas one day be a historical mecca like the twisting, cobbled streets of York? Or even the thousand-year-old hamlet of Porlock Weir?

"Yep," Brody had said often over the years. "You have to respect the staying power."

"I suppose I have to be grateful the British stereotype has protected me from the overt prejudices many other immigrants experience," Sam continued. "I've never been accused of taking someone else's job, or of burdening an education system, or of trying to influence the US culture to fit my own needs." She'd never felt the need to inflict the United Kingdom on the United States. The United States always showed more interest in British goings-on, from pop stars to period films, than Sam could ever possibly have propagated herself. "But I'm every bit as foreign as some of the accented taxi drivers, college professors, restaurant owners, hotel workers, or technical support staff I've encountered here. Despite the occasional linguistic faux pas—just try going into a stationery store and asking for a rubber—I'm easily understood, which helps." Sam knew her accent had provided shelter. She wasn't sun-kissed or mathematically or gastronomically or directionally gifted (her non-existent sense of direction led her to believe all taxi drivers were Mensa members), so she hadn't stood out in any non-vowel-related manner.

Until now. Now she felt uncomfortably exposed as the foreigner she really was. Not since she'd been asked if she were the nanny while trying to sign her young children up for story time at the affluent Connecticut Shoreline Library had she felt this way. Only this time it was at the hands of the one person who was supposed to accept her completely for who she was. Her reunion with Brody was beginning to feel less like *entente cordiale* and more like afternoon tea in Boston.

With a big sigh, Sam filled in the pie paperwork while Joan shooed the twins out of the dog baskets and slapped the dog hair off their clothes. Sherlock and JB staggered out of the kitchen, covered in kisses, and escorted the girls to the front door. *"Nice to see them come,"* Sherlock wagged. *"Nice to see them go,"* JB panted. After one more hug, the girls left, barking, to hunt more pie sales.

Trying to distract herself from tomorrow, Sam went inside to the office and pulled out another photo album, its pages yellow enough to make her feel like she was the product of the Victorian era. *What did they call the Victorian era in France?* she wondered. Probably the same, seeing as Britain ruled the world back then. Speaking of British arrogance …

Minus Seventeen

Sam and Polly didn't meet M. Mucharde their first evening in Provence, as he was on a wine-buying business trip in Bordeaux. Because that's what he did. He bought wine for large grocery chains all over the world. And got to travel to exotic places. For which he was obviously paid large amounts of money. And even got to take his dogs with him. To this day, Sam had never come across a non-horse-related job that made her more envious.

Knowing it had been a long day for the girls, Mme Mucharde set up a light evening meal in their cottage: cheeses, cold cuts, salad from the garden, and, surprisingly, a bottle of wine. Mme Mucharde caught Sam and Polly looking at each other. "Ah, yes. I forget sometimes my British friends take a little longer to discover the grape. There is orange juice in the refrigerator." She left the girls staring at the wine bottle, which they carefully placed in a cupboard as though it were a ticking time bomb. Which, of course, it was.

The next morning, Mme Mucharde began the tour by opening a large wrought-iron gate into the most beautiful L-shaped stable block with a small fountain in the centre of the courtyard that splashed a trickle of water gaily into a stone basin. An inquisitive head poked out of each stall.

"There's Argo, Colette, and Toujours, the ladies. Then the boys: Beau, based on his attitude, still mad about being gelded, Poirot, and Passepartout." Sam covered a snicker. While reading *Around the World in Eighty Days*, her dad had told her the story must be fiction because you'd never get a Frenchman to serve an Englishman. And it turned out Dad was right. Passepartout struggled to follow any and all directions in English, French, or Universal Curse. Then they met the pony boys: Digby, très English, and Gucci, très French. *Très* was a word Sam used frequently to validate her five years of classes.

Behind the stables was a long, low building where the wheelbarrows and garden supplies were kept. Sam and Polly called it the hatchery, as one side was completely taken up with rabbit hutches.

"I've tried to talk Nicole into getting rid of them," Mme Mucharde said with a sigh. "But she insists on keeping them. Some of them are actually quite rare and this one, Borak, is Nicole's favourite. The name means 'lightning' in Arabic, by the way, so keep your eye on him and the door closed." She pointed to an enormous grey-and-white speckled rabbit with pink eyes and floppy ears that trailed along the ground. Borak twitched his nose rapidly as he reclined on his straw bed, looking every bit the spoiled, pampered *Oryctolagus cuniculus* he was. "Bunny" didn't seem to apply. The idea of Borak bolting anywhere was difficult to imagine, as his multiple chins and sagging belly spoke more of languishing.

The most challenging charge was tied to a rope on a verge outside the stables: Tintin, the goat. Tintin looked Sam straight in the eye, and from that first second, Sam knew he'd be trouble. He stood four square, straining at the rope, and then took a few steps back only to charge forward until the rope snapped tight and his front legs left the ground, introducing the girls to Le Head Butt. Sam trod all over Polly as Tintin wound up for a second try.

"Tintin! *Arrête!*" shouted Mme Mucharde as Polly grabbed her foot and hopped around for a minute. "He can be a handful," the embarrassed host continued. "But he's so useful for keeping the weeds down. Just make sure you keep him secured. He lives in the end stable at night, with both top and bottom doors bolted shut."

As they headed back to the stables, Sam turned to see Tintin watching them, eating with that lateral, staccato chewing motion goats have that gives them a look of real purpose. Sam knew he was plotting something. She would hear his mocking bleat in her head for the rest of her life.

Sam would also forever hear the parrot, thankfully not named Polly but appropriately Echo. Due to his daytime perch by the fountain in the stable yard, Echo quickly learned to mimic his English caretakers' pathetic attempts at French, followed by a head-bobbing screech of derision. And more embarrassing still, usually a corrected version. Like he was some kind of feathered UN translator.

৵৽

On their third day at the farm, Sam and Polly were just finishing up the mucking out while discussing new concepts, like croissants and sunny weather, when they were snuck up on by an enormous white snowman of a dog. She lumbered up to the girls and leaned into their legs to be petted, a regal expression on her enormous face, staring into the distance as the girls stroked her thick coat. Next, a wild, yapping terrier-type fur ball hurtled around the corner, checked his stride for a second when he saw strangers, and then lambasted the laughing girls for paying attention to the other dog. He sprung into the air, all four feet off the ground, with as much verbal explanation of his existence as he could fit into the ten seconds between his arrival and that of M. Mucharde.

"I see you've met Yoyo and Clairette," M. Mucharde chuckled as he shook hands. "Bet you can't guess which one is Yoyo," he continued, in perfect English, as the explosive fur ball incessantly bounced from floor to chest height without seeming to put forth any effort at all.

"Clairette is a Great Pyrenees and named after one of our regional white grapes. She's getting up there in years now, but never was a quick mover. If you need her to get out of the way, you'll need to book in advance."

It was nice to have finally met every human and animal associated with their new lives, and with the exception of Tintin, Sam and Polly were well pleased with their lot. Sam couldn't help feeling a mite guilty that she was with all these animals so far from Dunster. But she knew Dunster understood the economics of sugar lumps. *Vive la République!*

∻

Polly and Sam quickly found one area that needed improving: the gorgeous stable needed a proper muck-heap. Currently, the stable waste, as Mme Mucharde so eloquently termed it, was thrown in a corner of one of the paddocks. It would simply not do.

Once the current pile had been removed by a local farmer, M. Faber, as he did every couple of months, Sam and Polly began shaping the pile into a perfect rectangle, coiffed on all sides. Sam and Polly had paid attention to every detail from their hedgerow classroom, and the result was something like a baked Alaska sponge base, but with corners. And not so sweet.

One morning, several weeks into their stay, Sam and Polly noticed an elderly gentleman watching them over the hedge as they worked on their manure sculpture. The next morning, there were two observers. By the end of the week, there was a bevy of spectators.

"What? They've never seen a muck-heap before?" Sam asked Polly crossly. She didn't feel so brave later that morning when Mme Mucharde came into the stable yard and asked to be shown the muck-heap. "Have we let WEC down already?" Sam muttered out of the corner of her mouth.

On turning the corner and seeing the heap, Mme Mucharde threw her head back and laughed. Sam looked at Polly, who had turned crimson in the face.

"It's beautiful!" Mme Mucharde exclaimed. "But now I see the problem. M. Faber knocked on the door last night and asked if he was still supposed to take this pile away. The gentlemen of the village had asked him what its purpose was." Mme Mucharde grinned. "Is there indeed some other purpose you had in mind?"

Polly and Sam exchanged glances again. "No, Mme Mucharde," Sam piped up. "This is just how we do things where we come from. Sorry for any confusion."

"Oh, don't be sorry," said Mme Mucharde. "You've provided hours of entertainment in the village. They've had a few choice things to say about the British. Something about if Churchill could have built walls that well, he wouldn't have needed the Royal Air Force."

◈◈◈

"Right. Better pay attention. These chaps are better trained than we're used to," Polly said as the girls tacked up Toujours and Beau. "Not that Dunster's untrained," she added quickly.

"He's just trained for different circumstances," Sam shot back. Like fancy dress shows, editing books, Christmas carolling, and getting Sam home when she was lost on the moors. Or deciding whether or not it was appropriate to eat suet pudding and custard. He was as highly trained in self-preservation as he was in dressage and show jumping. These French charges were more used to having good choices made for them, so Polly and Sam had to be the grown-ups in the human-equine dynamic. But Sam and Polly were treated well as they jogged down the lanes and cantered sedately beside rows of olive trees and vines. They weren't used to the sound of the hoof beats on the hard surface of the trails and missed their soggy, mossy, peaty sprints.

Afternoons off were spent in the medieval village of Les Baux. The village had beautiful shops, windows decorated with bunches of dried lavender, prints of olive trees, colourful bottles of skin lotions, bolts of floral fabric, and pottery in every shade of sunshine as found in all parts of the world that considered sunshine a right rather than a freak occurrence. Though lovely, those trinkets didn't tempt Sam or Polly to blow their wages. It was the *confiserie* and the *biscuiterie* that threatened future financial security.

"Cor blimey, look at those!" Sam's nose was practically stuck to the window of the *confiserie*. Copper pails were piled high with sugared figs, peaches, dates, pineapples, and ginger chunks. Huge bricks of chocolate were stacked like Jenga blocks, along with beautifully decorated tins and boxes filled with delightful selections of handmade chocolates.

"It's enough to tempt the gods!" Polly gasped next to Sam. "And this isn't your average trip down the Tesco's biscuit aisle either!" Two noses were now stuck to the window of the *biscuiterie* next door. Trays of uncovered biscuits were displayed at a forty-five-degree angle with each biscuit placed precisely in rows, looking like a beautifully tiled roof. "Hazelnut, sage, lavender, ginger, chocolate. Where to begin?"

"They even let you taste them first!" Sam exclaimed as the assistant snapped samples in front of her face to demonstrate freshness. It was like a wine-tasting event for all ages. Only with no loss of cerebellar functioning. Well, maybe just a little.

The wine wasn't bad either, the two girls from Scrumpy country decided.

"Spend it on something very French, and very frivolous," Mrs. Althorp had said. And so they did. And they did again.

৵৵৹

Emma Weston had posted on the WEC brochure, so the girls now knew how much they needed to save. They brushed off their maths skills to look at M. Mucharde's newspaper for currency conversion rates, francs to sterling. Misplacing a decimal point could elicit groans of "Oh, we'll never be able to afford that!" or "Great! We've got more than enough saved now!" Neither conclusion was appropriate.

"You're luckier than me," Sam said to Polly one evening as she counted her francs—again. "Your horse expenses ended with your trip to France."

"Well, Charlotte's family is paying for Dunster's keep while we're gone, aren't they?" Polly replied.

"Yes, but I'll have to pay again once I get home. I could still have to choose between WEC and Dunster." The thought kept Sam awake at night. She didn't know why, as there was no choice to be made really. The only question was what was she going to do once she got home if she wasn't going to WEC?

∂∕∝

It wasn't all sunny weather and *joie de vivre*, a phrase Echo used each time a wheelbarrow full of manure passed his perch.

Tintin was loose. Again.

"Surely weeds growing up to our necks couldn't be more bothersome than that bloody goat!" Polly cursed as she ran.

"And would weeds really look worse than the headless dahlias and the decimated vegetable garden?" Sam puffed as she tried to corner Tintin against a wall. It was uncanny how that goat seemed able to untie any knot, eat through any rope, slither through any gap. "It'll be a miracle if goat du jour isn't on the menu tonight." Tintin had just munched the greenery in the newly installed window planters. Mme Mucharde screamed and flapped her apron at the unfazed rebel, who even had the nerve to give a malicious-sounding bleat when Polly and Sam ran around the corner in hot pursuit. He was towing the new chain attached to the enormous corkscrew-style metal stake that had been purchased after other fiascos. Seeing his gaolers, he took off towards the garden gate through which Clairette was just entering. Clairette stood stock still, filling the gateway with her solid stature. Tintin kept running. Clairette processed that information at the speed of a Great Pyrenees, which meant she wasn't moving this week. *What exactly does happen when an immoveable force meets an unstoppable—?* Sam didn't have time to finish her thought.

"I can't look," squeaked Polly. Turned out the unstoppable force had failed to factor in the consequences of his chain getting wrapped around the base of the washing line. With inches to go before contacting Clairette's formidable bulk, the chain snapped taut and Tintin was flung backwards, as though hit by an explosion. Landing upside down under the patio table, Tintin had only a split second to look confused before Sam and Polly were on him. Trussed up like a convict in a straightjacket, he was hauled off to solitary, stable doors slammed shut and double bolted.

"Hope you enjoyed the flowers cuz I'm not feeding you again today!" Sam yelled though the door.

The gardener was apoplectic about the planters. With chin jutting defiantly, he gave the family an ultimatum: "Moi, ou la chevre!" Tintin spared Mme Mucharde the decision when later that same day she'd had to follow the girls in the car as they chased Tintin down the road towards the village, sending cars swerving. Luckily, he hadn't reached the *confiserie*. Anyway, it was decided to relieve Tintin of his weeding duties and send him off to stud with a local farmer. Rumours drifted back to the stables that Tintin may not have made the breeding cut, based on his "difficult personality traits."

"To be honest," Polly said, "I couldn't care less what happens to him. Life will be so much better without him."

෫෬

"The rabbit's dead!" Polly yelled as she charged around the corner of the stables.

"What? Who? I've been with you the whole time!" Sam gasped. "How'd you get knocked—"

"No, you wally!" For a moment, the bunny crisis was usurped by a glare at her best friend. Then back to the disaster at hand. "Borak's dead! I fed him last night. Fine. This morning? Dead! Like he just woke up and said to his little rabbit self, 'I think I'll die today.'"

"That's all well and good for him, but what are we supposed to do?" Sam wailed. "International incidents happen over stuff like this!" And less, as time would show. Sam bit her nails. "So what's our plan?"

"Taxidermist?" Polly threw out desperately, palms raised. "Stuff him and prop him up in a corner?"

"What's 'taxidermist' in French?" Sam heard herself say before coming to her senses. Not a long-term solution.

The terrified girls slinked up to the back door to break the news to Mme Mucharde, expecting lots of that arm flapping they'd witnessed after the Tintin incident. Surprisingly, their boss looked relieved. "A bit how the bank manager looked," Polly told Sam later.

Minus Sixteen

Mme Mucharde offered to take the girls Christmas shopping in Avignon. So they got the chores done, scrubbed themselves clean, and tried to find outfits that looked even vaguely chic. And failed.

"What do you think of the scarf?" Polly asked, modelling the long, knitted, multi-coloured scarf she'd made in her home economics class.

"Er … cosy," Sam said. But not chic.

"Right. Riding boots, wellies, tennis shoes, or flip-flops?" Polly continued gamely. "If it's too cold for flip-flops, I could wear my toe socks with them."

When they arrived at the kitchen door, ready to go, Mme Mucharde was dressed in a simple linen skirt, fitted blouse, leather belt slung jauntily low over her trim hips, leather boots, an elegant diamond bracelet and a gold watch intertwined on one wrist, and a silk scarf thrown casually around her throat, finished with a simple knot. For the life of her, Sam could never replicate that knot without looking like she'd tried too hard to impress a Boy Scout. To her credit, Mme Mucharde didn't look the girls up and down, but she did pull a small vial of perfume from her sage-green leather handbag, the one that pulled the whole outfit together by drawing from the colours in her scarf and contrasting with the brown boots and belt.

"This is a new fragrance," she explained. "Would you like to try some?" Truly a beautiful way of telling the English *unchiclettes* that, even after a good shower, they still smelled like horses. A spray later, the girls smelled chicly equestrian. Or was that equestrian chic?

Addition to Grand Scheme: the ability to dress like a Frenchwoman. Of all Sam's aspirations, this appeared the least likely to be fulfilled. Driving around with George Michael was a shoo-in compared to that.

❧❦

Avignon was a bustling city, mixing old Roman buildings with modern streets. After leaving the car, Sam and Polly followed Mme Mucharde until they emptied out into the Place de l'Horloge, the heart of the city. The huge carousel, a fixture in so many French towns, was spinning slowly, a million Christmas lights were strung across trees and buildings, ready for dusk, and the wide avenue heaved with people. The stores were a mass of colour, the cafes exuding enticing smells, and the French language engulfed them on all sides. They saw signs to the Palais des Papes, which Polly slowly and painfully translated into "Palace of the Popes." Echo would have bust a gut.

"Let's meet back at the carousel in three hours," Mme Mucharde stated as she walked off with her perfect handbag swinging and not a crease in her outfit, leaving the girls to fend for themselves.

"We should leave a baguette crumb trail so we don't get lost," Polly said. "Oh wait. Pigeons."

"Okay," Sam declared bravely. "Let's follow the signs to the Palais des Papes first and work our way back."

"Right," said Polly. "I don't really need much time to Christmas shop, so we needn't hurry." The Dalcs had sent a Christmas card saying Polly wasn't to waste money sending them presents.

"Well, Mum, I'm happy to prove I can actually follow parental directions," Polly said with a grin after reading the card, which arrived on Guy Fawkes Day, November 5, as though the Porlock post office had advised Helen that the letters would be walked across France by friars on donkeys.

The Palais des Papes was impressive in size, though much more fortress-like than they'd expected a religious palace to be. Polly and Sam got giggling as they pictured the cow from *Monty Python and the Holy Grail* flying over the battlements. Though Sam remembered the actual castle in that scene was in Scotland, and no Scotsman would have wasted good beef like that. Not the only implausible scene in the film, of course.

History not being the girls' forte (thanks again, Echo), they didn't pay to go inside the palace but wandered outside for a while. They watched the French teenagers, marvelling at their outfits.

"Chic starts young in France," Sam sighed.

"And just listen how well they speak French at such a young age," Polly said in awe. "Must have better French teachers in France than in England."

The girls heard some English tourists talking about a bridge. A bridge of Avignon. Being *sur le* bridge. And dancing *sur le* bridge.

"What the heck?" Sam puzzled.

"Oh wait!" said Polly. "That actually does sound familiar from French classes. Of course! Sur le Pont d'Avignon! I had no idea that was about *this* Avignon! Or even really about a bridge." Finding something their friends back in England may actually be impressed to hear about, they followed the English couple down more winding streets past a hundred souvenir shops, all selling the same medieval knights costumes, swords, coats of arms on plaques, and postcards. It looked suspiciously like the merchandise at all the British castles.

"Well, that was a rip-off," Polly moaned after paying to go on the Pont d'Avignon and finding it wasn't even a complete bridge, stopping halfway across the river.

"And not a single soul's dancing on it," Sam lamented. Some camera-toting tourists were trying to get their photo subjects to "on y danse tous en rond." But the kids weren't having any of it, all scowls and folded arms. Sam took a generic photo of Polly but doubted they'd show it to anyone.

The girls retraced their steps, arriving at the carousel in the Place de l'Horloge with ninety minutes to spare. They heard an American with his head in a tour book say, "Any historian could live for years in this one Roman enclave and never get bored." The girls felt bored for a moment and then daring. They decided to attempt to get something to eat at one of the cafés. Mrs. Althorp's money was a godsend, and Sam vowed to send her another letter really soon. (However, Mrs. Althorp's next mailing from Sam was a wedding invitation, about seven years from France.)

The girls both read the menu outside the café and then practised ordering *"le chocolat chaud et un croque-monsieur."*

"How can 'chocolate' be masculine," Polly asked, "when men couldn't care less and women worship it?" On being shown to a seat, practicing their phrase under their breath all the way, they looked up at the waitress and opened their mouths to speak.

"Wha' ud ya like, chooks?" the waitress asked in broad Yorkshire. Sam looked at Polly's toe socks and didn't bother asking how the waitress had known.

The meal finished, the girls left the restaurant feeling very chuffed as they managed a "Merci, au revoir" to the hostess at the door. They completed their Christmas shopping in about five minutes, using pointing, not words. They chose a plastic sword for M. Mucharde (for hurrying Clairette along, hoping Clairette would see the joke) and a gift box of the biggest meringues they'd ever seen for Mme Mucharde. Well, what do you get the woman with a perfect wardrobe, house, life? Splitting up for a few minutes, they picked gifts for each other and then met up with Mme Mucharde.

In the cottage that evening, they considered their foray

into the big city a complete triumph of themselves over the foreigners. Though truth be told, it was more like Yorkshire 1: Exmoor 0.

⊱⊰

The only marker of progress in Sam and Polly's assimilation into the French culture was their new habit of wearing scarves during their time off and even when riding sometimes. Mme Mucharde had given each of them a selection of accessories for Christmas—scarves, belts, and bracelets—that they attempted to throw casually around their necks, waists, and wrists as they saw the French do. The effect was … close … ish.

Before they knew it, spring arrived, though harder to distinguish in Provence because it had been early summer almost the whole time they'd been there. Emma told Sam in a letter that the wind wasn't quite as biting and the rain not quite as soaking in England now, a sure sign of spring. Or at least a sign of April 12 that particular year.

Nicole returned from America a few days before Sam and Polly were due to leave for home. Her first question was "Where's Tintin?" Sam and Polly were busy during Nicole's first visit to the hutchery.

Nicole filled them with stories of the American show-jumping circuit, indoor shows in the autumn in New York City and Washington DC, and the winter circuit in Florida. It all sounded so glamorous, and the photos filled them with admiration for Nicole's bravery. They couldn't even begin to comprehend the distances driven to get to shows, a journey of two or three days without stopping in a massive convoy of horse trailers, mobile homes, and supply trucks. Nicole told them that if they ever wanted to visit her friends in the States, she'd be happy to connect them.

"Maybe Nicole wasn't as attached to Borak as Mme Mucharde thought," Polly whispered in Sam's ear.

Neither Polly nor Sam could even contemplate going to America. A ferry and a couple of trains seemed exotic. A plane seemed more like a magic carpet ride. "Besides," Polly said that night before bed, "I've already got a pretty good grasp on what life's like in the USA. I watch a lot of *Starsky and Hutch*, and *Dallas.*"

On their last evening in France, Polly got out her journal and wrote a title page: "First Foray into Foreign Culture." (She didn't count the trip to Amsterdam, as it was mostly spent watching the telly on the highest floor of a hotel.) Dividing the page in two, with "Success" written on one side and "Failure" on the other, the girls decided on the following: Muck-heap—Success. Goat—Failure, presumed dead. Rabbit—Failure, definitely dead. Horses/ponies/dogs—Success, all survived. Parrot—Success, almost fully bilingual. French language acquisition—Failure. Attainment of French chic? Third column added: "Catastrophe."

Chapter Seventeen

Couldn't blame Echo. He did his best, Sam chuckled to herself. She imagined researching the hierarchy of lingual intelligence, where she expected to find *psittacines* above British *Homo sapiens*. Border collies would also rank higher, she supposed.

Midlife-Minus-Ten Sam sat with the photo album on her knees, *hireth* bringing her further *to* her knees with each viewed image. Young Sam was going home.

That young, excited, though somewhat jaundiced, Sam in the photo album was going home. With wide eyes and heart beating rapidly, the teenager undertook her perilous journey through foreign lands with foreign foods and foreign tongues and foreign clothing accessories. She'd been surprisingly ambitious for one who hadn't been accustomed to travel and who was, quite frankly, as content with her Exmoor lot in life as any youngster could be. It was Dunster who'd encouraged her to put herself out there in the world. Certainly, Sam had imagined riding white stallions down the hallowed driveway of WEC before Dunster. Stroller the Wonder Pony may have been responsible for many of the early dreams. But Dunster had, in effect, brought those dreams out of the realm of fantasy and into the realm of attainability. He'd precipitated practical responses and actual steps towards her goals. Well, all right, maybe trying to be an author hadn't turned out to be as practical as Sam had hoped, but it was still a step towards something. Because the step away from the potting shed was a step towards a French cottage. Towards a Wisconsin house on a hill.

But something else allowed her to leave also. Sam stroked the edge of the photo album. She knew the sanctuary of Porlock Bay would always be there for her when she was ready to return. The confidence and security of knowing home would always welcome her back had allowed Young Sam to branch out, to experiment and dream. Because if all else failed, what was the worst thing that could happen? She would go home.

Going home was the worst thing that could happen.

Sam said this over and over. In her head, under her breath, and finally out loud. "What's the worst thing that could happen? I could go home. What's the best thing that could happen? I could go home."

How weird was that?

ॐ✧

Not terribly enthusiastic about going out later, but realizing it really was the best thing to do, Sam went to take a bath, trailed by the dogs who flopped themselves down on the tile and slept sentinel next to the tub. As the water cascaded from the new waterfall tap, magically turning blue gel into a million white bubbles, Sam caught her expression in the steamy mirror. There it was, a midlife crisis in progress. The opening shot of that clichéd film adaptation of her fictional autobiographical short story— the fictional part being the writing of it, not the content.

Oh. My. God, Sam thought. *I've aged ten years since Thursday's dinner.* Because now the crisis was real, intense, life-changing. She wasn't ten years from anything. She was right in the thick of it.

With rising panic, the misty face in the mirror tried to focus on the positive, see herself as others saw her: a lucky world traveller, a novelty with a built-in conversation starter. And it was true. Sam was lucky, having seen so much of the United States, either as she followed Brody's banking career from coast to coast and the current centre, or on family holidays to Key West or Bar Harbor or Big Sur. On trips to England with the children, she and Brody had agreed to always take them somewhere new so that Exmoor didn't become synonymous with "The Rest of the World." From Paris, Oslo, and Madrid. To Edinburgh, London, and Tintagel. How lucky were they?

But the face in the mirror didn't look lucky. It looked jealous. Jealous of the "homebodies," as some of her co-workers had called themselves during lunchtime chats about holiday plans. Sam felt envy for those who were living where they'd always lived, close to family, blending in; none of them looking to be repotted, but to remain planted in their native soil.

A flash of something shiny and familiar appeared in the steamy mirror. It was so real Sam jumped and wiped the glass to get a better look. Then she bowed her head and began to smile. It was a mental image of the Christmas present Polly had given her in France. A keychain. A Union Jack keychain. Sam recalled the circular stand in the gift shop in Avignon, displaying key chains from, it seemed, every country on Earth. She'd walked past it, trying to find something French for Polly, though her gift to her friend had ended up being a pair of parrot-shaped earrings. Polly's gift was so much more perceptive. She'd gone all the way to a foreign place with her best friend and realised the only thing Sam really needed was a remembrance of her homeland.

And Polly had kept sending Sam small tokens of her homeland each birthday and Christmas. Every year. For twenty-six years.

Minus Fifteen

The friends set off on the reverse of the trip they'd taken eight months before.

They took photos of themselves between trains next to a sign that said "Paris," as this was the closest they got to the actual city. They linked arms, heads together, and stretched the camera away from themselves—selfies were not a new phenomenon, just newly named. These early examples, however, would not be beamed around the world in a Facebook second. The girls assumed they'd like one copy of the photo each and that maybe their mums and dads would get a chuckle out of it. Then the photo would be thrown into an album under soon-to-be completely yellow plastic and never seen again.

Mr. and Mrs. Dale were waiting at Dover to pick up the girls. Sam picked them out dockside. Polly's dad stood silently, smiling, which denoted intense joy in his case. Helen waved frantically, yelling, "Bonjour!" every bit as well as Sam and Polly could say it.

The girls watched from the boat deck as Helen covered her mouth to hide a scream when the huge ferry gently tapped the dock fenders as though the Titanic had just hit the iceberg right in front of her. Polly gave a sigh and said, "I haven't missed that." But the girls had missed the hugs and familiar faces and being able to understand everyone and the smell of dockside fish and chips. And the pathetically un-chic appearance of all the British tourists waiting to visit that fashion Mecca just twenty-two miles away. Two nations separated by a sense of colour and the ability to accessorize.

ॐ

Dunster looked tiny! Sam raced across the road to see him as soon as she got out of the car, having remembered to first hug her mum and dad.

"Have you shrunk?" Sam said into Dunster's soft cheek. "When was I ever small enough to ride you?" In throwing her arms around his neck, he seemed almost to disappear. Of course, she had to remind herself that she was now used to the full-sized horses in France, and it was not Dunster but her perspective that had changed. She would find this to be the case in other contexts too. Dunster sniffed at the alien French Sam and must have caught a whiff of the other horses, as he appeared to turn his nose up slightly, eyeing Sam suspiciously for a moment. But the carrot Sam found in a bag in the feed bucket soon got the relationship back on track. She told Dunster a few stories, mainly about Tintin. It would be a long time before she could call Dunster stubborn again.

The English spring was colder and wetter than Polly and Sam were now used to. It was April, but Sam wore a sweater and jacket while her dad was walking around in his shirtsleeves.

"Are you ill?" Emma asked when she found Sam warming her hands in front of the gas fire that hadn't been switched on since March.

Supper that first night home consisted of fish fingers, mashed potatoes, and baked beans followed by chocolate-covered Swiss rolls, one of Sam's favourite meals before being exposed to *boeuf bourguignon* and *clafoutis aux cerises*. After helping with the dishes, Sam walked down the familiar bridle path to Mrs. Althorp's, the birds singing and the azaleas nodding cheerfully.

Sam actually knocked at the front door, it having been such a long time. Mrs. Althorp's head popped up in the sitting room window, and Sam found herself enfolded in a big hug before becoming aware that she was filling the space two spaniels should have filled.

She didn't ask. She just bent down to stroke Mixie and Maynard, Mixie's eyes looking back at her, a cloudy blue squint.

"Arthur went first, just after you left," Mrs. Althorp stated, matter-of-factly, though with an exaggerated intake of breath as she commenced. "Tilly went just after Christmas, both at home and in their sleep, so a blessing really. Bit of a shock to the rest of us, though."

Mixie and Maynard gazed up lovingly at their mistress's face and reflected the sadness behind her eyes.

"But enough of all this!" she exclaimed. "I'll put the kettle on, and you can fill me in on all your adventures. Well, not all of them tonight but enough to get us through a cup of tea or two."

～∽

"That daft scarf's hardly going to keep you warm," Larry said a few days after Sam arrived home. It was the first and last time she tried to accessorize for supper. She looked down at the tangled rigging of a knot she'd attempted and vowed to give up on chic. Nothing wrong with a woolly sweater and jeans anyway.

"So, what now?" Larry asked as the family ate. Sam had prepped for the question as she and Polly paid their earnings into the local bank.

"I'm applying to the Weir Equitation Centre," Sam stated with more courage than she felt. "And so is Polly. The next course starts end of June. I know I don't have quite enough money yet, but I'm close, and after paying the deposit, I'll have some time before the next payment's due. I've spoken to Geraldine, and she says I can help with her horses to pay Dunster's keep and try to get the rest of the money saved." Sam looked hopefully from her mum to her dad and back to her mum again. Her parents looked serious but open to discussion. Not yet a yes. Not yet a no.

"She's done a wonderful job saving money, dear," said Emma, looking at Larry. "She spent hardly a single penny of her earnings in France, which shows a great deal of maturity and commitment on her part, don't you think?" They didn't know about Mrs. Althorp's money.

"Of course," replied Larry. "A credit to you, for sure. But it's going to be a stretch for you. And you'd have to be on the Working Pupil course to be able to keep Dunster too. I'll bet there aren't many students down there paying their own way and the upkeep on a pony too. Are you all right with that?"

"I am," Sam said with conviction. Refusers-to-sell-their-pony couldn't be choosers.

"Then you should go ahead and apply," Larry said. "But if the courses are already full for June, you'll have to find full-time work until the next one starts in September."

Sam leapt out of her chair and pulled the already completed application paperwork from behind her back, along with a letter of recommendation from Mme Mucharde and a cheque for the deposit. She ran around the table, hugging her laughing parents. She felt like running down the road to put the application directly into the hands of the WEC office staff right then.

"Now, don't get overexcited," Emma said. "Don't want you disappointed if you don't get in."

"Oh, get excited!" Larry said. "And of course you'll get in! You've got international experience!"

ॐ∽

Mrs. Althorp was equally as optimistic.

"Oh, my dear! Of course you'll get in!" she exclaimed the next day when Sam told her she'd posted the application. "And how exciting it will be to have two local girls training close to home. So many come so far to train here, then take their new skills to every part of the world. You'll be able to share your talents with us. Won't that be lovely?"

Sam agreed, out loud. And she was so happy to be back on Exmoor. But at the same time, she couldn't help considering the possibility that she, too, may like to use her new skills as a ticket to see more of the world. Her travel bug, dormant for seventeen years, had been cultivating during her time in France as though in a Petri dish, multiplying with each story M. Mucharde told of his adventures from around the world. Sam pictured herself riding through rivers in Canada, across deserts in Africa, over mountains in Peru, and even cantering through New York City traffic on horseback like Dennis Weaver in the TV show *McCloud*. Sam wasn't sure what the frozen, isolated village in Alaska or the indigenous tribe on the Amazon River needed with a riding instructor, but she wasn't prepared to rule anything out yet. The only things she knew for certain was that no matter where she went in the world, horses would be part of her life. And that her trips would be brief.

Chapter Eighteen

Sam sank lower in the bathtub, listening to the bubbly white noise. She looked around the newly remodelled room, squinting her eyes to reinstate her American lenses. *How huge this bathroom would seem in England!* Of course, there were plenty of stately homes dotted about, and Sam was sure her bathroom would look miniscule in one of those. But the typical cottage conversion didn't allow room for two-person tubs and separate showers, with water pressure strong enough to exfoliate the skin. Sam looked at the shower stall. Definitely enough room to lift your elbows over your head without knocking the soap dish off the wall. In fact, room to store ten types of shampoo and five conditioners and a TV, safe, and mini fridge in case it needed to double as a tornado shelter for a family of six. One got used to the size of everything in America. But "getting used to" couldn't be confused with contentment.

Sam let the bubbles trickle between her fingers as she pondered. Maybe she'd found that soulmate of a home too early in life to understand what that meant. Trying to convince herself as a young twenty-something she didn't need to run off to America would have been hard. Like trying to convince your parents that you'd found your one true love in the boy with the tattoo at the bus stop at the age of fifteen. Or announcing to the world at the age of five you were going to be an astronaut. "That's sweet, dear," they'd say. But no one believed you. Maybe you really had found true love, and maybe you were destined to be an astronaut, but the devil was in the convincing. Convincing others. Convincing yourself. Sam had found what she loved and then run away from it, just so she could waste time and energy missing it, going back, only to leave again. But she hadn't just been running away. She'd been running towards Brody too. And between him and the children, she had plenty of great reasons to shuttle between lives and worlds. Equal amounts of pull on both the British Airways arrivals and departures schedules.

Her toes peeping out of the water conjured up an image of the pebbles on Bossington Beach. She heard the sounds of the crash and tumble of stones being buffeted to and fro. The waves first heaved the pebbles up the beach as though casting them out with disgust, only to change their watery minds and suck the pebbles back down again, stony fingers groping for the shore in a futile attempt to stop the constant indecision.

Maybe she'd learned everything about life from those pebbles, her mind tossed first onto one shore, then another, as her prune-like fingers groped for … what? She and the pebbles were rolled into a good spot, and then with barely time to recognize a comforting, familiar fit, they were once again hurtled through space, bedraggled and spluttering, to another spot that didn't quite feel right. Sam liked to think she had a little more say than the wave-tossed pebble. But at that moment, she felt she had as little control over her destiny as a wind-blown blade of grass watching the approach of grazing sheep.

Minus Fourteen

Waiting for the letter from the Weir Equitation Centre was excruciating. Sam helped Geraldine, gave Charlotte riding lessons on Dunster, and did odd jobs for the neighbours to earn money. She also worked part-time at the Beech Tree Bed and Breakfast cleaning rooms and helping with dishes. Mrs. Evans seemed determined to convince Sam her future was in cleaning rooms as opposed to stables.

"These rooms don't smell as bad as a stable, and it's always warm and dry in here," Mrs. Evans said. "And just think about the risks you're taking each time you climb onto one of those brutes! Much safer in the bed-and-breakfast business." She obviously hadn't been cornered while trying to replenish the in-room tea tray by that drunkard in room six. Never would a riding crop have been more useful. Luckily, lifting hay bales and wrestling goats had given Sam surprisingly good upper-body strength, and the lunatic had hit the floor pretty hard. He was too drunk to remember what had happened, so Sam didn't have to explain anything. Lucky for Mrs. Evans, Sam needed the money. She didn't begrudge anything, though; Grand Scheme trumped all hardships. But she did miss being able to ride across the moors on an appropriately sized horse. Walking on foot up the combes around Porlock, struggling to see over hedges and leaping manually over streams, wasn't quite as exhilarating as it used to be on Dunster.

Sitting on a bench one evening, just before the crest of Ley Hill, Sam scanned the panoramic view across the vale eastwards, then north to Wales, and then west to

Hawkcombe. Familiar hamlets dotted the scene along with specks of sheep, a plume of smoke from a controlled burn on the top of North Hill, and the sun glistening off the whitewashed church of Selworthy. The gorse added cheerful accents to the somewhat-hazy palette of green and grey-blue. She heard the steady chomp of grass and the soft padding of hooves on peaty soil and a snort off to her left and then the sight of a head rising as it caught wind of her. The pony and the girl maintained a respectful silence and stillness. The pony blended effortlessly into Sam's collective sense of Exmoor. She hoped she did into his. At that moment, she was as at home as she had ever been and would ever be for many years to come. The line from "Desiderata" about having a right to be here, just like the stars, lingered on the tip of her tongue. There was complete peace and acceptance as they, the pony and the girl, shared the breeze and the birdsong and the ancestors.

Those knowing eyes looked into Sam's, shared one more thought, and then ambled off. Sam wondered if her presence was instantly forgotten by the pony, absorbed into the collective experience of the day like a meeting with a fox, a new smell, or a tasty patch of grass. To the pony, she was just as worthy, or unworthy, of further thought as those other entities. She just belonged.

ॐॐ

Sam and Polly received letters from the Weir Equitation Centre on the same day, reading in part:

> We are happy to inform you that you have been accepted to the Working Pupil Course commencing June 27. We would also like to congratulate you on being chosen by an anonymous donor to receive a scholarship covering 50 percent of the courses fees. We feel confident that this donor's trust is well placed and look forward to your attendance.

The girls crashed into each other and themselves, waving the letters wildly over their heads and leaping around in the road, making enough noise to induce Dunster to shuffle to the fence to watch. For a split second, the girls held back, not sure if the other had received a scholarship too. But switching letters briefly and scanning the text, Polly's next word was "Who?" and Sam's was "Why?" Then all the "wh" questions tumbled out of their mouths as they gasped and cried at their good fortune.

"It must be Mme Mucharde!" Sam exclaimed. "Maybe Nicole wasn't mad about the dead rabbit, and maybe the garden looks better without Tintin after all!"

"But it doesn't make sense," Polly pondered. "Why would Mme Mucharde want to remain anonymous? Why not just tell us she wanted to pay half the course fees?"

"Beats me," Sam replied, too grateful for this amazing windfall to question too deeply. "All I know is Dunster's safe and we're going to the Weir Equitation Centre! Can you believe it?"

Watching the two girls from across the road in his paddock, Dunster lifted his top lip in the air like he was pondering the significance of what he'd just heard.

ॐॐ

Sam shared the news with Mrs. Althorp that evening, both the acceptance letter and the mysterious scholarship.

"It could only be Mme Mucharde," Sam said. "I'll write to her straightaway and thank her. But what if it wasn't her? How embarrassing would that be? But it must be her."

"I'm sure she'd tell me if she'd done it," replied Mrs. Althorp. "Why don't you let me ask her next time I call."

"Great idea," Sam said. "Thank you. But, really. What an amazingly wonderful thing for her to do. We didn't talk much about Dunster, but this really takes the pressure off. Charlotte's going to ride him for another year, but I still have to plan for after that. Oh, this is all too good to be true!" Sam collapsed her head back onto the couch cushions and revelled in the grandness of life.

Her grand scheme had never, to this point, included anonymous benefactors. However, she decided to add them to all subsequent schemes. They were quite handy.

Chapter Nineteen

As Sam got out of the bath, her steamed mind switched focus to the recently terminated conversation with Thomas Sunby. Exmoor evaporated to be replaced with loneliness. She towelled off and threw on a bathrobe. Without bothering to dry her hair or even brush it, she plonked herself down on the sofa, eyeing the biscuit crumbs still on the table. *Even the dogs are letting me down.*

A light knock on the back door was followed by the creak of the hinges and a somewhat cautious "Hello?"

"I'm in here," Sam called back, feeling no need to get up. Gail was as welcome as a lottery win at that moment. Gail took one look at Sam, observed the state of her and the table, and sighed, "Joan told me Thomas had been over." She placed a chocolate éclair cake on the table and went to get plates, forks, and napkins, like she'd just walked in on a heart attack in progress and was coordinating emergency response teams.

Gail never criticized a fellow chocoholic. She'd watched Sam demolish an entire box of chocolates for breakfast one nasty hospital supervisor ago without so much as a raised eyebrow. She just quietly went into the bathroom, found the scales, and hid them under Sam's bed.

No words were spoken during the first slice of cake. Just studious concentration on their plates as the gooey prescription did its job. During the second slice, Gail occasionally glanced sideways at Sam, like she was waiting for a saline drip to reduce the delirium of dehydration. Third slice …

"What I don't understand is how I missed this," Sam started, fork upside down in front of her mouth like a microphone. "How did I not see that I was unacceptable in certain circles in this town? That I was suspicious to the electorate? How did I allow myself to feel so … comfortable?"

"Could it be because the committee is full of crap?" Gail countered, cutting a fourth slice and sliding it onto Sam's empty plate. "Could it be that there was nothing to miss because all this needing-citizenship-so-your-husband-can-run-for-office stuff is ridiculous?"

"Is it?" Sam's sad eyes skimmed over the remains of the cake on their way to Gail's concerned face. *Wow, Gail's eaten a lot of cake.* (Gail had stopped eating two slices ago.) "My community, and even my own husband, wants me to 'switch allegiance to the flag of the United States of America and from the Monarchy to which I subscribe, being one nation under Elizabeth, with Typhoo tea and healthcare for all'! And you're saying I didn't miss anything?"

Gail's suppressed giggle exploded into a hooting laugh. "How long have you been working on your own pledge?"

Sam finally cracked a smile. "Pretty good for off the top of my head, wasn't it? Must be good cake." Sam spent a moment or two sliding her finger around the plate to catch the last of the custard filling, licking a blob off her wrist.

"Seriously, do you really think any of your friends worry about whether or not you get citizenship?" Gail asked.

Sam sighed. "Well, this time last week I'd have said no. But having now heard it from Thomas, Brody, and Macy, who seemed very excited about a party to celebrate my crossing over from the Dark Side, I can't be sure anymore. How many others at the committee meeting agreed with the plan? Did anyone stand up and question whether it was necessary for me to change anything? Did anyone look at the manual to see if there were any requirements for the conversion of loved ones or its possible impact on electability? Have there been any elections where the only variable was the citizenship of the spouse? I highly doubt it. In fact, I'm going to google that very question right now."

Sam headed for her laptop, asking Gail to cut just one more tiny slice of cake for her. Returning from the office, Sam threw herself back on the couch to wait for her ancient laptop to boot up. It sounded more like a tractor as it whirred into life.

"I'm actually not sure what we're trying to prove here," Gail said as they waited. "Is it that you can continue your life here as normal, or is it that you are allowed to miss home?"

"Good question," Sam said and then returned to watching the computer screen.

"Or are you trying to justify a decision you've already made?" Gail's question snapped Sam's eyes back to her friend's face.

"Good question." Again, no answer.

"You know, I've never been to Europe," Gail continued, "and I'm just trying to sort out what I'm supposed to be helping you sort out. So what do you miss about England? Apart from family, of course."

Gail's question took Sam back to those first few weeks of being home in England after her stay in France. She'd found herself viewing Exmoor like a newborn, rediscovering the views and sounds, revelling in the familiar. It would be only the first of so many re-entries.

"Clotted cream, the kids' English accents." It would only take a week or two for her children to stop laughing each time they heard "loo."

"Blimey!" Ben had yelled as his little boots filled with Bristol Channel during one walk on the beach.

"The plot of *Coronation Street*, though I can probably predict it ten years out. Church bells, Cornish pasties, Prime Minister's question time in the House of Commons—a complete riot. If you've never watched it, you should."

Gail smiled but her eyes said she doubted she would.

"The birds—they sing differently in England. Cricket. Not because I like the game but because I love the ambiance—village greens with spectators watching from the clubhouse or the pub's benches. The clatter of spoons on saucers in the tea shops. The slopping sound of wellies in mud ..." Sam's voice trailed off. Gail allowed her a moment to regroup.

"What do you like about America? No one could have stayed as long as you have without finding something to keep them here."

"To start with, it was the food!" Sam's demeanour brightened. "I was so amazed when I first arrived in New York to find restaurants open all night, breakfast pancakes at three a.m. that were piled so high with fruit, cream, and sauces they defied gravity. Those plates looked like an entire Bossington birthday tea for three people to me, but in the US, it was just breakfast. For one! I truly thought I was in the land of milk and honey. I even called my first American puppy IHOP. Oh, and hamburgers that took several minutes to order due to all the extras—bacon, three choices of cheese, various buns, pickles, lettuce, tomato. And rare, medium, or well done. In England, my mum tipped a frozen beef patty out of a box and served it lukewarm next to oven chips and baked beans. No customizing that. More's the pity."

"You certainly picked up on the best the US has to offer," Gail grinned. "No wonder you want to go home."

"Well, obviously, there's lots more to love. The informality, bigger ... *everything*. I was going to say diversity, but maybe today's not a good day to discuss that. But can I? Can I go home?" Hearing it out loud was a jolt.

Until now, it had been a distant hum in Sam's head, like a train a long way off in a tunnel. But the spoken word brought the train out into the light at great speed, the shriek of the whistle proclaiming its arrival.

Sam recognised the yearning that typically began on the ascent out of Heathrow, the M25 turning from a monstrous, snake-like deathtrap to a rather quaint ribbon tying London up in a gift package. Then the patchwork quilt of fields would recede into square dots, villages into brown splodges, and the mist in Sam's eyes and the clouds outside finally blocked home from view. Rocketing through the cloud layer and out over the Atlantic to the sound of the seatbelt sign being turned off, Sam would once more be surprised that the sun was actually overhead all the time in England, though frequently invisible. One could forget about it in a way one couldn't in the US. It was always her first indication she had fallen through the looking glass. Again.

"How is it possible to feel Exmoor is the only place in the world where I can take a full breath, sleep deeply, be home? This irrational notion of home—and yes, it's irrational because I've been away so long—is responsible for my discontent. It's causing *hireth* as surely as smoking diseases the lungs. What is going on with me?"

Luckily the laptop fired up, sparing Gail the need to declare her friend insane. After a few minutes of searching, Sam let out a relieved exhalation of breath, like she'd been dreading the results. "Well, I'm here to tell you, you can search 'foreign spouses of elected officials' and any manner of convoluted sentences or questions containing the words *elected official, non-citizen spouse, foreign-born spouse, citizenship criteria for spouses of elected officials*, and you'll be completely underwhelmed by the results. Apparently, only President John Quincy Adams was brave enough to marry a woman born in England, and even then her father was American. Old Abigail wasn't impressed. It says here she thought her European daughter-in-law lacked the sturdiness of an American woman. All I know is, if I can survive a Midwest February ten times, I'm as sturdy a woman as any czar, congressman, king, emperor, prime minister, president, or first town administrator could possibly need. On second thoughts, Bill Clinton needed more sturdiness from his women than I could ever have supplied. But anyway, there's no precedent concerning the need for me to get citizenship. Going all the way back to 1776, thank you very much." Sam threw the laptop on the couch beside her and folded her arms with a harrumph.

"Alrighty then," Gail exhaled with relief. "Let's get that in front of the committee ASAP." The ladies sat in silence for a moment. "So what exactly have we proved again?"

"I have no idea," Sam almost spat out. "Wait! Yes, I do. I proved I have a choice here. No one gets to dictate anything based on the evidence."

"Well, that's great! Right?" Gail seemed to expect a lightening of the mood, which wasn't exactly forthcoming. She changed tactic. "I wonder if Brody would have got British citizenship by now if you'd lived in England."

"Definitely not," Sam shot back. "I looked it up last night. To get British citizenship, you have to be of sound mind. And you have to meet requirements for knowledge of the English language. Brody couldn't fake either one." Sam's mouth twitched in an effort to contain the smugness.

"So we can laugh about this then? Good to know. I thought we were going to have to be all politically correct from now on." Gail smiled. "Look, this will all blow over soon enough, and you can get back to making fun of our accents and royal obsessions, and continue to tell us how laughable our gas prices are. And we'll make fun of your steak and kidney pie, tea cosies, and Guy Fawkes Day. Brody will be elected or not based on far more important issues, and all of us will move on with our lives." Gail paused, causing Sam to look up at her. Gail was obviously waiting for a tinge of conciliation to sparkle in Sam's eyes.

Nothing.

"Look," Gail sat forward in her chair and clasped her hands. "Maybe you've misjudged how much this position means to Brody. It's not like him to push his needs over yours like this."

Sam nodded in begrudging agreement. She knew she'd followed in Brody's geographical wake because he'd paid the bills through her school years and supported her non-negotiable requirement that the kids were to spend more time with her than at day care. They'd followed Brody to the comfortable lifestyle they now led. They couldn't up and move to England on her part-time earnings. As Sam's mind opened to allow the old Brody back in, she recalled he'd never suggested they give up on living on Exmoor one day. And he'd always been apologetic that an upcoming transfer wouldn't take them to England. "Maybe the next one," he'd say, and Sam knew he meant it.

"So talk to him," Gail pleaded, causing a softening in Sam's eyes. "Get yourselves back on the same page. You're the best international negotiating team I know. But you must promise me you'll teach the committee your new pledge."

Sam snorted down her nose at the thought.

"See you at seven," Gail said, as the friends hugged. Gail made her way to the kitchen with the dishes and let herself out.

Sam settled back with a sugar hangover and a cushion held over her bloated stomach. Her eyes caught one of the few photos she had on display of her time at the Weir Equitation Centre. She was riding side-saddle through Porlock village on a beautiful grey mare.

"How perfect is that scene?" Sam said. "How could I ever have left? Damn it, Brody!"

So much for the softening.

Minus Thirteen

The big move may only have meant going two miles down the road, but to Sam it was like getting ready for space travel—new worlds, new frontiers. New boots.

"Did you hear I'm going to WEC?" Sam asked Mr. Bishop, the saddler, as soon as she and her mum pushed through the saddlery doors.

"Er … yes. You told me. A few times," replied Mr. Bishop, winking at Emma.

Up until now, Sam had only worn short jodhpur boots. The transition to sleek, leather high riding boots was as exciting as taking the training wheels off a bike. The boot selection at Porlock Saddlery was huge, the price tags even bigger. Emma patted her hair as she looked around.

Without even being asked, Mr. Bishop proceeded to get a selection of boots in Sam's size. She'd remembered to wear her riding breeches and appropriate socks, so she got stuck into the process of finding the perfect boots. Three trials in, Sam reached into a box and pulled out a soft, glossy pair that just spoke to her of rosettes and pirouettes, victory laps and newspaper write-ups.

"Oh, these are lovely, Mum," Sam purred. They took a great deal of effort to get on, however.

"Maybe you shouldn't force …" Emma's words petered out as Sam's foot juddered into place, with instantaneous regret. Her calf started to swell, her toes started to scream, and the bridge of her foot started to throb. Gamely, she tried to stand, but the additional weight caused major agony.

Sam attempted to remove the boot. First by hand. Then using the wooden boot pull. Then asking Emma to help. Then Mr. Bishop astride her leg, pulling on the boot, Sam pushing against his large derriere with her other foot. Then lying on the floor with legs up against the wall, hoping the blood would drain. Then with ice packs on her leg. Sam pictured mucking out, sleeping, bathing, marriage, childbirth, and death in a permanent leather leg shroud as the minutes ticked by with still no sign of release. She also pictured hacking to pieces the entire footwear budget and trying to get a waiver from WEC to ride in her jodhpur boots. Emma just stared, shaking her head.

Finally, after thirty minutes and a final, rather brutal pull by Mr. Bishop, the boot gave up and came off. Relief and sweat covered the brows of all. With embarrassment and apologies, the Westons backed out of the shop, and Sam hobbled barefoot up the road, for the first time finding it in herself to sympathize with Cinderella's ugly stepsisters.

Once Sam could walk down the bridle path again, she told Mrs. Althorp about the boot disaster. Mrs. Althorp squinted at Sam's feet, then got up and walked upstairs. She didn't return for quite a while. Sam listened to bumping and thumping above her head until she almost gave up on ever seeing her friend again. Finally, Mrs. Althorp reappeared, breathless, with cobwebs hanging off her glasses and a blackened smudge across her cheek.

"Try these," she panted, handing Sam a pair of riding boots that weighed about a ton each. There was a wooden knob sticking out of each boot. Sam put the boots on the floor and felt the knob, like she was expecting some kind of secret passageway to open up if she rubbed it and said, "Abracadabra."

"Those are boot trees, dear," said Mrs. Althorp patiently. "You pull that knob and the centre piece will come out, and that will allow you to remove the other two pieces. They were made to fit the boots exactly, which helps the leather to maintain its shape. I doubt those boots would still be in one piece without those trees. They must be thirty years old."

Sam looked at the boots. Beautiful, buttery, soft leather, not a scratch on them. Not quite as shiny as the boots she'd seen at the saddlery, but thirty years will take the bloom off skin. Ask any woman.

Sam looked at Mrs. Althorp in confusion.

"Try them on, dear," Mrs. Althorp encouraged. "I've got some boot pulls somewhere. They look like they may fit, but let's see."

Sam rolled up her jeans and slid her foot easily inside the boots. She heard a small gasp from beside her, something like the Prince made when Cinderella's foot slid effortlessly into the glass slipper.

"That's truly amazing!" exclaimed Mrs. Althorp. "Those boots were custom-made for me years ago, a gift from my husband. I could never fit into them now, even if I were to ride again, but I truly believe it's fate that they should fit you. I'd be so happy to think of them doing dressage, hurtling over cross-country fences, and galloping across the moors again. It would be a bit like I was riding with you. Please take them."

"Oh, I just couldn't!" Sam said breathlessly. "These are exquisite boots. I'd be scared to breathe on them, let alone get them muddy or trodden on. Surely you want to keep them as a memory of Mr. Althorp."

"Nonsense!" replied Mrs. Althorp. "Langdon never believed in owning museum pieces. I remember spilling tea on a new sofa once and being so upset. But Langdon said to me, 'Everything is meant to be used and enjoyed.' Use and enjoy those boots, Sam. Use and enjoy."

As Sam walked home down the bridle path, cradling the boots like they were babies, she found herself unable to believe a pony's needs, a writer's cabin, a foreign job, and a pair of boots weren't cosmically connected. How could one stranger have given her so much? Been exactly what she needed at so many junctures of her life? It was … uncanny.

∂∽⩰

Sam was now working full-time on the farm; Geraldine had suddenly got very busy with liveries and training. Sam just knew this upswing in business was because people had heard she was going to WEC. "Would you like the alfalfa hay or the regular, because knowing the difference got me into WEC." Her subtlety led sometimes to congratulations and sometimes to eye-rolls.

Reading ferociously on all horsey topics from colic to quittors, from Japanese tread bandages to bran mashes, Sam had determined to go into her training already not needing it, according to her dad.

"If you can get all the information you need from the library, why are you spending all that money at WEC?" Larry had asked one evening.

"Well," Sam explained, "a book will take me so far, but I can't complete the old adage 'Fall off six times, get on seven' by reading about other people falling off horses, can I?"

"Oh," said Larry. Discreetly, he counted on his fingers the number of times he'd seen Sam showing another bruise to her mum while telling her how no one could have sat that buck. "More than seven," Larry muttered.

"But Dunster didn't mean it," Sam would always say, quickly covering the bruise in case Emma mistook Dunster's high spirits for mean spirits. He was always happy when they hacked along the moorland trails. And he always stood waiting for her to get back on, not exactly contrite, but at least helpful.

Minus Twelve

June 26. The day before *the* day. Sam was a mess of anxious energy, her hyper-preparation leading to frayed nerves, snippy comments, little sleep, and lost appetite. Sam felt elated at the thought of living in the country house, meeting the horses she would take care of, impressing the instructors, and going to horse shows in the fancy lorry. Then the flip side: the fear of humiliation, of disappointing others, and of coming home with her tail between her legs if she failed the final exam. Fear of reality not matching the dream. Fear of letting down that star-struck little girl sitting in the hedgerow.

Unsure of all that lay before her, Sam decided to spend that last free day alone on the moors. Pushing a sandwich deep into her jacket pocket, she strode purposefully through the village, up Doverhay, branching off towards West Luccombe, and onto the Granny's Ride trail. Initially a wide bridle path with stunning views over the vale, the path narrowed and wound up through Tolken-esque forests full of gnarled trees and low-growing holly bushes, down steep gullies, across streams, and up the other side of the combe with trickling water testing water-resistant hiking boots to the fullest. The moss was so thick on the ground it was like walking on cotton wool, the spongy carpet creeping up the tree trunks and tumbling over stone walls. Watching the birds swooping to and fro, singing, singing, singing, Sam wondered if they were swapping stories of the current day or making plans for tomorrow. "Meet me at the sycamore tree for worms when the yellow ball touches the broken branch." Or were birds as lucky as dogs were presumed to be? Completely in the moment, no worrying about tomorrow. But that wouldn't explain migration, so birds must be forward-thinkers. Sam pondered the universe some more, trying to take her mind off her own changing galaxy.

On the hilltop, where the wooded combe met the moor, Sam ate lunch at her all-time favourite spot: a simple bench made of two logs and a single, wide plank. The aged grey patina suggested antiquity without degradation. A large evergreen holm oak stood guard next to the bench with a stone five-mile marker half hidden in the moss at its roots. Sam always conjured up highwaymen when she saw it. Sitting on the bench, her back to the slopes of Dunkery, Horner combe channelled the eye to a triangular view of Porlock Vale, the tip of Hurlstone, and the water beyond. Sam had felt since childhood the three hundred and sixty-degree view from that bench framed all she held most dear: the teashop at Bossington, Horner Water chasing to the sea, the promise of Porlock village just out of view, the purple hue of Porlock Hill in the distance to her left, the trees of Webber's Post to her right, the Grand Dame Dunkery protecting her back. A perfect world.

In all her visits to that spot, Sam never failed to see a few ponies. Today was no exception. The gentle munching of three mares and a foal continued, undisturbed by her arrival. The shade of the tree next to the bench was usually welcome after the steep climb, but today's breeze contained a slight nip, telling of changes to come. Sam moved into the sunshine a few yards from the bench and lay down, that bed as soft as her mattress at home but with a blue, clear canopy and curtains decorated with splashes of yellow gorse.

"Tomorrow … tomorrow … tomorrow …" Sam's mind raced. But Exmoor worked its magic, slowly calming Sam's thoughts from hurricanes to wafts. "Now, just now, just here …" A bee bumbled by, lulling her subconscious.

A subtle layering of sound on sound, the bee's hum under a birdcall, the gentle breeze catching in leaves only to break free with a grateful wheeze and whoosh and rattle of dry twigs. A gust of wind from the fields at the top of Ten Acre Cleeve carried the bleat of lambs, the calls swept over the moors again as though they never really existed. A stream, just audible from way below her cloud-topped perch, added the white-noise undercurrents to the symphony of the moors. Not a single sound made by mankind; the last vestiges of consciousness before Exmoor took over completely.

ॐॐ

"She's prob-ly dead."
"Na. Just drunk, I reckon."
"Couldn't ha' made it up that hill drunk."
"Couldn't ha' made it up that hill dead, neither."
"Fell off 'er 'orse, maybe?"
"Dumped up here, more like. I seen the news outta London."

Disjointed fragments of dreamy dialogue became more insistent, like Sam was swimming to the surface through a gramophone horn. A smattering of light broke through her slowly opening eyelids, first bright with no dimension, then condensing and clarifying into … tweed cap, brown teeth, glasses, and tip of a walking stick in the periphery. Sam stared into the weather-beaten face of an elderly farmer, a few of his peers behind him, their tweed jackets tied with baler twine, and a sheepdog sniffing at her pockets. Sam gasped and sat bolt upright, startling the men into taking a step back, particularly the man who'd pronounced her dead.

"It's alright, luv," the closest face said. "Take it slow now. You're on Exmoor and the Queen's still on the throne, so it'll be all right." Those words would echo in Sam's head for the next thirty years. But first she had to explain to a few sheep farmers why she'd been caught sleeping. The concept of a nap during working hours was as foreign to these farmers as morris men were to the rest of the world. Merv and his friends moved off, shaking their heads at what the world had become. He looked back at Sam, knowing he'd never have dared wake his own wife.

～∂∙⧂～

That night, Sam spent an hour with Dunster, apologizing that she was going away again, even though she knew she would still be close enough for him to smell her if the wind was right. She also apologized for the fact the book hadn't brought in the dough, his photo wouldn't appear on the cover of a bestseller, and he wouldn't be moving into a real stable at his very own farm for a while yet.

"You'll have to stay in the shelter with the wonky roof for a bit longer," Sam explained.

Dunster suggested he'd rather be in the paddock anyway by walking away from Sam to eat a blade of grass he'd missed during the day. Maybe he was just being polite. Once he'd nibbled that blade, he came back over to Sam and nuzzled his head into her chest, rested a hind leg, and settled in for a long chin rub and neck scratch.

Charlotte had been delighted to have Dunster on another year's loan. She loved showing him, and he enjoyed cruising along the moorland paths with her. No growth spurt in sight for Charlotte, thank goodness, though Sam supposed she had to be thankful for hers now. Otherwise she'd have been heading to Chepstow or Ascot for training rather than WEC. And a flat-out gallop on a barely contained missile of a racehorse, being jostled by other missiles to left and right, wasn't her idea of a good time. Polly said she wouldn't be caught dead on a racehorse.

ॐॐ

And so Sunday morning arrived, the day all the new students were expected to gather, ready to start their courses the next day. Some had been flying for twenty-four hours, struggling with luggage on trains, then buses, then taxis, to get to the gates of a place they had only seen in the photos of a brochure or on a film screen. Sam and Polly could have walked from their front doorsteps, and they knew, or thought they knew, every inch of the place. But there was commonality between all the new students: a dream.

When the Westons and the huge trunk arrived at the gates of WEC, Sam asked if she could get out of the car at the top of the drive. With a puzzled look, Emma and Larry headed down to the car park to wait for her. Sam stood a long time looking down that driveway. She saw lifelong friends, pony noses over gates, riding lessons through hedgerows, dancing stallions, Dunster, abandoned writing cabins, French goats, and a special lady, more special than Sam even realised at the time.

It had been an amazing journey to make it just two miles down the road. As her foot moved tentatively across the threshold, Sam felt she was stepping into the one place on Earth she'd stay forever. She couldn't know then forces within that same place would lead her away for an eternity.

Chapter Twenty

Sam stood up slowly, still queasy from the cake, and took the side-saddle photo off the wall. She ran her fingers over the outline of Luna Mist, always beautiful but one of the crankiest mares she'd ever known. Sam traced the hills in the distance, mentally filling the gaps outside the frame. Dad. His empty chair still waiting after ten years for him to flop himself down on the faded cushions to read the rugby results. Mum. Living in a smaller cottage now, overlooking the bowling green, with perfectly coiffed hair and a busy life of walking, volunteering at the village information centre, and ever improving her skills with Twitter and Facebook. Her irritated comments about grandchildren being so far away had morphed into tech-speak about new ways to keep in touch. "Twenty-six years will take the piss and vinegar out of a fight and have one looking for alternatives," she said. Many warring nations could take a leaf from Emma's book.

Sam placed the photo reverently back on its hook. Surveying her office through the door from the sitting room, her eyes fell on her desk, life's command centre. She noted all the chargers for various phones, iPods, and cameras. Downloading photos to send to foreign shores was a full-time job, especially around the holidays, a consequence of having children and puppies and special events far from home. Frequent flyer cards, dog wormer prescriptions, National Trust membership renewals, and paint swatches, all jumbled together in a Union Jack-themed storage container. An American life wrapped in

Britannia.

Sam eyes flitted to the framed English scenes on the walls, British knick-knacks, and cottage-inspired floral furniture fabric. She smiled at the ceramic Nessie, actually four separate pieces, but placed on a flat windowsill, it looked like the prehistoric monster's humps were looping in and out of the wooden waters of Loch Ness. She reached for the leather strip hanging by the window frame, attaching four horse brasses together. They depicted sheaves of wheat, a Windsor Gray, a grazing horse, and an Exmoor pony. Rubbing the brasses between her fingers while inhaling the scent of the leather produced vivid flashbacks to the proud Clydesdales at the county shows. Back when they were still associated with farming traditions. Not beer.

Arms folded over her chest to stop her heart from bursting, Sam strolled from room to room as though at a museum. Copper kettles sat on top of the kitchen cabinets and Wedgwood blue teacups, a quintessentially English colour that Sam had tried hard to emulate in her bridesmaid's silk dress. A Peter Rabbit cup and bowl bought for Ben's first birthday, a silver picture frame with Tori's smiling face snuggling an Exmoor pony. A shelf covered with miniature ceramic teapots; Sam's favourite had scones with jam and clotted cream painted around the rim.

All this British-ness.

Interspersed with her homeland memories were the kids' high school diplomas, photos of red Midwest barns, American cookbooks, US Navy submarine memorabilia from Brody's service to his country, and Remington statues of cowboys on broncos.

All this foreign-ness. But which bits were foreign and which bits native? *Brody and the children aren't foreign, are they? Their memorabilia aren't foreign. Are they?*

Last week, if Sam had given this hodgepodge of stuff a second glance, she'd have lingered only long enough to think it all needed dusting. Today, she saw incompatibility: Prince Albert botanicals battling Pier 1 in the china cabinet; Laura Ashley fighting for global domination over Ralph Lauren; Nessie in head-to-head battle with the broncos; the Brontës, Hardy, and Austen offering up prim resistance to Melville and Hemingway on the bookshelves. P.G. Wodehouse standing sentinel on the battlements, overseeing the field as commander in chief. No one dared touch him. No one.

Unable to take the chaos inside anymore, Sam threw open the back door and headed into the garden, bare and colourless, as April didn't denote spring in Wisconsin. She loved gardening, a gift from her mother wrapped in pastels. But today, the war spilled out the door behind Sam. Her attempts to create her Midwest version of Stourhead gardens in Wiltshire struck her as pathetic. The vinyl siding on her blocky midwestern house made fun of Cotswold stone. Sam had tried to mask the siding with trellises of roses, rhododendron shrubs, and clumps of lupines, hollyhocks, and foxgloves. The perennials became annuals, one tour of duty enough. The climbing roses fought valiantly against the brutal subzero winds, but the rhoddies petered out at about two feet tall, and only survived to that height if wrapped in burlap for all six months of winter. Sam's dreams of producing thirty-foot high competition to the ones at Stourhead were shattered each spring, as dead branches were ceremonially removed and sent for burial with full honours. Stella de Oro lilies, those hardy mainstays of the Midwest garden, laughed gaily as the English bluebells Sam had planted by the hundreds abandoned their posts and failed to show up even once for muster.

Sam gazed at her sleeping flower beds. Even imagining them at their fullest in summer, she finally saw her garden for what it was: a misplaced resident's sorry attempts to bring her home to her house. On this foreign battlefield, claimed in the name of Her Majesty, Queen

Elizabeth II, Patron of the Royal Gardens, Sir Union Jack had his hands around the throat of Mr. Star Spangled Banner, squeezing, all the while looking around with a serene smile as though nothing was wrong. Mr. Banner looked unimpressed at the effort, knowing it was just a matter of time before Jack gave up. It was a battle to the death, one bulb, one knick-knack at a time.

Sam didn't know at that moment whether to thank Thomas Sunby for bringing the war to her attention or chastise him for destroying the outward semblance of *entente cordiale* she'd managed to present to the world for so long. Either way, something was going to have to be done to reconcile nations. And souls.

Minus Eleven

Those first months at WEC were brutal. Horsemanship hadn't looked so exhausting from the leafy observation deck. Watched over by Stable Manager Edgar and Chief Instructor William, the students soon found, no matter how experienced they thought they were when they arrived, they had a lot to learn. Between Edgar, William, and the other instructors, not a corner of the yard was left unmonitored. Shrieks of startled surprise were frequently heard from a student, who, thinking he or she was alone, tried to take a breather for a moment. Nothing got by those instructors. Nothing. And if the principal of the centre, Col. Hollerford, was around, they had to look sharp. He had a distinctive step, one footfall slightly heavier than the other; the heel clips on his boots acted as an early warning siren. If your horse and stable weren't perfect, your tack wasn't gleaming, and you didn't have your answers down pat to any question he deemed to ask, head for the bomb shelter.

Building monumental muck-heaps, swilling down the main yard, picking stones from the fields, unloading hay and straw lorries, brushing equine coats to a mirrored shine, picking out hooves multiple times a day, weeding the areas around the stables, polishing high-set brass tie rings, and lifting saddles onto the highest racks in the tack room way above their heads left the students' arms so weak they had trouble cleaning their teeth at night. If one blade of straw was found on the main yard after it had been swilled down with buckets of water and swept clean, Edgar would make everyone wait until the water trough had refilled from the slow, ancient hosepipe. Then he would demonstrate the correct way to chase that single piece of straw down the drain, using nothing more than four hundred buckets of water and ten students with brooms.

"Now, *that's* what a properly swilled stable yard looks like," he would say as he glared around the exhausted group of sweepers. There was nothing worse than hearing the bell for dinner ring out from the main house, knowing that one piece of straw was costing you your precious stew and pudding. On more than one occasion, Sam considered grabbing the single offending straw, stuffing it in her mouth, and swallowing it to save time. And possibly starvation.

Weekly horse inspections were particularly traumatic. The inspection was conducted, one horse at a time, in the main yard on a Friday afternoon. No one was allowed to leave for dinner until each horse had completed the white glove test. Literally. Edgar wiped his gloved hand over and around every inch of each horse, checking his glove periodically for dirt. Every inch happened to include the sheath area of all the geldings.

Sam had been assigned Militaire, a 17.2 hand-high, ex-three-day eventer with an angry disposition and a fierce cow kick. Now Sam knew Dunster had a sheath. But clean it? Not on your life! "Dunster has survived to a ripe old age without me ever having touched that part of his equine person. And no empires have fallen," Sam said to Polly one night. Not the case at WEC. Every sheath had to be cleaned, up inside, with a soapy solution and a sponge, to get all the chunky gunk out. The smell was revolting, the chunky gunk gag-inducing, and the risk to life and limb extreme if your charge happened to be Militaire.

"I've tried everything!" Sam huffed. "Food bribes, threatening, stealth attacks disguised as back-hoof picking. It's no good. Militaire's sheath is hardwired to his very precise cow kick." Sam looked around the tack room, hoping for inspirational ideas from the other students.

Nothing. "Oh well. I shouldn't worry about it because if I can't touch it to clean it, Edgar can't touch it to inspect it, right?"

As Sam led Militaire up to the inspection area, she thought she caught the exchange of a smirk between Edgar and the observing instructors. And Militaire was in on the joke. He stood perfectly still for the entire inspection, four square, not so much as a blink, as Edgar wiped the inside of the sheath with his gleaming white glove. Sam stood open-mouthed as the glove reappeared, all chunky gunky. Edgar could have hung a crib mobile from Militaire's sheath and let a tiny baby bat at it in complete safety. Sam now had a new number-one equine humiliation.

ം⍣

The very first time Sam rode into the large indoor school, she heard the sound track from *2001 Space Odyssey*. The giant doors slowly opened, and the blinding light emitting from within dazzled the trembling riders as they were beamed up, engulfed by the sheer and total awe of the occasion. *Boom boom boom boom boom boom dah dahh dahhhh! Da daaahhhhh!*

The working pupils only rode for one hour a day, but what an hour! In the early weeks, every back, shoulder, abdominal, and gluteus muscle, which apparently the students had all their lives, was somehow newly discovered and tormented, bullied, berated, and stretched into positions never before known. Military-straight spines tore intercostal muscles, soft skin between fingers bled through gloves and onto reins, and calf muscles cramped under blistered skin. "How is it even physically possible to have a leg appear virtually straight from the side view when a horse is barrel shaped and wider than a girl's hips?" Polly had lamented, face down on her bed because her bum hurt too much to turn over.

"And how the heck can I 'Sit deeper in the saddle,

Sam!' when my seat bones feel like burrs spiked on medieval torture gadgets?" Sam truly expected to tip blood out of her inherited boots after each lesson. She and Polly weren't alone. There were times all the students needed help just to get up the stairs to their dormitory bedroom over the stables. Many of them moved like ninety-year-olds that first month, groaning and crying as they lowered themselves gently into a bathtub in the evenings, despite the cotton wool padding they'd worn in their underwear.

"Trench warfare and Scott's trip to the Antarctic must have been worse," Emma said during Sam's first day off while offering antiseptic lotion through the bathroom door for Sam's blistered … well, whatever.

"I don't want to hear it," Sam muttered, dabbing delicately. "Though I think I've got permanent hearing loss, like many troops." The instructors' decibel level rarely dropped below an incredulous yell. Sometimes, a manoeuvre in the indoor school would be followed by the sound of a flock of birds being startled off the roof by a blood-curdling scream. Someone had just jeopardized the future of the universe by losing a stirrup or not getting enough inside bend through the horse's body on a twenty-meter circle. Sam wondered what exactly they were being trained for, as she thought cavalry warfare was a thing of the past. William's nickname became Basil Fawlty, as every single day at least one student got to feel like Manuel. No one cried during lessons, as wiping the tears would have required losing the horse's outline; a deadly sin. But at night, sniffles were often heard from a darkened bed. The terrifying words "Quit and cross your stirrups" were muttered during nightmares for at least three months.

Slowly, excruciatingly, and with teeth-gritting determination, muscles conformed, skin hardened, and spines straightened. Dismounting was no longer a painful leap to one's death onto jelly-like legs. Tinnitus lessened, rooftop birds slumbered longer between flights, and occasionally, very occasionally, the words "Well done" escaped the lips of an instructor. Progress. Wrapped in cotton wool.

It was four months before the working pupils were allowed onto the cross-country course. Sam gasped as William opened the gate to the field, knowing she was about to live a seven-year-old's dream. Polly gave her a terrified glance as they lined up at the bottom of the hill that was known as The Slide. A solid-looking telephone-pole jump stood at the top of the steep slope. William called it a slope. Sam called it a cliff. An even more solid-looking stacked log fence stood a stride out from the bottom of the slope/cliff/deathtrap. Overhanging tree limbs jutted out between the two fences to wipe the smile off your face if you wobbled off course on the way down.

"These are Olympic fences, for crying out loud!" Sam muttered in Polly's direction. She noted Polly's clenched teeth and felt her own stomach drop. If the 1952-style Olympic fences frightened her, there was no hope of her surviving later versions.

Dry mouthed, with chests heaving, rider after rider was sent along the banks of the stream, briefly out of sight around the back of the hill to appear (hopefully) from behind the trees in a (hopefully) strong trot in (hopefully) the centre of the first fence. Encouraging murmurs rippled down the line as each rider faced his or her own personal god, gathered reins, and booted horses into gear when ordered to go.

"Look way out over the channel," William instructed beforehand. "This will prevent your back rounding and your head dropping forward, which will offset your balance and result in a fall over the horse's shoulder." What channel? Every rider had his or her eyes closed. Most horses did too.

It wasn't pretty. Refusals and run outs were standard, and in one case, the rider didn't appear from behind the trees at the top of the hill at all. William had to go in search, and he found poor Cecily vomiting into a rhododendron bush. Sam's confidence took somewhat of a turn for the worse after that. She weakly patted her mount, Gordon, hoping upon hope that the song all the students were singing around the yards about a Gordon hadn't been written about this particular Gordon. About then, William appeared to feel it was time to make the riders more afraid of him than the jumps, so the screaming got worse, the threats more dire, and the consequences of failure more life threatening than any fall could have been. "Sam! Your turn!"

I NEVER WANTED TO RIDE IN THE OLYMPICS! Sam wasn't sure if she'd said this out loud or not but robotically gathered her reins, along with what was left of her wits, and headed up the hill. A good stiff trot, out of the trees, the centre of the jump, head up, looking out to sea, back flat, seat low, heels down, over the telegraph pole, into a haunches-down slide through the muddy descent, kick, one stride and over the bottom fence, still on top! Gordon was *not* a moron!

A cheer from the crowd, and a spooked horse shot sideways. Sam toppled off, losing her velvet riding cap, to be struck in the head by a flying metal stirrup and then a hoof. Right before she passed out, she thought she saw a snooty-nosed, seven-year-old girl shake her head with disdain in the hedgerow.

❧❦

"Sam. Sam. Wake up! You're having a nightmare!" Polly's voice came through the fog.

Am I dead? Sam thought. But Polly's hand on her shoulder felt real enough. Glancing at her alarm clock, Sam saw the fuzzy outline of 3:46 a.m. in red, but being unable to place the numerals in any particular order (a throwback to many a maths exam), she leapt out of bed and grabbed her jeans off the floor. Polly gently took Sam's arms and guided her back down onto the bed.

"It's okay, Sam," Polly soothed. "Not time to get up yet. Just didn't want you yelling the place down."

"What was I yelling?"

"Something about 'Stroller's down! In the water! Stroller's down!' followed by 'Not part of bloody Grand Scheme.'"

Snippets of the dream came back. Stroller the Wonder Pony, so close to gold, leaping to clear the last water jump and falling in up to his neck. Not easy, seeing as the water obstacles on a show-jumping course were about four inches deep. Even Stroller was taller than that. Anyway, it had been very traumatic for all the spectators watching in their pyjamas.

Sam laid back down, now able to pick out the outlines of the windows and the other sleeping students in the darkness of the attic dorm room. Intermittent moonlight from behind clouds shone on piles of clothing beside each bed, bits of straw everywhere, open packets of biscuits on bedside tables, and notebooks opened to the stable management and minor ailments lecture notes being studied for Friday's test. Friday's test! Sam just knew concussion-induced memory loss wouldn't be considered an excuse.

Friday arrived, the whole day marred by the prospect of that day's test. Tempers frayed on the yards, and overreach boots were put on upside down, and on the wrong horse. Riding lessons turned into Chinese fire drills as lead riders turned the wrong way, circling horses collided, and pile-ups and mayhem abounded.

"You look like the bloody Keystone Kops!" William yelled during the working pupils' dressage lesson that day. Then two horses were found wandering in the apple orchard unaccompanied. But you can't study your notes, lead a horse to the paddock, and remember to shut a gate. Or so Sam heard.

The bell finally rang to call the students to dinner, but not a soul went to the dining room. They all bolted for the dorm to cram. Sam threw riding gloves, dressage whips, and boot polish tins off her bed to find a spot to sit down. Polly swept a week's worth of muddy socks into her bedside drawer to do the same.

"I'm going to throw up," Polly wailed, fighting through the hairnets that were hung over her lamp like cobwebs in order to turn the light on. "I've no idea what a quitter is or how to treat it, and if they ask me to put on a double bridle, I'm doomed!"

"Let's calm down," Sam ordered, addressing her remarks to all the students in the dorm. Some nodded in agreement, others didn't move. Sam waved her hand in front of Patricia's face, who appeared to be in a catatonic stupor. She then attempted to model slow breathing for Roseanne, who was hyperventilating into a leather glove.

Sam looked around the musty attic dorm room at the motley crew. From all over the world, aged from sixteen to twenty-eight, all heights and weights, and with experience levels from backyard pony owners to hardened competitors, the rigorous expectations of WEC had reduced them all to bundles of grubby, callused, exhausted raw nerves. The Americans were still trying to work out how the movie version of the training centre bore any relation to actual events. The Italians were wondering how sleek, dark hair could turn to frizzy, fog-induced curls. And the poor Aussies were still trying to get over their first experiences with rising damp. Complaints of exhaustion were universal. The Brits felt obliged to defend themselves at times.

"You know Disney doesn't make documentaries, right?" Sam told a sobbing Texan.

"You could try wearing your hairnet to the pub." Gilda from Rome glared back at Sam's comment as she tried to flatten her frizzy locks.

"At least you don't have to check your boots for deadly spiders or snakes," Polly cheerfully offered Becky from Perth as she rung out her sodden socks. Polly had already checked all the Aussies' boots for imported deadly spiders and snakes.

"This is what put the Great in Britain," the Brits would say as another five hundred bales of straw arrived to be unloaded at nine o'clock at night, or while they were all standing in a chilly barn making wisps out of twisted ropes of hay.

"Stiff upper lip, Jackie!" a voice would encourage, as once again Jackie failed to get her jacket unbuttoned, taken off, swirled around her head, and put on again, all while jumping down a grid of six fences.

"You know Jennie Loriston Clark, David Hunt, Lester Piggott, and Lucinda Prior-Palmer all had to be able to do this before winning anything, right?" Sam encouraged, not quite sure she was on solid ground there.

Anyway, the encouragement seemed to work as most students felt lucky to be part of it all, even if they lived in dirt and chaos while their equine charges lived like kings and queens. If the instructors had judged the students' living quarters as they judged the yards, they'd have escorted the students to the top of the driveway and left them to the grockles. But the choice between clean, healthy grooms and clean, healthy horses was no choice at all really. No one had the energy or interest to choose both.

෨ఄ

Everyone survived the stable management and minor ailments test, of course. And the first attempts at riding lateral moves. And the first time they got to teach each other, though it was so much harder than it looked. Not only were there directions to give in plenty of time to avoid pile-ups in corners of the arena, but each individual rider had to be watched closely enough to offer some kind of advice. "Er … Jill, turn your shoulders a smidgen. Pam, you're leaning back too much. Ummm, Polly, open your inside rein more." Sam couldn't believe anyone would listen to her, seeing as her own shoulder position/seat position/rein contact was questionable, at best.

But supporting each other was vital, to the point where the student riders would actually translate the trainee instructor's directions to avoid embarrassing her. ("She can't have meant turn down the centre line, as I'd collide with the other riders. So I'll do a long diagonal instead.") They all mucked in and mucked out, watched one another's backs, swapped advice, dried tears, and cheered on successes. It would be the most collaborative environment Sam ever experienced. Those muddy, bloody, exhausting, terrifying, hilarious, exhilarating experiences bonded the students forever. *Magical* was a term used over and over again in decades to come as they reminisced about their journey to horsemanship.

If energy and time allowed, Sam would sometimes jot a quick letter to Dunster in her notebook, thanking him for some small lesson he had taught her that helped her though the day. She couldn't decide if Dunster would have been better off if she'd known when she first got him what she knew now. He'd have eaten less, galloped on rocky pathways less, and been groomed more. Sam wouldn't have laid down on his back to read a book when he was napping. She'd have won more rosettes, checked his teeth, and always faced forwards when riding through the tunnels instead of sitting backwards, watching his tail swing side to side. She'd have worried more, and Dunster would have had fewer opportunities to teach and protect her. Would she have seen him as less of an equal and more of a subordinate, his life more in her hands and hers less in his? No, Sam would always be grateful she learned from him as a novice rather than taught him as an experienced rider. Though "experienced rider" seemed a long way off in those early days at WEC.

But one thing Sam knew for sure. No way would she *ever* have cleaned Dunster's sheath.

Chapter Twenty-One

Sam clasped the silver chain round her neck, a Freudian choice of jewellery, she thought later, and did a quick twirl in front of the mirror. An unfortunate incident involving a skirt tucked into knickers precipitated the OCD-like twirl before each dressy exit from the house.

Sam thought of Brody returning tomorrow from his "boys and their toys" trip. She never begrudged him those weekends. He worked hard, played hard, gardened hard, and opined hard. If staring at a chrome exhaust pipe or V8 engine helped him understand the principles of global economics and the unfathomable rules of American football, she was all for it. "Good job he was away this weekend," Sam told her reflection. "Not sure we'd have survived as a couple if Brody had been here for Thomas's visit." She was almost sure beating a town elder to death with a shovel while setting fire to one's spouse was grounds for deportation.

The thought of dinner wasn't that appealing, as the cake still took up vast quantities of digestive real estate. But she was glad to be going out. She turned lights on for the dogs and, as an afterthought, tidied up the coffee table, where she'd strewn the letters she'd written to Dunster. As she moved to place them in the box, she spied some white-bordered photos peeking out of a faded envelope. Pulling them out, she stared at herself and Polly at a train station, "Paris" emblazoned on a sign behind them. Polly and Squirt with Sam and Dunster at Luccombe Show, grinning and waving rosettes at Dad's camera. Polly and Sam with all the other working pupils, standing on top of a giant muck-heap at WEC. Must have been the period when the lorry drivers went on strike and there was no muck-heap collection for months. Usually the heaps were hauled away to the local mushroom farm every few weeks; the reason Sam still didn't eat mushrooms. But in the old photo, the muck-heap was ten feet high, probably the first-ever horse-made structure visible from space. The students posed like Egyptian pyramid builders on their massive sculpture, only without the eyeliner.

And one more photo. Polly and Sam. Arms wrapped around each other, cheek to cheek, both of them obviously crying. It was the day Sam had arrived home from America that first time.

"Over a man? Seriously?" Sam rolled her eyes at herself. After everything they'd been through, how could she have bolted off instead of standing her ground and fighting for her best friend? Just the thought of it, even after all these years, made her feel sick.

Minus Ten

The guy was a jerk (American term). A dill (Aussie term). A pucko (Scandinavian term). A pillock (British term). Because every language in the world had a special word for Bedwyr Llewellyn. He'd galloped into WEC on a three-month Riding Club scholarship like Saint David himself. (In reality, more like Monty Python's King Arthur, cantering sideways down the driveway accompanied by clacking coconuts.) But men were always vastly outnumbered in that equine tinderbox of estrogen, so it was hardly surprising that war broke out.

"Talk about delusions of grandeur and the distinct possibility of a *coup d'état*," Sam said to Polly when they looked up the strange words at the library. "Bedwyr was a knight of King Arthur, and Llewellyn meant 'leader.' How could an underling knight of King Arthur be a leader too? Poor Art had enough to deal with, worrying where Lancelot and Queen Guinevere were." Polly didn't appear to be listening.

It didn't matter that Bedwyr was arrogant, or that he never pulled his weight on the yards, or even that he invited girls out for drinks at the local pubs, which they ended up paying for. All that mattered was the competition. Polly wasn't Bedwyr's first choice—or even the sixth. But she was eventually anointed Queen of Chepstow, and from then on, students had to make a lot of noise before entering the hay barn if they couldn't stomach watching thirty-minute Welsh kisses.

"For a girl with an emergency escape plan for every

eventuality, Polly certainly hasn't thought this one through," Sam told Dunster one evening after sitting through Polly dreamily recounting the latest soapy episode of *The Young and the Senseless*. Or *Aberystwyth Street*.

Polly gave the evil eye to other girls on Bedwyr's course as they rode with him to the indoor school. There was even talk that a particularly pretty German student was having trouble finding her tack before classes and was frequently late. Just rumour. It was a relief when Bedwyr's group took the exam. After a rousing speech on the manicured lawn from Col. Hollerford about spreading the glory of WEC to every corner of the globe, Bedwyr and his cohorts rode one last time up the driveway and into lucky stable yards, both near and far.

Bedwyr wouldn't go away, though. He took the bus from Chepstow to Taunton on his days off to meet Polly. He just wouldn't go away.

ॐॐ

In the blink of an eye, one of the greatest years of Sam's life was almost over. British Horse Society examiners arrived from various locations around the country. Students scurried around the yards, heads down, reciting poultice recipes and first-aid procedures under their breath, and made one last check of the position of the curb bit over the snaffle on a double bridle. Or was that under the snaffle? Oh God! Someone! Help!

By 5:00 a.m. on the day of the exam, all lights were on in the stables as manes and tails were plaited up, last-minute stains removed from hocks, and hoof oil applied. Examinees appeared in glistening leather boots, bleached breeches, and brushed velvet caps. Jacket lapels were straightened and ten trips to the toilet were completed just in time. Divided into small groups, some students went to the lecture room to take the written exam, some went to the indoor schools to ride, and some remained on the yards to demonstrate their stable management skills. The teaching part of the exam would follow in the afternoon.

After a whole year of training, it seemed inherently unfair that everything hinged on only a few hours. One hour to show you could ride; forty-five minutes to show you could identify common ailments; fifteen minutes to mount a rider and spin them around in both directions while providing some semblance of useful instruction; and about fifty seconds to prove you could jump a round of fences. There was no room for error. No do-overs. No excuses. Just the honour of the Weir Equitation Centre at stake, whose reputation for excellence now rested on quaking shoulders. Or seat bones.

The day was a blur to Sam, a terrifying blur of physical exertion, mental toughness, and emotional outbursts about what would happen if she failed, let the team down, let parents down, Mrs. Althorp down, Mrs. Althorp's boots down, Dunster down, the entire British equestrian tradition down. Four o'clock teatime was a silent affair, each student hugging a mug of tea and ignoring the cake, waiting for the results to be posted on the message board. Then, the first screams of joy, hugs of relief, and deep shock, hugs of comfort. It was all over. For some because they'd passed the exam and now faced the reality of leaving the hallowed cobblestones to find jobs. For others because they'd failed and had to search their souls to determine if another attempt was worth it or if a different career path was calling. Maybe something cleaner. With fewer opportunities for injury. Which ruled out the bed and breakfast industry.

Sam and Polly looked at their neatly typed names on the notice board for a long time. Next to each name was a row of Ps, denoting they'd passed every discipline. They were now officially British Horse Society Assistant Instructors. They were the last to arrive on the lawn, arm in arm, for Col. Hollerford's speech. Sitting on the worn stone steps of the veranda, their backs to the grand old mansion, they looked out over the paddock walls, the jumping grids, the beach, and the channel.

Words from a magical book found in an attic, and from a fundraising book that raised no funds but scripted a guardian angel, blended into the babbling brook of a story that was Sam's life. She just couldn't hear the words from the next chapter yet. But she knew there'd be horses in it. As a new instructor, she promised herself she would remember the early days so she'd never scare a timid rider just because she thought what she was asking them to do was easy. She promised to consider the horses that way too. Take it slow and build firm foundations. Never put the whole fancy dress outfit on before introducing the parts, gently and respectfully.

And Sam knew Exmoor would be in the rest of her story too, the best playground in the world for child or adult alike.

"So we're part of the equestrian world. With a certificate to prove it." Sam spoke with wonder.

"Wow. We have an employable skill," Polly sighed back.

"So what's next?" The girls sat in surreal silence.

Chapter Twenty-Two

What were the odds of me doing the same thing— marrying a foreigner? Sam wondered as she finished tidying and searched for her shoes. "You know the irony of it all?" Sam asked the slightly chewed heel. Sherlock refused to make eye contact. "I'd never have met Brody if not for Bedwyr." The physical desertion of her homeland had been an unintended consequence of Polly's marriage to Bedwyr, with all its dire warnings, long-distance commutes, and talk of interracial children. No amount of explaining to Helen Dale had been able to alter her mindset that the Welsh were practically an alien species.

The dogs, aware they were not invited to this evening's shindig, were piling on the guilt trip with deep sighs and puppy eyes and presumptive steps towards the door each time Sam moved. "Oh, stop it! I know you'll be asleep upside down on the couch as soon as I close the door." Brody had a point about the expensive doggie beds in the kitchen being a complete waste of money. He was right about a lot of things, Sam had to admit. And he was usually an excellent judge of her needs. But the last forty-eight hours or so had wiped out all the Brownie points accrued over two and a half decades. *Completely fair,* Sam thought, pulling on her shoes. Except for the wonderful-father bit. And the caring-husband bit. And the fun-at-parties bit. And the way he'd apologised for his behaviour at Windsor Castle. *All right, so he can keep most of the Brownie points. Not that I'll tell him that tomorrow.*

Their issues wouldn't have dissolved by tomorrow, no matter how calming the car show or good the éclair cake. Sam knew she needed an ironclad argument as to why she shouldn't, or wouldn't, change citizenship. Or a reason why Brody shouldn't run for office, thereby skirting the question of citizenship. Or … what? An agreement to take an oath with her fingers crossed behind her back?

"Could I really say those words? Even for Brody's sake?" Sam leaned on the wall, staring at her car keys.

The dogs looked imploringly up at their mistress. *"Does that mean we're coming with you or not?"*

"I know I still love him," she said, relieved to know that. Too many memories, on both sides of the Atlantic. A quarter-century's investment. A two-child investment. An international investment. "So we've got to work this out." She placed a hand on the door. The dogs, sensing defeat, turned to walk towards the couch.

Sam turned suddenly and spat out, "It's not like my life depends on it, or my children will only be released from the clutches of an evil tyrant if I switch allegiance."

"For barking out loud!" JB stopped in his tracks to scowl back at his beloved, but needy, mistress.

"It's not like Brody would stop loving me if I didn't get US citizenship. Would he?" Was this a deal breaker? An addendum to "Til death do us part" that read "or til you refuse to further my political career by sacrificing your British identity?"

Sam knew she was being told to change something very fundamental about herself in order to please others. "No! No! No!" She stamped her foot and headed into the garage. Any mother knew the feeling: her needs morphing into the need to satisfy others. "But I'm not Brody's mother. I've brokenheartedly accepted the severing of the daily natal ties to my grown children. But I don't have to coddle Brody." She hit the garage door opener, slammed the car door, jammed the key in the ignition, and hit reverse a little more forcefully than she'd intended, almost hitting the still-raising garage door. "Why am I being expected to shape-shift again? Haven't I done that enough over the last twenty-six years? Do I have to document it and sign it and swear to it too? It's too much to ask!" Defiant eyes glared back at her from the rear-view mirror. As she placed the car in drive, she realised she didn't mean the years she'd been away were too much to ask; she had followed that path with volition. But that little piece of paper, that chant, that whopping great lie? That was too much to ask. "I won't abjure one Iowa of my Britishness. For any reason. So help me God."

As the garage door closed on one war, the door to a restaurant opened on another.

"Eat, drink, and be merry, Sam. For tomorrow we may die."

Minus Nine

"I almost wish I'd failed," Sam said morosely. "Could have repeated the course." Polly nodded distractedly, as though she had another plan percolating in her head.

As the girls left the veranda and crossed the grass, William called Sam into his office.

"Col. Hollerford and I have been impressed with your skills and wondered if you would consider staying on to train (static crackle), a small stipend, (static crackle) teach students (static crackle)." Sam could see his lips moving, but everything after "staying on" was completely redundant.

After hurtling out of the office and into the stable yard, screaming something incoherent at Polly and hugging the breath out of her, Sam ran the length of the bridle path that led from the victory lawn to Mrs. Althorp's. She hoped William had translated the scream as a yes. She arrived at the cottage panting and dusty.

"Good gracious, dear!" Mrs. Althorp exclaimed. "Whatever's the matter? Is someone hurt?"

"Well, my lungs are about to explode," Sam gasped, holding her side, "but everything's wonderful! I passed the exam, and I'm staying at WEC to train for the British Horse Society Intermediate Instructor's exam! They want me to stay! I get to stay! I can't believe it! I can stay!" She sunk down on the deep sofa, laid her head back, and cried. She spared a brief thought for Polly. Nope, she wasn't giving this chance up.

"Oh, how wonderful!" Mrs. Althorp exclaimed,

kissing the top of Sam's head, then offering to make tea. On her way to the kitchen, Mrs. Althorp walked over to her desk and quietly scrunched up a piece of paper, tossing it into the wastepaper basket.

A few minutes later, tea and biscuits appeared, just like on every other occasion that required celebration or commiseration. The tray was placed on the table, and Mrs. Althorp hummed as she poured. It was only when she handed Sam the cup that she saw the now-flattened-out paper from the wastepaper basket on her young friend's lap.

"You paid for our scholarships?" Sam asked, voice weak and shaky. "And you were setting up another so I could stay on for further training? You let Polly and me think that Mme Mucharde helped us and you never said anything? I don't understand."

"Well, I never corrected your assumption, which is not the same as not telling the truth, is it?" Mrs. Althorp seemed a little miffed as she looked at the discarded letter. "And who taught you to go through other people's rubbish, may I ask?"

Sam looked at the contents of her lap. It was a look on Mrs. Althorp's face that made her think the letter concerned her. Satisfaction? Relief? Disappointment? She wasn't sure. But now, was she glad she knew who the anonymous benefactor was? Or was the guilt too much to bear for having spent a year not thanking this amazing woman every single day? With her head down and china teacup wobbling in her hands, she whispered, "Thank you."

"We are kindred spirits, you and I, Sam," said Mrs. Althorp, simply. "Or as my mother would say, we're 'children of the heather.' It's been such a pleasure listening to your stories, reliving my youth in that glorious place. I feel I gained more than I gave." With that, Mrs. Althorp sipped her tea and stared at the fading photographs on the bookshelf.

෧෧෯

The M-word was mentioned, much to the horror of Polly's parents and Emma Weston.

"No eighteen-year-old should be allowed to make a commitment like that," Emma stated over tea one evening, shortly before the formal announcement. "Marriage is like a tattoo. No one remembers what on earth they were thinking when they committed to the Hello Kitty shoulder ink as a teenager. Nor will Polly remember why she picked that pimply-faced foreigner twenty years on. We should all talk her out of it."

"Bedwyr isn't pimply, Mum," Sam said, hardly able to believe she was defending the jerk. "And being Welsh is not exactly being foreign if you have a United Kingdom passport." But if Emma's comments were negative, Helen Dale's were positively frightening.

"She'll be sorry she married a foreigner when she can't understand her in-laws and they all think she dresses funny," said Mrs. Dale with a hankie held to her mouth, slurping tea in the Weston's kitchen the day after the engagement was announced.

"They'll think she dresses funny if she does the dishes in the bed gown, shawl, and wide-brimmed top hat of the traditional Welsh rural woman," Sam muttered, unheard. But jeans, she believed, were pretty standard in Chepstow.

"My grandchildren will have funny accents, and they'll be teased at school about their mum. And Polly doesn't even like leeks!" Helen wailed, dabbing at her eyes.

"Polly won't have to eat the leeks, just wear them on her helmet every Saint David's Day," Sam blurted out, quickly grimacing at her own comment that was every bit as ridiculous as Helen's.

"And when will we get to see her?" Mrs. Dale ploughed on. "Where the heck is Chepstow anyway?" The hankie came out again, with a dramatic blowing of nose and wiping of tears.

"You go to Bristol, hang a left over the Severn Bridge, sharp right, and you're there," said the ever-practical Emma.

"Have you seen that Severn Bridge?" Mrs. Dale wailed. "Deathtrap! Unlikely to last the week. I'd never set foot on it." Well, the bridge had its issues, but it wouldn't stop most people from a jaunt across to Wales to see the grandkids.

Sam's theory, developed over the next few years, was that Polly's concept of danger was much more vivid than most people's. Years spent making emergency plans for all manner of outlandish scenarios made her oblivious to the dangers wrapped in less-spectacular packages. Bedwyr didn't look like a meteor or an alien or a runaway school bus. He appeared more like a butter and sugar sandwich, all sweet and satisfying. But underneath, full of tooth rot and diabetes.

As it turned out, none of the commuting worries or foreign-accent issues would matter. But the general consensus at the time was that Polly shouldn't marry Bedwyr. So Polly *had* to marry Bedwyr. Because that's what being a teenager meant. You were honour-bound to get Hello Kitty tattoos and marry men from foreign lands against your family's wishes.

Minus Eight

The wedding was lovely, just three months after leaving WEC, with Polly's cherubic face under lace and Bedwyr's pimple-free face under the influence.

"That rain will never hold off," said Helen to cloudless skies. "There's not near enough food," she said to groaning tables. "The marquee'll not hold up in this wind," she said to the gentle breeze.

"They didn't understand a word of the service!" she said to the vicar while nodding at Bedwyr's parents.

"The stitching on your dress just may hold up for the day," she said to the bride. So that was a plus.

Sam carried off her duties with dignity, despite nearly wetting herself at the altar when Bedwyr referred to the vicar as "Your Highness." Slurred speech or not, the happy couple was pronounced husband and wife, the little flower cousins picked their bouquets to pieces all over the prayer cushions, the bells pealed, the photographer herded, and all the married women cried. All the married men stood by helplessly, holding their tongues and praying for nothing more than an open bar.

Before heading to the paddock that night, Emma had first forced Sam to change out of her bridesmaid dress. "Like I'm ever going to wear this 'Chelsea Flower Show meets *Upstairs Downstairs*' creation again," Sam had muttered. Not for the first time, she thought their trip to France had been completely wasted.

She sat on the fence stroking Dunster's velvety nose after taking out the wildflowers she'd woven into his mane and tail for the occasion. Charlotte had held him in the road as Polly's wedding party left her parents' house. As Sam sat looking at the stars, it really hit home: Polly and Sam, the Dynamic Duo, was over. Polly was a new partner to someone, but Sam had just been demoted to gooseberry. A phone call. A birthday card in the post. It was hard to imagine. Then Dunster twitched his ears and nuzzled his nose deeper into Sam's cupped hands to remind her that she was still a partner. Still half of a dynamic duo.

Sam wrote Dunster a letter that night, the first one in a while. "From Batman to Robin," she wrote.

のくの

Both Bedwyr and Polly worked at the Chepstow racecourse as newly-weds. All that work on a deep dressage seat, long leg, and light rein contact usurped by a bum-in-the-air, pull-as-hard-as-you can stance that was both exhilarating and terrifying, according to Polly.

"Remember when you couldn't even get Squirt to stop eating?" Sam teased. "And you were terrified of little jumps? Look at you now, you and your emergency plans! Yet you voluntarily strap yourself to a rocket and light the touch paper." Helen only knew of Polly's duties as a groom. Obviously, or she wouldn't be humming as she did the ironing right then.

Sam loved being an instructor. She never forgot walking out of the office to teach her first professional lesson. She had steel heel clips put on her riding boots so the new students would hear her coming as she strode importantly across the cobbles. She had to suppress a giggle as she saw students scurry at the sound. *Click-clack. Mind your back.*

There had still been so much to learn, and always would be, Sam discovered. The first lesson wearing spurs was terrifying, as the punishment for making any kind of mark on the horse's side was death by firing squad. (As it should be.) Then there were more advanced dressage moves, higher fences, choosing the best new horses for the school, and finding multiple ways to explain a half halt. It was almost as overwhelming as those first days as a student.

And it was a little lonelier than being a student. The camaraderie wasn't as close. There was a certain image to protect, and there was a little rivalry involved in building up a private client base. Most of all, though, Sam missed Polly. Never, since the age of two, had they been apart for so long. Sam felt the constant urge to point something out to Polly, or find her friend when she was sad or embarrassed or happy, or when she felt the need to reminisce about something from the old days. Like last year. But there was still Dunster, and he was happy to oblige. However, his reduced penchant for cream teas was detrimental for completely filling Polly's shoes. Mrs. Althorp had to take up that slack, trooper that she was.

Minus Seven

"You want me to join the quadrille team for Dunster Show?" Sam heard the incredulousness in her voice bounce off the main yard walls, a year after becoming a WEC instructor. "And I'm to ride side-saddle?" What was a word for "more than incredulous"? "All right then," she said while performing internal cartwheels.

The three ladies were to ride side-saddle, each accompanied by a gentleman in top hat and tails. Sam borrowed a side-saddle habit and spent a hilarious afternoon learning to mount in full habit from the mounting block. It took a certain amount of coordination to sweep the skirt out of the way, avoid getting completely tangled up on the fixed head and leaping head pommels of the side-saddle, and lower one's self gracefully into place.

Mrs. Althorp was beside herself with excitement. "Oh, I can't wait!" she exclaimed, circling the date on her calendar.

"Maybe you can't," Sam said. "But I've only got a few weeks to learn to ride without twisting to one side, sit elegantly at the trot, and strike off on the correct canter lead when there's no leg to help on the right side. Oh, and I have to remember a complex routine of dressage movements paced in time to the music. And Mum keeps asking why I'm not sleeping!"

The day of the show dawned warm and cloudless, not a given for August in England, so welcomed gratefully. Manes and tails were plaited up and horses loaded onto the lorry.

"Why are you wearing your top hat in the car?" William quizzed Sam.

"Terrified to forget it somewhere," Sam replied, terrified of so much more than that. Dunster Show was one of the biggest in the west of England. Sam's stomach flipped as the convoy drove through the gates past the dog show rings, farming equipment displays, the huge tents full of prize-winning jams, cakes, flower displays, and quilts, and the llamas, sheep, cows, pigs, and fowl. Past the trade stalls selling everything from jewellery to handmade woollen sweaters to shortbread to equestrian prints. And past an enormous crowd of spectators, waiting expectantly in bleacher seats and on the sloping banks around the main ring.

You're not in Bossington anymore, Sam. As she mounted up, arranged her skirt, and began to warm up with the other riders, she stole a look at Dunster Castle.

"To think it's gazed majestically down on this patch of earth for a thousand years," Yvette, one of the other riders, said to Sam, catching her awed glance. "Makes you feel small, doesn't it?" Sam felt very small indeed at that moment, even as little girls gawked at her.

Once in the arena, it didn't matter that the lead riders forgot part of the routine, requiring shouts of "Turn now!" from some panicked followers, or that they were behind the music, or that three of the six horses took the elegance factor down a notch or two by lifting their tails to the giggles of the little children. It didn't matter that the horses weren't white or the hats weren't pointed. It didn't matter that there was only one air above the ground, an accidental Courbette when a balloon popped next to William's mount. It only mattered that Sam felt the presence of two little girls in an indoor viewing box, bowing with reverence to waltzing stallions. She was dancing on horseback under the battlements of an ancient castle, with her own pony waiting to hear all about it when she got home. As the riders saluted gracefully on their way out of the arena to great applause, the tears streamed down Sam's face, matching those of two spectators: Mrs. Althorp and Polly.

Sam didn't miss the *Sachertorte* at all.

Chapter Twenty-Three

Sam pushed the door open at Bernie's and warm, hop-filled scents engulfed her as she sidestepped through the throng to the bar. Gail was there already with a glass of wine.

"It's going to be a bit of a wait for a table," Gail said. "Who knew the whole world would want to eat here tonight?"

"Oh, they're probably celebrating the conversion of a wayward Brit," Sam said. Even to her ears it sounded a little bitter.

"I see," Gail replied through pursed lips. "It's going to be a night of doubles then. Double gin and tonic, Brian, please." The drink arrived as Sam hung her coat on the back of her chair.

"Cheers," Gail said as glasses chinked. "What are we drinking to?"

"To immigrants and émigrés," Sam said. "May we never confuse the two."

"You may need to explain that one to me." Gail screwed up her eyes and furrowed her brow. "But not until we've had a couple more drinks. Hubby's at his mom's, but I saw Jacob's cab outside earlier if we need him."

"We might," Sam replied. "It's been a long day of soul-searching. Not sure if alcohol will clarify or confuse, but there's only one way to find out." She took a large swig and enjoyed the burn in her mouth. She glanced up and caught the end of a trail of refugees wandering across the television screen above the bar. There was a discontented mutter from a couple of patrons, so Brian switched the channel.

"Think about all the immigration issues lately," Sam began. "About building bigger walls, making citizenship harder, turning more away. The perception is that everyone's trying to get in. Did anyone ever consider that some may be trying to get out?"

"Certainly occurred to me," Gail said. "As of today."

"Not all émigrés are fleeing other worlds. And I'm an émigré, not an immigrant, by the way. It all depends on whether you're emphasizing the 'coming from' or the 'going to' part of the equation. Some of us just floated along for a while on a river cruise, saw something shiny— or dressed in a fancy uniform—and stopped to stare for a while. We only found out later that the shiny object was a key, opening one door and closing another." Sam took another drink. "But this particular accidental emigrant," she said, stabbing herself in the heart with a finger, "was completely unaware of the consequences, always assuming that one day she could just turn around and resume the old life."

"Rather poetic," Gail said with an appreciative nod. "But you make it sound like you regret meeting Brody. Can that be true?"

"No, no, I don't mean that." Sam stared into her glass, twirling the ice cubes with her finger. "I was so lucky to meet him, to walk into this country with a loved one, to be handed the key with barely a murmur of opposition. Well, except from the grumpy immigration officials at every airport, but they're paid to keep the riff-raff out. And everyone in that immigration line is riff-raff until begrudgingly proven otherwise." Sam looked at Gail, realizing she needed to stop sounding so anti … everything. "Horrible job, though. Glad someone does it."

"We need more of them, if you ask me." A suited man sitting next to Sam with his tie loosened and the collar of his jacket twisted up on one side looked at Sam over his

Scotch and then through his Scotch as his head got too heavy to hold above rim level. Sam scooted her stool around to show him more of her back.

"Brody was my Person from Porlock, I realised today," Sam continued. "Disrupting my writing ... all right, maybe a bit of a stretch there ... but my equestrian career, and definitely my dream of having children with proper English accents."

"Bastard!" Gail spat out in her best *Downton Abbey* accent.

"I know, I know," Sam sighed. "I sound really ungrateful. There are so many others from foreign lands who had to beg for the key to a new country, work to exhaustion for the key, and nearly die for the key. This griping is all so unfair of me."

"Many came here outrunning terrors, that's true" Gail said. "But it doesn't mean you have to see it as a haven if your heart is elsewhere. I know England is pretty special to you."

"Pretty special! It's the greatest nation in the history of mankind!" Sam's grin said she was only partially joking. "I know. My British superiority complex is hardly appropriate in the company of those who've survived wars and their entire families, refugee camps, and treks across continents as solitary teenagers, young families, or elderly couples. You see the tears in their eyes and the holes in their hearts for the lives they left behind. I arrived with blessings and wedding gifts and healthcare and job opportunities. Others arrive with nothing more to their name than a reason to search for better and, in many cases, an enviable work ethic that puts mine to shame. I really shouldn't be feeling so ... hard done by." Sam noticed her drink had been refilled. Scotch, sitting next to her, had a refill too.

"Soooo ... you're an imm-i-grant," Scotch said carefully into his glass as his eyes rolled over Sam's face. "You just never know where they'll show up next."

Gail tugged at Sam's sleeve, but Sam ignored her, already turning to face the suit.

"An émigré, actually. Big difference. And you? Not from around here?" Sam couldn't believe she'd just used the line all her patients at the hospital used on her.

"Nope," said Scotch. "And wouldn't wanna be. Tooooo many imm-i-grants here."

"Oh? And where might you be from? Or should I ask, how long has your family been off the Mayflower?"

"Long time. My family practically discovered this place."

"Funny, you don't look Native American." Sam felt more tugging at her sleeve and a quiet "Careful now" in her ear. Gin was very practised at ignoring good advice, however.

Scotch snorted down his nose. "So why'd we let you in? Peasants chase you out of the castle? Did we have to give you royal ass-y-lum?" Emphasis on the "ass."

"What makes you think you're so fan-bloody-tastic?" Gin retorted.

"You tell me. You're the one wants to live here instead of where you came from."

For a drunk man, Gin had to admit, Scotch had a good point. His smirk said, "I rest my case."

"Well, I may just be going back soon," Gin stated haughtily. "And many here will miss me."

"Bet they'll throw a party." Scotch waggled his head as he snorted again, signalling Brian for another. "I'd come." Gail frantically gestured the hostess for a table.

"Well!" Gin couldn't believe it. Neither could Sam. She was being treated like … like so many other immigrants. With disdain. With no knowledge of her story, or why she had come, or what she felt, she was being judged, stereotyped, and dismissed. It felt … awful. It *was* awful.

"Well!" Sam stammered again, as Gail grabbed her coat and her arm and pulled her off the barstool. "Speaking of immigration officials, certainly need more of them at the borders of this town! You know, to keep the riff-raff out!" The bar had gone quiet. Gail pushed Sam from behind towards a table. Scotch raised his glass to the ladies and took a big swig.

"Are you related to Bedwyr by any chance?" Sam threw her parting shot over her shoulder before tripping down the step into the restaurant.

Gail slapped the menu down in front of the drunk immigrant. "What is this? A Trump rally?"

Sam's bravado seeped away. There was no need to be *that* rude.

☙❧

The clock by the bed showed 10:30 p.m. It had been a slightly earlier night than she'd anticipated but understandable given the slightly frosty dinner. Unfortunately, she was sober enough to remember everything. A mug of hot chocolate was cradled in one hand, and the photos from the coffee table were spread across the comforter. The Dunster Show display team smiled out at her, six beautiful horses in a row, Dunster Castle in the background.

But the crowning glory of Sam's equestrian career had signalled the beginning of change. Real change. Lasting change. Her second year as an instructor at WEC had begun with a growing sense of dread. She would have to contemplate the walk back up that gorgeous driveway to a life beyond the stone pillars. If she had known then just how far she'd travel from those gates, just how long she'd be away, the dread she'd felt at the time would have been magnified exponentially. It would simply have been unbearable to leave. She *was* that place, woven into the heartbeat of the vale like the tangled valerian roots that bound themselves to the stone walls. But she was a friend too, she remembered, and the future would bring a choice between a place and a friend.

She clasped her stomach as she lay in bed. To stop *hireth* from spilling out. But it wouldn't be stopped, as it seeped from her pores, soaking the sheets and trickling over the photos. She gave herself a mental slap. *Stop it! You can always go home.* But could she? Responsibilities and ties to one place, years and changes from another. All surmountable, surely? She was unlike many other immigrants who longed for home but could never return, not because they didn't want to but because there was no home left. How easy that pledge would be for some, how willing they'd be to take it, wholeheartedly, with fingers uncrossed, if only they had the chance. But Sam didn't want what thousands of others dreamed of. Life was so unfair.

Sam pictured WEC from the beach, framed by the green slopes behind and surrounded by neat hedges and whitewashed stables. The country house looked both serene and everlasting. Like a child of the heather. Turned out it wasn't. But was she?

Clearing the photos and rolling over in bed, Sam turned out the light and closed her eyes to block out the oncoming storm.

Minus Six

Not twenty yet, Polly seemed much older to Sam now. "The rent's due, and there's a fight over whose parents get us for Christmas," Polly sighed as the friends picked their way through the Chelsea Girl lingerie department during a meetup in Taunton. Lingerie, another concept that made Sam feel positively childish. "Need any of this yet?" Polly raised her eyebrows at her friend. Sam just blushed. With the exception of a few dates, Dunster was still her only male companion, which even Sam had to admit sounded somewhat pathetic. No offence to Dunster.

The fallacy of the freedoms of adulthood had hit Polly head-on. Apparently, Bedwyr wasn't fluent in English, certainly not in his understanding of more abstract vocabulary like "monogamy" and phrases, such as "Til death do us part." Polly's teary phone calls became more frequent; the long weekends "visiting" her parents trailing into Tuesdays. The friends' once-jolly walks filled with tales from the racetrack and WEC, punctuated with hoots of laughter, became silent, ambling attempts to slather Exmoor balm onto open wounds.

"Come on, you'll feel better after a cream tea at Horner and a foal sighting on Dunkery," Sam encouraged during one of Polly's stays.

"Oh, look! Ffŵl even looks foolish!" Sam nudged her friend jokingly at the library during another visit. They'd gone to look up "fool" in Welsh after a particularly bad row with Bedwyr over the phone. But the Dynamic Duo's camaraderie wasn't part of daily life anymore. It was just an interlude from Polly's other life, with all that foreign world's cares and worries.

❧⚜❧

Sam came out of Mrs. Althorp's cottage after sharing the news William thought she was more than ready to take the Intermediate Instructor's exam, which was a nice way of saying "Sam, you've been here long enough. It's time to move on." Never had a pat on the back felt like such a fatal shot to the head. As she joined the road from the bridle path, her raincoat hood made the rain sound even heavier than it was. With hands in pockets on her way to check on Dunster, Sam saw the back of Polly disappearing up the front steps to her house with an armful of riding gear in a laundry basket. Through the window of Polly's rusty Vauxhall estate, Sam saw familiar, still-wrapped wedding gifts in boxes.

"Polly!" Sam called, initially happy for a surprise visit. But the slow head turn, limp smile, and Polly's resigned expression left Sam's raised hand lifeless as it slowly dropped to her side. Polly shrugged as rain dripped off her nose and slowly closed her door.

Dunster was lying in his shelter but scrambled up when he saw Sam approach. He gave one of those deliciously satisfying pony stretches—arched neck, chin to chest, followed by one hind leg thrust straight out behind him, then the other. With a final snort and a shake, he looked at Sam, sniffing the air. Sam ducked under the wonky, though waterproof and protective, roof and hugged Dunster's face. He breathed patiently in to her neck.

How do they know? Sam thought. Every animal lover had asked this question at some point or another. How did their four-legged friends know when to remain still and ask for nothing? To wait for others to bring up what ailed them? To quietly absorb the tears without pushing for explanations?

And without bringing up the fact they'd told you so. Because if anyone had bothered to listen, Dunster had told them this Bedwyr thing was going to end badly. He'd told them from the get-go, being a connoisseur of stable characters. He'd tried to show the girls what he instinctively knew by pushing Bedwyr's hand away, ears turned slightly back, head more erect, clearly declaring, *"Parts of that immaculate muck-heap will hit this particular fan hard."* "I told you so" wouldn't help. So Dunster said nothing, just blew gentle, comforting breaths into Sam's cheek, grieving quietly for, and with, his friend.

అఫ్ఆఙ

Polly got a job with a livery stable in Wheddon Cross, which was nice because it meant Sam had an excuse to borrow her mum's car every other week to drive up over Dunkery on their days off. But Polly was grieving, and it didn't matter how many pork pies, packets of crisps, Swiss rolls, and bottles of bitter lemon you had in your picnic basket, at some point you had to stop eating and talk. *Mind you,* Sam thought, lying on her back on a woolly blanket, stuffed to the gills, staring at the puffy clouds chasing each other over Webber's Post, *this certainly beats talking turkey in a therapist's office.* Speaking of turkeys …

"He wants to do what?" Sam exclaimed, sitting bolt upright as Polly's words sunk in. "Move down here to start over? He has to be kidding! Can't wait to watch you kick him hard in the Brecon Beacons and send him back to Snowdonia. If you need help, just call."

Good to know all Emma's lectures had sunk in about not running Bedwyr down or making decisions for Polly. "After all," Emma had said to her daughter, "they aren't officially separated yet, so don't go saying words you'll have to swallow if he turns up again."

"You're being thick, Mum," Sam had replied. "As if Polly would be dense enough to have that road apple back."

"So I thought we should try it," Sam thought she heard Polly say but couldn't have because … like Polly would have *that* road apple back. "What do you think?"

Sam opened, then closed, then opened her mouth again. Then her mum shut it for good, but Sam's eyes twitched in protest.

"He's changed, he says. Misses me, he says. And how can we give up so soon? The wedding gift subscription to the *Exmoor Gazette* from Auntie Minnie hasn't even expired yet. And it was only a two-year one," Polly lamented.

"Right. I … I see," Sam stammered. *Talk about role reversal. Thought you were supposed to be the pessimist?* "Well, obviously, I'll support you in any decision you make. People can change. Second chances, and all that." Sam cleared her throat and stuffed another Swiss roll where the advice should have been.

In a paddock by the sea, an Exmoor pony rolled his eyes.

ॐॐ

"Wotcher, Sam," said Road Apple, strutting into the pub, fifteen minutes late. Bedwyr attempted a peck on the cheek, which fell flat with an audible *thwack* as Sam swatted a non-existent fly.

"Sorry. Hello," Sam said, not meaning either one. Why she had to be there she had no idea. The reconciliation was between Polly and Road Apple, not her. But somehow Sam knew that wasn't strictly true as she stared coldly at Bedwyr. Whether you break a heart, or go bankrupt, or get caught shoplifting, or make a fool of yourself in any of a million ways, the ripple effect knows no bounds. The whole Family and Friends Pool gets choppy. Bedwyr had to face Sam, and Mr. and Mrs. Dale, and His Highness, the vicar, and the baker who made the wedding cake, and Dunster at some point. And Dunster wasn't mincing his words.

Sam had no idea what to say next. "How are you?" Already knew. A jerk. "What's new?" Already knew. Monogamy. "Nice to see you." *Don't get me started ...* But Polly was looking at her best friend with beseeching eyes, so Sam asked about the racehorses and Bedwyr's new job as a veterinary assistant in Minehead and how the new flat over the saddlery was working out. He asked about the exam Sam was due to take next month, and they spent an unpleasant hour recalling the names of all the horses at WEC. Several times.

"Did I say Prestige already?'" Road Apple rubbed his stubbly chin.

Yes, you did, and you don't deserve to breathe the same air as that gentle, though somewhat neurotic, soul. Did I mention you were a road apple? Looking at Polly, Sam really hoped she hadn't said that out loud. She hadn't, but Polly had seen it on her face, and Sam was ashamed. She'd promised to support her friend and she meant to pretend that this, the very worst of any contingency plan Polly had ever devised, was a winner worthy of its own red-covered binder and a place on the shelf of every Emergency Response and Recovery agency in England.

Yes, sir. We're in the clear now.

Minus Five

"What do you know about fitness regimes for a three-day-event horse, Dunster?" Sam sat in the straw with her twenty-six-year-old study partner.

"Well, I can't remember ever doing anything but graze for three days straight. But I can speculate it will involve a brisk trot up Porlock Hill, trying to stay ahead of the coach staggering up behind." It was amazing what Dunster could convey in a look. But Sam had to disagree with him on that one. Porlock Hill without horseshoe crampons and a rope harness was a ridiculous proposition. But she appreciated him listening carefully while she rationalized her thought process. He flicked an ear at an error. Snorted at a just plain dumb guess. Drooped a lip when it all fell into place. *"Just hope all this is worth it,"* his sleepy eyes said.

One evening, about a week before the exam, Sam was interrupted in her wonky-roofed classroom by a deep, baritone voice and a warning flick of Dunster's ears. Bedwyr had seen Sam as he left the pub on his way to Mr. and Mrs. Dale's house. Why he was going there was unclear, as the flat he shared with Polly was in the opposite direction. "I assume Scrumpy helps with the whole fifty-fifty-ninety thing," Sam whispered to Dunster. The wary pony was momentarily interested in the smell of fermentation that preceded Road Apple's swaying climb over the fence and expletive-laced walk through his namesake-splattered paddock. Dunster sniffed at the scent of cider on Bedwyr's breath, then directed his nose to the stains spilled down Bedwyr's trousers.

"Hellooooo, Shammy," Bedwyr cooed as he lowered himself down on the straw beside Sam and tried to make eye contact. With what, Sam wasn't sure. "Thought I'd check to shee how you were, shee if you needed me to help with anything. I'm a grrrreat horseman, you know. Ask me anything. Go on." With that, Bedwyr half-closed his eyes and assumed the facial expression of a great thinker ... under anaesthesia.

"I'm fine," Sam responded, gathering up her notes, pulling herself up, brushing all the straw off her jeans, and hugging Dunster goodnight. Dunster watched Bedwyr closely. "I'm off home, but I'll help you over the fence first." Not a friendly gesture on Sam's part, but one designed to get Bedwyr away from Dunster. Bedwyr heaved himself up and zigzagged his way to the fence.

They parted, so Sam thought, on the road, and Sam headed to her parents' door, looking forward to spending the night in her own bed. But the smell of apples appeared close to her neck as she reached for the handle.

Bedwyr reached forward, grabbed Sam's arm, and took in a deep breath ready to say ... what? Apologize for his behaviour towards her best friend? Beg forgiveness? Promise to do better?

"I always knew you were the one for me, Sham," Bedwyr enunciated slowly, focusing all the while on the horse head doorknocker over Sam's shoulder.

You hid it well by going through the populations of England and Wales first, Sam had time to think before feeling the fury rise. She took a breath to give Bedwyr a piece of her mind, but Bedwyr read this as a prelude to a tongue-heavy kiss and leaned in with a lopsided smile.

He licked paint. The door slammed so hard between him and Sam as to leave no ambiguity. Sam looked triumphantly at the still-vibrating door, her head erect, arms by sides with fists clenched, feeling her Boadicea heritage course through her veins.

"You slimy, Scrumpy-infused bastard!" Sam shouted through the door. She had a story to tell Polly that would seal Road Apple's fate forever. Polly would be so grateful and the two friends would ride off into the sunset, the Dynamic Duo once again, to set up a world-class training stables. With attached cream tea shop.

It would all have been so perfect if not for the trapped coat sleeve Sam noted just below the door latch. She stared at the fabric. Would it dissipate like breath on a winter's morning if she prayed hard enough? Would Bedwyr just take the jacket off and leave it as a permanent reminder of his despicable behaviour? This outcome seemed less likely when Sam noticed the blood. Not a lot, but enough to make even her realise she had to open the door again. That double glazing had been worth the cost apparently because on opening the door, the language produced behind it was atrocious. The cleaned-up version Sam would recount to Polly included something about a female dog not being worth his time and see if said female dog would ever get his generous offer again. She couldn't believe even that nail short of a horseshoe thought his offer was anything close to generous. Sam huffed as the bloodied jacket sleeve turned sharply and flapped away from her. She watched Bedwyr lurch down the road, still spitting curses into the twilight.

It would have been so perfect if not for the fact that Jenny from the post office was walking by at the time. Apparently, to the casual observer, there was plenty of ambiguity as to what happened, and what was said, on that doorstep. Jenny gave Sam an odd stare as she paused in the road and then walked on. But Sam was too busy framing the *coup de grâce* conversation she'd have tomorrow with Polly to worry about Jenny. So Sam just turned her euphoric grin briefly towards the passing post mistress and slammed the door.

"Think I'll leave the blood on the paintwork," she said triumphantly to her reflection in the hallway mirror. Her father had once told her about the English regiment that left a uniform button unpolished. It was to remind them that Nelson's blood once fell on the button of one of their regimental ancestors. "England expects that every man will do his duty."

"And I shall do mine, Nelson," Sam said, marching proudly up the stairs, saluting her bedroom door. Except she wasn't a sailor. And the vanquished Bedwyr looked nothing like a Spaniard. And the blood would be hers.

It was a shame Polly needed stamps the next morning.

છ્

"She's shut me out, Mum!" Sam wailed after her epic failure to save her friend from further damage. "How could she believe him over me! She's choosing pride over a lifetime of friendship!"

Emma believed Sam's version. Mr. and Mrs. Dale believed her version, based on their compassionate glances. Dunster, of course, knew all the facts but once again was not called to the witness stand. Larry was ready to clock Bedwyr, being about as wound up as Sam had ever seen him because "No one, NO ONE, calls a Weston a liar!" Sam felt a warmth towards her father that day she hadn't felt since she'd found Dunster in the garden.

"Sit down, Larry, and finish your bacon," an infinitely more sensible Emma said. "Sam, wait things out, focus on your exam, and trust that Polly will come to her senses." Good motherly advice. And with Polly refusing to see her distraught ex-best friend, to answer the phone, or to accept long, anguished letters hand-delivered to her door, Sam had no choice but to wait it out.

છ્

The exam came and went with no good-luck hug from Polly before it and no celebratory scream after it. How many times had the girls met in the road between their houses, leaping, skipping, and grinning, sharing life's joys? But it was like the Berlin Wall had gone up overnight. Right there on the scenic Toll Road. Quiet footfalls, a twitch of a lace curtain before venturing out, eyes averted. Scurrying past the saddlery. A cold war indeed.

The celebrations at Sam's house and at Mrs. Althorp's cottage weren't quite the same. But Dunster treated the victor as he would have the vanquished, with a welcoming nicker and a soft cheek. And just as he had many times before, he instilled in Sam a sense that he knew all things, that he saw a silver lining to her suffering. Just a few years down the road.

Minus Four

"Where should I go?" Sam asked Mrs. Althorp. It was a week after the exam, and Sam had given herself a month to find a new position. She figured it would take her that long to get over the trauma of packing up her things and staggering, shell-shocked and dazed, up the driveway of WEC for the last time. Never had anyone found success so earth-shatteringly sad. But the instructors were right. It was typical to branch out before taking the full Instructorship exam.

"Luckily, you've got lots of choices," Mrs. Althorp replied, looking at all the training opportunities Sam had been offered. "Dubai, Sydney, Hong Kong, and New York. Gloucestershire, Wiltshire, and Surrey. It's going to be a tough decision."

Sam focused on America. "Well, I speak the language" (or so she thought), "and as far as I know, New York doesn't have as many deadly reptiles and spiders as Sydney. The Upstate Equestrian Center looks gorgeous. It's tempting." Sam waved the brochure at Mrs. Althorp. The opportunity to travel all over the United States, combined with the grant money being offered, was a big plus.

But if Sam were honest, it didn't really matter where it was as long as it was far away from Polly and Bedwyr. Even Surrey seemed too close. The Polsam Livery Yard and Tea Shop was dead in the water. Sam couldn't imagine staying within gossip distance of the village, or even in the country, at that moment. She remembered the last time she'd run away overseas; it had turned out okay. Maybe it would this time too.

Though "Bedwyr the Plonker" as Larry had anointed him, had the smarts to look sheepish if he passed Sam in his car, avoiding him and Polly was a full-time job. The pain of knowing her best friend was in danger and that she, Sam, couldn't save her was agonizing. So Sam sat on Mrs. Althorp's couch, waiting for a solution. Because Mrs. Althorp had never failed to give the perfect advice. Until now.

"Yes, I think you should go, dear," Mrs. Althorp replied. "And not because you are running away from Polly's problems—and you need to understand they are Polly's problems, not yours—but because this is a wonderful opportunity to learn and grow as a rider and teacher."

Sam remained quiet.

"It's only a year's commitment. You've seen how fast a year goes. All this with Polly will have blown over by then, one way or another. And you'll be able to take the British Horse Society Instructor's exam and finally set up that livery yard together. Everything will still be here when you get back. Not much changes in the space of a year on Exmoor, after all."

Sam hated this advice. She didn't want to go. She wanted to stay here with Polly and Dunster and Mrs. Althorp and Exmoor. Sam leaned her head back on the couch and closed her eyes. The reality was she wouldn't be going because it was a great opportunity. She'd be going because she didn't feel she could stay. It wouldn't be because Mrs. Althorp was right. It would be because her life there was all wrong.

But what about Dunster? He was twenty-six now. A little stiff, a little slow, happy to mooch around in the paddock, and flick the flies off a shelter-mate's nose. Life was good for him, and Sam could afford to pay his keep with the money she'd earned at WEC. He'd wait for her.

Exmoor ponies live well into their thirties. And Mrs. Althorp was always right.

᷾ᵒ᷾

The following weeks were full of packing and paperwork for student visas. Sam had no idea then the whole visa/immigration game would be a recurring theme in her life. She spent hours writing out instructions for Dunster's care because, strangely, he'd become more and more fragile as she became more and more educated. "Whoever said ignorance was bliss wasn't kidding," Geraldine mumbled, as she walked away with another binder of notes.

"Take photos of Dunster every week, Mum, and send them on to me, please," Sam begged. She'd almost added instructions for her mum to take photos of Polly, too, so Sam would be able to see in her friend's eyes the moment Polly finally believed her. On second thoughts …

Sam wrote Dunster a letter the night before she left for New York, leaning against his warm back as they both lay in the straw of his shelter. "A year goes really fast," she'd written, quoting Mrs. Althorp's last words to her as she'd left the cottage earlier. She put the envelope in the rafters with the remains of the ones she'd placed there before leaving for France. Mice, birds, wind, and rain had left their mark, but no human had ever found them. Dunster knew they were there, though, and he watched with kind eyes as Sam tucked the new letter on top of the old. The message was the same: "Thank you. For a million things."

"One more year and I'll be back for good," Sam told him. She inhaled the scent of his cheek and kissed his nose. He did the same to her.

She stayed awake all night, watching Dunster in the paddock, the solid, comforting outline of Hurlstone against the twinkling sky. Hurlstone blacked out the stars like a gaping hole that Sam felt she was about to fall into. But it was also the route back home, a two-way gaping hole, to see again the moonlight on the still waters of Porlock Bay. Lights twinkled over in Wales, then faded with the sunrise. Sam tried not to think of Chepstow.

The dawn sky broke pink and wispy. Suitcases were once more loaded into the car as Emma and Larry checked the route to Heathrow.

Just head for the bright lights, Sam thought.

She glanced briefly up at Polly's old bedroom window, willing a vision of a wave, the sound of a sob. Nothing. Would there be a sob in a room above the saddlery, turned away from a supposed partner?

An already-homesick Sam didn't dare go and stroke Dunster's nose again. So the pony and the girl just looked at each other for a moment over the gate, a silent acknowledgement of a forever bond.

An ending. A beginning.

As Sam climbed into the car, she felt it—a tiny tear in her heart. Too late.

Dunster raised his head and sniffed the air. His eyes flashed a warning to the receding tail lights. Too late.

Chapter Twenty-Four

Twenty-eight years and four thousand miles from that farewell, the tear had become *hireth*. It was 11:15 p.m., and the storm raged on.

Polly. On her second marriage. Three children. A successful livery stable on Exmoor. Sitting in her queen-sized bed with en-suite bathroom, great life, great friends, great kids, loving husband, financial security, and holiday plans, Sam had never felt so jealous of Polly. Not since seeing that bright orange space hopper in her garden. It was too late to phone her now with the six-hour time difference. Or rather, too early.

"Did I wake you?" Sam said two minutes later.

"Don't be silly," Polly replied with a slight echo from the international connection. "The horses never need feeding on a Sunday, so I usually stay up all night." Sam missed that British wit. "Are you all right? You never normally call this early just to chat."

"Fine. Well, not fine, but nothing scary. Well, a bit scary, but not life-threatening. Though could be life-changing," Sam blurted, sounding like the confused mess she was.

"Start at the beginning," Polly breathed into the phone. Sam heard the click of a door closing and pictured Polly tiptoeing downstairs to the kitchen so as not to disturb Jack, who'd been forgiven years ago for being the son of a butcher. A gush of water followed as the kettle filled, then the chink of a mug on the counter; preparations for a long conversation. Sam closed her eyes and conjured up Polly's kitchen with its pine table, red AGA stove, saddle pads drying over the backs of chairs, and one whole wall completely covered with rosettes. The large kitchen window looked out over Dulverton's rolling fields and the beautiful livery yard Jack had built Polly with his own hands; a monument to his love for her. He was a breath of fresh air each time the McClintocks went to stay. He showed the kids how to drive a tractor and bottle feed a lamb. He discussed hay prices with Brody. And he comforted Sam over steaming tea out of cracked mugs. "It'll still all be here when you're ready," he'd say. Sam would have traded her whole Wedgwood tea set to hold one of those mugs at that moment.

"I just need an objective opinion, so please listen carefully." Sam took a couple of deep breaths. Without judgement or emotion, except for the occasional "He's being a complete arse!," "Who the hell does he think he is?," and "This whole bloody country's insane!," interspersed with suppressed sobs, Sam recounted the entire story. Brody's version may have been a little different, but Polly was Sam's best friend, so she accepted Sam's version.

"Blimey," Polly gasped. "Just … blimey! I figured something was up when I didn't see you on Facebook yesterday. Never dreamed anything like this was going on."

"They think it's like getting a dog licence or paying the gas bill!" Sam wailed. "Just paperwork. But how can you swap one country for another and just override the heritage gene?" She paused to draw breath. "It's all far from simple. Remember how hard it was to get a green card? About as convoluted and frustrating as herding cats into a checked box. And they hate me here! I sat next to a jerk in the bar who acted like I was one of an army of immigrant zombies, attacking the border fence!" Gin still had some influence over the story, apparently. "And the nerve of 'The Committee!'" Sam's fingers twitched quotation marks. "As though America's the only Eden on Earth where anyone wants to live!"

"You're right," Polly concurred. "I don't remember anyone in Porlock Junior School waving the stars and stripes and yelling they wanted to be an American when they grew up."

"Exactly!" Sam felt triumphant. "It was just a stupid three-hour cruise that turned into much longer." *"Though without the theme song,"* Gin added wisely.

As Sam's breathing slowed, her momentary hostility towards her adopted homeland waned. She was typically grateful for all America had offered her. But she had never planned to live here for decades. After the wedding in England, coming back to the US had felt more like leaving for an extended honeymoon, nothing more. Bathing in the newness of love and marriage, holidays in England had been enough. When the children were younger, extended summer visits home were exciting, and showing the kids the other half of their heritage was a joy and an honour, not to mention an eye-opener for Sam. She'd never been to half as many castles, cathedrals, or museums, or eaten so much fish and chips, before moving to the States as after. Something about distance and time made you appreciate your heritage. Or maybe it was the need to prove Britain was in fact more than a slow-moving US aircraft carrier. Although the leaving after a holiday could be agonizing, Sam always felt in her heart that it was just another temporary separation. She'd never considered herself to be an immigrant. Just a misplaced British resident abroad—an accidental émigré. But they won't put that on your green card. Apparently, the rules state you must be called a Lawful Permanent Resident.

"So what on earth do I do?" Sam whined. "Walk away from my country? Or walk away from my husband?"

"Oh, surely it's not that black and white? Would Brody really choose an elected position over you? Would you really leave him for a cream tea?" The attempt at humour fell flat. Polly had walked away from a husband and struggled for years with the consequences. Sam knew Polly took this seriously.

"I don't know, Polly. I just don't know what to do. But right now I really feel like I met the right guy in the wrong place."

"Well, first we need all the facts," Polly started. There she was, the emergency coordinator. Sam pictured her friend reaching for the manual she'd probably prepared on Sam's wedding day for just such an eventuality. "How much do you know about getting US citizenship?"

"That's just it! I can't get past the first line of the pledge to look much deeper. 'I hereby declare, on oath, that I absolutely and entirely renounce and abjure all allegiance and fidelity to any foreign prince, potentate, state, or sovereignty of whom or which I have heretofore been a subject or citizen.' I mean, bloody hell! Can you imagine me saying that? Even though apparently you can say it with your fingers crossed behind your back and it doesn't 'technically' mean you've renounced prior citizenship. I just can't say the words!"

"Blimey," said Polly again. "That does sound a little … final, doesn't it? Unless your fingers are crossed, in which case it just sounds … ridiculous. Either you do or you don't renounce prior allegiance, correct?"

Polly had taken a vow seriously once, only to find it meant nothing to certain others. The two friends had spent many nights on the phone in the early days of Polly's divorce talking about how fragile the meaning of words could be unless you put your whole heart and soul behind them.

"So what do you get in return for all this renouncing," Polly continued, "apart from the right to flip the switch on the Christmas tree lights?"

"Well," Sam said, "if I become a naturalized citizen, I can vote, and I agree that's important. It's the one thing I've always felt guilty about, as it reduces my right to complain." (Which was not to be confused with not complaining.) "I could get a federal job. And become an elected official ... hey, I could run against Brody! Fun!"

Polly giggled in the background, which, when combined with the echo on the line, made Sam chuckle too.

"And I could live outside the US for over a year at a time, which apparently I can't do now, as I'm not 'naturalized.' Can you believe it? According to the US government, I'm unnatural!"

"They may not be alone in that sentiment, Sammy-kins."

That wasn't British wit. That was just rude.

"Yeah, thanks for that," Sam said. "I'll be honest, though. I'm feeling a little used. America spins this whole yarn about welcoming all with open arms. But, according to the committee, she's pulling you into an embrace against a steel breastplate, blocking admission to the heart. I guess the breastplate just gets hidden under the robes of Lady Liberty."

"That's a little harsh, Sam. You've always spoken very fondly of the way you've been treated everywhere you've lived over there. Especially in the Midwest. 'Friendliest people I've ever met,' you've said on many occasions. But you've also made it clear, at least to me, that your heart is on Exmoor, despite all your years abroad. So who's really wearing the breastplate?"

Ouch. A zinger.

"Here's what you need to do," Polly stated after a few moments of silent airtime. "Find out more about the process of citizenship, find out more about how your town folk really feel about you being 'foreign' with regards to it influencing their vote, and find out why Brody really wants to run for office. Finally, ignore all that and ask yourself the only question that really matters: If you belong anywhere your heart says you belong, regardless of any piece of paper or official title, where do you, Samantha

McClintock, belong?"

$\approx$ $\approx$

Early morning on a Sunday was not something Sam normally witnessed. Sleep being her drug of choice, she typically woke to the smell of pancakes around 9:00 a.m., Brody having already been for a run with the dogs, read the paper, and fired up the griddle. But this particular morning, Sam was in charge of letting the dogs out (and they knew better than to expect a run down the road from her, smart pups). She trudged downstairs, gripping the handrail to prevent herself from ricocheting off the walls, buffeted by the dogs around her legs. Carrying the empty hot chocolate mug to the kitchen sink, she let the ecstatic hounds outside. The two brothers bounced around the garden, peeing on everything and chasing the birds off the feeder. Well, someone had to do it.

Heading back into the sitting room, Sam thought with self-loathing of yesterday's cake and biscuits. And gin. She decided to have fruit for breakfast. And lunch. And dinner. Until Tuesday. Make that June.

Sinking down on the sofa, Sam began drumming her fingers on the armrest. Unable to settle, she returned to the kitchen where she paced, arms folded, unseeing, while the kettle boiled.

What was she going to say when Brody got home? Though she knew it was not really *what* was she going to say but *how* was she going to say it. To make it seem inoffensive, plausible, reasonable, and not a knee-jerk reaction. Not running away from anything but running toward something that she'd always wanted. Something she and Brody had both agreed to many years ago. It wasn't a change in plan as much as it was an acknowledgement that now was the right time to implement an old plan, one Brody had helped formulate when he married an English girl who was never an immigrant, just a misplaced resident.

What about the kids? Of course, the kids came first. Were they ready to see themselves as never more than a plane flight from their parents? Was Sam ready? It had taken a year to stop buying so much milk, and there'd been tears when she'd had to put a loaf of bread in the freezer for the first time because it wasn't eaten fast enough. But her children had been travelling since they were born, far more at home in an airport than at a bus stop. The idea of "visits" from the kids was something Sam had struggled to come to terms with, as neither of them was in the Midwest anymore. Any sighting of either one of them had to be planned and coordinated, which would be no different if their visits were to a neighbouring state or a neighbouring country. In the case of a country, the cost would be higher, the time commitment longer, but the mindset was the same. And in Sam's experience, the kids were happy to visit their parents anywhere as long as the parents were prepared to foot the bill.

Ben and Tori both loved Exmoor, Sam knew. As children they'd spent plenty of summer holidays sleeping in Sam's old room, playing outside the coastguard hut, riding ponies, and smearing clotted cream on each other. *Lucky devils never had to take an oath*, Sam thought as she considered their dual citizenship. They had a much different view of the size of the world than Sam had had at their age. The world was accessible to them, familiar and open for exploration. Today's travellers barely had to plan ahead at all. Just a quick look at the calendar, and "Oh, I'm free next weekend." Then an online search, and their ticket was at the airport in about a third of a second. Their parents could be informed via text and waiting at Heathrow before the ink was dry on their boarding pass.

So I could live anywhere now without guilt. Sam nodded her head slowly, processing that information. She knew there would really be some guilt, like when the kids' car broke down or the flu hit. But she also knew she couldn't reach them from where she was now quickly enough to help with those inconveniences anyway.

"It's all right to think about my needs, my wants, my home, right?" Sam said to the teapot on the Welsh dresser. "It's all right to ask others to follow in my geographical wake once in a while, isn't it?" She'd made a home for her family, full of laughter and holidays and encouragement, along with nagging and screaming and top-notch tuition in the art of sarcasm. And yes, sarcasm was an art form, no matter what Oscar Wilde said. Considering her kids were only half British, they'd overcome that drawback amazingly well, Sam would always think, as another bone-dry zinger whipped across the dinner table. So proud.

"Right then." Sam rubbed her hands together. "I've done my duty to my children, to my husband, and to my adopted country. But what about to myself?"

Minus Three

Six months and two days after she'd left for the States, six months and two days of amazing horses and experiences and travel, Sam got the call. Mrs. Althorp was wrong. Exmoor had changed.

Leaning against a brick wall in the aisle of a beautiful stable block in upstate New York, clutching the phone, slowly sliding to the floor, Sam cared nothing for all the grooms and riders trying to help.

"No! No!"

Barely holding the phone now, Sam heard the screams in her head. *But I'm getting you away from the wonky shelter! I'm getting you a nameplate over a custom-made stable door, cut low enough for a little Exmoor pony! Just a little longer! Wait just a little longer!*

Sam never even considered that bereavement leave wasn't appropriate. She was bereaved, wasn't she? She booked a flight for the next day and arrived at Heathrow with her pockets stuffed full of a compassionate flight attendant's soggy tissues. The attendant had never had a pony, she'd said, as she'd begun a tale about her childhood bunny. Sam's distraught face silenced the tale.

Emma and Larry were at the airport, with a card from Mrs. Althorp to read in the car. It wasn't read in the car.

Geraldine was waiting as the car pulled up across the road from the paddock and Sam tumbled out. Geraldine opened her mouth to speak. A slamming door, running feet, reminiscent of an eighth birthday. A choked sob. Polly flung herself into Sam's arms. No words. Cheek to cheek, a vague recollection of a click in the background. Larry, as sensitive as ever, took the photo Sam would find decades later, tucked in with the letters in a Midwest attic. The Dynamic Duo once more. Reunited in grief over the only male figure they'd ever both loved.

Sam put her hands up to block Geraldine's explanations of how. It was the why Sam needed. Like that mattered either.

Dunster wasn't in the paddock or the shelter. Sam's eyes paced back and forth while Geraldine commiserated. Sam saw and heard as though through thick mist and auditory treacle. Where was he? No, she didn't want to rest first. No, she didn't need to eat first or wash first or do anything first. Back in the car, Polly gripped Sam's hand tightly as they drove along a narrow lane that wound and climbed along the edge of the moors to Oaktree Farm. Wanda Waverly lived there now with her new husband. Apparently, Wanda was Charlotte's cousin. Funny how that worked.

A large hole had been excavated in a corner of a field with stunning views towards Dunkery in one direction and, in the distance, a glimpse of the sparkling waters of Porlock Bay. Goodness knows how, or at what cost, but Dunster was lying there, with the comforter from Sam's bed tucked around him. Sam was about to climb into the hole when her mother gently took her arm and handed her a pile of letters, battered and torn.

"Geraldine found these in the shelter when they were clearing it out," Emma said. "Seems like they'd been with Dunster for a long time. He'd like them with him now, I'm sure."

Sam stared at the letters. They were all copies, except for the one she'd written right before leaving him for the last time. She didn't need to read them again, as she knew them by heart. At that moment, she was sure Dunster knew them by heart too. Sam knelt in the hole, smoothing the whorl on Dunster's forehead, sinking her fingers into his coat, trying to get his thick mane to lie down flat. It had never worked in life so probably wouldn't in death. Sam placed the letters between his front legs, nestled close to his heart. A solitary bird sang, the weak winter sun twinkled in his eye, and the gentle breeze blew, ruffling the hairs on Dunster's neck for the last time. His little girl placed her cheek on his.

Grand Scheme: Get a pony and keep him forever. Check.

Minus Two

"You have to go back," Mrs. Althorp said gently over tea and cake two days later. For the first time ever, a chocolate cake was just being pushed around Sam's plate, crumbs smooshed with a fork but never lifted to her mouth.

"Your wants are still the same: to take the BHS Instructor's exam and run your own riding stable. Your training in America can help you do that. It's the need that's changed slightly. You don't need to do it to provide Dunster with a home anymore. You're doing it just for you now. You still love horses and riding and Exmoor. You still enjoy teaching others. Dunster cemented these passions in you, but I don't believe they went away because Dunster did."

Sam thought about those words a lot. Was it true that her wants were still the same? Because it certainly seemed like something big had changed. Just the thought of Exmoor without Dunster was painful. A little girl turning up for a lesson with Sam on a pretty Exmoor pony was out of the question. Sam knew death was part of working with animals. She'd seen horses injured and taken some old show horses to be "put to sleep." Such a gentle term for such a brutally hard decision. But those other horses weren't Dunster. They weren't Sam's giddy, galloping childhood and accomplice and guide as she discovered the moors. They weren't there during her teenage angst, or part of her bond with Polly, or her reason for living abroad. Twice. They hadn't motivated her foray into the world of writing, which had precipitated a special bond with the lady who was looking at her now with such compassion over her teacup. No, this was different. If Sam began to untangle Dunster from her being, what would be left?

৵৽৽

On the plane during that first Dunster-less flight, rattling the Queen's afternoon teacups at Windsor Castle, passing over Bristol, then Wales, then Ireland, Sam saw little. Too homesick already. Too bitter at being forced to go by the simple, cruel impossibility of staying. For the second time in a year, America would harbour her after the loss of a friend. Even with Polly back in her life, and committed to leaving Bedwyr for good, Sam knew she couldn't stay and look across the road at the empty paddock. She couldn't watch an Exmoor mare trot along a Cloutsham path followed by her foal, or train a young child for her first Bossington show. Not yet. It was slightly less agonizing to go back to the United States than to stay home.

So once again, Dunster, or now the lack thereof, combined with input from Mrs. Althorp, directed Sam's life, taking her away from Exmoor, in person at least. For how long Sam could never have guessed. But Dunster and Mrs. Althorp were busy setting other wheels in motion; still the running border on the Bayeux Tapestry of Sam's life.

Minus One

The first months after Dunster died were tough. Sam craved the comfort of familiar people and places, yet found the thought of those people and places distressing. Her grief clouded exciting rides on lovely horses and prevented her from letting the many joys of America touch her heart. But slowly a new normal developed. Not a better or worse normal. Just a new one. The old normal got put on hold after a meeting with a tanned Californian US Naval officer wearing military whites on a New York Harbor cruise.

"Cute accent," he'd said.

"I don't have one, but you do," she'd shot back.

Apparently, they shared Celtic ancestry; a great pickup line. This stranger was also three thousand miles from home, so the bonding topic of homesickness was discussed during that first meeting while gazing up at the Statue of Liberty.

The long distance romance blossomed, despite Brody's absences to defend his country below the surface of the Atlantic. Despite Sam's returns to England to meet visa requirements. Despite the proposal being made over the phone and wedding plans being drawn up between deployments. Despite her mum's warnings of homesickness and Polly's tears that she'd be living so far away. Despite Helen's attempts to defend King George against the colonists. Through it all, never, for one moment during that two-year courtship, did Sam think she was emigrating.

"I suppose you could visit the Empire State Building," Helen had said to Polly when she mentioned she'd like to visit Sam. Polly looked at her mother in disbelief.

"You'd have a heart attack if I got on a plane or in an express elevator," Polly said.

The wedding in Saint Dubricius Church in Porlock turned out to be an eye-opening experience for both families and locals alike. Brody's parents cooed ecstatically over everything except the showers, and Larry's long-winded introduction to the rules of rugby at the rehearsal dinner. Oh, and the narrow lanes.

"What do you mean, these aren't one-way streets?" yelled an ashen-faced Bill McClintock as he'd come to a screeching halt in his rental car, grille to grille with a Range Rover. "Our driveway's wider than this!"

The US submarine force took over the local pubs and refused to accept clotted cream on top of jam on top of scones as real food. And forget about happy hour being time for tea. To quote the best man, with a smashing English accent: "How can a nation that produces such good beer possibly think it acceptable to have tea as the national drink?"

"Do we really sound like that?" Polly mouthed quietly to Sam across the bouquets.

"Apparently so," giggled the bride.

Sam had always pictured Dunster at her wedding, bedecked in flowers, waiting outside the church. He'd have been stopped, repeatedly, from eating the garland around his neck, and he'd have rested on three legs, droopy lower lip, waiting for his charge to appear as Mrs. Whatever. But no matter the age or name, he'd have looked at her the same, always a child to him. And so Sam pictured Dunster that day as she stepped out of the cool, dark church to greet the sun and the pealing bells and the rice, looking up into Brody's face to settle her gaze on a new set of loving eyes, Polly next to her in leg of mutton-sleeved attendance, and Mrs. Althorp in the family photos.

శావ

That first entry into the United States of America as a Conditional Permanent Resident had been traumatic. Sam had flown in several weeks after Brody, as he had to get back to his ship, and the immigration paperwork had been a nightmare. The trip to the US Embassy in London involved a litany of accusations as to her motives, though Sam had to admit it probably wouldn't have been any different if Brody had been sitting at the British Embassy clutching a tree's worth of paper. At JFK airport, Sam was pulled out of line and taken into a separate holding area. There she sat with other tired souls on hard-backed chairs before being numbered, photographed, fingerprinted, and spat out into baggage claim with a "Welcome home" that felt far from welcoming. And far from home. Sam had searched for Brody's face in the crowd and kissed it with love, gratitude, and just a smidgen of resentment.

But her accent was cute and her British ways adorable. Her early attempts at shepherd's pie, Bakewell tart, and roast beef dinners were highly sought-after tickets (but these were single naval officers who ate submarine food, so the bar wasn't set very high). And once Sam had accepted that four o'clock in the afternoon would never see a teapot, the happy couple settled in to chase the American Dream. This meant finding Brody a career after the navy, as Sam had refused to raise children by herself. Brody's switch from nuclear engineering to banking was deemed necessary if they wanted to live in quaint New England towns. Said towns refused to build nuclear reactors to accommodate Brody's skill set. New England seemed a natural choice to set up home, as it was the midpoint between their respective birthplaces and as close to England as Sam could feel in the States. She found a riding stable to teach at part-time (the young riders called her Mary Poppins, of course), but under the weight of home repairs, nappies, and motherly exhaustion, her equine lifestyle quietly extinguished itself.

With the children a little older, Sam set off to university to become a speech-language pathologist, mainly because of the job security she saw in three hundred million people who couldn't produce a single-syllable word in less than three.

"Fu-ra-yuns! I never worked in Fu-ra-yuns!" Sam fumed, wondering how the French would view this massacre of their country's name.

Brody looked at his wife in the passenger's seat as they drove home after a dinner party. "I don't know why I feel a strange urge to apologize for my southern bank president. I should be defending my fellow countrymen. You know they make fun of your accent, right?"

"The difference being that's unjustified," an aloof Brit snapped back. She'd had to soften her views when her children began curling their tongues back for the R sound and pronouncing "vitamin" to rhyme with "fight." She couldn't keep telling her children they sounded like foreigners, Sam had concluded. Begrudgingly.

The McClintock's enjoyed searching for property during each visit to Exmoor, and they'd peruse the local newspapers for suitable jobs. Then it would be back to the States with renewed British spirit and suitcases full of chutney and Cadbury's finest. They'd go furniture shopping and drag home Welsh dressers and floral print sofas and tapestry wallcoverings sprinkled with lions and unicorns, all pieces that would make much more sense under a thatched roof once they'd put them on that container ship and sent them down the M5 motorway to Somerset. The fact these pieces didn't quite look right in their Connecticut barn-conversion home, followed by their Spanish-style California home, followed by their contemporary Wisconsin home wasn't missed by either of them. Or their visitors.

"Oh, look! How … ancestral," one banker's wife had exclaimed on arriving for dinner.

"I say, what! Where'd you put the suit of armour, old boy? Ha ha." Sam could still hear Thomas Sunby's dreadful English accent as he slapped Brody on the back.

At regular intervals during the build-up to, and beyond, their silver wedding anniversary, Sam and Brody had looked up from the life they lived to search for the life they'd planned to live. They said they would move back to England once Brody was out of the navy, once they'd saved a little money, once Tori was born, once Sam had her degree, once the kids were through school.

Once ... twice ... twenty-six.

Chapter Twenty-Five

There's not much more to say about the American years really, Sam thought tearfully, leaning on the kitchen sink as she watched the dogs cavort on the lawn. Outside of a great husband, two amazing children, and a lot of history. Hardly insignificant. Her family were her pride and joy, no matter which country they happened to be in at the time. Which spoke volumes. But nothing of her old life was forgotten; everything was still missed.

That Sunday morning in her war-torn house, battle fatigue clouding her eyes, Sam couldn't believe she wasn't in England. She and Brody hadn't changed their minds about living there; they'd just been distracted, that's all. Waylaid by mortgages and school plays and career paths and a creeping sense of normalcy. That normalcy now laid shattered in the bottom of a Portmeirion bowl coated with breakfast Ben and Jerry's cookie dough ice cream, a perfect blend of two cultures.

"Can I have it all? What I want, where I want it?" Sam straightened up and took a couple of deep breaths. Tea made, still without milk, she pulled a sweater off the back of the counter stool and threw it over her pyjamas. The sun shone on her face as she pulled out a chair at the kitchen table. Light glinted off the Union Jack keychain she'd found in the box of letters. Hanging the little, shiny symbol on the hook by the door had seemed brazenly confrontational last night. Slightly pathetic this morning.

This isn't a war against Brody. The realisation hit her with such relief she closed her eyes. She saw an image of her husband, munching on a cheese and Branston pickle sandwich as he gazed contentedly across the purple-coated moors. Another of him, hands in the air, shouting, "Wheeeee!" as they'd negotiated the steep cliff-side descent of Countisbury Hill into Lynton, and then him ducking without complaint in the low-ceiled bed and breakfast inn. He held ponies in the rain, watched the changing of the guard in the rain, cued in the rain. She recalled him trying on a sporran in a kilt shop in Scotland and never once recalled him searching an English menu for a burger. He patted dogs under bar stools, asking, "Why don't we allow this in the States?" Even the narrow winding lanes didn't faze him.

When in the States, Brody cheerfully acknowledged the British vibe in his home: getting up in the middle of the night to watch royal weddings, wearing a flat cap while watching Royal Ascot (top hats were harder to find), and saving some Fourth of July fireworks for Guy Fawkes Day. He'd even been known to choke down the occasional full English breakfast if Sam was feeling particularly patriotic on a Sunday morning. He would lament the death of a British celebrity he'd never heard of because the loss of that personality impacted Sam in a way she couldn't fully understand, explaining it only as another tie to home withering away. The point was, he fit in, seeming sometimes more adaptable than she was. When she was considering whether he was The One, she could picture him being The One in England too, and this had taken much of the fear out of her decision. Her world looked good on him. He was comfortable there. She wanted him there.

We can make this work, she thought. Then out loud: "We can make this work."

෴

Sam dressed nicely, brushed her hair, and tidied up a

bit. Small olive branches. Brody walked through the door around lunchtime. He usually looked refreshed after these weekends, which Sam couldn't understand, as the idea of finding something new and exciting to say about the millionth tailpipe or chrome bumper seemed exhausting to her. But this time, Brody looked sheepish, and Sam looked sheepish, and the dogs, sensing sheepiness, slunk off to meditate on the couch, sprawled on their backs with all four legs splayed out. The sleep of the innocent. And the immodest.

Sam prepared a guilt-free salad, served on generic plates with no obvious connotations of either England or the US, the People's Republic of China playing the arbitrator.

"I'm sorry," they both started at the same time, awkward smiles covering the first inklings of victory.

Brody looked like he could taste First Town Administrator.

Sam could smell warm scones and damp Exmoor ponies. "You first," she said. Magnanimously.

"Okay," started Brody. "I'm sorry I didn't discuss what running for office meant to me in more detail. I'm sorry I didn't realise how big a transition it was from Lawful Permanent Resident to citizen. I'm sorry I assumed citizenship was a relatively small cog in the wheel for me getting elected. I'm sorry I appeared to speak for you. And I'm really sorry about the cake. That bit I seriously didn't know anything about, but once I heard Thomas's choice of red velvet cake, I really understood the depth of your anger." Brody gave one of his irresistible boyish grins.

Dear God. Red velvet. Worse than she'd ever imagined. Flashback to other cakes, some flying, some eaten as encouragement while writing in a little cabin, giant towers of cakes in tea shops, or eaten out of backpacks on the moors. So many special memories tied in with cake.

Brody was looking at her expectantly.

Sam took a deep breath. "I'm sorry I downplayed the importance of the first town administrator position. I know you love a challenge and that your heart is really in the right place. We love this town, and I'm proud of the fact you want so much to help your community. I'm sorry I belittled your Scottish heritage. And I'm really sorry I called you Buck."

Obviously, the next move was Brody's. "So I'm withdrawing my candidacy." Or "So I spoke to the committee today, and we agreed you didn't have to change a thing." Or, and Sam's personal favourite, "Let's get you home."

Instead, thunderous silence. It hurt the sleeping dogs' ears, making them twitch. The teacups trembled and rattled ominously inside their Welsh fortification. But Sam's years in assisting with communicative interactions had taught her to be patient. She tried prompting her husband with a wide, dazzling smile.

Looking back on the next five seconds, Sam could only assume Brody saw that smile as a prelude to her pulling the completed application for citizenship out of thin air, twirling it gaily around her head, and grabbing him for a makeup kiss. Because he didn't withdraw his candidacy or absolve Sam from deserting the Queen. Or offer to take her home.

Brody leapt from the table shouting, "So you'll get citizenship then?"

The dogs woke with a start, flipping right-side-up, quickly assessing the situation. They slowly pivoted their heads from Brody's pumping fists to Sam's frozen face.

"That guy can be a real jerk sometimes," Sherlock whined.

Chapter Twenty-Six

With the slamming door and the wailed, "I'm sorry! I thought …" still echoing around the valley, Sam strode towards town, then quickly reversed direction and headed off into open farmland. Usually while walking Sam liked to sing to herself. She never felt she picked the song; her mind would just hit "shuffle" and something always popped up. Country walks typically chose calm melodies: Simon and Garfunkel, Enya, James Morrison. But today the melody was no lullaby. Exploding inside her was the "1812 Overture" overlaid with "Bohemian Rhapsody." Pounding feet and heart provided the baseline, clenched jaw and fists filled in the lyrics.

What was going on? When did Brody change from a loving, supportive husband to a complete jerk devoid of feeling, sense, or even a rudimentary understanding of his wife?

"Breathe. Breathe," Sam said to the roadside dandelions. "Entertain the possibility that you, Sam, are the one who's changed. Breathe. Entertain. Breathe. Entertain."

Her paced slowed a little, and her heartbeat calmed somewhat. The soundtrack faded to a dull roar, replaced by the rhythmic pulse of her footsteps. Rational thoughts crept back in, replacing the hatchet murder of a husband and the forced re-colonisation of a backward nation. She finally looked up from the angry road surface and gazed around her.

"Breathe, entertain," she panted, making a conscious

effort to look on her adoptive surroundings with appreciative eyes. The red Dutch barn with its distinctive roofline, a classic silhouette in the Midwest. The ditch lilies that would fill the roadsides with their cheery orange glow in the summer; such an elegant invasive weed. The dairy cows, lowing mournfully, though chomping happily enough on lush grass between laments. Green fields. Rolling vistas. It was beautiful. And tranquil. But as Sam absorbed the sights, the red wooden barn morphed into thatch and stone, the ditch lilies into gorse, lowing cows into bleating sheep. The road here looked too wide, though equally as rural as the lanes around Porlock. The spring sunshine was slowly repairing damage on the snowmobile trails rather than the horseshoe divots on a muddy bridle path. Similarities in reality. Differences in the heart.

Another melody appeared, at first distant, as though heard through a stone cottage wall, then seeping louder and louder into Sam's space through a newly opened door. Calm in tempo, but its lyrics more disturbing. Dido's "Life for Rent."

"Am I just renting this life in America?" Sam preached to the sky, lifting her arms and standing still in the middle of the road. "Have I never really bought into the dream? Is this nothing more than a place-saver, an interlude from my real life on Exmoor?" Sam suddenly felt like she'd abandoned painting the walls because it was just a rental house, abandoned timely oil changes because it was just a rental car. Abandoned any notion of support for her husband's role in this community because she was just passing through. "Could this be true?"

She collapsed onto a makeshift rocky bench on the side of the road, head down, arms hugging knees. Never had she felt so lost while knowing so exactly where she should be. Breathe. *Hireth.* Breathe. *Hireth.*

Lifting her head slowly, Sam felt so alone. But she knew at that moment her alienation had nothing to do with Thomas Sunby and his making out like everyone thought she didn't fit in. It had nothing to do with Brody's ambitions. It was all about her. She was refusing to dance at this party because somewhere, she thought, was a better one. But she'd helped to stage this event, setting up the chairs, booking the DJ, planning food, and sprinkling confetti on the table cloths. Now she had stepped back, looked around, and found she was at the wrong ball in the wrong dress. Nothing to do with the guests being glad or not she was there. The realisation was crushing.

"But I'm not a changeling," Sam said to the cow that had dawdled up behind her and stood looking at her with patient, familiar, liquidy-brown eyes. "I was always this. Always just trying to get home."

A breeze ruffled her hair and stirred a memory of the wind on Bossington Beach.

Of grand schemes, set in stone. But nothing was ever set in stone, it seemed. Certainly not career choices or locations or loneliness or bottomless grief. Or divisions between two people who loved each other, til death did them part.

Chapter Twenty-Seven

"We need to talk," Sam said. "Obviously."

Brody looked like he'd been pacing the porch since she'd stormed out, his head carrying the telltale marks of fingers repeatedly drawn through his hair, something he'd always done when frustrated or angry. As the hair thinned, the grooves of the finger trails got wider and were less likely to spring back. Not a good time to mention that.

"This is not just about you running for office." Sam started, sinking down onto the porch bench with no idea how to get the next part out without breaking down. "I suppose I'm more homesick than I realised. I suppose I've been going through the motions for too long. Acting settled. Trucking through each day like it was normal. This whole citizenship thing has stirred up the mud to the surface. But the mud was always there. Turns out it's peaty Exmoor mud, not Miami fine sandy loam." Even Sam had no idea how she knew that was the type of soil prevalent in this part of the Midwest. Hardly came into play in the container-planting classes she'd taken. But she could see she was losing Brody. He was trying so hard through squinty eyes and twitching mouth to relate mud to citizenship. Men really don't do segues the way women do.

"It's *hireth*. Plain and simple," Sam tried again, producing nothing more than panic on Brody's face as he tripped from soil types to foreign languages. His eyes darted from Sam's to her mouth and back again.

"What the heck is she talking about?" his eyebrows

asked.

"Sorry," Sam mumbled. "*Hireth* means homesickness with a sense of longing. With the addition of loss." Addition of loss sounded confusing even to Sam, but she ploughed on. "It means I'm more than homesick. I'm yearning to go home but at the same time scared that the home I miss may not be the home that's there anymore. Nostalgic for lost places and times. I can't settle here, and I'm worried that if I go back there, 'there' may not be there anymore. Even though Mrs. Althorp says 'there' doesn't change much. And I feel in my heart that 'there' is still there and always will be there. All I know is, I can't severe a tie to that life while I'm trying to work out what that tie still is. Does this make any sense?"

"Yes." Bless his heart. It was the most confused-looking affirmative anyone had ever seen on a loving face. But yes was enough for now.

❧

The late afternoon was still. Birds were rushing around in the gathering twilight, finding a last beak full of dog hair for the nest (plenty under the kitchen table if you need it, fellas), a last snack from the birdfeeder, and a last aerial assault against that puffy-chested male that had been hanging around the wife. Sam and Brody watched it all from the porch under a blanket as Sam shared so many stories she'd never shared before: Lipizzaners, James Cuthbertson, Mrs. Althorp's boots. And every detail of Dunster. The written letters that had never seen the light of day since Dunster died. Even the internal letters she'd written in thoughts throughout the years. Brody took it all in.

"While you were gone, I sat here thinking," Brody started, rubbing Sam's palm with his thumb. "Thinking about how I'd have fared living in England. What would I have loved about your country, what would I have missed about this one? Would I have blamed you for taking me away, or thanked you for the opportunity to live a life I'd never imagined? How quickly would the novelty of being 'different' have worn off? I started to feel a bit queasy, to be honest."

"Queasy?" Sam queried.

"Queasy because I realised I'd done you wrong. You'd made it quite clear from the beginning you belonged in England. I knew it and avoided it for, what? Twenty-six years? Perhaps you made it look too easy, living a foreign life. I'd see your joy on our holidays, feel your tension as we boarded the plane to leave again. I should have known how much effort it took. And been more grateful to you for sacrificing for your family."

"I had choices, you know," Sam replied. "You weren't exactly holding me hostage. I wanted to be here with you, and I wanted the kids to have all the wonderful things America's given them. I haven't been resentful or unhappy here. This may just be all about timing. Let's face it, something would have triggered this. If not your run for office, something else. Maybe the demise of Cadbury's or the passing of the Queen. Or something simpler, like a pony's face on a postcard. Your request for a formal severance of ties just collided with a stupid crossword puzzle. And the time to think about home more." With each empty bed came more empty time to reassess life's choices.

"Well, simple or not, here we are," sighed Brody. "And yes, timing may have something to do with this. I guess I've felt a little … empty lately. I look around, and the kids don't need me anymore, and I can do my job standing on my head. And life's become a little staid, for want of a better word. I don't mean I'm bored with you. Never with you. But with me. This first town administrator position was mentioned and I just grabbed at it for excitement, I think."

"Rather than a Ferrari or a young secretary then, Mr.

Midlife Crisis?" Sam tried to grin, but the thought of either alternative was too unappealing.

"Something like that," Brody continued. "Though if a Ferrari's being offered ..."

Sam tipped her head towards her Subaru in the driveway and raised an eyebrow. "Speaking of upgrades ..."

With dual smiles, a few moments of quiet sat calmly between them.

"You know," Sam started, "if it's a challenge you're looking for, how about a run for the border instead of a run for office?" She glanced sideways at Brody, head on one side. *Please see the segue ...*

"Way ahead of you," Brody said, squeezing Sam's hand. "I've always known you were my greatest asset, not because you *sound* British, but because you *are* British. Because being British makes you so many of the things I love about you. With the exception of Yorkshire pudding, which still sucks, no matter what you say." This earned Brody a backhanded smack.

"So I think I should repot you. British roots, American pot, not working anymore. You need some native soil, a drenching of English rain, not Wisconsin snow. And you need feeding up on clotted cream. Put the bloom back in your cheeks."

"You know clotted cream's nothing but fat, right?" The first negative comment Sam had ever made about that delightful concoction. *Why would I bring that up now?*

"No, Sam. It's more than that. It's home. Your home. And hopefully, soon, my new home."

Sam looked up at her husband, his face all twinkly and blurred through the tears. He was right about everything. Except the bit about thinking he was the gardener. No more following others. She would repot herself. But she'd dig two holes in the soil, side by side.

They had sat on that porch so many evenings, Mr. and Mrs. McClintock, with the children as tweeners and young teenagers when they had first arrived from the East Coast. Then just the two of them as the grown-up children slowly extracted themselves, root by root, from the potting soil that was their family home. It *had* been a home. A real, loving, and happy home. And it still was. Just not *the* home. Something in the wind had changed. With that thought, Sam felt a sudden urge to giggle as a vision of Mary Poppins came to mind, pulling her umbrella from her carpetbag and watching for the weather vane to shift direction before flying off to … wherever she went.

"Spit spot," Sam giggled.

Brody demonstrated an amazing ability to follow this particular segue, given that Sam had said nothing else out loud. In his best Cockney accent, which, by the way, was so much better than Dick Van Dyke's, Brody said, "You 'ain't bin from 'round 'ere in a long toyme. Iz aboit toyme you was frum 'round 'ere agin." Which, when Sam really listened hard, sounded more West Country Somerset than Cockney. But you hear what you want to hear.

෴

Sam and Brody spent hours going over options during dinner. Brody was sensible enough not to complain about whether or not frozen pizza constituted a real dinner. Pros: many (heart-related), cons: many (brain-related). But the happy couple knew lists, plans, financial considerations, logistics, including moving two large dogs across continents—none of it mattered. Sam was going home because she had to. Just like she'd had to leave England after Polly deserted her or Dunster died, Sam felt she had no option but to return now. This was not a midlife crisis. There was no buying a red convertible to get over this one. This was about being true to herself, and it had been in the works since she was twenty-three years old. The heart was packed already. It was all sorted.

"I do worry that you'll be disappointed somehow,"

Brody said gently over wine. "I mean, you won't be living in a country mansion, galloping over Exmoor whenever you want to. Maybe we'll get a glimpse of the water, but we won't be overlooking the entire coast. You'll be working in a hospital, not your own livery yard. Your dad won't be there. Polly won't be next door. Dunster—"

"I know," Sam cut in. She'd already contemplated that the Sweet Shop Sam, the Galloping Sam, the Dynamic Duo Sam had been permanently replaced by the Dieting Sam, the Sensible Sam, the Coupon-Cutting, Hatchback, Middle-Aged Sam. That wasn't America's fault. That was life's fault. And it scared her a bit. "It won't be the same. But it will be heartwarmingly familiar. I truly believe I'm still the Exmoor Sam." She rolled the words *Exmoor Sam* around inside her head for a moment, savouring the feel. "But I worry it will be harder on you than me, as you've never lived in a small cottage with nineteenth-century plumbing. But taking a shower with all the water pressure of a slow leak in a hosepipe will preserve what's left of your hair. So many benefits."

"I'll chose to ignore that last one," said Brody, patting his forehead, or "fivehead," as he called it now.

"And you can walk to the pub if you get claustrophobic in our little cottage. And you'll have all the space for a car they thought necessary in the 1840s," Sam continued, meaning a square of grass on the verge outside the cottage.

"But seeing as the vehicle will be the size of Tori's old Barbie car, I can just pick it up and hang it on a hook in the hallway if the grass verge gets muddy," Brody chuckled, though his wince conveyed the pain of losing his massive Ford Explorer.

"Very funny. But when you've paid those European petrol prices for a week, you'll be so glad of the fifty mile-per-gallon engine. Pushing me and the Barbie car up Porlock Hill may get old for you, though."

"I didn't tell you we're getting the upgraded Mustang

version, did I?" Brody countered. "Pink pompom wing mirror accessorizes and all."

"You'll like the convertible in all the rain," Sam added, silently kicking herself for giving Brody all these reasons to second-guess his decision to request a transfer to England. But she could tell from the smile on his face that he knew what he was in for. Maybe better than she did. He loved her enough to take her home. She loved him enough to take him home.

As Sam got ready for bed, she couldn't believe that this time last week she was preparing for another Monday at work, no inkling that the week would bring such cataclysmic lows followed by such euphoric highs. And a whole new Grand Scheme. Or was it the rebirth of an old one? What a roller coaster life could be. Thank goodness someone was around to force you to put your hands in the air and just let go sometimes.

"You know what's going to be the hardest bit about leaving?" Brody said as he turned out the light. "Thanking Thomas for saving you ten years."

Sam laughed. She couldn't wait to thank Thomas Sunby. The irony of trying to force a bond that instead severed it wouldn't be lost on him.

Chapter Twenty-Eight

The cake was chocolate with alternating ganache- and raspberry-filled layers. A little airplane was perched on top of a meringue cloud with a "Bon Voyage" streamer jetting out the back. The plane was flying towards a photo of the Queen pasted on stiff cardboard to make her stand up. HRH was holding a little sign that said, "Welcome home, Sam!" on one side and "Clear off, Yanks!" on the other, Brody's first taste of being the foreigner in the duo. Of course it would all have looked better on sky-blue icing, which would have necessitated a vanilla or lemon cake. But English skies were often not blue, and besides, it was Sam's choice, so that was that.

Sam watched Brody work the crowd of friends in the tavern on Main Street and felt a twinge of guilt. He'd have been a great first town administrator. She knew he'd pictured a gathering like this, only with "Vote Brody McClintock" on the cake and pencils standing in jelly jars on each table with "#1 Hometown Choice" printed down the side. Gail was there, tearful for herself, smiling for Sam. Gail knew of Polly, and Polly knew of Gail. They were truly a union of the Old World and the New World. But one of the friends always seemed dream-like, somehow unreal, depending on which side of the ocean Sam found herself at any given time. Sam so hoped they would all meet some day over a cream tea in the shadow of Dunster Castle or Hurlstone Point, knowing that when Gail really did visit, it would probably be both. More than once.

Ben and Tori were there, flying in from various

geographical locations, catching up with high school friends and saying goodbye to the old homestead, while at the same time expressing genuine excitement at welcoming a new one.

"Amazing kids," Sam gushed to Gail. "A perfect meld of Old and New World DNA, if only third-generation American DNA on Brody's side counts as New World." There was something truly special about those red-headed dual citizens with a stronger allegiance to the world as a whole than to any one place. It would serve them well in their global lives. Sam felt another twinge of guilt. Had she taught them to rent space rather than buy? But her children were comfortable everywhere, worldly wise and tolerant of differences, noticing them with curiosity, interest, appreciation, and acceptance. But not fear. They were comfortable on planes, in transit, arriving anew, surging forward, seeking change. She'd taught them that too.

"Don't worry, you'll see them as often as you do now. You promised to pay their airfare, remember?" Brody kissed her cheek. *He always could see right through me*, Sam thought.

"I'm more than happy to have a homey base to go to on Exmoor," Ben said, handing his mum another drink. "It's my heritage too." Sam rejoiced at the words. But she knew the kids' lives were full and busy and exciting, little time for old mom and pop, no matter how close or how far they lived from each other. *Just the way it should be*, Sam thought, with deep regret and great relief.

"Your old toys will be there," Sam told Ben, who looked slightly confused. Waiting for the grandkids, of course. Brody had said he couldn't even believe they were packing those darned toys but he didn't put up a fight. *He's finally learning*, Sam thought. *But dogs are so much quicker to train than husbands.* She couldn't wait to see JB and Sherlock splashing through the Exmoor streams, sniffing the wind, rooting through heather. Learning to bark with English accents.

Brody's bank had been wonderful. Never before had Sam been so grateful that Brody understood the connection between sterling and the dollar and London docks. She was so glad she'd allowed all those pecks on the cheek and seat-of-honour rides in the recliner. They had facilitated the support of Chairman Sunby in pushing Brody's transfer through to the Bristol office.

"Bristol? Is that close enough?" Brody had panted nervously after bursting through the door three months earlier with the news that he'd been accepted for the transfer.

Sam considered her new perspective of geographical closeness and said, both laughing and crying, "Yes, that's close enough."

The euphoric call Sam made to Polly the night they got word of the transfer had all the markings of an eighth birthday: glass-shattering frequency, jumping around, the promise of so many adventures to come. Not much changes on Exmoor.

"How ironic," Polly had said, when she could finally draw breath. "Their attempts to make you one of them convinced you of the fact you never could be."

But as Sam stared around the bar full of loyal friends, six months from that fateful introduction to *hireth*, she couldn't believe all this had started with the premise that she was an outsider. How could she ever have believed that for a second? She'd been wrapped in midwestern kindness for ten years now and in American hospitality for twenty-six. And would miss it tremendously. It wasn't that she wasn't grateful. It was just that she wasn't home.

There was one more order of business before clearing up the paper plates and heading back up the hill to spend one more night sleeping on the floor. Thomas cleared his throat. He never could resist an audience, tipsy or otherwise. "He'll make a good first town administrator— with a little sensitivity training," Sam whispered into Brody's ear.

"And his wife has the right pedigree," Brody grinned back. "I plan to vote for him again if he runs for a second term, based just on her heritage." Sam dug Brody in the ribs. "But I'll be voting by absentee ballot."

❦

Sam wrote a letter to Dunster that night by the light of a lampshade-less bulb on a borrowed air mattress, the first written letter in a couple of decades. She was still a great literary imaginer, seeing pen and paper but rarely touching them. Talking to Dunster had been, and always would be, a comfort. It seemed appropriate to include him, her homing pony, in this moment. It was his calling, after all. So many complex emotions floated through Sam's consciousness, she found she couldn't articulate anything. But that was the beauty of Dunster, wasn't it? He knew it all already. She felt him nuzzle in her pocket as the simple written words took shape.

Dear Dunster,
Be home soon. Wait for me by the gate.
Love, Sam

Epilogue

Exmoor, England. 2016

The flight path from Chicago to London arced up over Canada and Newfoundland, out over the Atlantic, brushing Greenland, crossing Ireland and the peaks of Wales, then finally followed the winding thread of the M4 before providing the Queen with her early morning wakeup call in Windsor Castle. *Bet she hates tourists*, Sam thought. She certainly would if she'd ever stood in line at the gift shop outside her front door.

Twenty-eight years from Dunster, Sam and Brody flew right over Porlock, dipping down to skirt the southern Welsh coast. It was daybreak, Sam's favourite time to fly into England. The promise of dawn lasted for hours as her shiny, economy-class chariot glided to greet the sun. She'd looked down through the wispy clouds, careful not to spill her plastic cup of tea, such as it was, because even the British airlines struggled to make decent tea at thirty thousand feet. Forget about the American ones. Over the rim of the steaming cup, she saw it: the coastline, where Exmoor kissed the waters of the Bristol Channel. Sam made out the expanse of undulating moorland, tinged purple, autumnal trees, and the arc of Porlock Bay, in whose glittering sphere she slept the best and breathed the deepest. Little blocks of white with grey roofs. The church. The harbour at Porlock Weir with its cluster of fishing boats. The Weir Equitation Centre. Or the shell of it anyway. Sam knew each curve, valley, river crossing, and beacon stone. Her mind's eye filled in every detail hidden by the intervening altitude: the little bird nests, the fawns, the bridle paths, the tea shops. The people, the ghostly ones and fleshy ones. She saw them all until tears blurred her vision. A gentle hand reached over to break the spell, or maybe to strengthen it. It was Brody, clutching Sam in one hand, his immigration documents in the other.

‌‌ಹ∽

"Ninety-five? How can I be ninety-five?" Hattie shook her head as she gingerly reached for the plate Sam offered. Sam had made the cake in the shape of a horseshoe, decorated with fondant icing roses in the exact shade of pink that fluttered outside the cottage window in the summer, with "Happy Birthday, Hattie!" written in shaky icing on top.

As she carried the offering from the kitchen, Sam looked down at the sticky words and smiled. She still called her friend Mrs. Althorp in her head, but out loud she had learned to call her Hattie after much insistence on Mrs. Alth—Hattie's part.

Hattie, Polly, Jack, Emma, Brody, and Sam sat on the faded sofas and window cushions, a small fire in the grate to ward off the late autumnal chill. Not much had changed in that sitting room.

Sam and Hattie revelled in the joys of their trips to the ice cream van on the top of Porlock Hill, or to the Bossington Tearoom, or the top of North Hill to look out over the Bristol Channel and down the Somerset coastline. They planned trips to spot the new foals on Dunkery once the spring came, followed by Dunster Show in the summer.

Sam felt a presence now when she surveyed these scenes; Exmoor not a place so much as a being. She didn't *go* to Exmoor, she *met* Exmoor. Anew. Every day. She walked Porlock High Street with a bemused smile on her face, cognizant of all the joys and somewhat fazed when she noticed others going about their business as though being here, in this magical place, was nothing special. Maybe it wasn't for those who'd been smart enough never to leave. The ordinariness of typical routines—the shopkeepers, delivery drivers, hikers, the mothers pushing prams, the vicar—all seemed in stark juxtaposition to Sam's quiet euphoria as she completed a simple errand, took a favourite walk, or ate a long-forgotten treat, Brody at her side, two sets of newborn eyes relishing every moment.

Much had changed, of course. Mrs. Althorp couldn't always be right. The pebble embankment down on the beach had been breached one too many times and victory had been declared for the sea. Saltwater now pooled where the sheep had grazed, and the salt marsh attracted new birds and wildlife. The village contained upscale interior design and antique shops, mingling with those that supplied the essentials. The junior school was a visitor's information centre, and the saddlery was closed. Some private cottages were now bed and breakfasts and some bed and breakfasts were now private homes. The pub menus included exotic dishes, like tapas selections, vegetarian nut roasts, and gluten-free desserts.

The Weir Equitation Centre had closed many years ago, now a corporate retreat with a driveway full of expensive cars. The dormitory above the stables was a luxury flat, smelling of potpourri rather than straw and muddy boots. The jumps were overgrown with brambles, cow parsley, and young oak trees masking old terrors. The remaining indoor school stood silent, a hole in the roof letting the spirits out. Sam brushed her fingers along the hedgerow each time she walked past the gates. The rustle of the leaves summonsed a parade of spectral school horses led by a lady riding side-saddle, her ghostly veil glinting in the sun. Sam heard the dinner bell on the wind and "Loose horse!" echoed around the combes. Happy ghosts, with pitchforks and deep dressage seats, and heel clips on their boots so you knew they were coming.

There were no dogs in Hattie's cottage, but Sam swore she still saw the occasional stray hair floating in the breeze that played around the happy group through the open window. Oh, and a few newer photos, if five-, or ten-, or fifteen-year-old photos could be considered new. Sam's children laughed out from assorted frames: on ponies, smiling at Mrs. Althorp in the garden or at Bossington Tea room, holding their scones high, saying, "Cheers!" together. Tea parties in the writer's cabin, laughing at their mum's stories about trying to write a book in there. The kids always loved their time with Auntie Hattie. The photos now stood next to the old, well-loved copy of *Moorland Mousie* that Sam had given as a gift on this special occasion. It seemed right it should reside in this room with this person. Though views of the book had morphed with changing views on hunting, the story's strongest message for Sam was still "listen to your pony, look after him to the best of your ability, never let him go." A timeless sentiment. Emma had said when the young girls found the book in the attic someone would come looking for it one day.

And so I have.

The gaping wound in the earth that had swallowed Dunster was now, to the unknowing eye, just a field; the ground absorbing one of Exmoor's own back into the collective psyche. To Sam's searching eye, though, there was, and always would be, a slight depression in the earth, a greening of the grass. A brighter ray of sunshine always seemed to mark the gravesite, a more fitting tribute than any grand mausoleum. The gaping wound in Sam's heart was simply patched over; she had no desire for complete healing. But sunshine shone out of the scar, leaving her warm and comforted. She wore the locket each time she visited. It held a photo of Dunster on one side and a few strands of his mane on the other. No one knew her dad had made the keepsake until Emma found it in a jacket pocket after Larry's death; so like him to forget something like that. Emma hadn't wanted to add to Sam's grief at the funeral, so the locket had been placed in a drawer gathering antiquity and then on Sam's kitchen table the day she and Brody closed on their new home in the village. Sam would stroke the locket as she shared Exmoor again with her pony. She always left a sugar lump on the fence post close by, knowing in these more enlightened dietary days it should have been an apple. The sugar was always gone the next time she visited, and Sam would smile. If anyone could find a way back across the Great Divide to get a sugar lump, it would be Dunster.

But so much was the same. The lanes were still too narrow, the church still stood sentinel, and the ubiquitous fish 'n' chips was still standard fare in the pubs. Dogs still slept under the bar stools, though joined now by a couple of American hounds. *"Look at all this food on the floor!"* their tails thumped. The clotted cream at the Bossington Tearoom, the robins fighting over crumbs, the colour of heather and gorse, the smell of peaty soil, and the sound of the wind as it swept around the stone beacon on top of Dunkery, all still the same.

While walking from Webber's Post to Dunkery earlier that day, Sam had come across a mare and yearling. They stopped grazing to watch her for a brief moment. The little colt with a mealy muzzle and soft eyes stared at Sam, unblinking. They'd met before. Sam's presence was acknowledged with the same interest as a breeze or a view or a starry night, and Sam knew what it was to be a truly naturalized citizen.

Focusing back on the sitting room, Sam watched her husband, mother, and best friends swapping birthday wishes and anecdotes about getting older. A border design flashed before Sam's eyes: a special lady, a pretty pony, heather, English oak leaves. They'd always been there. But she now saw something new: at regular intervals, interspersed with the events of the past two and a half decades, little stars and stripes showed up, colourful and proud. Fondly remembered. Sam knew she wouldn't have traded one Iowa of her American experience for anything.

"I have something for you, dear," Hattie said quietly once the cake was finished and the china plates washed. The other guests wandered out into the evening garden as shaky hands pulled a thick envelope from the desk drawer. The paper burned Sam's fingers like acid. She didn't want to touch it; a lawyer's name and address was embossed on the outside.

She couldn't read it. Nobody spoke.

Dunster and Mrs. Althorp. Words unnecessary.

The rest of the family began the walk along the bridle path in the thickening dusk, going to new homes now that didn't overlook Dunster's paddock. The swayback shelter, looking just as rickety and just as solid as it ever had, protected other dreams for other children. Sam took a different path, alone: the overgrown zigzag up to the writer's cabin, which Hattie had left untouched. Expectantly waiting. The leather chair, cracked and bleached, the sewing table, the rug, frayed and musty. Descendants of the spiders that had been unceremoniously evicted by an excited broom all those years ago had returned to lay claim. Sam caught a fleeting peripheral flash of freckles, seen no more. The trees that framed the window had filled in again, the view not quite as large. But Sam knew exactly what lay beyond the leaves.

She sat down at the sewing table, wrapping her jacket more tightly around her. Through the hazy glass, she watched the last of the sunlight slip away like lemon treacle puddling on the ground and oozing along the gravel path until swallowed by the shadow of the cottage. She wondered what her Grand Scheme was to be now. And then she realised: it would be the same as it had always been—not to have a pony or be a famous rider or live in a certain house or write books. But to find home.

After all, life is just a long journey looking for home,

isn't it? The little bits and pieces, creature comforts, ambitions, parts of the whole, were not the grand scheme. The feeling that seeped out of her as she sat on a wooden chair in a dusty potting shed was the culmination of all her grand schemes. Being back on Exmoor was like breathing again after holding her breath, like feeling her resonant frequency after a disruption in the electromagnetic force field of her life. Find home. Never let it go.

"Where I sleep the best and breathe the deepest," Sam exhaled out over the vista.

Hireth? Could you go home again? Was it still there? Sam drew circles in the dust as she pondered. Some of it. She smiled, knowing that she had indeed come back to a new reality, but with enough of the old to change yearning for loss to appreciation for what was left. So much was left. All the sentiment was still there if not all the physicality, and it spoke of her home clearly and decisively. So, yes, in her soul, home was still there, and it had always existed and would always exist.

"Maybe I'll have a go at writing," Sam chuckled, then sighed deeply. Did it matter whether anyone else knew?

"You're on Exmoor and the Queen's still on the throne, so it'll be all right." She wasn't sure where Merv's voice came from, but it echoed around the cabin to rest easy in the twilight.

Sam picked up a cobwebbed pen and blew dust off a yellowed notebook. She looked up in time to catch a shooting star streak across the sky, disappearing into the stratosphere beyond Hurlstone Point.

"Dunster," Sam whispered. He'd known all along where this story would end, not written in stone, but etched across her heart.

Acknowledgments

I had no idea how many team members it took to get this far. I mean, you hear authors are solitary creatures, writing in fingerless gloves in lighthouses and abandoned castles, shuffling into the local grocery shop once a month to get the essentials—and cat food. They avoid eye contact and push children facedown on the way back to the beat-up Volvo. About once a decade, they stagger to the post office to mail their latest offering, and *voila!* The bestseller appears. Or is this just my view? Anyway, I couldn't make my dream of this kind of authorship come true. No Volvo. Or castle. But here are the people who destroyed the rest of the illusion. Meanies.

Diana Schramer, my editor, for your confidence and our external discussions about internal dialogue. *You get me.* Sometimes you just have to put down *The Chicago Manual of Style* and go to lunch.
To Shaun "Can you right click?" Dow, Debbie Troxel, and Nicolette Pierce for all things technical, explained patiently and without laughing. To Anita B. Carroll for the beautiful book cover design. I cried when I first saw it. It says everything.

I have fallen off galloping horses, nearly drowned at sea, and survived the teenage years of two children. But nothing has been more terrifying than other eyes on my first novel. This book only exists in its physical form because of the following: Gail Anderson, Sarah "The Bard" Baird, Toni Goodridge, Holly Read (the prologue queen), and Anita "You can do better, Tracey" Shaxson. Your honesty and encouragement have meant the world.

To Betty Howett, Penny Challis, Nicola Thornton, Steve Howes, and Tony Fitzcosta for accommodations, chocolate, transportation, photo shoots, chocolate, encouragement, chocolate, and chocolate. You are my rocks, my Dairy Milk rocks.

To Rebecca Harmer, for encouragement beyond words.

To my expat Facebook friends, though we've never met in person, for sharing your tears, joys, traumas, and sagas of living a foreign life and wondering out loud, "What if I'd stayed home?" You have been family.

To the Moorland Mousie Trust, Juliet Rogers, Bridget Major, the Exmoor Pony Centre, the Westcotts of Lower Hook Hill, and Sylvia Beaumont of the North Berwick Ponies for your patience with my questions and the chance to hang out with the greatest ponies in the world. No, really. In. The. World.

To Mum, for the love of reading. To Dad, for the love of travel.

To my children, Alex and Kerry, for … life itself.

To my husband, Scott, for the freedom to write. I couldn't have dreamed this story without you.

To England, my once-and-future homeland, and to America, my current abode: I have loved you both for what you've taught me about being a global citizen.

To Exmoor: I am a moth to your flame.

And lastly, to my patients and students in a former life. You taught me that if I have something to say, I should say it now.

About the Author

Born in England, Tracey is kindly referred to as an "undecided" by her eye-rolling husband and two grown children. Her trans-Atlantic lives have included roles in speech-language pathology and professional horse riding. She travels extensively whilst acknowledging geographical indecision is costing too much. Tracey currently divides her time between Wisconsin and Exmoor—and Facebook.

25731482R00188

Printed in Great Britain
by Amazon